LOVE'S LAST KISS

A DEADLY FORCE NOVEL

SHARON WRAY

Toban
Books

Published by Toban Books Publishing Company LLC, Fairfax, VA, 22033

Library of Congress Control Number: 2022906249

Print ISBN: 978-1-958197-00-4

E-Book ISBN: 978-1-958197-01-1

For my husband Patrick ...
Who taught me that Happily Ever Afters do exist.

ALSO BY SHARON WRAY

THE DEADLY FORCE SERIES

Every Deep Desire (Book 1)

One Dark Wish (Book 2)

In Search of Truth (Book 3)

~

Love's Last Kiss (a standalone novel in the Deadly Force world) takes place after **Every Deep Desire (Book 1)** and before **One Dark Wish (Book 2).**

PROLOGUE

Rose Guthrie sat on the edge of her brother's hospital bed, not sure she believed his story.

She didn't trust fairy tales or favors or freebies. She knew the truth of the world. No one gave away anything for nothing. No one could be trusted. Ever.

"Timmy." She handed her eleven-year-old brother a wet washcloth. "Tell me again why you have chocolate all over your face?"

"The man brought me ice cream." Timmy used the washcloth to wipe his mouth, missing most of the sticky sauce around his lips. "This man brought all the kids on the floor ice cream. He also wore a white eye patch. And he bowed."

"He bowed?" She took the cloth and placed it on the table next to his hospital bed. "Like a butler?"

"Like a pirate! He had an eye patch and brought ice cream and bowed." Timmy used two fingers to cross his heart. "I *swear*."

"I believe you." Rose took his hand and squeezed. "It's just that a bowing pirate with ice cream in a pediatric unit seems weird."

Timmy withdrew his hand and sank against the thin pillow. "I didn't mind."

She stood and crossed her arms over her chest. She knew better than to hover. "How did this bowing man get in? Did the nurses see this man giving away ice cream to kids?"

Timmy shrugged. "Dunno."

Although he didn't smile, she noticed he'd lost another tooth. He was only eleven, but she always thought of him as older.

"*Hmmm.*" She nodded toward the empty Leopold's Ice Cream cup on the rolling bedside table. "You know you shouldn't take food from strangers."

"The man said he was visiting all the sick kids, handing out ice cream." Timmy wiped his mouth with his arm, transferring the sticky chocolate onto his pajamas. The same superhero PJs she'd fought the pediatric nurses over. But the jammies had been worth the fight. They'd been a gift from Harry, a family friend, and made Timmy feel more at home. More comfortable. More like a normal kid.

She nodded, not wanting to push the free ice cream issue. She'd take it up with the nurses before she left. "At least this bowing man brought you chocolate."

"Chocolate *fudge*. My favorite." Timmy grabbed Teddy Hawkins—his mangy brown bear with one ear almost torn off —and held it to his chest. "I wonder how the bowing man knew?"

She rubbed Timmy's head. "Maybe the same way Santa always knows what you want."

He frowned until she withdrew her hand. "I don't believe in Santa."

The way he said it, so definite and decisive, made her angry. Not at him. Never at him. Just furious with her parents. Her uncle. Her cousin. Everyone in general. But she'd never let

Timmy see her bitterness. He could never know how hard she fought for their daily survival.

"I know you don't believe in Santa. I'm sorry if I treated you like a baby."

"*Rose*." Timmy tilted his head, his hazel eyes appearing more green in the room lit by fluorescent bulbs. "I'm eleven."

She nodded, and it was her turn to cross her heart with two fingers. "I promise to remember that."

What he didn't realize was that she'd remember everything. The fact he was born during a hurricane. The way he cried for weeks with colic. The night he turned blue, and her parents rushed him to the emergency room. The oh-so-many times she'd almost lost him to cardiac failure. The horrible truth that he could die before receiving the heart transplant he needed.

Her eyes welled, and she turned away. *I will not cry in front of him. Not again.*

The room lights dimmed, and she was grateful for the cover to wipe away a tear. Lately, the city's power had been fluctuating on and off with no explanation from anyone in charge. When the lights returned to normal, a nurse appeared to check all the machines hooked up to her brother.

Grateful for the reprieve, Rose went to the window overlooking Savannah's darkening sky. She didn't want him to see her so emotional. He needed her to be confident and courageous. Not a trembling mess who'd no idea how to either save him or go on without him.

The nurse took his temperature, and Rose focused on the world outside. The setting sun gave her enough light to see Timmy's view: an adjoining rooftop covered in humming HVAC units and rusty water towers. A nearby helicopter pad outlined in flashing red and white bulbs. Old, battered antennas that probably didn't work. She sighed, wishing she had the money to pay for a private room with a better view.

Condensation had formed on the window's edges, caused by the too-hot outside air in conflict with the too-cold room. While the nurse spoke softly to Timmy, Rose used one finger to inscribe their combined initials. Then she wiped it away with her fist. The irony was that Timmy probably liked the view. He enjoyed taking old things apart and rebuilding them. He loved steel and concrete and glass. And bell towers. Especially bell towers.

If she were being honest, right now she'd rather take in the industrial ugliness than acknowledge the newly stripped bed next to her.

She rubbed her forehead. The low-grade throbbing couldn't block out the images of what the previous patient had left behind on the bedside table: a worn stuffed lamb with one eye, a superhero water bottle, two comic books, and a blue brush with dark hair within the bristles.

The one-eyed lamb studied her, forcing her to acknowledge the truth. Kids who went home didn't leave behind personal items.

"Miss Guthrie." The nurse came up next to her. "Timmy's temperature is still elevated."

"I don't feel hot," Timmy said from the bed. "I want to go home."

The nurse touched Rose's arm. "The doctor won't release him—"

"I know." She knew the game. They'd been playing the same one since Timmy was four months old. "He can't be released until he goes twenty-four hours without a fever."

"The doctor will be in tomorrow morning. You can talk to him then."

"Thank you." When the nurse left, Rose faced Timmy, making sure to keep her shoulders up and her gaze on his. "It's just one more night."

He frowned at her. "You always say that."

She held out both hands, palms up. "What can I do to make this better?"

He arched an eyebrow. "Bring King George."

Is he daring me?

"You know I can't do that. Not after the last time. We got into tons of trouble." They'd both learned the hard way that nurses didn't approve of smuggling white, semi-feral cats into hospitals.

Timmy shrugged, but she could tell from his crossed arms that he was disappointed.

Her sinuses felt tender, and the low throb in her head became a steady drumbeat that made her eyes hurt. Hell, even her teeth ached enough to fill her mouth with a bitter, metallic taste.

"Do you want some water?" She poured a drink using a spare glass and the pitcher from a nearby rolling cart. Except her hands shook, and she dripped water on the table.

"No," Timmy said. "I want King George. He helps me sleep."

She grabbed some tissues to clean up the spill. "Maybe I'll sneak King George in next time."

"You always say that too." He clutched Teddy Hawkins and closed his eyes. "Can you tell me an Iria story?"

"Of course." She sat on his bed again and clasped her hands in her lap. "Eleven years ago, an alien pod landed in Savannah, Georgia. It was a dark night, so no one heard the crash, except for me. After running outside in my nightgown and bare feet and prying open the pod, I found a baby boy. But when I removed him and his teddy"—she looked at Teddy Hawkins, which Timmy now used as a pillow—"the pod disappeared.

"Luckily, the instructions hidden within Teddy Hawkins were clear. Whoever found the baby was to take him into their family and raise him until he became a man. Except he'd be no ordinary man. You see, this baby was really a rogue alien warrior from the planet Iria. He'd been sent to Earth to hide from his enemies. Before I could take the baby inside, I had to swear an oath that I'd keep him safe, help heal his heart, which had been damaged during the trip, and promise to give him a family of his own."

Timmy smiled, his eyes still closed. "That promise is my favorite part."

The tightness in her chest eased. All because of that ridiculous story she'd made up after he'd been born, when she'd been *twelve*. She'd originally invented the tale to make him feel unwelcome. Because, seriously, what middle schooler wanted a pregnant mother and a baby brother? But over the years, it'd become their history.

Their canon.

"That's why my heart is bad and no one can fix it." He opened his eyes and met her gaze. "I'm a dangerous rogue alien waiting for my real family to send me an Irian cure."

She fought to keep from grabbing his hand. How she wished that story were true. An Irian cure was far more accessible than a pediatric heart transplant for a congenital ventricular septal defect.

Especially when she couldn't afford the legally-required private health insurance to cover the million-dollar-plus procedure, and the extra two million dollars needed for a lifetime of anti-rejection drugs. Especially when she had less than five hundred dollars in the bank. Especially when she wasn't even sure of her rights as Timmy's guardian. "I just wish we had a way to contact the Irians."

"Contact who?" The male voice came from the open doorway.

"Hey, Mr. Dolan!" Timmy waved in Kade Dolan, a six-foot-four man with a shorn head, scruffy facial hair, and the bluest eyes she'd ever seen.

She stood and smoothed down her white blouse.

"We're talking about my secret alien family," Timmy added. "If I can contact them, maybe they can fix me."

She met Kade's concerned gaze.

"That sounds like a plan." Laughter tinged Kade's voice as he beelined for the bed. Tonight he wore his standard work uniform of black jeans and T-shirt. As usual, his clothes outlined a perfect masculine form that turned heads everywhere he went. And she had to admit she wasn't immune to his blue eyes, easy-going smile, and sexy scent.

She wiped her palms on her jeans. At least she'd put on lip gloss and brushed her long hair into a high ponytail. "What are you doing here?"

Kade held up a brown bag in one hand and a can of lemonade in the other. "Samantha told me Timmy was in the hospital..."

He paused, and Rose heard his unspoken *again.*

"That was nice of Miss Samantha." Timmy sat up, tucked Teddy Hawkins next to him, and tightened his blanket. "I like it when she visits. She makes me laugh."

Rose frowned. She'd told her friend Samantha, in confidence, about Timmy's readmittance. Rose had good reasons for not sharing her life with the others she worked with, mostly because Timmy didn't know what she had to do to support them.

"Samantha makes me laugh too. But not like your sister." Kade sent Rose an exaggerated wink and handed Timmy the lemonade can. The condensation dripped onto the blanket. "I also brought you these."

Timmy put the can on the table, accepted the bag, and dumped its contents onto his lap. Small action figures fell out. "Whoa! Attacktix battle figures! These are awesome!!"

There were at least twenty brightly painted and heavily armed sci-fi soldiers.

"Thank you, Mr. Dolan!" Timmy smiled at Kade. "Are you and Rose working tonight at the hotel? Can you take her? I don't like it when she walks alone."

Kade's eyes narrowed, and Rose took his wrist. "We'll be right back, Timmy."

"Okay." Timmy was already setting the figures on the rolling table and making battle sounds that drowned out the beeps of the blinking machines hooked up to his small body.

Once in the hallway, and after making sure Timmy couldn't see them through the door's small window, she released Kade. "How did you get onto this floor? It's restricted."

"I spoke with a nurse downstairs, and she let me up." He nodded toward the narrow hallway behind her. "This is the tiniest hospital I've ever seen. I didn't even know it was here in the city."

"It's a specialized pediatric unit. Years ago, the Prioleau family chose this location in the historic district, hoping it would feel less institutional." She squinted at him. Considering he could win a Greek-god competition, she wasn't surprised the nurse relented. He'd probably left the woman speechless. And for some reason, that annoyed Rose. "That present was generous, but—"

"Don't worry. Samantha hasn't told Deke or anyone else at the club where you've been for the past few days." He glanced at Timmy before meeting her gaze again. Only now his blue eyes had darkened. "You haven't told your brother the truth about where you work?"

She shook her head. "He knows I work as a waitress at the Mansion on Forsyth Park."

"What will you do if Timmy finds out you're also working at Rage of Angels club as a—"

She touched Kade's lips with her fingers. "I can't worry about that now."

He nodded, and she said, "Thank you, Kade."

Kade took her hand, and she inhaled sharply. Yet she didn't fight him. His grip was firm, although not painful. With his gaze fixed on hers, he lowered his head until his warm breath tickled the inside of her wrist.

It was the first time he'd initiated any kind of intimate contact, and the sensation of his lips so close to her skin flooded her with heat. Her lower stomach clenched. Every breath she'd ever breathe again stalled in her chest, and the world around her dimmed until all she could perceive was the man, and the heat he released, towering over her.

"Kade?"

He squeezed her wrist, and the action made his massive bicep flex beneath his T-shirt. She exhaled in short bursts. The blue depths of his eyes, filled with so many emotions, sent a pain into the center of her heart.

He dropped her hand and began to pace the hallway, taking his heat with him. The air around her felt cooler, and she took a few more deep breaths.

He ran his hand over his head and continued moving as if on a private mission. As if he couldn't stop himself. As if afraid of what would happen if he did stop. "Deke is asking questions about the time you've been taking off. You're the best the club has, even Deke knows that, but there is a line of women who'd love to take your place."

Because the money was so good. Yes. She knew. She leaned her shoulder against the cold, concrete wall, grateful for the reprieve from Kade's body temp. She was glad he'd pulled away. The last thing she needed was another complication.

She focused on the long stretch of silent hallway behind him. "Hopefully Timmy can come home tomorrow. As long as he's stable, I'll be at the club every night for the rest of the week. That should shut Deke up for a while."

Kade paused in front of her, stared at her lips, and paced

again. "Deke is also busy tormenting the two new bouncers he hired. They're smart and strong. Two things Deke hates about other men."

"Great. Deke feels threatened. That will make life easier for all of us." She swallowed and lifted her chin. That might explain the weird text Deke had sent her earlier, asking if she needed another way to make money. She wanted to hear what he had to say, though, before giving him a firm answer.

Kade stopped in front of her for a third time and started to reach for her face but dropped his hand. That's when she noticed a series of scars along his forehead.

She closed her eyes and licked her lips. What was she doing? Noticing such personal things about a man she barely knew?

"*Rose.*" Her name came out as a plea hidden beneath a whisper, and she opened her eyes. He moved closer. So close that his lips hovered over hers. So close that everything around her heated up again. So close that she had to raise her head to meet his blue gaze. "How can I help?"

"You *can't.*"

His eyelids lowered, and she felt his short, choppy breaths brush her cheek. "You don't have to do what you're doing. There are other jobs—"

"There aren't." She stood taller, despite shame's heavy weight. She'd do whatever was needed to save her brother. "I barely finished high school and need to make money as quickly as I can. Besides the medical costs, I also have legal fees and everyday living expenses."

He took her elbows and drew her in until she leaned against his chest. He was so much taller, and her head barely reached his chin. She inhaled his masculine scent—a combination of leather and bourbon—and a tear traced her cheek.

Slowly, she moved her hands to his waist.

Kade wrapped his arms around her shoulders and rested

his chin on her head. She fought against drawing herself in closer when all she wanted was to burrow into his warmth and cling to his strength. That was the thing with shame. It didn't just strip away your dignity, it left you cold and alone.

Shame left you naked while reality snapped the whip.

And in her case, reality was a bully named Deke who managed Rage of Angels, Savannah's infamous Goth nightclub.

"You don't always have to be strong."

Instead of laughing at his ridiculous statement, she tried to pull away.

Kade tightened his hold and whispered against her hair, "It's going to be okay."

You don't know that. She didn't say the words because she didn't want to move, didn't want to break the peace of the moment.

She'd met Kade nine months ago when she'd started working at Rage of Angels, and she still knew nothing about him. While he'd helped her get the second waitressing job at the hotel where he bartended, they'd never dated, nor flirted, nor even held hands.

Yet, in the past few weeks, she'd become hyperaware of his presence. No matter if he was bartending or bouncing, she always knew where he was and what he was doing. She'd even begun looking forward to seeing him at work. A miracle since the club was the sleaziest—and most violent—place in town.

When she heard his indrawn breath, she withdrew from his embrace and wiped her eyes, disappointed that he wouldn't meet her gaze. Instead, he stared down the hallway.

She turned just as the overhead fluorescents flickered. For a brief moment, in between the blinking lights, it looked like a man in a black T-shirt was coming toward them with a...*gun.*

The lights went out. Kade threw her against the wall, using his larger body to shield hers. When the red emergency light flared, she noticed another man behind the gunman. The second man wore a black hoodie and a white eye patch. He also held a thin sword against his thigh.

The red emergency bulb, tucked within an iron cage, pulsed. The man in the hoodie now held the gunman with one arm and slipped the thin sword into his neck. The gunman fell to the ground, and she screamed until Kade covered her mouth. Slowly, the man with the sword lifted his head to stare at her.

Then he wrapped one arm around his waist and bowed.

A moment later, the emergency light burned out and everything went black.

CHAPTER 1

Six weeks later, Rose wiped down the counter of Screamin' Perks Coffee Bar and turned on the neon CLOSED sign. Then the café's lights went out.

Using her prepaid cell phone's weak flashlight to guide her way through the dark, she grabbed the baseball bat her boss kept behind the counter. A few seconds later, the power came back on. She exhaled and sank into the one chair she hadn't flipped onto a table yet. The city's power grid got flukier by the day. Every time the lights flickered, she remembered that night in the hospital. With Kade. And the bowing man who'd killed the gunman.

It didn't help that within the past six weeks, a heroin crisis had hit the city hard. The hospitals were full, and crime had skyrocketed. Although the police said the situation was under control, there'd been too many break-ins in this area of town to agree.

She put the baseball bat away and began to sweep the floor. The strangest thing about that night in the hospital hadn't been the murder they'd seen, the fact that Kade had almost kissed her, or that Timmy had been upset because he'd missed the entire thing.

The strangest thing had been that after the lights turned on, the bowing man and gunman had disappeared. Things got worse when she'd called the nurses and police and no one believed her. Then, when Detective Garza had asked to speak to Kade, he'd already left. He'd slipped away like he'd never been there.

The next day at the club, she'd tried to bring it up, but he'd blamed the event on the city's rapidly-rising heroin problem and reminded her she had other things to worry about. Which, to be honest, was true. No one had believed her story that night and, after Detective Garza had left, Timmy's fever had spiked.

So she'd done what she'd been doing for the past ten years. She focused on her own problems and how to help Timmy. The gunman—and the craziness in the city—wasn't her problem, and the bowing man could obviously fend for himself.

Once she put away the broom, she texted Samantha.

ANY WORD ON WHEN ROA WILL REOPEN?

Samantha texted back,

NO. I WOULDN'T COUNT ON THE CLUB, OR THE HOTEL RESTAURANT, REOPENING FOR A WHILE.

Rose stared at the phone. What were the chances that in the last week both her employers—the restaurant at the Mansion on Forsyth Park and the Rage of Angels Club—would shut down?

Although she'd scored the job at Screamin' Perks Coffee Bar, it didn't bring in nearly what she'd made before. What she really needed was the money the club's manager, Deke Hammond, had promised her two weeks ago.

HAVE YOU SEEN DEKE? I'VE BEEN CALLING AND TEXTING, BUT I CAN'T FIND HIM ANYWHERE.

DEKE IS GONE. STOP LOOKING FOR HIM.

I CAN'T.

She took a deep breath to control the rising anxiety. Timmy was back in the hospital, and every day brought them closer to the moment when surgery would be the only option. A surgery she couldn't even get Timmy on the list for because she didn't have the necessary health insurance and carried too much medical debt.

Once her breathing evened out, she texted back,

DEKE PROMISED ME A CHANCE TO MAKE MONEY IF I DELIVER SOMETHING FOR HIM. NOT DRUGS!

PEOPLE DISAPPEAR ALL THE TIME. LET IT GO.

Samantha's texts paused before she changed the subject.

HAVE YOU HEARD FROM KADE?

Rose pressed a hand against her lower stomach. It ached every time she remembered the last time she'd seen Kade in the club, two weeks ago when... It didn't matter now. Until she found Deke, nothing mattered.

NO WORD FROM KADE.

I KNOW THIS IS HARD TO BELIEVE, BUT EVERY-THING WILL BE OKAY.

Said the woman who didn't have tens of thousands of dollars in medical debt with more piling on every day.

Samantha sent a heart emoji.

ANY WORD ABOUT GETTING TIMMY ON THE TRANSPLANT LIST?

TIMMY CAN'T GET ON THE LIST UNTIL I PAY OFF HIS MEDICAL DEBT, PURCHASE INSURANCE, AND GUARANTEE THAT I WILL HAVE THE INCOME AND INSURANCE TO COVER A LIFETIME'S WORTH OF ANTI-REJECTION DRUGS.

Then there was the issue of the right-sized pediatric heart becoming available at the perfect time. A situation that meant another child, around Timmy's age and size, with the same rare blood type, had to die.

Rose teared up and wiped her eyes with her free hand.

Samantha sent a crying emoji.

WHAT ABOUT A FUNDRAISER?

PEDIATRIC HEART TRANSPLANTS, AND ANY OTHER MEDICAL DEBT RELATED TO THEM, CAN'T BE PAID FOR WITH FUNDRAISING MONEY OR WITH GIFTED FUNDS. I HAVE TO HAVE INSURANCE. THOSE RULES COME FROM FEDERAL PEDIATRIC ORGAN ANTI-TRAFFICKING LAWS. IT'S ALL SO COMPLICATED.

I AM SORRY.

Rose sighed and sniffled. She was sorry too.

IF YOU HEAR ANYTHING ABOUT DEKE, PLEASE LET ME KNOW.

She put down the phone and was about to mop the floor when she noticed a man walking by the coffee shop. Although it was after ten p.m. and dark out, she recognized his red tracksuit with neon green stripes. For some reason, Antoine only wore tracksuits that'd been popular in the 1980s.

Besides being a local thug who ran this street in the sketchy part of town, Antoine had also been a friend of Deke's.

She opened the door and paused. This idea was risky, but she had no choice. "Antoine?"

He turned and sauntered back toward her. "Whatcha need, beautiful girl?"

Ugh. She had to hold her breath because he reeked of garlic and body odor. Then she tried not to stare at his overly bleached hair with black roots. "Have you seen Deke?"

Antoine's brown eyes narrowed. He checked the street around him and came into the coffee shop. "Why you askin'?"

She wasn't thrilled that he'd come inside, but she needed information. "Deke was supposed to give me something. Except I haven't seen him since—"

"Since they closed the club after that stripper got murdered?"

"Yes." Rose forced a smile. *That stripper*, a woman named Sally, had been Rose's friend. "I know you and Deke are buddies..."

She paused because Antoine moved toward her, forcing her to back up until her hips hit the bar.

He frowned and then snapped his fingers in front of her face. "You worked at Rage of Angels?"

She nodded.

"Well, fuck me." He stared at her body as if he could see through her jeans, white Screamin' Perks T-shirt, and black logo apron. "You're one of Deke's strippers."

She tried to move past him, but he grabbed her arm. His grip was so tight she had no doubt it'd leave a bruise. "Let. Go."

"I'm remembering now." Antoine leaned in close enough for his body to trap hers. His whispered leer landed in her ear. "You're one of Deke's whores."

❦

KADE MOPPED the floor of Iron Rack's Gym in time to Papa Roach's *Dead Cell*.

The old-school rap metal song blasted through the cheap sound system with enough anger to tear apart a magazine full of bullets. Perfect metaphor for his fucked-up mood tonight.

He glanced at the gym's wall clock. The gym had closed an hour ago, and he should have left already. But since he was getting paid by the hour, he'd decided to stay and clean up. His mop sloshed water around the dingy gym that the previous boss—an old man and hoarder—had decorated with pirate-themed flags and memorabilia.

While Kade had never cared about the décor, lately he'd

come to hate the place. Come to hate everything associated with Savannah's pirate history. Or maybe he'd just come to hate Savannah itself. Since that moment two weeks ago when he'd walked in on Rose and Deke in the club and found them —he kicked over the bucket and water rushed toward the boxing ring in the center of the gym.

"Dammit!"

It took him ten minutes to grab towels from the broom closet and soak up the dirty mess. When he was done, he dumped the towels into a laundry basket near the locker room door.

After putting away the mop and bucket, he found the broom. He swept the front of the gym despite those mind-numbing mental images of Rose and Deke that broke down his mental defenses.

How could he have been so wrong about her? He'd been so sure that night at the hospital that she...what? Liked him? Cared for him? Was attracted to him?

Then again, he'd ditched her after the police had arrived for reasons he'd never be able to explain. Reasons that could cost them both their lives. So he couldn't blame her for turning to someone else. But Deke? Rose despised him.

His broom hit a leg of the front desk, and it wobbled. Because, like everything else in the gym, it was a piece of shit.

Fuuuuck. He needed to pull himself together. But how was he supposed to do that when every time he closed his eyes, all he could remember was Rose's honeysuckle scent? When all he could see was Rose's soft red lips? Rose's beautiful hazel gaze. Rose sitting on Deke's lap.

With another loud, "Dammit," Kade forced himself to change his mental convo. Because if he didn't, he'd break the broom in half. Then he'd set the gym on fire.

As he swept, another question rumbled through his brain. *What the hell happened to Deke?*

The manager of Rage of Angels had gone quiet since the club closed a week ago. Not that Kade was missing the asshole. Deke's ghosting act was just unusual.

"I'm telling you, Nate," Pete White Horse said as he came out of the front office with his buddy Nate Walker, "stop worrying."

"Easy to say, hard to do." Nate tossed a file folder onto the front desk and closed his eyes. "Can someone shut off that music?"

Pete moved behind the desk and hit a central switch.

Kade exhaled, grateful for the sudden silence.

Nate opened his eyes. "Thanks, bro."

Both men wore jeans and combat boots. Where Pete had braided black hair that reached his ass, Nate kept his long blond hair tied behind his neck. Kade had met them weeks ago at Rage of Angels, figuring they were either down-on-their-luck bikers, weight lifters, ex-military, or all three.

They'd handled the club's security until the club had closed. Now? They were two of eight managers of Iron Rack's Gym who'd agreed to let Kade keep his *very-part-time* job working as a referee for the boxing ring and janitor. The rest of the open, warehouse-type space held serious lifting stations and dusty treadmills that didn't need his help.

Pete crossed his arms tatted with tribal ink and stared at Nate. "Deke is gone."

"But the club—"

"Is still closed." Pete stopped talking when he saw Kade come out of the shadows. "Hey, Kade. I thought you'd left."

"I'm about to." Kade raised his broom. "Wanted to finish this first."

"Cool." Pete clapped Nate on the shoulder. "I'm going upstairs to shower and change. I have a date with Samantha. I'll be back tomorrow morning. In the meantime, get some sleep. You deserve it."

"Sure." Nate picked up the laundry basket filled with Kade's dirty towels.

Kade hung the broom in the storage closet near the front office. Once Pete went upstairs to the dismal living quarters that now housed Nate and Pete and their six other buddies, Kade offered to do the laundry.

Nate frowned. "You sure?"

"Yes." Kade wasn't offering just because he needed the extra hour's wage. He was offering because the brother seemed seriously strung out.

Nate, with dark circles beneath his green eyes, ran a hand over his head like he wanted to pull out all his hair, and the scar on his cheek had deepened. He also wore a long-sleeved black T-shirt that had a minty, antiseptic scent. Like vapor rub. Or maybe a burn balm.

"Nate?" Kade asked. "When did you last sleep?"

Nate dropped the basket and picked up a clipboard from the desk. "I haven't slept in years."

Kade grabbed the abandoned basket and headed for the locker room. Except he paused and glanced back. "How much do you know about the previous owner of this place?"

"Other than the fact he hadn't thrown anything away since JFK's assassination, nothing. A friend of mine handled the, uh, business details." Nate looked up from the clipboard. "Why?"

Kade debated about what to say, then opted for a vague, "No reason."

Before Nate could respond, Kade headed into the locker room. Calum Prioleau, the new owner whom Nate and his friends worked for, had started badly needed renovations on the gym. And one of the most important changes had been a modern washer and dryer in the laundry room adjacent to the men's locker room.

Since no self-respecting female would ever come to Iron Rack's, there was no women's locker room.

When he turned the corner, he saw two men standing an inch apart, fists pressed against their respective thighs. Both men were not only tall and heavily muscled, they were buddies of Nate and Pete. Hence, they were also Kade's new bosses.

He really didn't need this tonight.

"You're a pig, Cain." Vane Tanner, who wore a pair of gym shorts and a black T-shirt, pointed to a pile of dirty towels on the floor at Cain's feet. "How many towels does one man need?"

"As many as it takes." Cain Marun, with his shaved head and enormous tattooed biceps, put his hands on his hips. He was dripping wet and bare-assed naked. "Who the hell made you the laundry police?"

Kade turned the knob in the shower Cain had been using. The older showerheads leaked unless the handles were jiggled correctly.

Vane pointed at the shower. "We're supposed to be conserving our resources—like hot water and electricity—not wasting them. Who do you think has to pay for all this laundry?"

"You're not my fucking mother." Cain moved closer to Vane. "So shut the fuck up."

Kade headed toward both men, just in case he needed to intervene. But they seemed oblivious to his presence. He also had the distinct impression this wasn't Vane and Cain's first fight.

"I'm telling Kells," Vane said. "Then you can explain to our boss why the water and power bills have tripled since we took over the gym."

"Run to the CO," Cain sneered. "That's what you always do."

CO? Kade watched both men carefully. The only CO

acronym he knew of stood for *commanding officer*. Which meant he'd been right all along. Nate, and the rest of his men, were former military.

"Enough!" Another man entered the room and forced his way between the two men. This one, Zack Tremaine, had long dark hair pulled back behind his neck, a tattooed dragon spread over both arms, and wore jeans and a blue T-shirt. "I could hear you two fighting from the office."

Cain scowled. "Vane is being a pussy."

Zack tilted his head. "For one night, can we please not piss each other off?"

Vane raised his chin and crossed his arms. "I'm the one trying to make this new shitshow of an operation work smoothly."

"Cain"—Zack closed his eyes and squeezed the bridge of his nose—"get dressed and meet me in the office."

"What the fuck for? None of this is my fault."

"Nothing is ever your fault," Vane replied.

"Cain?" Zack opened his eyes, and his dark gaze skewered the naked man who was built like an Abrams tank. "Office. *Now.*"

"But—"

"Your wife is on the phone." Zack mouthed a *sorry* at Kade and left the room.

Cain's face softened and, within a second, he'd pulled on sweatpants and followed Zack.

The air suddenly felt lighter, as if the space had released a huge sigh.

Vane tossed Cain's towels into a laundry basket and headed for the laundry room. Kade followed with his basket.

"I'm sorry you had to see that." Vane tossed the towels into the washing machine. "Things between us have been tense since we moved to Savannah."

No kidding. "I didn't realize Cain was married."

"Cain's wife, Charlotte, is still at Fort—North Carolina. Once she finds a job here, she'll follow. Then she and Cain can get an apartment, and we won't have to pick up after him anymore." Vane chuckled. "Unless she finally tosses him out on his naked ass."

Kade emptied his basket into the tub, added soap, and hit the *on* button. "You and Cain and the rest of the men... Have you known each other long?"

"*Yeah.*" Vane glanced at him, all traces of laughter gone. "Why are you asking?"

"You fight like brothers."

Vane chewed his lower lip, and he suddenly found the detergent container on a shelf above the washer the most interesting thing in the room. Finally, he dropped his empty basket and started filling it with towels from the dryer. "I guess we do."

Kade, recognizing the sudden shift in Vane's mood, helped him fold and stack. Although paranoia and suspicion were two of Kade's best friends, he pressed on. Something was *off* about these men he worked for. Not bad, just...emotionally strained and stretched like a tightly drawn metal cable about to snap. A cable that, if broken without warning, would recoil with enough force to kill. "I'm just not sure how your boss, Kells, fits in."

"Kells is in charge. No one fights with him." Vane handed Kade a basket with clean, folded towels, picked up another basket, and led the way back into the gym. "Have you worked here long?"

Kade wasn't surprised by the deflection and played along. "A few years. I ref the ring and do odd jobs."

Once in the main part of the gym, they placed the clean towels on a rack near a powerlifting station.

Suddenly, Vane said, "I've been clearing out the former owner's office."

Okaaaay. "Don't go into the back room behind the gym." Kade grimaced. "I've seen rats."

"I know." Vane handed Kade the last stack of towels and then went around turning off the power switches until the only light streamed through the front windows from the streetlamps outside.

While Kade moved the empty baskets near the lifting stations, Vane checked the two training rooms and the office. When he returned, he had a darker, more intense, almost secretive look on his face.

"I found a binder." Vane cleared his throat. "Before I ask, I need you to know I would die for my friends."

Kade raised an eyebrow.

"In the binder, I discovered this." Vane pulled something out of his back pocket and unfolded it. It was an advertisement for the next tournament at Doom, Savannah's illegal underground fight club managed by Iron Rack's Gym.

Fuck. Kade thought he'd destroyed all of those flyers last week after the gym had been sold. Until Doom's sponsors knew what kind of men managed Iron Rack's, the fight club had to remain a secret from the new managers.

Doom's sponsors had been very clear about Kade guarding that secret, or else he'd lose his gig as referee. A gig that paid a hell of a lot of money.

When he didn't respond, Vane continued in a voice that carried a heavy weight. A deeper blackness. Maybe even a threat. "I want in on the fight. None of my buddies can know."

Kade took the flyer. Below the image of a fighting ring, he read his own name in small type. *Referee: Kade Dolan.*

He didn't want to have this conversation. Except Vane, who hadn't moved, wasn't going anywhere without an answer.

Kade studied Vane. They were almost the same height and width. Vane's powerful build proved he carried enough muscle. The scars on his forearms told their own story, a story that had to include serious street tussles. "It's illegal."

Vane snorted. "I figured."

"Sometimes the action goes beyond a knockout. You gotta be okay with that."

"I've killed men before." Vane pointed to the ceiling above the gym. "We all have. But I think you know that."

Yeah. Kade had figured, but it was nice to have clarity. "This isn't combat."

Now it was Vane's turn to raise an eyebrow.

Kade folded the page and shoved it in his back pocket. This was not how he'd expected the night to turn out. Then again, nothing had been going his way lately. He grabbed his gym bag from a small locker beneath the reception desk and paused near the front entrance. "There's a buy-in."

Vane followed and lowered his voice even more. "How much?"

Kade shrugged. "Depends on what the sponsors want."

"I don't have any cash." Vane rubbed a fist across his forehead. "How do I—"

"Look." Kade adjusted his grip on his gym bag. "Just show up, and I'll see what I can do. Do you know where it is?"

"No idea."

"Tomorrow night, meet me in Johnson Square. I'll text you the time. Don't be late." Kade pushed open the door and headed outside. The hot, humid air echoing with faraway thunder promised a summer storm.

"Hey." Vane stuck his head out of the door. "Thanks."

Kade waved, annoyed at himself for agreeing to help Vane. Without warning, all the streetlights flickered and blinked out. Kade moved against the building and unzipped his gym bag so he could grab his weapon if necessary. Since the attack at the hospital, he made sure to keep his gun as close as possible.

A moment later, the lights came back on. He paused

beneath a flickering yellow lamp with bugs buzzing around the glass and breathed in the damp air. This part of the city, on the worst side of town and close to the river, had a particular smell—damp bricks, urine, and mildew. Also known as rot and decay. He'd always hated the scent. But would he miss it?

Although he'd yet to tell Doom's sponsors, tomorrow's fight would be his last. He had only six months left of freedom, and he didn't want to spend it wiping other men's blood and other bodily fluids off his face.

He closed his eyes and ignored that heavy feeling in his chest. A feeling that had been growing for weeks now. A feeling he hadn't been able to shake off no matter how hard he fought in the ring.

Could he actually leave with Leonato and Sampson, the warriors who'd released him from prison early? Or face the rest of his life sentence?

Since Kade didn't want to do either, he opened his eyes, zipped his gym bag, and crossed the street. He'd go home. Read. Sleep. And pretend he hadn't completely fucked up his life.

His stomach growled. He hadn't eaten in hours and decided to swing by Screamin' Perks at the end of the block. He could really go for a sandwich and a coffee, and that café was usually open late.

He paused in front of the neon CLOSED sign and noticed movement inside. Through the door's window, he saw the local asshat Antoine with...

Kade flung open the door with such force the glass shattered.

CHAPTER 2

Kade dropped his gym bag, grabbed Antoine by the scruff, and threw him onto a nearby table. "Get off of her!"

Antoine rolled and landed on his knees. "What the fuck is wrong with you?" He used his forearm to wipe the blood from his split lip. "I was just having fun."

Rose rushed past Kade and kicked Antoine in the face. "I wasn't having fun!"

Antoine fell onto his side and sneered at Rose. "What's wrong, honey? I'm sure whatever Deke offered, I can double—"

Rose stepped on Antoine's balls, and he curled into himself, whimpering.

Kade took Rose's arm and drew her away so they could whisper in private. Her long red hair, which had been tucked into a bun, had come loose. Now silky strands framed her face. "Are you okay?" he asked.

She wiped her arm across her forehead and nodded. But she didn't meet his gaze.

"Look at me." He gently tugged her elbow. "What happened?"

She closed her eyes and took a few deep breaths before answering. "I needed information and hoped Antoine could give it to me."

"Information?"

She opened her eyes. Although normally hazel, her eyes were deep green tonight. A sign of her temper that he'd seen in the club when she'd had to deal with difficult customers. "I have to find Deke."

Kade dropped her arm. Hearing Deke's name felt like a punch to the gut. The kind that forced all the air out of a man's lungs and left him gasping. "Why?"

She lifted her chin. "Deke promised me money."

Now Kade stepped back. How could he have forgotten what he'd seen two weeks ago? "The club is closed, and Deke has disappeared."

She shook her head, and more red strands fell from her bun. "I have to find him. I need to know what to do next."

"What you need to do next is find another job." One not so close to Iron Rack's. "Because after this"—he pointed to Antoine, who was still whimpering on the floor— "you can't stay in this neighborhood."

She sank into a chair and put her head in her hands.

Shit. Was she crying?

He looked up, stretching his neck. Six weeks ago, the night of the weirdness at the hospital, he could've sworn they'd had a connection. A connection he'd probably shattered when he left her alone with the police. He'd never be able to tell her why he disappeared, but he'd had no choice. Still, she was the most beautiful and kind woman he'd met in a long time, and he honestly thought he could get past the fact she'd been a stripper at Rage of Angels.

Not just any stripper. *The* stripper. The one who'd made

the best tips, gotten the best times on the floor, brought in the longest lines. But that was *before.*

Before he'd seen her with Deke.

Deke had handled the strippers, but he'd had three side gigs with his now-almost-ball-less-buddy Antoine: drugs, betting, and prostitutes.

Kade's hands landed on his hips, and he stared at the brown water spots staining the ceiling. When had he become such a fucking, judgmental hypocrite? "Rose, please don't cry."

He had no idea what to do with a woman's tears.

"I'm not crying," she said without raising her head. "I just don't know what to do."

"You bitch," Antoine moaned from the floor. "Wait until my boss hears about this."

That's when Kade realized he needed to get Antoine out of there and contact Antoine's boss before he did. "Rose? I'll take Antoine away. But don't leave until I get back. We need to talk."

She sniffled, looked at him with watery eyes, and nodded.

Kade lifted Antoine over his shoulder and left Rose alone.

ONCE KADE LEFT WITH ANTOINE, Rose went into the restroom.

She removed her Screamin' Perks apron and washed her face. Then she released her failing bun and finger-brushed her hair into a high ponytail.

When finished, she gripped the sink and stared into the white porcelain. *What am I going to do?*

Instead of coming up with plans, her mind focused on Kade. She was still annoyed with him for leaving her alone with the police that night at the hospital and not wanting to talk about what happened. But she was also ashamed. She hadn't seen him since he'd caught her with Deke two weeks ago, and she didn't want to know what he thought of her.

Actually, she did want to know. The real problem was she didn't want to care. Because no matter how handsome, no matter how many times he came to her rescue, no matter how desperately she craved his masculine leather-and-bourbon scent, caring for Kade Dolan wasn't an option.

She had no room in her life for anything other than hunting down Deke so she could save her brother. And she wouldn't allow anything or anyone to distract her from that goal.

If she didn't find Deke and get the money he'd promised her, which would help her pay off the medical debt and purchase the required insurance, she could lose her brother forever.

Since her parents were dead, she honestly wasn't sure she'd survive the guilt and blame if Timmy died under her care.

She took a deep breath and went into problem-solving mode. First, the front door.

She called the owner and told him the door had been shattered while she'd been distracted. A lie, but she wasn't about to answer the difficult questions that came with the truth.

Luckily, considering the city's heroin crisis, the owner wasn't surprised by random vandalism. He told her to use cardboard and duct tape from the storage room to cover it, and he'd deal with it in the morning.

It didn't take long to tape the cardboard over both sides of the broken door and sweep up the glass.

She was just hanging up the broom when Kade strode in. Tonight he wore his low-slung jeans, worn out in all the right places, with a dark blue T-shirt that matched his eyes.

She had to admit she was glad to see him. "What did you do with Antoine?"

"Left him with a buddy." Kade ran a hand over his head, and she couldn't help but watch his massive arm muscles flex. "I'm serious about getting a new job, Rose. Antoine runs this street. He could make your life miserable."

She nodded and grabbed her pink backpack from behind the counter. "Thanks for dealing with him."

"Wait." Kade blocked the door. "Where are you going?"

"To the hospital to check on Timmy."

Kade touched her shoulder. "Timmy was readmitted?"

"Yes." She moved until Kade dropped his hand. "He has a cold, and the doctors are worried about pneumonia."

Kade crossed his arms and stared at the floor. "How much did Deke promise you?"

She paused, not sure how much to tell him. "A lot."

Kade took her hand in his. "I'll drive you to the hospital. I don't want you going alone."

She hesitated, but kept her fingers within his. She knew what he'd seen when he'd walked in on her and Deke in the security room two weeks ago, and she had no excuses. She'd do anything to save her brother. Period. Still, she wasn't stupid. Without a car, or cash, she'd have to walk to the hospital on the other side of town.

With all the dealers and addicts that swarmed after dark, the streets were dangerous. Besides, she was tired and would appreciate the ride. "Thanks."

Fifteen minutes later, Kade parked his truck a few blocks away from the children's hospital. The hospital had limited, paid parking, and she didn't want him to incur any fees on her behalf.

Before she could get out, he came around to open her door and helped her down. They hadn't talked much on the way over. She'd filled him in on Timmy's ongoing health issues, and Kade had mentioned he had picked up more hours at Iron Rack's Gym.

They'd both lamented the loss of their jobs at the hotel restaurant and the club. While there'd been a murder at the club, the hotel had suffered an unexpected gas explosion the next day.

A few minutes later, he held the hospital door for her. She could tell from his pinched lips he had something to say.

"Tell me," she said as they headed for the elevators. "Just get it over with."

"I don't want to start an argument about how you earned the money Deke promised you..." They got into the elevator, and he waited until the doors shut before adding, "But Deke has disappeared. Asking his dirtbag friends or boss where he has gone is a bad idea. It's dangerous."

"How did you—"

"Know that you were going to ask me about Antoine's boss?" Kade let her leave the elevator first. "You don't back down when it comes to those you love."

"If this boss has information about Deke—"

"Even if Antoine's boss does have information about Deke, you'll never find Deke on your own."

"You seem to know all about this boss."

"I do. None of it good."

"Wonderful." She stopped near Timmy's door and straightened her shoulders. "That's exactly what I needed to hear tonight."

CHAPTER 3

Thirty minutes later, Rose kissed Timmy's head, promised to feed King George, and left the room only to find Kade sitting on a chair in the hallway. "What are you doing here? It's after midnight."

"It's creepy here at night." He motioned to the hallway where, six weeks earlier, they'd seen the two men.

She dropped her backpack on the floor, leaned against the wall, and closed her eyes. She wanted to ask him about his disappearing act that night, but she was too tired. She craved a hot bath and her soft bed. "I can't stop thinking about the man with the gun. The other with the sword. Their disappearance. It almost seems..."

"Ghostly?"

She opened her eyes. "Maybe I could add it to my ghost-tour exam."

"Samantha told me the Got Ghosts? exam is a killer." Kade smiled wryly. "But if you can pass their history test, working as a tour guide for Got Ghosts? isn't a bad gig. It beats working at Screamin' Perks. And you'll have flexible hours."

"Tour guiding doesn't make as much as the club did." She picked up her backpack and walked toward the elevator. "I need to get home."

"Miss Guthrie?" A nurse came around the nurse's station, holding a blue sweatshirt. "I found this in the Lost and Found box. I believe it belongs to you."

Rose took the sweatshirt and smiled. "Thank you. I've been looking for this."

The last time she'd seen it had been the night of the gunman, police report, and Kade's disappearance.

"You're welcome." The nurse glanced at Kade, blushed, and returned to her desk.

Rose tamped down her irritation and slipped on the sweatshirt. When she zipped it up, he said, "Do you have friends at Yale?"

"No. But my parents went to Yale." She picked up her backpack and hit the button for the elevator. "This was my mother's."

It was one of the few things she still had that belonged to her mother, and Rose was happy to get it back.

He followed her into the elevator, but his eyes seemed darker than before. "I'll take you home."

Considering his emotional distance, probably a reaction to her coldness, his offer surprised her. "You don't have to do that."

"I know." He punched the button for the first floor. "I want to."

Even after you know what I did with Deke?

She didn't ask the question because she was a coward.

By the time they rode the elevator downstairs and hit the humid night air outside the hospital, the tension had become too much. "I understand you don't want to talk about Antoine's boss—"

"He's dangerous."

"I don't even know his name."

"And I'm not telling you." Kade took her hand, making her stop on the sidewalk. "Deke is gone. He probably never had the money he promised you. Even if he did, you're *never* going to get paid."

She pushed past him and headed toward her house a few blocks away. "I can walk from here."

"I'm serious, Rose." Kade fell into step next to her. "I heard Nate and Pete—"

"Those two bouncers from the club?"

"Yes. They manage Iron Rack's Gym now. I heard them talking about how Deke left Savannah. Permanently."

That couldn't be true.

"So even if you could talk to Antoine's boss—who was also Deke's boss—it wouldn't matter. You have to let the money go."

She didn't respond because her throat had closed up.

For the next ten minutes, Kade walked with her despite the fact he'd parked his truck in the other direction. At one point, he'd taken her arm and made her cross the street to avoid vagrants sleeping on the sidewalk.

She paused at the corner of East Liberty and Abercorn streets. She rented an old house sandwiched between St. John the Baptist Cathedral and Colonial Park Cemetery. Stuck between the praying hopeful and the long dead. An irony she often contemplated.

Kade shoved his hands in his pockets. "May I check out your house?"

She adjusted her backpack on her shoulder. "There's no need. Antoine doesn't know where I live. And, as you've said a dozen times, Deke is gone. Besides, I have King George."

Kade lifted one eyebrow.

"My vicious guard cat." She hurried up the stairs to the front porch and halted beneath the light. A white cat appeared from behind the balustrade and hissed at Kade. "Thanks for walking me home."

He ignored the cat and came up the steps, moving close enough for her to see the porch light reflected in his blue eyes. They reminded her of photos she'd seen of the Caribbean Sea, varying shades of vibrant blue that shifted with the shadows. He had no right to have such beautiful eyes, especially since her hazel ones could never choose one color for long.

He touched her face, bent in so she could smell his leather-and-bourbon aftershave, and whispered, "Rose—"

His buzzing cell phone interrupted, and he pulled away to check it. A moment later, he shoved the phone into his back pocket.

Even in the dim light, she saw his eyes narrow and his nostrils flare, as if he was annoyed. "Good night."

Before she could respond, he left her porch and disappeared into the shadows.

Of all the emotions battling for dominance in her heart, one stood out. Unfortunately, it was one she didn't want to admit to. *Disappointment.*

She sank into the rocking chair near the front door and touched her lips.

Kade had almost kissed her. Again.

She closed her eyes and began to rock. A slow *creak, creak, creak* as the runners hit the loose floorboards. Her breaths came out in short spurts, and she gripped the chair's arms. The weathered wood left small splinters in her palms, but she didn't care. In fact, she embraced the pain. She needed the pain to remind her not to lose focus. She needed the pain to remind her of what was important. And in the midst of her life's mess, the last thing she wanted was Kade Dolan's kisses.

Which was a complete and utter lie.

King George meowed. When she didn't move, he hissed.

She opened her eyes and scolded the white cat lurking

behind her potted lavender. "Be nice." Not that he ever listened to her.

King George took off across the street for the cathedral's bell tower. His home away from home. That meant, in about an hour, she'd have to go rescue him.

In the meantime, she'd make a cup of tea and study for the Got Ghosts? exam. As she unlocked her door and went inside, she noticed an unread message from Samantha on her phone.

Hey! I forgot to tell you. There's a nonrefundable fee to take the Got Ghost? exam. Five hundred dollars. Will that be a problem?

No.

Rose snorted and threw the phone onto the kitchen table. Of course it landed on top of Timmy's legal documents and hospital bills. She wasn't surprised she'd have to pay to take the test. Because the Fates, apparently, hated her.

As she boiled water for her herbal tea, she considered her options. She hated asking for help or money, but she could call Harry for the testing fee. Harry, her parents' best friend, had been her guardian angel since her parents' deaths. His checks for groceries and rent were random, but they always came when she was the most desperate.

She had no idea what Harry's financial situation was, yet he'd once mentioned that he couldn't help with Timmy's medical bills. So she was grateful for the money he could send her.

Now too restless to sleep or study, she let the tea steep and grabbed the iron key from the hook near the back door. Then she went out the kitchen door and headed for the cathedral across the street. She might as well retrieve King George before he set off the church's alarm. Again.

She didn't need another visit from the police. Although that would be a fitting end to a difficult day. A day made more miserable by the kiss she'd never received from the strong and sexy Kade Dolan.

KADE HAD ALMOST KISSED ROSE.

Once he turned the corner, he headed down the street to retrieve his truck. The entire walk, besides dodging sleeping heroin addicts, he fought a brutal, internal battle. Leaving Rose before things got complicated had been the right choice. At the same time, everything inside him urged him to turn around, take her in his arms, and help her.

No. If he was being honest with himself, everything inside him urged him to take her in his arms and kiss her.

He'd noticed her brother's setup in the hospital and knew from experience that that kind of medical care cost money. Money he was sure Rose didn't have.

Yet he couldn't forget what he'd seen two weeks ago at the club: Rose half naked on Deke's lap in the security office. Deke's hand on her breast, her long red curls draped around her shoulders. It'd been the first time he'd seen her hair down. Usually, she wore a wig while she stripped in the cage above everyone's heads. And when he saw her otherwise, she always wore her hair braided, in a ponytail, or in a bun.

Never undone.

When he'd walked in on that scene, he'd wanted to pound everything in sight. And that violent craving had returned tonight when he found Antoine hurting Rose.

Now that Kade knew Deke had promised her money, Kade didn't want to think about what she'd done to earn it. Yes, that made him a colossal, judgmental asshole. But he'd been hurt.

He almost tripped over a curb as he crossed the street. He had to get his shit together and leave the Rose mess behind.

He'd no business getting involved with a woman who had more emotional baggage than he did.

So maybe that text he'd received from Leonato moments before he'd kissed Rose had been a blessing. Something Kade had never, *ever* considered before.

He got into the truck, tossed his phone into his gym bag, and drove across town to his apartment. Between that moment with Deke two weeks ago and Antoine's attack tonight, Kade knew of only one thing that would help him sleep. A bottle of tequila. Which he didn't have and didn't want to waste money on.

A man ran into the street in front of his truck, and he slammed on the brakes. The burning adrenaline rush broke him out of his stupor, and he had a moment of clarity. He gripped the wheel and counted his breaths until the drunk man in the road wobbled away. Then he hit the gas and kept going.

That look in Rose's hazel eyes—two weeks ago with Deke and tonight with Antoine—hadn't just been anger or surprise or embarrassment. It hadn't even been regret.

It'd been blow-to-the-gut shame.

A few minutes later, Kade parked, grabbed his gym bag, and was walking toward his apartment when he heard a male voice say in a deep Australian accent, "'Tis a beautiful night."

Kade gripped the bag's handle. Before this meeting, he'd shoved his gun in his back waistband and tucked his knife in his boot. A man always had to prepare himself before a parley with a Fianna warrior.

Leonato emerged from the shadows dressed in a black T-shirt and combat pants. His white eye patch reflected the light from a streetlamp. Unlike the night in the hospital when he'd killed the gunman, now he wore his long dark hair loose. Silver hoop earrings hung from both ears, and tattoos of concentric dots decorated his arms.

"What do you want, Leonato? We weren't supposed to meet until tomorrow night." Kade studied the surrounding shadow. "Where is your sidekick, Sampson?"

Kade still didn't know a lot about Fianna warriors, but they always worked in pairs. Leonato and Sampson were the unlucky Fianna warriors assigned to Kade's stubborn, insolent ass.

"Alas"—Leonato moved closer—"Sampson is engaged with grief."

Kade stopped himself from backing up. Despite the fact he was taller and wider, Leonato moved with an eerie gait that took enormous strength and control to achieve. The same way all Fianna warriors moved. Like Kade would move one day if he didn't get his shit together and figure a way out of the mess he'd been in for the last two-and-a-half years. "What the fuck does that mean?"

Leonato wrapped an arm around his waist and bowed, proving his status as a full-fledged Fianna warrior who worked for the Prince. Leonato and Sampson were deadly assassins who walked with a strange, deadly grace and spoke only in verse—straight out of the pages of Shakespeare's plays. "Our brothers, Balthasar and Escalus, have met their demise."

Kade dropped his gym bag. It hit the sidewalk with a thud. This was the last thing he'd expected. Especially since Fianna warriors—assassins whose brotherhood dated back to the Celtic Druid warriors of ancient Ireland—were almost impossible to kill. "When?"

"A week past."

"*Soooo... that sucks.*" He was being even more irreverent than usual because he was tired and just wanted Leonato to go away.

Leonato straightened and frowned. Probably because of Kade's inability to give a fuck. "Pray tell, have you finalized details for the fight tomorrow hence?"

"Yes." Kade tried to keep the annoyance out of his voice. Didn't he always take care of Doom's details? "Vane, one of the new instructors at Iron Rack's, wants in. I haven't run a background check, but from what I've seen in the classes he teaches, he's strong enough."

"I know of the soldier Vane." Leonato took out his phone and texted. A moment later, he said, "The Prince will allow it."

Although surprised by the decision, Kade wasn't about to contradict a Fianna warrior. Since Leonato showed no signs of leaving, Kade felt compelled to ask, "That night at the hospital six weeks ago—you killed that gunman?"

"Aye." Leonato hit his chest with his fist. "The gunman may have been seeking Lady Tempest."

"Who?" The Fianna referred to women, even those they didn't know personally, with old fashioned titles. But he didn't know anyone named Tempest.

"Lady Tempest *Rose*." Now Leonato crossed his arms over his chest, as if annoyed. "Lady Temp—Lady Rose lost something. Something the Prince requires you to help her retrieve."

Oh. Fuck. No. "Does Rose know about the Fianna?"

"No."

Relieved, Kade released a long breath. He'd spent years balancing his godforsaken life on the thinnest of high wires. Half of his world committed to the Fianna and the other half to appreciating his precarious freedom. "My agreement with the Prince was only about managing the fights at Doom. For three years. Then I must join the Fianna brotherhood or return to Leavenworth." Kade swallowed so he could add the words, "I have six months of freedom remaining."

"The Prince understands your reluctance to join our brotherhood." Leonato held up his hand before Kade could speak. "Yet you still owe him for your release."

"You and Sampson showed up at Leavenworth and got me

out. I never asked you to come, never contacted the Prince about my situation."

Hell, Kade hadn't even believed the stories about the Fianna or that they really existed. He'd thought the Fianna were only a myth based on a legendary Celtic fighting force formed in Ireland to repel the Romans.

From the gossip he'd heard during his time in the army, this force supposedly died out during the Third Crusade. But that night in Leavenworth, when the warden had called Kade into the office, Kade had learned the truth. The Fianna existed. And if a Fianna recruit made it through the training and gauntlet, he tithed to the Prince—the leader of the Fianna— for life.

"Yet"—Leonato snapped his fingers in front of Kade's face —"that night, Sampson and I, on behalf of the Prince, gave you a choice. Work for the Prince here in Savannah for three years and then become a warrior. Or dismiss the Prince's offer and return to your cell."

True. And Kade had chosen his freedom. But what man wouldn't do anything to leave hell and start a new life? "My agreement with the Prince is simple. He got me out, and I referee the fights at Doom. Just like my grandfather did. Then I must join you."

Leonato's dark eyes narrowed. "The three years is almost expired."

"I have six months, four days, and two hours of freedom left."

Leonato smiled, except his gaze remained devoid of all emotion. It was as if Leonato smiled because it was the acceptable thing to do, not because he cared about putting Kade at ease. It was the kind of demeanor that sent a warning of imminent danger.

Kade let out an exhausted exhale and stared up at the sky. The city lights and the clouds obscured the stars. Why did he always feel like he was stumbling around in the dark? No direction. No hope. No redemption. Always screwed by the Fates. "So I help Rose find this thing, or go back to prison?"

"No."

Kade refocused on Leonato. "I don't understand."

A common occurrence when dealing with the Fianna.

"You and Lady Rose must find a box and offer it to the Prince by noon on Sunday. If you do this, you may win your freedom. Forever."

Whoa. Kade breathed in until his lungs filled to capacity. "Tonight is Thursday." He glanced at his watch. It was after midnight. "Friday."

"I am aware of the time."

"If I find and deliver this box, the Prince will release me from my vow? No more threats about joining the brotherhood? I can leave Savannah and go anywhere I want?"

"Aye."

Kade sat on the steps leading to his apartment. Partly because his legs were about to fail him, partly because his head spun like he'd done a double run on a Tilt-A-Whirl. The irony was Kade didn't have much. But what he did have, he didn't want to throw away to live a life of extreme penance punctuated by acts of extreme violence. "I don't..." He cleared his throat to gain some verbal traction. "How?"

Leonato squatted in front of Kade. "The Prince is surprised by your reluctance to join a brotherhood that has stood the test of time for over two thousand years. Yet he was also impressed by your presence of mind during the incident at the hospital."

Where Kade had protected Rose. He shook his head to clear it. "Let's back up this chaos train for a minute."

Leonato stood and frowned. Again.

"You said the gunman may have been at the hospital for Rose. Does that mean Rose is in danger?"

Instead of answering the question directly, like a regular person, Leonato stepped deeper into the shadows. "If you don't aid Lady Rose in her search for this box before the other man searching for this box discovers her identity, he will destroy her."

"Who the fuck is this other man?"

"I cannot say."

Kade stood. A surge of heat blew through his veins, and he pressed his fists against his thighs. "How am I supposed to protect her when I don't know who is after her?"

"'Tis a quandary."

"You know what, Leonato? Fuck you."

Leonato didn't comment, blink, or show any emotion whatsoever. Yet his stillness felt more deadly than any fighting stance Kade had ever encountered. And he'd encountered a lot.

At that moment, Kade didn't care if the Prince considered Kade's attitude as an act of war. He was sick of the Fianna games. And the irony wasn't lost on him that he wasn't even a warrior yet.

He swallowed and considered his options. If he could keep his temper in check and do this job, maybe he'd win his freedom after all.

After a few deep breaths, he narrowed his gaze on the warrior. "Does this box have anything to do with the money Deke promised Rose?"

"Deke was to give her this package so she could deliver it to another. After which, she'd be paid."

Kade crossed his arms over his chest. "Rose is a courier for a box that the Prince, and another man, are looking for?"

"Aye. She was to be paid, by a third party, upon a successful delivery."

So three people wanted this box. Awesome. "How much?"

"Forty thousand. Yet the box has been misplaced."

No wonder she was desperate to find Deke. "If I find this box and give it to the Prince, will the Prince pay Rose instead?"

Leonato shook his head.

"Why?"

"I do not know."

"And if I can't find this box?"

"The Prince will require you to end her life, and you will join the brotherhood two days hence."

The cathedral bells rang out, signaling the early morning hour. For the first time since Kade had left Leavenworth, he wished he'd made a different choice.

Leonato continued, "If you find the box and offer it to Lady Tempest Rose instead of the Prince—"

"I know." Kade closed his eyes. The Prince would order him to kill Rose. If he refused, the Prince would kill both of them without a single thought, a single regret, or a single shred of remorse.

"If you speak about any of this with Lady Rose, both your lives will be forfeit."

Kade's throat went dry, and by the time he opened his eyes, Leonato had disappeared.

Kade wanted to go after the fucker and drive a fist through his shiny whites. Then tell the Prince to fuck off. In the years since Kade's release, he'd put up with a ton of Fianna bullshit. Their strange, formal speech. Sudden appearances and disappearances. Ridiculous demands.

But the fact remained, Kade had made a deal with the Prince. Release from Leavenworth in exchange for refereeing fights and passing intel back to the Prince, and eventually— after three years—becoming a full-fledged warrior.

Although Kade hated lying to Rose about what they'd seen in the hospital six weeks earlier, he'd stayed silent to keep her safe. The less she knew about things like Fianna warriors, Princes, and illegal fight clubs, the better.

As he unlocked his apartment, he thought through his next move. How to help Rose find this box, while keeping her safe and without telling her the truth, so that he could hand it over to the Prince and finally be free.

Yet the only thing he could focus on was the fact that Rose —the beautiful woman with fiery red hair and sexy honeysuckle scent—was named Tempest. And how he wasn't at all surprised.

CHAPTER 4

$\mathcal{E}$arly the next morning at Screamin' Perks, Rose said goodbye to the handyman who'd fixed the front door and returned to the bar to take orders.

It didn't take long to clear her line. As she wiped counters, Samantha entered the café wearing a white ruffled skirt and a black lace camisole. Her strawberry-blonde hair was tied up into a messy bun.

"Hey." Samantha usually wore a wide smile, but today her frown could cover the state of Georgia. "I talked to Pete, who spoke with Kade."

Rose groaned, annoyed at Kade for telling everyone her problems. "I'm fine."

"Don't be mad at Kade. He's trying to help you."

"I'm sure he is."

Samantha grabbed Rose's arm—with a surprisingly strong grip—and pulled her into the back room. They kept the door partially open, and Samantha spoke in a harsh whisper. "Antoine, Deke's buddy, attacked you last night? And you're bitching about Kade caring?"

Rose closed her eyes because that somehow made the

previous night's events easier to handle. It wasn't that what had happened wasn't a big deal. It was that compared to everything else going on, Antoine's attack seemed minor. "I asked Antoine about finding Deke. Instead of giving me information, Antoine got...fresh."

"Fresh?" Samantha dropped Rose's arm. "What does that mean?"

Rose opened her eyes. "Rough. Before I could handle it, Kade appeared and took care of the situation."

Samantha waved a hand toward the front door with blue tape on the new glass panels. "A situation that broke glass? And you have this under control?"

"You know what I agreed to do for that money. Even if Deke is in hiding, I know he has the box. He would never walk away from the kind of money we are supposed to receive once I deliver it to the right person."

Now Samantha closed her eyes. "I have to tell you something, but you can't tell anyone. Ever."

Rose glanced into the shop, and when she didn't see any new customers, she closed the door. "What?"

Samantha opened her eyes and paced the room. "Deke is never coming back to Savannah."

Rose tilted her head. "Why?"

"I can't tell you." Samantha didn't even blink. "Stop looking for him, Rose. I mean it. Forget about the money he promised you for delivering that package he never gave you."

As much as Rose disliked Deke, this wasn't good news. "If I can find the package and deliver it, maybe the people I need to give the box to will pay me."

Samantha put her fists on her hips. "Rose—"

She held up a hand. She'd had enough lectures. "Do you have any idea where Deke might've hidden the box he was supposed to give me?"

"Probably at the club. That dump was his life." Samantha

lowered her voice. "Only bad things will happen if you get involved with what Deke was doing. And with whom he was doing it."

Rose peeked out the door and noticed a customer. "I have to go back to work."

Samantha touched Rose's shoulder. "You're going to let the whole Deke-box-delivery-money thing go?"

Rose smiled tightly. "Sure."

Samantha chewed her bottom lip. "Could you ask Harry for extra money?"

"I've thought about it. I just hate asking him for money." Harry was generous, but also sporadic with his checks. Sometimes she'd get small amounts throughout a month, then she'd hear nothing from him for almost a year. "I'm not even sure why he sends us checks. It's not like we're his kids. He was just my dad's roommate at Yale."

"Maybe he's lonely." Samantha kissed Rose's cheek and they returned to the main shop. "Oh, I also heard there may be an opening for a waitress at NOG. It's closer to your house."

Rose exhaled. Nectar of Gods was the newest coffee shop that specialized in cocoa and coffee concoctions. While waitressing didn't bring in enough money, maybe the tips would be higher in a trendier café. "Thanks. I'll stop by on my way home later today."

Once Samantha left the shop, Rose made two iced lattes and warmed up scones. Yet all she could think about was what Samantha had said about the club being Deke's life.

And she knew what she had to do next.

~

SIX HOURS LATER, after finishing her shift at the coffee shop, changing her clothes, and checking on her brother, Rose slipped beneath the yellow police tape guarding Rage of Angels club.

During the day, tourists avoided this edge of the river walk littered with empty warehouses and abandoned homes. The recent murder of one of the club's strippers hadn't improved the area's reputation.

She ran through the side alley and opened the back entrance's metal door. Apparently, no one had bothered to lock up after the police left.

Once inside, she took the flashlight she'd borrowed from the coffee shop out of her backpack and dropped the bag on the floor. The club had a few windows, and she didn't want to turn on the lights.

No one could know what she was doing.

She swung the light down the dark hallway. Where would Deke hide valuables?

She stopped in front of the women's locker room and shined the beam around a room that looked like someone had driven a tank through it. Some lockers had been knocked over, others had dented doors. Bowls on the dressing table had been shattered, covering the floor with broken glass, hairpins, and silver-packaged condoms. Sparkly boas decorated a dressing chair that lay on its back, legs up. Glitter powder left a sheen on the floor.

Samantha had told Rose there'd been an incident with Deke and a security guard the night of the murder, but Rose had left early. From the destruction in the locker room, the incident had been a brawl.

Although she *really* missed the money she'd once made here, she was relieved to be done with this sleazy club.

Thirty minutes later, after checking out the main club rooms, the VIP room, and the storage areas, she paused near the security office. It had an encrypted keypad, and she didn't know the code.

What would Deke, a narcissistic, sadistic, misogynist asshole who hated the world, choose as his passcode?

Having no idea, she closed her eyes and leaned against the door. A moment later, the unlocked door swung open, and she fell into the room, landing on her backside.

Once she got up, she hit the light switch and shut the door. Fluorescents flooded the windowless room, and she sneezed from the moldy stench. Folding tables edged one wall. A couch covered in a plaid blanket stood against the opposite wall. An unplugged microwave sat on the floor, and a chair lay on its side. The water cooler had emptied, staining the cheap wood floor. It didn't take her long to search the room and find nothing.

Defeated, she sank onto the couch and held her head in her hands. Deke's box wasn't—

She heard a sound and raised her head. She stood just as a man entered the room, holding her pink backpack and a gun.

Kade.

~

KADE RAISED one finger to his lips in a shushing motion and kept the door partially open.

When he'd gotten the call from the security company that the club's alarm had been tripped, he'd figured it'd been a false alarm. Or one of the local heroin addicts had found a way inside. Or the electrical system had shorted. He'd not considered that Rose had tripped the alarm. But he should have.

He shoved the weapon into his jacket pocket when he heard Nate call out from the VIP room down the hallway, "Hey, Kade? Find anything yet?"

"No." Kade dropped Rose's backpack onto a table and stepped into the hallway so his voice would carry to Nate as well as to Pete, who was checking out the women's locker room. "Why don't you both head to the front, and I'll recon the kitchen?"

"Good idea," Pete said. "The sooner we do this, the sooner we can get back to the gym."

"Yeah." Nate was now in the hallway, near the VIP room door. "Vane has been bitching all day about us not being around for his refresher self-defense classes."

Pete came out of the women's locker room and pointed at Nate. "I'm not the one he's worried about."

When both men disappeared in the direction of the main part of the club, Kade went back into the security room and shut the door. "What are you doing here?"

She sat on the couch again, and his heart contracted at the deep circles beneath her hazel eyes. She'd braided her hair and twisted it into a knot at the base of her neck. Still, rogue red strands framed her pale face. "I can't find it."

He knelt in front of her and took her hands. He inhaled her honeysuckle scent, and his lower half woke up. He wasn't thrilled with his reaction. But there wasn't anything to be done about it at the moment. "Can't find what? Deke?"

She shook her head until more strands of red hair fell around her face. "A box Deke was supposed to give me."

So Leonato had been right about the box. Kade had hoped, with this morning's light, that his meeting with Leonato had been a figment of an overactive imagination. "Drugs?"

"No." She pulled her hands out of his, stood, and pushed by him to pace. "I told Deke I wouldn't touch drugs."

"Money, then?"

"I don't know," she said as she moved around the small room, waving her arms. "Maybe. Eventually."

He stood and had to admit he enjoyed watching her move. In her denim shorts and fitted black T-shirt, there was no doubt she had a rockin' body. A great ass. And a waist he could span with his hands.

He stared at the buckled floor. His reaction to her was so much more than that. It wasn't just how her hair shone with a million shades of red, or the grace with which she moved. It was how passionately she fought to protect those she loved.

When she passed him, he took her arm to stop her. "What does 'maybe eventually' mean?"

"I was supposed to deliver a box for Deke. In return, the recipient was going to give me money."

Nate's conversation with Pete sounded from the hallway, and Kade whispered, "You were going to be Deke's courier?"

Although he already knew that, he acted surprised.

She nodded. "Deke was supposed to give me a box. After I received a message about where to deliver it, I was going to receive two hundred thousand dollars."

Holy. Fuck.

Kade sank onto the couch and rubbed his eyes with his fists. Had Leonato been lying about the payout? Or had the warrior not known how much money was at stake? Kade leaned forward, hands clasped, and studied Rose's cheeks, which seemed paler in stark contrast to her red hair.

No wonder Leonato had tasked Kade with helping her. If Deke told anyone else about the box, and that Rose was supposed to deliver it, every lowlife in the city could potentially come after her.

He exhaled hard, surprised to find he'd been holding his breath. As was usual with Fianna requests, this task was so much more than a treasure hunt. He'd love to know more about the box. But the fact that the Prince wanted it told Kade it had to be bad or important or priceless. Or all three. Adding to this growing disaster of a mission was the fact he had no idea about the details surrounding the box. And working blind was a situation that, in a combat zone, was to be avoided at all costs.

Rose wiped her face with her fingers.

"Rose? Are you sure about the two hundred thousand dollars?"

"Yes." She sat next to him but refused to meet his gaze. "Except Deke has disappeared. I've no idea where he hid the box. And even if I could find it, I don't know who to deliver it to or how to go about delivering it."

Her voice sounded strained, but he had a more immediate problem. Her scent was wreaking havoc with his libido. His erection pressed against his zipper, and the air in the tiny room felt hot and clammy. He shifted in his seat, but that just brought his body closer to hers. It was as if his body had a plan of its own, regardless of the danger they were facing.

Although they weren't touching, he could feel the coolness of her skin. Needing to get his shit together before he threw her down and covered her body with his own, he studied her defeated posture. She'd tucked her hands between her knees and stared at the water-stained floor.

"Rose?" He desperately wanted to touch her shoulder, but he didn't dare move. He didn't have that much self-control. "What else do you know about this box?"

"I was told it would be in a black drawstring bag and be small enough to carry."

"And you searched the entire club?"

"Yes. There's no place else to look." She raised her head and looked at him. "What are you doing here?"

"You tripped a silent alarm. I was working at Iron Rack's when I got a call on my cell phone from the security company. Apparently, I'm on their contact list. I told them the place was closed but that I'd check it out. When I told Nate and Pete what I was doing, they wanted to come along. I couldn't say no."

She threw herself against the back of the couch and closed her eyes. "Are you going to tell the security company? Or have me arrested for trespassing?"

"No." Kade pulled out his burner cell phone and sent a text to the alarm company telling them all was well. Then he paused, not sure if he should voice his idea. But her body language screamed dejection and sorrow. "Have you checked Deke's apartment?"

It took a moment for her to meet his gaze. Another moment for her to sit upright. A third moment for her to say, "I don't know where it is."

"I do." Kade checked his watch and stood. He still had a few hours before meeting Vane and heading for Doom. "I'll take you. But you have to stay hidden here for a while. I'll get Nate and Pete back to the gym, make up an excuse to leave work, and return to get you. Deke's apartment isn't far from here."

Kade held out his hand, and she placed her much smaller fingers into his. Her hand felt so cold and shaky. He closed his warmer fingers around hers and held on tight.

"You're going to help me?" she whispered. "You have a plan?"

"Yes."

She licked her lips. "Why?"

Since he couldn't tell her the truth—that he was an agent for a mysterious Prince and his fucking Fianna warriors—he improvised. "Whatever Deke was doing, it was probably dangerous and reckless as hell."

She nodded in agreement, but a smile edged up the corners of her red lips. "Probably."

"Most likely, we're going to fail spectacularly." The story of his life.

She tilted her head. "Most likely."

"There's no doubt I'm going to regret this."

"No doubt." Now laughter tinged her whisper-soft voice. "But we have a plan, and we're in this together?"

"Since you're going to follow through with this plan anyway"—he kissed the back of her hand— "there's no way you're doing it alone."

CHAPTER 5

An hour later, Rose followed Kade into Deke's apartment in a renovated warehouse near the club. *Renovated* being a relative description considering the warehouse had been built in the eighteenth century, and the apartments had been constructed during the Great Depression.

"How do you have a key to Deke's apartment?" she asked.

"No comment." Kade flipped the light switch.

When nothing happened, she took the flashlight out of her backpack and handed it to him. He turned it on and cast the beam over the living room and galley kitchen. Deke's sparse apartment was meticulously clean.

She rubbed the back of her neck and tried not to think about Kade's working relationship with Deke. Kade had been a bartender at Rage of Angels, often helping the bouncers when guys got rough. About eight months ago, he'd helped her out with a difficult situation at the club. And he worked at Iron Rack's Gym.

She didn't know anything else about him other than he'd taken an interest in Timmy and had been kind to her until the day he'd walked in and found her with Deke.

Although she assumed from the Army Ranger tattoo she'd once seen on his back that he was ex-military, he was still a mystery.

As she roamed around the small, sparsely furnished family room with a leather couch and ottoman, she couldn't help but think about Deke's unsavory side gigs of drugs and prostitution. Had Kade been involved with those as well?

Kade swung the light, exposing the galley kitchen with a door in the back corner. Deke favored black cabinets and gray paint. One thing he didn't have? A television.

"There's enough daylight coming through the kitchen window," Kade said. "Why don't you start there, and I'll check the bedroom."

Before she could respond, Kade disappeared through the door. For a moment, she wondered what Kade would do if he found the box before her. Would he take it for himself?

She hated that she didn't trust him. Although he'd been kind to her, the weird incident at the hospital six weeks ago, as well as the fact Kade had a key to Deke's apartment, meant she had to strengthen the walls guarding her heart.

People couldn't be trusted. Her uncle had taught her that when he'd stolen her inheritance. Her cousin had taught her that when he'd sold her parents' house and filed for legal guardianship of Timmy after her uncle's death.

She sighed as she checked out the cabinets. The past didn't matter now. She'd just watch Kade carefully.

It didn't take long to search the kitchen and the living area. Deke had few personal items, and all of his cabinets and drawers were neat and orderly. Nothing out of place and no dust. Had Deke cleaned before he'd disappeared? It was an odd thing to consider, but then, no one ever knew for sure when they left the house that they'd return.

Fifteen minutes later, she found Kade in a closet in Deke's

bedroom. Boxes were piled outside the closet, lids open. "Find anything?"

Kade pointed to the desk. "Deke's planner."

She opened the black journal and flipped through the pages. "There are a few pages missing."

"I'd bet all the money I have that those missing pages are the ones we need."

Kade was probably right. She tossed the planner onto the black satin duvet covering Deke's bed. Nothing seemed overtly strange about the planner, but she'd take it with her. "Did you check the bathroom?"

"I did." Kade shoved two boxes into the closet. "I rifled through every drawer, box, and the trunk." He pointed to the steamer trunk at the end of the bed. "I also went through the pockets of his clothes and searched under the bed. Nothing."

Besides the chair, trunk, and bed, there was a desk beneath a window and a bookshelf that served as a bedside table. She went over to read the titles: All three The Lord of the Rings books. A complete set of John Flanagan's Ranger's Apprentice series. Brian Jacques's Redwall series. And a single-volume, *The Complete Works of Shakespeare*. If not for the latter title, she would've assumed Deke's reading matter hadn't progressed past middle school.

She'd read all of those series to Timmy over the years. "I didn't know Deke was a fan of Shakespeare."

Kade grunted and moved the last box into the closet.

She pulled out the book of plays. Many of the pages had been bunched together with multicolored paperclips. Tucked in between Sonnets 116 and 117, she found a business card and a folded-up newspaper clipping. "Deke liked love poems."

Kade scoffed and pushed the last box into the closet. "I doubt that."

The white business card had the name Hezekiah Usher printed on the front along with a phone number. "Look at—"

A noise came from the living room, and they both stood. She put everything into the book and shoved it and the planner onto the shelf before Kade dragged her over the boxes and into the closet with him. He kept one arm around her waist and held her against his chest. His breaths pumped out in a rapid-fire movement, while she tried not to inhale his sexy leather-and-bourbon scent.

A moment later, they heard a male voice.

"You're late." The man spoke in a thick Southern drawl.

She covered her mouth with one hand to prevent a squeak. It sounded like her cousin Magnus. A man both she and Kade despised.

"Shit." Kade whispered.

"'Twas I who summoned you," the second man said in an Australian accent.

"*Fuck*," Kade whispered against her hair. "If they find us, let me do the punching."

Punching?

She felt his gun pressed against her lower back, and the situation suddenly felt real. As in, maybe they could get hurt. Or worse. She took a few deep breaths and nodded. Except if there was going to be any violence, she wasn't going to stand back and let Kade get hurt.

KADE KEPT Rose close and his weapon ready. "*Fuck*."

In the other room, Leonato, the Fianna warrior, faced off with Rose's cousin, Magnus Guthrie. Magnus, besides being a respected lawyer and a major asshole, also worked a secret side gig as Antoine and Deke's boss. But Kade was pretty sure Rose didn't know about Magnus's other life.

Rose squirmed until Kade pressed his lips against her hair. He needed her to stop moving her soft body against his. And if there was some way he could extinguish her honeysuckle scent which drove his libido insane and made him sweat like he'd run a marathon, he'd do it. Even if it meant joining the Fianna that moment.

"Leonato?" Magnus's Savannah drawl was so thick he was hard to understand. "What the fuck do you want?"

Kade held his breath. A man didn't speak to a Fianna warrior that way unless he was tired of breathing.

"To make an offer, Lord Magnus," Leonato said.

"A deal with the Fianna?" Magnus scoffed. "I'm not insane."

"A fool thinks himself to be wise," Leonato said in a low, tight voice. "Alas, Hezekiah Usher requested the box from the villain known as Deke. Except both man and box are missing. I understand you still seek the box. If you recover it, the Prince will extend an offer to preserve your wretched, wasted life."

"Will the Prince pay me for it?"

"Possibly."

Kade bit his tongue to keep himself still. Leonato—*that fucker*—was double-dealing behind Kade's back. A move Kade should've seen coming. The Fianna could *never* be trusted.

His life—and now Rose's—depended on remembering that truth.

"Unless you can give me a number—a six-figure number —then run back and tell the Prince I happen to love my life." Magnus's voice held a tremor of anger that Kade knew well. "I also know, from notes I tore out of Deke's planner, that Hezekiah is willing to pay at least two hundred thousand for that box. So you and the Prince can fuck off."

Leonato chuckled. "If thou dost play games with my lord, thou wilt lose."

A moment later, the apartment door slammed shut. Then he heard Magnus's voice, apparently on a phone call now.

"Antoine," Magnus said. "Leonato wants me to find the

box and hand it over to the Prince. With no guarantee of recompense. I told him to fuck off."

Magnus regaled Antoine with what had happened and finished with, "Are you sure Rose said that Deke was supposed to give her the box?" Magnus paused. "I have searched this place twice. And it's not at the club. I need to find that box before Rose." Another long pause. "If Rose hadn't asked you about the package last night, we never would've known that Deke betrayed us. It's a good thing Deke has disappeared. Otherwise I'd kill him."

Deke had betrayed Magnus?

Rose looked up at him, and he placed his lips near hers to keep her quiet. She nodded and rested her head against his chest.

"Did you find Deke's cell phone yet?" Magnus paused. "No, idiot. The one he used to take the bets for Doom."

Mother. Fucker. Kade closed his eyes and held his breath to tamp down his anger. So Deke was the one who'd been taking illegal bets on the fighters at Doom. Kade, along with one of Doom's sponsors, had been wondering about that for months but hadn't found a single clue.

"Fuck," Magnus said.

Kade heard a loud bang. Magnus must have kicked something.

Magnus cussed again. "If Deke didn't hide that damn box —and that cell phone—at Doom, we're both fucked. Remiel Marigny is expecting my call. If we don't have the box to give him, he won't be happy. And we could end up dead."

A moment later, a door slammed shut.

～

After a minute, Rose released her breath. She pressed her cheek against his chest, and Kade's chin rested on her head.

She heard his rapid heartbeat and felt the gun he held against her lower back.

"Are they gone?" she whispered.

"Let's give it another minute."

She nodded. At least she now knew for sure that the box existed. Although she wasn't happy that others were looking for it. Least of all her cousin Magnus.

Magnus and his father, Isaac, had already stolen everything from her.

Kade's breathing evened out, and she raised her head. Her eyes had adjusted to the low light that seeped around the edges of the closet door, and she realized Kade's focus was on her lips.

She licked them and heard his sharp inhale.

His masculine scent filled the small space, and she fought back a moan. It'd been so long since she'd been this close to a man. And she'd never been this close to a man as sexy as Kade.

He shifted, and that's when she realized his body had...hardened.

She swallowed and tried not to hyperventilate. But his sexy scent and the fierce strength that rolled off of him like a heat wave made her feel small and vulnerable.

Slowly, he lowered his head. When his lips touched hers, she was surprised at how soft they were. Because he was made of only muscle and bone, she'd expected his kiss to be hard. Demanding. Forceful.

Instead, it was gentle and giving. The sweetness of it touched something in her heart, and she melted against him.

A tentative surrender. A temporary stay of all the rules she forced herself to live by.

A trial search for human connection.

He lifted his head. "*Rose.*"

Her name came out loaded with meanings she couldn't comprehend. Meanings she wasn't sure she wanted to decipher. With so many worries in her life, she had no business making promises to anyone. She had no business kissing anyone. Especially the man who'd seen her at the lowest moment in her life—the night she'd begged Deke to give her this opportunity to deliver a stupid box.

An opportunity that was slipping away with each passing moment.

She pulled out of his embrace and opened the closet door, grateful for the cooler air that cleared her head.

Kade followed her out and didn't say anything. She grabbed the planner and Shakespeare book off the shelf. She wasn't sure if either book was a clue, but they were all they had.

Kade led her into the living room, weapon first. "They're gone."

She placed the books on the kitchen table. "I can't believe my cousin Magnus is involved with all of this, and that he wants my box."

Kade scrubbed a hand over his eyes. "Magnus has been out of control since his father died nine months ago."

"I won't ever forget that fight you and Magnus had outside the club, not long after Isaac's death."

"Magnus came into the club, pulled you out of your cage, and hit you." Kade's voice sounded darker than she'd ever heard before. "I had no choice but to fight him."

"I'm still angry he got you arrested."

"Magus is a powerful lawyer." Kade shrugged and dropped his hand. "It's the way of the world."

The police had held Kade overnight, and she was ashamed that she never asked him how he'd been released so quickly. "I never thanked you for saving me that night."

"Magnus deserved every hit I gave him." Kade met her gaze, as if just realizing something. "How well did you know your Uncle Isaac?"

"Too well. After my parents' deaths ten years ago, Isaac became my and Timmy's guardian. I was twelve, Timmy was six months, and Magnus was a nineteen-year-old bully. Magnus's mother died when he was a baby. So Isaac spoiled Magnus as a way to make up for rotten parenting."

Kade muttered, "*Fuuuuck.*"

She watched Kade carefully. Her uncle had been a cruel, hard man who'd hated children. And Magnus was emulating his father's dirty behavior. "Did you know Isaac?"

Kade crossed his arms over his chest. But now his gaze seemed focused on the tipped-over ottoman that Magnus must have kicked. "Isaac used to come to Iron Rack's Gym."

"Really?" Isaac had been one of the most influential lawyers in Savannah, next to Calum Prioleau, the wealthiest man in the city. "I'm surprised my uncle didn't use one of the higher-end gyms in town."

Kade raised an eyebrow. "Isaac wasn't there to work out."

"So why—"

"Isaac dealt drugs." Kade spoke with no inflection or emotion. Just a bold, flat statement.

"Oh." She moved to stare out the kitchen window. It gave her a view of only the neighboring brick warehouse, but she needed the distraction. She wasn't surprised her uncle had been a dealer. At least it proved what she'd known all along: Her uncle had been a lying bastard. Unfortunately, during those years after her parents' death, no one had believed her. "I heard Magnus took over his father's place as head of the law firm Isaac founded. Did Magnus take over his father's extracurricular activities as well?"

"Yes." Kade cleared his throat, and she glanced at him. "You don't seem surprised by your family's unsavory businesses."

"I'm not. Isaac and Magnus are"—she tapped her finger

against her cheek—"wasted wretches. Just like that man Leonato said."

"I would've gone with 'evil fucks'." Kade flashed her a half smile filled with pity and concern. "I'm just sorry you're related to them."

"So am I." She returned to the Shakespeare book on the table and pulled out the business card. She needed to change the subject. "On a less-dreary note, look at this."

Kade took the card. "Hezekiah Usher. That phone number has a Boston area code."

"Magnus mentioned the name Hezekiah Usher as a potential buyer of the box." She touched Kade's arm. "Do you know him?"

"No." Kade placed the card on the counter.

From the way he avoided meeting her gaze, she knew he was hiding something. "Do you know Leonato? Or the Fianna? And who is the Prince? Or the guy that Magnus mentioned he needed to call... Remiel Marigny?"

Kade closed his eyes and pinched the bridge of his nose. "Rose—"

She hit him in the stomach, and he didn't even flinch. But he did open his eyes. Then he put his hands on his hips and sighed as if he'd just fought ten rounds in a fighting ring.

"I don't know anyone named Remiel Marigny."

"And the others?"

"Leonato," Kade paused, shook his head, and then cleared his throat. "Leonato, the man with the Australian accent, works for the Prince, who is the leader of the Fianna, a secret army of brutal Celtic Druid assassins that dates back over two thousand years. Except now they recruit the fiercest soldiers from every army around the world."

She opened her mouth, then closed it. A secret army of Druid assassins? For real? "You can't be serious."

"I am." Kade pointed to the apartment's closed door. "If

you get in Leonato's way, he'll kill you. If you tell anyone about him or the Fianna, he'll kill you. If you get in the Fianna's way, they will destroy your life."

"How do you know that?"

Kade paced the room with long strides, which meant he made rapid turns. It was almost as if he was at war with himself. "Leonato is the man we saw in the hospital hallway all those weeks ago."

All the air rushed out of her lungs, and she sank onto the couch. "*What?*"

Kade picked up the ottoman. The top was opened and blankets had fallen out. As he refolded the blankets and stacked them on the couch, he said, "Leonato is a Fianna warrior, and he killed that guy who was coming after us with a gun."

"Are you sure?"

"Last night, I met Leonato, and he confirmed it." Kade paused for a long moment before adding, "I kind of work for Leonato. Odd jobs and such."

She blinked a few times, trying to process everything. "You're just telling me this now?"

"I wasn't going to tell you at all." Kade grabbed a remote and something else that had fallen out of the ottoman. A prepaid cell phone. He opened it, but the screen was locked with a passcode.

She took the phone out of his hand and held it behind her back. Considering everything she'd just learned about him, he owed her more information. "Please continue."

He found her pink backpack on the floor and shoved the flashlight, planner, business card, and Shakespeare book into it. "Leonato, under the Prince's orders, wants me to help you find that box before Magnus does."

"It sounds like Hezekiah Usher is the person I'm supposed to give the box to."

"Maybe." Kade handed her the backpack and pulled his own phone from his back pocket. He started typing, not realizing a folded page had fallen out of his pocket.

She slipped Deke's cell phone into her backpack. Then she picked up Kade's paper. She honestly didn't know what to think about everything he'd just divulged. It was so outrageous, and she had a hard time believing it could all be true. "What are you doing?"

"Research." He kept typing. "In 1647, Hezekiah Usher was the first publisher and purveyor of books for the thirteen colonies. He had a store in Boston."

She stood on her toes to read over his shoulder. "Is there anything about a current-day Hezekiah Usher?"

"Nothing."

"They could be related. Who else would name their kid Hezekiah?"

"Good point." Kade found the business card on the counter and dialed the number. Then he hung up. "The number has been disconnected."

Why was she not surprised? She was about to hand him the paper he'd dropped when she noticed something. "What is this?"

"Nothing." Kade tried to take it from her, but she'd already opened it.

She held up the ad for an illegal fight club named Doom that listed Kade as referee. "Magnus mentioned Deke might've hidden the box at a place named Doom." She pressed the paper against Kade's chest. "How do we get there?"

CHAPTER 6

$\mathcal{K}$ade held the pink backpack on one shoulder and helped Rose out of his truck.

After spending thirty minutes in Deke's apartment arguing about what to do next, Kade and Rose had called a truce. As a compromise, they'd decided to go to Rose's house and come up with a plan. First, he'd taken them to a convenience store and bought them both new prepaid phones. Even though she already used a burner phone—probably because it was cheap—he'd explained to her that, when dealing with dangerous people, it was a good idea to switch out phones frequently.

Then he'd driven them across town and parked a few blocks away from her house. He'd also thrown his Fianna phone—the one Leonato had given him years ago—into the glove box.

Kade had no idea if Leonato and Sampson were tracking him, but he wasn't taking any chances.

Now, as they waited for traffic to slow so they could cross the street, the church bells rang, signaling it was four-thirty p.m.

Rose took his free hand and pulled him along the crosswalk. "I miss the real bells. Those digital bells sound so hollow."

He couldn't tell the difference, but he was too distracted by watching her walk to respond. She had a gracefulness that caused every breath to shorten and sweat to drip down the back of his neck. The clouds obscured the summer sky, making it appear later in the day. A warm, humid breeze blew by, and he inhaled the city's summer smells of roses, mildew, and Rose's honeysuckle perfume.

He held her scent deep in his lungs and watched her climb the steps to her small house. He loved the swing of her hips, the gentle bounce of her long braid. No wonder she'd been such a favorite at the club. She moved like a ballet dancer who skated on ice. Sheer, feminine perfection.

Kade couldn't imagine how horrible it would've been to be raised by Isaac and Magnus. Kade had dealt with the Guthrie men when they'd been at Doom and sometimes at Rage of Angels or Iron Rack's Gym. Those infrequent moments had been more than enough for Kade.

He hadn't been joking when he'd called Isaac and Magnus evil fucks. Kade had spent enough time in the world's most violent shitholes to see the worst of humanity. But even those experiences—hell, even his time in prison—hadn't prepared him for Isaac and Magnus. As far as Kade was concerned, Isaac's death had been a gift to the world. Unfortunately, Magnus seemed committed to becoming an even more violent bastard than his father.

Then there'd been Magnus's talk about the Fianna, the Prince, and Leonato. Kade knew the unpleasant punishments for spilling any intel about the Fianna, but he'd told her anyway. Although he'd held back on a lot of things, including his deal that he hand the box over to the Prince in exchange for his freedom.

He still wasn't sure why he'd told Rose what he had, but he suspected it was because he felt sorry for her. She'd had a tragic life and was up against forces she was defenseless against and had never heard of. Although he didn't want more trouble with the Fianna, the pain and trauma in her hazel eyes hurt his heart.

Maybe he'd hoped that having a sliver of truth would convince her to trust him. He needed her trust to complete this mission despite his attraction to her that made speech difficult and left him breathless. Between kissing her and divulging secrets, his plan to keep his shit together had failed. Miserably. He just hoped his speaking about forbidden things wouldn't cause their untimely deaths.

He adjusted her pink backpack on his shoulder. While he wanted to ask more questions about Rose's life, he had another problem—Rose wanted to go to Doom, and he couldn't allow that. Now he had to figure out how to get to Doom tonight without her following. Except he had a gut-wrenching feeling it would be easier to walk to the moon.

"Since you don't have to be at Doom until eight p.m.," she said as she unlocked her door, "that gives us time to eat and plan and go through the clues we found."

While he had no intention of taking her to Doom, he appreciated her optimism about their supposed clues.

King George appeared in the hallway, purring, until he saw Kade. If Rose hadn't picked the beast up, Kade had no doubt the animal would've sprung, claws out, and gone for Kade's jugular.

She nuzzled the white cat and entered the house.

He locked the door and followed her into the kitchen. A window over the sink exposed a garden and, beyond that, Colonial Park Cemetery. Gnarled oak trees divided her home from the dead lying twenty yards away. From the window in the kitchen door off to the side, he saw the cathedral's bell towers.

"Are you hungry?"

"Yes." He paused when he realized Rose had been speaking to the cat, who was still in her arms and snarling at him.

She chuckled, dropped the cat, and took a tin of cat food out of the cabinet. Then she found an apron in a drawer and put it on. "I'm sorry about King George. He's a feral rescue and hates strangers. He'll feel better once he eats."

Wouldn't they all. Kade dropped the backpack onto the table covered with stacks of papers, moved her blue Yale sweatshirt, and sat in a chair. He tried to keep the incredulousness out of his voice. "Of all the strays in the world, you picked King George?"

"Timmy picked him." She filled a bowl with cat food and placed it on a floor mat decorated with Union Jack flags. "Timmy has a tough time with other kids—"

"Bullying?" Kade surreptitiously read some of the papers spread across the table. Legal documents and medical bills with amounts most people couldn't pay off in a lifetime.

"More like ignoring. It's as if they're afraid Timmy's congenital heart condition is contagious." She washed her hands and wiped them on a dishcloth. "Timmy spends too much time alone. And he enjoys hiding, probably because he knows how his isolation upsets me. He's a preteen, so he's at that contrary age."

"Where does Timmy go?"

She pointed to the church's bell tower visible through the kitchen door's window. Only part of the white spire sparkled in the fickle sunlight. "The church has been undergoing renovations, and Timmy found a secret way up to the top of the spire, where he found a loft and a stray cat. The workers took down the bells temporarily, so the space was empty and quiet.

While I thought Timmy was in after-school art class, he was using the tower as a tree house, until one day I got a call from the church. They'd found Timmy and King George. Luckily, they didn't charge Timmy with trespassing—"

"He's eleven." Kade took the new burner phones out of her backpack and used his pocket knife to open the plastic packages.

"I know." She shrugged and retied her apron, tightening it around her waist. The action showed off her perfect female form.

He looked away and set up the chargers on the counter. After plugging them in, he attached the burner phones. Then he threw away the packaging. He had to stay focused before his attraction to her became a more serious problem. "What did the church do?"

"I was worried the church would call CPS. They didn't, but they insisted that Timmy take the cat with him. Once King George moved in with us, he never left. Although, whenever he can, he returns to the tower." She pointed to a brass key tied to a piece of twine hanging next to the kitchen door. "The church gave me a key to the exterior door of the closest tower so I could retrieve him on my own."

"That's nice of them."

"The church has had problems with break-ins and vandalism." She opened the refrigerator door and stared at the contents. "They don't need the stress of a stray, feral cat who bites parishioners."

Kade whistled at the surly animal. King George looked up from his bowl and glared back. It was as if the cat knew they were talking about him and didn't give a fuck. An attitude Kade reluctantly admired. "I'd heard there was trouble at the cathedral last week. Was that King George's fault? Or Timmy's?"

"No." She took two cans of tuna fish, mayonnaise, a block

of cheese, a tomato, and a loaf of bread out of the refrigerator and placed them on the counter. "I have no idea what happened, although the police were there for hours."

Kade wanted to ask why the church would call Child Protective Services, but that seemed too personal. "How come the art teacher didn't tell you Timmy wasn't in class?"

She took two plates from a cabinet and placed them near the sink. "The class was held in one of the art rooms after school, and he always made sure to be back before I picked him up. Since I didn't have to be in the art room with him, I didn't realize he'd unenrolled himself from the class. Apparently, he told the teacher that the doctors didn't want him spending more time in school than was necessary. It was a ridiculous excuse, but the teacher didn't know that."

Kade sat in one of the kitchen chairs and stared at his scuffed black boots against the yellow linoleum floor. "It's not easy being a parent. Especially a single one."

"Technically," she said as she opened a can of tuna and dumped it into a bowl, "I'm not even a temporary guardian. I'm just the sister Timmy lives with."

"Why?"

She tossed a glob of mayo into the bowl and mixed it with a spoon. "Ask my uncle Isaac."

Since he had known Isaac, Kade wasn't surprised by that dick move. He surreptitiously moved the bills on the table. While appalled at the amounts owed, he was more worried about the immediate Doom situation. There would be no way to get her in, and he didn't know how to break that news.

When he didn't respond, she changed the subject. "Do you have siblings?"

"Four brothers." He tilted his head to read an itemized bill that cost more than his yearly salary while he'd been in the army. "All older."

She faced him, holding a spoon of mayonnaise, her eyes—

now an incredible shade of green—had widened. "Your mother had five sons?"

He chuckled beneath his breath. He'd never thought about it that way. "Yep."

"Wow." She shook her head and added Worcestershire sauce to the bowl. "Just wow."

"That's what Nin—my grandmother who raised us—used to say."

She laughed and started slicing tomatoes. "I'd love to meet Nin one day."

"Nin would've loved you." Rose turned, probably because of his use of past tense, and he changed the subject again. "I'm going to Doom alone."

"No." She popped bread into the toaster. Then she filled two glasses with water and placed them on the table. "I'm going with you."

He frowned while he sipped the water that soothed his parched throat. "Doom isn't a movie theater. You can't just buy a ticket and walk in."

"We'll figure it out." She stacked the bills and legal papers on the table and shoved them into a tote bag lying on the other chair. Then she hung the bag and her Yale sweatshirt on a hook next to the church key. "I hope you like tuna sandwiches."

"Love them." He didn't, but she'd refused to stop for takeout on the way here, and he was hungry. He hated eating her food when he knew she was struggling financially.

While she made the sandwiches, he clasped his hands on the table and tried to think of a different plan.

"I hear you mulling," she said as she spread mayonnaise on the toast. "You might as well stop. I'm—"

"Determined to come with me."

She layered tuna over the mayo and topped the sandwiches with sliced tomatoes and cheese. Then she added some lettuce she'd pulled from the refrigerator's crisper. "You don't have to sound so defeated."

"Rose." Shit. He rubbed his chin with his fist. "Doom is dangerous."

She sent him a smile that melted his heart. "I've seen *Fight Club*."

"This isn't a damn movie. It's real life. It's brutal. And..." He waited while she put the plates, napkins, and a bowl of potato chips on the table. She'd given him two sandwiches, while she'd taken only one.

"And what?" she prompted as she sat across from him. "It's scary?"

He picked up a sandwich, took a bite, and closed his eyes. Besides cheese and tomato, she'd added a seasoning to the tuna that made it surprisingly delicious. After he swallowed and wiped his lips, he opened his eyes to meet her gaze. "No women allowed."

She wrinkled her nose. "Why?"

He shrugged. "It's always been that way. I can't even imagine why a woman would want to go."

"Has Doom been around long?"

Kade tossed a bit of his sandwich into King George's bowl. Kade wasn't above bribery. Besides, it annoyed him when animals didn't trust him. King George ate it and then presented his tail. "Doom has been around since 1770. Maybe even earlier. The fighters used to meet below the original Tondee's Tavern on the corner of Broughton and Whitaker streets."

"There's a Tondee's Tavern on East Bay Street."

"That one is newer and named for the first."

She wiped her mouth with a napkin. "Below this original tavern, someone formed an illegal fight club? Named Doom? In 1770."

"That's the legend."

"Nothing surprises me anymore," she muttered as she sipped her water. "You referee these fights?"

"Ref and facilitate."

"What does that mean?"

"There's paperwork before the fight starts. Every fighter has to be vetted and sponsored. Rules have to be reviewed. Bets made."

She paused with a chip in her hand. "Magnus mentioned Deke's cell phone that he used to take bets on."

"Yeah." Kade shook his head and sighed. "Illegal book-making has become a problem. For months, one of the sponsors and I have been trying to track down the source of these bets. I know there's a website on the dark web, but we've had no luck finding any information. I'm hoping Deke's cell phone will give us some answers."

She nodded and asked, "Sponsors?"

"There are four sponsors who act as the bank." He took a handful of chips and dumped them on his plate. "All legal bets are underwritten and approved by the sponsors. They also make and enforce the rules regarding how Doom works for both patrons and fighters."

"Do these sponsors pay you?"

He started his second sandwich, grateful for it since he was still hungry. "The sponsors pay my fee, and I take a cut of the book—the bets made."

She tilted her head, as if contemplating something. "Is it a lot of money?"

"It can be." He paused mid-bite as a horrible thought appeared. "They're not hiring. Besides, no women allowed. Remember?"

She wrinkled her nose and grabbed a few more chips. "That seems sexist."

"I don't know if it's sexist or just..." How could he explain the culture of violence and fear and straight-up testosterone that ruled Doom? "It's the kind of thing that most women not only don't know about, they probably don't *want* to know about. Besides, after a night of fights in an underground room, the place stinks to the point where I can barely breathe."

"I guess it would." Laughter tinged her voice. "So, how are you going to get me in?"

"I'm not." He finished his sandwich, sat back, and watched King George circle Rose's chair with his tail high, his fierce glare focused on Kade.

She nibbled her sandwich and kept her head down. Since she ate slowly, he took the planner, Shakespeare book, and cell phone out of the backpack and laid them on the table.

She took the book while he flipped through the monthly planner.

"Apart from the missing pages," he said in between sips of water, "I don't see anything in this book except for the hours Deke worked at the club. And a phone number for a company called Beaumont, Barclay, and Bray, with the initials A.L. next to it."

She wrinkled her nose as she read the newspaper clipping she'd pulled from the book. "It's a law firm based in New Orleans. I remember Isaac and Magnus arguing about it not long before Isaac died. But why would Deke need a lawyer?"

"No idea. But let's find out." Kade got up to grab his new burner phone from the charger.

"Why did we get new phones again?"

"Because when you deal with the Fianna, you tend to become a bit paranoid."

"Makes sense, I guess. Although I'm still processing the fact that the Fianna exist, and that you work for them. Kind of."

"I'm still processing that truth as well." He called the Beaumont, Barclay, and Bray number only to hang up a minute later. "It's been disconnected."

"That's strange."

"I agree." He flipped through the rest of the planner's pages but found no other notes. Deke's planner was as neat as his apartment.

"Oh my gosh!" She handed Kade the newspaper clipping. "This was in the Shakespeare book."

He skimmed the article from the *Georgia Historical Journal*. "What is this?"

"The *Georgia Historical Journal* is one of the most prestigious history publications in the state."

"So?" He reread the synopsis about a historian who'd found something in Savannah's Preservation Office.

"See the photo at the bottom?"

The photo showed a pretty woman holding a rectangular wooden box decorated with silver plates around the corners, sides, and top.

Rose stood, moved behind him, and tapped the photo with one finger. "That is my box."

He read aloud, "'Sarah Munro, a historian on loan from the Smithsonian, found a rare eighteenth-century puzzle box hidden in the Savannah Preservation Office.'"

"That box"—Rose pointed to the photo again—"belonged to my mother. My mom was an historical architect, and she worked part time in the Savannah Preservation Office."

"I don't understand."

She paced the kitchen, pushing strands of hair behind her ear. "Whenever someone renovates an old home, historical architects make sure everyone follows strict building codes. If someone wants to renovate in a historically accurate way, they call in experts like my mom to ensure everything they're doing is correct according to the time when the home was built."

"Sounds like a lot of rules."

"You have no idea." She waved a hand around the room.

"The point is, my mother worked at the Savannah Preservation Office. When I was twelve, she discovered that puzzle box in a New Orleans antique shop. She brought it home, and my parents were so excited about it. The box sat on my dad's desk for a week before it disappeared."

"What happened to it?"

"I don't know." Rose paused near the sink and stared out the back window. Her voice shook, as if she was remembering something difficult. "When I asked my mom, all she told me was that she put it someplace safe."

The pain in her voice made him ache to take her in his arms and hold her close. Despite their unbelievably erotic kiss, they barely knew each other.

He let out an explosive sigh and clasped his hands behind his neck to stretch his arm muscles. His entire body felt hot and tight. "Your mom hid the box in her office, and this historian found it. That's good news, right?"

"There's something else." She faced him again with her arms wrapped around her waist, and tears streaked her face. "The day after my mom hid the box, my parents died."

ROSE UNTIED HER APRON, threw it onto the counter, and paced the kitchen some more. "This can't be a coincidence. I'm supposed to deliver a box, and Deke has an article about my mother's box tucked in his book?"

"Rose." Kade spoke firmly yet softly, as if knowing her head was about to explode. "What is going on?"

She took a deep breath to calm her erratic breathing so she could speak calmly. "My mother's box. Deke. Magnus. It's all connected. I just have no idea how or why. But that box in the article—my mother's box—has to be the one Deke wanted me to deliver. Otherwise, why would Deke have hidden the article?"

"Rose." Kade stood, took her arm to stop her movements, and gently drew her to her chair. Once she sat, he said, "Start at the beginning. What do you know?"

She'd eaten only half of her sandwich, but now her stomach felt like it'd been twisted into Celtic knots. She pushed her plate toward him and said, "I can't eat this. You should."

He pulled his chair around the table so he could sit across from her. Then he placed a hand on her knee. "I wish you'd eat it."

She shook her head. "I can't. Please. You need to eat for tonight. I don't want it to go to waste."

"Okay." He took the half sandwich and finished it in two bites. "Now, what's going on?"

His hand on her leg was rough and scarred, yet his touch was so gentle she felt his warmth more than any pressure. "One day, I came home from school, and the box—the one in the article—that had been on my dad's desk was gone. I didn't think much about it." She glanced at him from beneath her lashes. "I was distracted by my plan to sneak out of the house that night and meet my girlfriends."

He raised an eyebrow. "You were a rebel?"

"Kind of." Her throat started to close, and she sipped her water. "There's a game kids play on the Isle of Grace called Dare the Witch."

"I know the game. You sleep in front of the tomb of a supposed eighteenth-century witch, and then, if you survive, you drink a beer in the morning."

She tilted her head. "Have you played it?"

"No." He squeezed her knee. "My grandmother Nin, who grew up on the Isle of Grace, told me about it. And I know my Aunt Mamie played it with my mother. Apparently, it was a big deal to make it through the night since the owner of the land was scarier than the ghosts."

"Old Man Capel was terrifying." She sighed. "We slept in front of Anne Capel's tomb—she was one of the isle's witches and supposedly murdered forty-four kids—but the sheriff caught us. He called our parents in the middle of the night." She placed her fingers on top of his hand that still rested on her leg. "My parents' car ran off the bridge leading from Skidaway Island to the Isle of Grace. They died on their way to pick me up."

Kade didn't say anything. It took a minute before she realized he'd matched his breathing to hers.

She swallowed, surprised when she tasted salt. She'd started crying and hadn't realized it. He handed her a paper napkin, and she blew her nose. "It was so weird and random."

"Weird how?"

"My dad was a surgeon. He never worked on cars or did any kind of hobbies where he could hurt his hands. He always drove new cars and kept them in perfect shape. Yet, according to the police report, his brakes gave out on the bridge." She sniffled and scrunched her napkin in her fist. "The first thing Uncle Isaac asked me after my friend's parents took me home was..." A lump formed in her throat, and she stared at Kade, his face fuzzy through her tears.

"What did Isaac ask you?" Kade prompted.

She lowered her voice because it seemed safer that way. "Isaac asked me where my mother hid the box."

CHAPTER 7

At seven forty-five p.m., Kade led Rose into the Johnson Square garden and squeezed her hand for the millionth time.

Although they'd spent only a few hours at Rose's house, he was emotionally exhausted. Their conversation had left him with little doubt that Isaac Guthrie had been involved in the deaths of Rose's parents.

Kade knew from firsthand experience that Isaac had been a *truly evil fuck.*

After the revelations about the box and her parents' deaths, Rose called the Savannah Preservation Office. Historian Sarah Munro had left for the day, but the assistant told them that six weeks after the article ran, someone had broken into the SPO and stolen the box. About the same time Deke asked Rose to act as courier.

As far as Kade was concerned, the box Deke wanted Rose to deliver had to be the same one that'd been stolen.

They'd also used Rose's second-hand laptop to do more internet research on Hezekiah Usher and discovered nothing. Rose's research on the Fianna and the Prince pulled up only a

Wikipedia page about an ancient Celtic order of assassin warriors. Kade had warned Rose not to bother researching the Fianna, because the Prince had a team that scrubbed information off the internet. The Prince even updated the page himself. As far as the world was concerned, the Fianna died off during the Third Crusade, and one of the Prince's many jobs was to make sure the world continued to believe that lie.

Then they'd researched the name 'Remiel Marigny' only to find an obituary about a man who'd been murdered years earlier. That's when Rose fell into a funk. After adding her contacts to her new burner phone, she offered to bake peanut butter cookies.

Apparently, she baked when stressed.

To cheer her up, he'd driven her to Leopold's Ice Cream and then to see Timmy in the hospital. Timmy adored the treat, despite being annoyed that they'd left King George behind.

After seeing Timmy, Kade took Rose to his apartment under the guise that he wanted to change and grab his gym bag. He'd just needed the driving time to think.

He had no chance of getting Rose into Doom. And now that it was almost eight p.m., he had to convince her of that truth.

Rose sat on an iron bench beneath an oak tree near the center of the square. She'd changed into jeans and a navy T-shirt that did little to hide her figure, and he wished she'd put on the blue sweatshirt she'd tied around her waist. She wore pink lip gloss and had pulled her red hair into a high ponytail. Backdropped by a garden of purple azaleas, white roses, and trees dripping with Spanish moss, she shimmered.

He swallowed. Why did she have to be so damn beautiful?

To distract himself, he dropped his gym bag and paced, fisting and unfisting his hands.

What am I going to do with Rose?

He'd told her, over and over, that she couldn't come into Doom. But she'd insisted that he ask. Since he didn't want her searching for that box alone, he'd agreed. Hopefully, after he asked for permission and got shot down, she'd believe him.

He stretched his arms and ignored the sweat streaming down his back. It was hotter than boiling tar despite the breeze that promised an incoming storm.

"Kade"—Rose grabbed his wrist when he passed her—"what are we doing here?"

He sat next to her. "Waiting for someone. A fighter." He checked his watch. "He'll be here soon."

"Have you figured out—"

Kade stood. "Here he is. I'll introduce you, but don't ask questions. He doesn't want anyone to know he's fighting tonight."

She nodded and rose as well.

Vane came toward them in black combat pants, black T-shirt, and boots. His long brown hair was tied behind his neck, and he carried a gym bag. He stopped a few feet away and nodded.

Out in the wild, Vane looked larger and fiercer. So much so that a woman with a stroller turned around on the path and hurried away.

After introducing Vane as Vin—the fight name Kade had chosen for Vane—Kade said, "Both of you, follow me. I'll point out where I want you to wait." He fixed his stare on Rose. "Don't move until I get you. Agreed?"

When she nodded, he said, "Let's go."

A few minutes later, Kade left Vane and Rose near a stoplight and crossed the street. He beelined for an iron gate next to the building marked 35 Whitaker Street. He was grateful to see a black Mercedes with shaded windows parked nearby.

He knocked on the driver's side window, and it rolled down.

Ivers, Calum Prioleau's butler, sat in the cool air conditioning and said, "How may I be of service, Mr. Dolan?"

Kade handed over the cell phone he'd found in Deke's apartment. "After the fight, please give this to Mr. Prioleau. I believe it may have the information he requested."

"I will." Ivers slipped the phone into the center console. "Good luck tonight, Mr. Dolan."

"Thanks." Once the window rolled up, Kade headed through the iron gate into an alley with a long staircase. He descended, stopped at a wooden door on the left, and knocked.

Once the doorman ID'd him, Kade handed over both of his cell phones, hurried down more stairs, and went through the metal detector. Weapons and cell phones were forbidden. To add to the security, the lights were high-frequency LEDs that interfered with phone cameras. Since all the members knew the *very* unpleasant consequences for breaking the rules, the bulbs had yet to be tested.

Despite the high-tech security, Doom was just a huge, colonial-era empty room with stone walls and rough-hewn roof beams. Pewter lanterns held lit candles that competed with the modern lights hanging from the ceiling. Alcoves had been dug out around the room's perimeter. Two of those alcoves had doors. One led to the Fighter's Hole where the fighters waited, and the other opened into an office where the four sponsors conducted business. There were also some darker, danker storerooms in the back.

The most interesting things about the main room were the floor-to-ceiling frescoes on the stone walls. Although stained with mold, the designs peeked through.

A Liberty Tree was on one wall.

On another, there was an early colonial flag with vertical red and white stripes and a blue field with eight-pointed white stars.

Someone had painted AUGUST 10, 1774 on the third wall.

The fourth wall held two lines from Shakespeare's Sonnet 116:

LOVE ALTERS NOT WITH HIS BRIEF HOURS AND WEEKS, BUT BEARS IT OUT EVEN TO THE EDGE OF DOOM.

Some members believed the place was haunted by the Sons of Liberty. And Kade didn't discount that theory.

Spectators filled the room around the pit—the center area consisting of a packed-dirt floor where the fights happened. Luckily for him, the main alcove/office had been renovated into a soundproofed room. A place of quiet. A reprieve in the center of hell. Especially in the summer when the club's underground coolness couldn't keep up with the lack of AC.

He entered the office, dropped his gym bag onto a metal shelf that held cases of bottled water and paper towels, and took a clipboard off a hook on the wall. Three of the four sponsors stood in the center of the small room, arms crossed, speaking in hushed tones. The man in a seersucker suit was Ivers's boss, Calum Prioleau, one of the four sponsors. Calum, having the confidence that came from being the richest man in the city, didn't bother with false names.

Meanwhile, the other two men, Selah and Gideon, used fake names. Since Selah and Gideon were the kind of men Kade would never encounter unless he was investing millions or selling BMWs, he didn't know them outside of the club.

Everyone avoided Doom's fourth sponsor because he was an asshole.

Kade cleared his throat and moved toward the three sponsors. "Like I mentioned in the text I sent you earlier, I have a new fighter interested in throwing down tonight. He is big and tough. Ex-military. Combat-hardened. Name is Vin. The audience will go batshit crazy."

Kade hadn't bothered texting Asshole Sponsor.

Selah shrugged. "Fresh meat always brings in more money."

Gideon took a long drink from his water bottle, a few drops falling onto his black suit. "You willing to vouch for this MF, Kade?"

"I am," Kade said.

"I'm okay with it," Calum said. "As long as Vin knows the rules and can meet the buy-in."

"He doesn't have any money." Kade pressed the clipboard against his thigh. "What is the buy-in tonight?"

Selah crossed his arms, wrinkling his blue cotton suit. "Ten grand. Purse is twelve grand for the winner, two for the loser."

"I'll throw in five grand for Vin." Gideon tossed his water bottle into the nearby trash bin. "Based on Kade's rec."

"I'll add the second five," Selah said. "I'm always looking for new excitement."

"Good." Kade breathed the sigh of the hugely relieved. "I'll bring Vin down. I have another question. Someone wants to come." He paused and swallowed hard. "A female."

All three men laughed at the same time.

Then, in a firm voice that demanded obedience, Calum said, "*No.*"

Rose tapped her foot on the sidewalk. What was taking Kade so long?

The man—Vin the fighter—hadn't said a word since their introduction. All he'd done was stand still, arms crossed, and stare at the ground.

She peeked at Vin. While not as handsome as Kade, he was as large and imposing. From the size of his biceps and the width of his shoulders, she wasn't surprised he was a fighter. She wanted to ask him questions about Doom, but since this was his first fight, he probably didn't know much. Unless he'd gone as a spectator.

She glanced at him again. Kade had told her not to ask questions, but still... "Do—"

Vin moved quickly and crossed the street. That's when she saw Kade on the other side of the gate. He let Vin in, and they both disappeared. Now she was alone. Wonderful.

Her phone buzzed, and she checked the ID. She'd only sent her new burner phone number to a few people.

The text was from Samantha.

You're all set for the Got Ghosts? test next Wednesday night. I'll drop off study materials. There's a ton to memorize. And you'll have to learn the tunnel map. Bring the $500 with you on the night of the test.

Although she hadn't asked Harry for the money yet, Rose texted back,

Thank you!

She was about to put her phone away when she thought of something.

Are there tunnels beneath Whitaker Street, near the original site of Tondee's Tavern?

Yes. They're closed off. Most of the tunnels in this city are too dangerous to walk through. And they're haunted!

Rose sent a laughing emoji.

Samantha responded, Why?

Rose stared at Samantha's single-word text. Before she could answer, Kade appeared.

"Hey." He crossed his arms and stared over her shoulder.

She knew male deflection well. "They're not letting me in, are they?"

He shoved his hands in his back pockets, as if not sure what to do with them. "They said no."

"It's not fair." Now she sounded like Timmy.

"I'm sorry." He finally met her gaze and touched her cheek with his fingers. "I promise I'll look for that box."

She scoffed. "I'm supposed to wait here?"

"I'd prefer if you go back home."

She grimaced. "Patience isn't my thing."

He chuckled just as the phone buzzed in her hand.

She hid it behind her back and smiled at him. "But it's okay."

He raised an eyebrow.

He had reason to doubt her. So she touched his arm reassuringly. "Meet me at my house when it's over. But please text me if you find my box."

"I promise." He pulled his truck's keys out of his back pocket. "Take the truck and lock your doors when you get home."

She bristled at the reminders but then remembered he was only trying to protect her. She accepted the keys. "I promise."

He fixed his gaze on her face as if he wasn't sure what to believe. Finally, he headed for the iron gate. A moment later, he disappeared.

Exhaling deeply, she put the keys in her pocket and walked back to Johnson Square. It was after eight p.m., and most of the tourists were ensconced in restaurants. Because it was mid-June, the sun was still up. Thunder rolled in distance. Between the dreary light and lack of people, she felt isolated in the city she'd grown up in.

After checking her surroundings for the third time, she texted Samantha back.

Can you meet me in Johnson Square ASAP?

Why?

I need your help to get into the tunnels beneath Whitaker Street. I need to find a place called Doom.

Once Kade left Vane in the office to meet Selah and Gideon, Kade headed for the fighting pit.

He had hated seeing the disappointment on Rose's face, but there'd been no other options. Now, as he studied the main space filled with men, his chest felt tight. And the constriction had nothing to do with his shallow breathing.

He just couldn't shake the feeling of unease that fueled his restlessness. Although the moments before the violence ramped up were always tense, this felt different. Tonight his emotions were on high alert, his senses heightened. Maybe it was because he couldn't confirm Rose had gotten home safely. Or that he was worried about how Vane's fight would work out, especially since Kade had vouched for the brother. Maybe it was the secrecy Vane required, or the flickering lights due to the city's random power fluctuations. Or it could even be from the storm-charged air, exacerbated by huge claps of thunder.

Kade honestly wasn't sure. All he knew was that tonight's fight felt strange with a side of expectancy. Maybe he was making things too complicated. Maybe the rising tension had to do with the wait for everything to begin. The promise of violence. The smell of blood and despair. The desire for victory or death.

Doom's air tasted tangy, like a combination of testosterone and whiskey.

While Doom hadn't had many deaths in the ring, there'd been some. A few had been due to random fist blasts that hit the perfect spot at the perfect time. Other deaths had been due to fighters who were encouraged by a blood-thirsty crowd and a sponsor with no moral objections. The former types of deaths had been unfortunate accidents that were cleaned up by patrons who happened to be law enforcement officers and EMTs. The latter deaths, always surprising, had been handled by people he had no interest in meeting.

Selah appeared and clapped Kade on the shoulder. "Vin is impressive. He's down with the rules, so I sent him to the Fighter's Hole to get ready."

"Great." Kade read the lineup sheet on his clipboard. For some reason, the second-round fight slots remained blank. "Is *he* coming tonight?"

Selah sighed as if disgusted. Another testimony of Asshhole Sponsor's awful reputation. "*He's* lurking around."

Gideon came up with a huge smile. "Hey, Kade. Looking forward to a great night."

"Me too, sir," Kade said with a fake smile.

After quick handshakes, Selah and Gideon headed for their reserved spaces around the fighting pit.

Once Kade made sure the sound system was working, he went into the office, grateful to find Calum there alone.

Calum laid his phone on the desk that held a monitor, the only way to watch the fight in the office. "Kade, why would you ask about inviting a woman to Doom?"

Kade placed the clipboard on the desk. "It's not important."

"Hmmm." Calum buttoned his suit jacket. Of course, despite the heat, the pants were perfectly pressed. Calum would never allow anything as mundane as a wrinkle to disparage his appearance. "Ivers told me you left him a cell phone."

"Yes, sir." Kade focused his attention on the wood plank floor that had probably been laid long before the American Revolution. "I found that cell phone in Deke's apartment today. I can't get past the passcode, but I thought you'd be able to figure that out."

"I know someone who can. The question is why do you think the cell phone is important?"

Kade met Calum's ice-blue gaze. "I believe Deke may be the source of the excess money flowing through Doom. That phone could lead us to his clients."

It'd been a situation that Calum, after having done an audit of Doom's financial records, had brought to Kade's attention two months ago. But neither one of them had solved the mystery.

Calum leaned a hip against the desk and crossed his arms, his gold signet ring glinting. "You think Deke is the man taking off-the-books bets?"

"It's possible," Kade said. "I also found something in his planner. A phone number for Beaumont, Barclay, and Bray. A law firm in New Orleans. He'd also included the initials A.L."

"I know that law firm, although I don't know any lawyer there with those initials. That firm gives corrupt lawyers a bad name." Calum sighed and pinched the bridge of his nose. "Thank you, Kade. I'll check into this. Hopefully, before these larger bets attract unwanted attention."

"Did you tell the other sponsors?"

"Tonight, before you arrived, I discussed the situation with Selah and Gideon. They were unhappy, but not surprised. After the last fight, they'd heard rumors of out-of-state people placing off-book six-figure bets. They want this situation handled as quickly and quietly as possible."

Fuck. "Seriously?"

Calum nodded. "That activity could draw attention from the IRS. But I'm more worried about nefarious types."

Like organized crime. Exactly the sort of attention Doom had spent centuries avoiding. Doom was an exclusive private club for a select group of men in the know. Those in the know weren't, by any means, the richest in town. In fact, most were local, working-class men. A few came from Charleston and New Orleans, but the majority of the clientele were from Savannah. And those men knew about Doom from their close male relatives. Even the old-man hoarder who'd owned Iron Rack's Gym had once fought at Doom. As had Kade's grandfather. "Have you told Asshole Sponsor?"

"No."

"Good. Because I think he's involved as well." Kade felt uneasy about not divulging the conversation he'd overheard earlier, but that would bring up questions he had no intention of answering.

Calum's eyes narrowed. "Before I confront anyone, I want to know who is placing bets higher than the club's agreed-upon limits. Who is keeping the books on that money? Where is the money being held, and how is the cash being transferred?"

"Maybe Deke's cell phone will help."

"One can only hope." Calum gripped Kade's shoulder. "In the meantime, I can't wait to see what Vin brings to the ring. I haven't met him yet, but I'm betting in his favor."

The office door opened, and Asshole Sponsor appeared with a frown plastered over his face. "What's this about a new fighter? I haven't agreed to anything."

Calum crossed his arms again. "A new fighter needs the

approval of three out of four sponsors. Since we agreed, we didn't ask you."

"I still should have been notified." Asshole Sponsor, with black hair brushed back from his face, crossed his massive arms and took up a mirror-image stance across from Calum. Unlike Calum, Selah, and Gideon, who always wore suits on fight night, Asshole Sponsor wore jeans, a black T-shirt, and a black leather motorcycle jacket. Either he enjoyed acting the rebel who had once fought in Doom's pit, or he didn't give a fuck about blending in and making friends.

Since Kade had been on the opposite side of Asshole Sponsor's fists, Kade figured it was both. With a fierce temper and unmitigated pride, Asshole Sponsor believed this town owed him everything.

"There is always next time." Calum smiled, but even Kade could see the annoyance behind his cold, blue eyes and in the tight lines around his mouth.

"Fuck you, Calum." Asshole Sponsor threw a glare at Kade. "What are you looking at, Dolan?"

Kade shrugged. "Just waiting for the fight to begin."

Asshole Sponsor scoffed, glanced at the clipboard on the table, and smiled. It wasn't a smile one would offer a child or a lover. It was the smile a man used when he had leverage over others. "I see round two is empty."

Since Doom's fight manager decided who fought whom, Kade said, "Not my problem."

"No?" Asshole Sponsor moved into Kade's personal space until he could smell the other man's sweet tobacco scent. "We'll see about that."

What the fuck does that mean?

Kade's stomach heaved. But instead of looking away, he sent a silent warning. *Back. The. Fuck. Up.*

Calum, with perfect timing, clapped Kade's shoulder. "It's five minutes until start time."

Asshole Sponsor scowled at Calum and left the room.

Kade exhaled and said to Calum, "You didn't need to come between us."

"No?" Calum picked up Deke's cell phone and slipped it into his jacket pocket. "I remember the last time you two fought."

"I was throwing him out of Rage of Angels."

"You broke his wrist. In return, he busted your nose and had you arrested for assault."

"Only because I let my guard down. I thought he was drunker than he was, and I didn't know he was a dirty fighter."

"Still"—Calum took a water bottle from the metal shelf—"take my advice. Stay away from him. He hates you."

Since Asshole Sponsor had far more money and clout, Kade relented. "All right, Mr. Prioleau. Next time, I'll be extra nice to Magnus Guthrie."

"Samantha?" Rose zipped up her sweatshirt, steadied her phone's flashlight, and stepped over a metal bed frame that blocked the tunnel. It was much cooler down here than on the street above. "Have you heard of Doom?"

After Samantha met Rose in the park, she'd admitted the barest details. Rose didn't want Samantha any more involved than she had to be, so she'd avoided mentioning the Prince or the Fianna. But when Rose had said that she believed Deke had hidden the box at Doom, Samantha had offered to come.

"I've heard rumors." Samantha used her own phone's flashlight to add more light to the dark and creepy situation. Like Rose, Samantha wore jeans, a blue T-shirt, and sneakers. And she'd tied her hair up into a tight bun. "But I never believed Doom existed."

Samantha grabbed Rose's shoulder so they didn't both fall on the rusted pieces of the ancient bed frames and filing cabinets.

"What is this trash doing down here?"

Samantha wrinkled her nose. "Years ago, the local hospitals used these tunnels as garbage pits. No one ever came down here, so no one noticed. It wasn't until the city needed to do some much-needed upgrades to the power and water utilities that they clamped down on the illegal dumping. But the city never cleaned the tunnels."

"How many of the tunnels are usable?"

"Ten percent. Maybe. The Got Ghosts? tour company paid for a lot of the cleanup of that ten percent. But they only worked on those that were structurally stable."

"And it's a coincidence that those tunnels are the ones with ghosts in them?" Rose laughed. "How convenient for the tour company."

Samantha, surprisingly, didn't laugh. "Ghosts always find a way."

Not wanting to irritate her friend, Rose changed the subject. "Where are we?"

"I'm not sure." Samantha stopped where the tunnel split into two. She moved the light between the pitch-dark options.

Rose heard scratchy, scurrying sounds. "Maybe this wasn't a good idea."

"Don't think about the rats." Samantha pointed left. "This way."

A few minutes later, after breathing only through her mouth to avoid the stench of decay, Rose paused as Samantha shone the light along the wall. "We're beneath Whitaker Street," Samantha said. "I think."

"How do you know?"

Samantha pointed to graffiti painted on the stone wall—a white skeletal hand holding a white pirate's cutlass. Red blood dropped down the blade to form words below: *Sans Pitié.*

"Without pity?" Rose whispered.

"Technically, it means 'no mercy.'" Samantha walked carefully around broken concrete blocks, gravel, and building debris.

"I've seen that tag around the city." Rose touched the cutlass's flaky paint on the wall. "But this looks like it was painted decades ago."

"It's the symbol of the Prideaux pirates, who used to terrorize this area in the seventeenth and eighteenth centuries, before the city was formally founded." Samantha took Rose's hand. They helped each other as they climbed over school desks that hadn't been used since the 1940s. "That tag means there is a nearby entrance into or out of a tunnel."

When she moved her flashlight, something glinted along one side of the tunnel. "What's that?"

Samantha used her light to illuminate the doorknob of a paneled door within the stone walls. Someone had carved something in the center of the wooden door. Rose used a finger to trace the indented image. Then she blew away the dirt.

"Use this." Samantha handed her a bandana she'd pulled from her back pocket.

Rose wiped off more of the grime and stood back with the light.

"It's a carving of a Liberty Tree," Samantha said. "Doom was built beneath the original Tondee's Tavern, where the Sons of Liberty used to meet."

Rose ran her fingers over the edges that felt smooth and worn with age. "This door could be from 1776."

"Or earlier." Samantha grabbed the brass doorknob cast with the initials JL tucked within a lily, and it turned easily. "Ready?"

Rose nodded. "Let's go."

She led the way through a tunnel that ended at a stone staircase. A reverb shook the ceiling, and dust fell on their heads. "Do you hear that?"

Loud male voices and hard-core rock music reached through the walls.

"I do," Samantha whispered.

Rose took two deep breaths and went up the stairs until she hit another door. A beam of light came through where the uneven stone step met the wooden frame. They turned off their lights and slipped their phones into their pockets. Rose took the decorative brass doorknob, similar to the one below, and paused.

Samantha touched her shoulder, giving Rose the confidence to push. She blinked from both the light and the smell. The stench of male sweat and moldy air sucked the breath out of her lungs. Kade had been right. The place reeked.

Samantha gasped and followed Rose. Luckily, the door opened into a dark storage area off of an open room. They tucked themselves against a wall lined with boxes of white towels and cleaning supplies that gave them a view of an open, central area. Unfortunately, so many men filled the floor, it was hard to see the action in the center. On the other hand, since the men faced the fighting ring, no one saw them. With the shouts and pounding rock music that could cause a brain bleed, no one heard them, either.

From what Rose could see, there were a few storage areas like the one she and Samantha hid in. Two had doors. The other alcoves, with no doors, remained dark. The center area was a huge open space filled with men. Considering the crowd, she'd have no chance to explore those rooms. And within the main area, there was no place to hide a small, wooden box.

The men roared and flung their fists toward the ring in

time to the music. The din made it impossible to hear individual words, so she had no idea what had happened.

Something bloodthirsty, probably.

Rose motioned to Samantha that she was moving closer. Samantha, with her hands over her ears, shook her head. Yes, it was risky. But she'd do anything to save her brother.

She left the shadow's safety and stepped onto a stack of concrete blocks near the entrance to the alcove. She didn't have a clear view, and the two fighters in the center ring moved in and out of sight. Vin and another man had stripped down to gym shorts. Their sweaty bodies only emphasized their sheer size, their bare feet gripped the dirt floor.

The men circled each other, and she held her breath. Although the music blasted through the room, the spectators quieted. It was as if the expectation of violence muted everyone's voices. The two fighters locked gazes as they moved, making it seem as if they were the only ones in the room. The way they flexed their hands, twisted their necks, and shifted their shoulders promised bloodshed. It was clear, even to a novice like her, these two men weren't random street fighters.

They were combat-hardened warriors who'd give no quarter and offer no mercy.

The moment Vin, with his long brown hair tied behind his neck, sent a roundhouse kick toward the other fighter's chest, the crowd screamed in unison. The room filled with a loud wave of sound that moved the stale air. The other fighter, shorter and wider than Vin, dodged the kick with a graceful gait and tremendous speed. This man also had long hair—black instead of Vin's light brown—with darker skin, tattooed dots on his arms, and a scar on his face that extended into one of his eyes. Vin's fighting style was strong and controlled. The other fighter's was fierce and deadly.

The scarred fighter slammed his fist into Vin's face. Blood spewed from Vin's mouth, and he fell to his knees.

The crowd roared, "*Leo! Leo! Leo!*"

Vin rolled and kicked Leo's legs out from beneath him. Leo fell but regained his posture quickly, pulling Vin up by his hair. Leo whaled Vin with massive punches, sending the crowd into a frenzy. Some of the spectators moved as one, pounding their fists in the air as the music got louder, screaming, "*Vin! Vin! Vin!*"

Others shouted, "*Leo! Leo! Leo!*"

Rose swayed on the block and reached for the wall to steady herself.

The fight continued with the violence in the pit ramping up with every hit. Each spurt of blood spurred on the crowd which, in turn, sent the fighters deeper into a cycle of violence she'd never known existed.

She gagged and moved back before falling into Samantha's arms. They collapsed on the floor, wrapped around each other. Rose knew they should leave, but she'd frozen in place.

No wonder this place was called Doom. It was the closest thing to straight-up violence she'd ever seen. And, to make it worse, Vin and Leo were in that ring voluntarily. They weren't just fighters. They were being used like rabid dogs for the entertainment of others.

The crowd exploded with, "*Vin! Vin! Vin!*"

Samantha took her turn on the concrete block. A moment later, she returned. Even in the dark shadows, Rose could see Samantha's wide eyes and labored breathing.

"We need to get out of here," Samantha whispered. "*Now.*"

Rose agreed and turned toward the door they'd used to enter...and stopped.

Another man must have come up the same steps they had, because he blocked their escape route, arms crossed. Jeans encased his thick thighs, and a black T-shirt outlined his massive muscles. He was tall, black, and had a bald, tattooed head.

He glared at Rose with startling green eyes. When he noticed Samantha, he tilted his head and said, "Lady Samantha."

The darkness in his voice carried shock and displeasure.

Samantha held up her hands, palms out. "I haven't said a word, Arragon. I *swear.*"

Samantha's voice sounded more stressed than Rose had ever heard before.

Arragon shifted his gaze back to Rose. Then he wrapped one arm around his waist and bowed.

CHAPTER 9

*K*ade stayed off to the side of the pit, whistle in his mouth, waiting to end the fight.

He swiped his arm across his forehead. The place had heated up, leaving him soaked in sweat. And the smell—no, *stench*—of hard-core male violence could smother an enraged bull.

Leonato pinned Vane to the ground. Kade knelt to watch Vane's broad shoulders hit the dirt. Leonato was the stronger fighter, but Vane put up a hell of a defense—better than Kade had expected.

Considering the cheers that overwhelmed the piped-in music, the crowd agreed.

On cue, someone—probably Magnus—turned up the volume on Static-X's classic thrash metal sound. Because exploding eardrums just added to the fun and games.

Vane found an opening and rolled until he crouched on one knee. When Leonato stood, Vane charged and took Leonato back to the floor. Fists cracked jaws, the fighters groaned and grunted, and Kade followed the action. He was now covered in splatter—blood, sweat, and saliva. But he stayed close, whistle ready.

Leonato tossed Vane off. Just as Vane scrambled to stand, Leonato sent a roundhouse kick into Vane's sternum. Vane fell, clutching his chest and gasping.

The crowd yelled over the pounding music.

Kade blew his whistle and ran to Vane. The fighter was on all fours, desperately trying to drag in oxygen.

Kade crouched, one hand on Vane's back. "Do you yield?"

"*No.*"

The audience shouted, "*Vin! Vin! Vin!*"

Kade touched Vane's neck. Blood from his nose dripped onto the floor. His entire body, like Leonato's, was covered with cuts and bruises. But none of that concerned Kade. His real issue was Vane's off-the-chart pulse. The fighter was moving into the stroke zone.

"I'm sorry, brother," Kade whispered. "I gotta call the fight."

Vane shook his head and used Kade's shoulder as leverage to stand. That hero move kicked up the crowd's blood lust. Kade glanced at Leonato. The Fianna warrior stood off to the side, chest heaving like furnace bellows, fists flexing against his thighs. His long black hair hung around his shoulders, his dark skin glistened, his gaze fixed on Vane.

When Vane stopped wobbling, Leonato raised his chin.

Neither man was going down unless it was a knockout. That meant the next call was all on Kade. He never forced fighters to yield, because he'd never yield. Besides, while bloodshed equaled money, time meant bonuses. The longer Kade could keep the fighters locked in combat, the more money they'd all make.

Kade stepped back, raised a hand, and whistled to resume the fight.

Vane tackled Leonato. They landed and rolled toward

Kade. He stepped aside as Leonato broke free and elbow-jabbed Vane in the windpipe.

Kade blew his whistle.

But the crowd's rhythmic chant deafened Kade's warning and spurred the fighters on. Vane recovered and sent a left hit to Leonato's nose. The sickening sound of breaking bone rivaled only the crowd's chant of, "*Vin! Vin! Vin!*"

Apparently, Leonato had had enough, because he slammed his fist straight into Vane's chest. When Vane fell to his knees again, Leonato followed up with a kick to Vane's head. Vane collapsed onto the dirt, his eyes closed, body shuddering. Still, despite his hyperventilating, he pressed his bloodied fists against the floor to get up.

Kade whistled and pushed Leonato away so he could check Vane's vitals. His heart rate was too fast and too irregular. "Do you yield?"

Vane shook his head, spewing blood and spit.

The crowd's frenzy was unlike anything Kade had ever seen before. The more Vane struggled to stand, the louder the spectators became. Except Vane couldn't get his footing and landed on his knees. When he fell onto his back and his shoulders didn't move, Kade blew his whistle again.

The fight was over. Leonato had won.

"*Leo! Leo! Leo!*" resonated throughout the space, except Leonato didn't do the victory walk. He wrapped an arm around his waist and bowed to his opponent. Then he left the pit in that eerie, silent way that made it seem like he was walking on water over glass.

Kade exhaled and wiped his forehead with the bottom of his T-shirt—the part that wasn't soaked with sweat or anything else. Once Leonato disappeared into the Fighter's Hole, Kade held a hand out for Vane. Except Vane didn't take it. Although his shoulders shuddered and his legs wobbled, he got to his feet on his own.

Aaaand the crowd screamed in approval, *"Vin! Vin! Vin!"*

Vane might have lost, but he'd become a fan favorite. A feat very few fighters ever achieved, especially their first time in the pit. He'd definitely be asked back.

Kade followed Vane out of the pit. Then Kade stripped off his shirt and tossed it to one of the boys—who were the teenage sons of longtime members—who rushed in to smooth out the dirt and add sand for the next fight. Kade grabbed a water bottle from a nearby table. He drank deeply and checked the fight chart on the wall above the clock where the fighters' names were written in chalk. There were eight rounds tonight, but the slots for the next round's names were still empty. Magnus stood near the ladder below the chart, talking to Selah and Gideon. Lots of hand movements were going on.

That can't be good.

Kade had twenty minutes before the next round and needed a few moments of quiet in the office. He turned and ran into Vane's back. Kade hadn't noticed that Vane had stopped outside the office door.

"Brother?" Kade touched Vane's shoulder. Usually, fighters couldn't wait to return to the strange peace of the Fighter's Hole. "You okay?"

Vane didn't say anything. He just stared through the office door's window, his lips forming tight white lines. Kade followed his gaze and saw Calum talking to Arragon, a badass Flamma warrior who made Leonato seem like the Easter Bunny.

At that moment, Calum looked in Kade's direction and frowned. That's when Kade noticed something else. Two people sat on chairs behind Arragon.

Samantha Barclay, a waitress from Rage of Angels, and...*Rose.*

∽

KADE TOOK two deep inhales and exhales before pushing open the office door.

He was surprised when Vane followed him inside, but Kade was more concerned with the two women who sat behind Calum. They held hands, yet it was Rose who met his gaze straight on.

Despite his need to confront her immediately, now was not the time. Instead, he forced his attention onto the other men in the room. Calum, with his arms crossed, threw glares around. Arragon, who'd moved to the corner of the room, seemed more spectator than participant.

Arragon might be a scary-ass SOB, but Calum was a sponsor with the power to hire and fire. And Kade needed to finish the night to get paid. "Is there a problem, Mr. Prioleau?"

Calum raised an eyebrow. "I guess that depends on how you define the word 'problem.'"

Rose dropped Samantha's hand and stood. "We're not a problem. Samantha and I were exploring a tunnel and found a door and ended up in one of your storage rooms."

"The same night Kade asked about bringing a woman to Doom?" Calum glared at Samantha, who tucked stray hairs behind her ear and stared at the floor. "I don't think so."

Kade shifted his weight and clenched his fists against his thighs. Rose had lied to him. She'd known when she told him she was going back to her apartment that she had an idea for how to get into Doom. He had to give her credit, though. Enlisting Samantha—who as a ghost-tour guide probably knew the tunnels better than anyone—had been a good idea. It's something he would've done. Except he would've been armed. And he'd never have gotten caught.

As angry as he was, he had other problems right now. He had to get the women out of there as quickly as possible. He had to get them out before Magnus saw them.

Kade nodded toward the clock on the wall. "I still have time before the next fight. Why don't I escort the women out and—"

"Kade"—Calum tilted his head—"did you beat up a man last night named Antoine?"

Rose gasped and covered her mouth with one hand.

Kade kept his shrug loose and nonchalant. "Antoine harassed Rose, and I took care of it. No biggie."

Arragon shifted his gaze to Rose. While Calum was now staring at Vane. Probably because Vane was leaking blood all over the floor.

Kade said to the fighter, "Why don't you get cleaned up? I'll pay you afterward."

Vane, who seemed completely focused on Samantha, nodded.

Do Vane and Samantha know each other?

It took a minute for Kade to realize the connection. Vane lived at Iron Rack's with Pete White Horse. Pete had also been one of the bouncers at Rage of Angels, where Samantha had worked as a waitress, and now they were dating. So Samantha knew Vane. Which meant Vane had to be sweating the fact that Samantha would tell Pete she'd seen him here. And Pete would tell Nate...and on and on and on.

But that was Vane's problem. Not Kade's.

Once Vane left the room, Calum asked, "Kade, did you know Antoine works for Magnus Guthrie?"

"Yes." Everyone in Doom knew Magnus sold dope on the side and paid twerps like Antoine to run the sketchier streets.

"*Soooo...*" Calum drew out the word as if searching for the right words. "Magnus, on Antoine's behalf, challenged you to a fight. Tonight."

What? "I'm not fighting tonight. And I'm sure as fuck not fighting Magnus."

"Your name is on the board," Calum said, "and the bets have been taken."

Kade opened the door, stared at the chalkboard on the wall with his name scratched in white across from Magnus's, and came back in. He slammed the door with such force he was surprised the window didn't break. "Fuck you, Calum."

Calum held up both of his hands. "While I understand your concern, all the sponsors have agreed to the fight—especially in light of the female incursion."

"Excuse me?" Rose moved into the center of the room. "Kade has to fight Magnus because of me?"

"If you mean because Kade saved you last night from Antoine and because you chose to trespass here tonight, then yes." Calum took off his suit jacket and laid it on the table. "While Kade fights Magnus, my butler, Ivers, will escort you and Samantha home."

"I'm not going home with anyone." Rose stared at each man in turn. "And Kade isn't going to fight anyone on my behalf."

Samantha took Rose's arm. "We need to leave. We've caused enough damage—"

"No." Rose pulled her arm out of her friend's grasp. "Samantha? Why are you agreeing to this?"

Samantha glanced at Arragon, and the warrior nodded. Then she looked at Calum, who gave her a wan smile.

"Samantha?" Rose softened her voice. "In that storage room, you knew Arragon's name. And you apologized."

"Rose," Samantha whispered, "you don't understand."

"Miss Guthrie." Calum cleared his throat. "There are things going on you have no clue about."

Samantha and Calum know about the Fianna? Kade rubbed his chin with his fist. *Interesting.*

"I don't care." Rose turned her scorching gaze onto Kade.

"I'm going to search this horrible place and find what I'm searching for."

"You will not." Arragon's deep bass voice filled the room. "Tonight's turn is unfortunate, and action must be taken to remedy the insult."

Rose's hands landed on her hips.

Before she could scold Arragon too, Kade said to Arragon, "If I fight Magnus, will the women be free to leave?"

"Aye," Arragon said.

"This is crazy." Rose threw up her arms. "I'm already free!"

"We're not," Samantha said sharply. "We're at *their* mercy."

Kade wasn't sure if Samantha's *their* meant the sponsors or the Fianna. Either way, she was correct.

Rose snorted and headed for the door. Before she could reach for the handle, Arragon blocked her way. She turned to Calum, who shrugged. Samantha went back to her seat and watched the floor. Then Rose switched her gaze to Kade.

"Kade?"

"Arragon won't let you leave on your own, Rose." Kade took another water bottle off the metal rack and opened it. He was so thirsty, he could drink the entire Savannah River. If he didn't stay hydrated, he'd never make it through the night. "Trespassing is against the rules. I told you that."

"You didn't tell me you'd have to fight if I got caught!"

"I didn't think it was going to be an issue." He took a long sip, appreciating how it soothed his dry throat despite being warm. While he hated berating her, especially in public, she'd brought it on herself. "You're supposed to be home. Alone. Waiting for me."

She clasped her hands behind her neck. Her high ponytail had lowered, and chunks of red hair curled around her face. "This can't be happening."

"'Tis almost time," Arragon said.

Kade looked at the clock. He had ten minutes to change. He closed his eyes and inhaled deeply. How had he ended up in this situation? That's right. Rose.

Except he couldn't put all the blame on her. If he'd ignored her the first moment they'd met, none of this would be happening. If he'd walked away the night he'd fought Magnus on her behalf, maybe he wouldn't have spent the last eight months dreaming about her. Wanting her. Worrying about her.

So, yeah, this wasn't all her fault.

He opened his eyes and sighed. "Calum, you're sure Ivers will get Rose and Samantha home safely?"

"Of course," Calum said with firm intent.

And that was good enough for Kade.

"I must attend to Leonato now." Arragon hit his chest with his fist, bowed his head, and left the room.

Once the warrior disappeared, Kade took Rose's arm. "Go home and wait for me there."

Before she could argue, he kissed her on the cheek. Then he headed for the Fighter's Hole.

CHAPTER 10

Rose touched her cheek where Kade kissed her and waited until he left the room before turning on Calum. "Mr. Prioleau, you can't make Kade fight—"

"I can and I will." Calum's blue eyes hardened. "And you will not mention anything you've seen here. Do you understand?"

"I don't care about what I've seen." She waved a hand around the sparse room. "I care about what happens to Kade. I won't force Kade into that horrible pit with my ghastly cousin because of my desperate choices."

Calum moved toward the desk. There was little furniture in the room. A few folding chairs, a desk with a monitor, and metal shelves holding water, paper towels, and a first aid kit.

"Unfortunately, Miss Guthrie"—Calum switched on the monitor—"it's too late. The bets have been made, and the crowd...Well, let's just say that Kade is a favorite. Since he hasn't been in the pit in over a year, I couldn't stop this fight even if I wanted to."

The screen showed the pit. Magnus was already in the

arena, walking around, hands in the air, trying to get the crowd to keep yelling, "*Magnus! Magnus! Magnus!*"

She swallowed a bitter taste. "You mean Kade has fought in the pit before?"

"Of course." Calum muted the volume. "Kade fought for almost two years before the sponsors voted him in as official referee."

Fought? In that human cockfighting pit? For years? Her heart ached at the thought.

"Don't worry, Calum." Samantha came over and touched his shoulder. "We won't say a word to anyone about anything."

"I expected better of you, Samantha." Calum smiled at her. "Especially after all that's happened."

"I swear," Samantha whispered, "we'll keep Vane's secret."

"Wait." Rose had the sudden feeling that something else was going on. "Who is Vane?"

"The fighter Vin," Samantha said. "His real name is Vane. He works at Iron Rack's with Pete and Nate—"

"Those two bouncers from Rage of Angels?"

"Yes," Calum said, "and Vane doesn't want his friends to know about this fight tonight."

Rose chewed her bottom lip. Kade had mentioned the same thing. "Vane's buddies will figure it out when they see his face. I'm kind of surprised he didn't think about his injuries before getting beat up."

"Vane is a strong fighter." Calum pulled out his phone and texted. "It probably didn't occur to him that he'd get so injured. That also means he needs a cover story."

"Make it a good one," Samantha said. "Pete can smell the smallest amount of bullshit."

"No kidding."

Samantha and Calum stood close enough to read his text. Close enough to be friends.

Shivering, Rose went back to the screen. Magnus pranced around in shorts, slapping his hands together to rile up the men. His bare chest shone with sweat. The tattoo of a black raven on his bicep appeared to move as his muscles contracted. Someone had increased the volume on the hard-core metal music, and the deep bass shook the floor of the soundproof office.

Was she surprised her cousin Magnus sold drugs and was one of Doom's sponsors? No. When she'd been twelve, and he'd been nineteen, he'd been a horrible, bullying teenager to her and everyone else around him. Now he'd grown into a vicious, vindictive man.

How am I going to get Kade out of this?

"No, Calum."

Rose turned to see Samantha pointing at Calum's phone. "Make it a random mugging."

Calum typed again. "What do you think?"

"It's good." Samantha squinted to read. "Send it to Vane before he leaves."

Calum hit a button and slipped his phone into his pocket. "Rose, before Ivers arrives, I want to know about this thing you're looking for. Arragon mentioned your search."

She scanned the room, looking for anything that resembled a fuse box. Maybe if she cut the power, they'd cancel the fight. "It's nothing—"

"We're looking for an eighteenth-century puzzle box Deke was supposed to give to Rose," Samantha said.

Rose spun around. She'd told her friend, *in confidence*, about the box while they'd gone through the tunnels. "Samantha!"

Samantha shrugged. "I have to tell Calum the truth. He knows about Deke's...uh...disappearance. Calum may be able to help us."

Calum sat on the edge of the desk. "Is the box the important thing? Or what's in it?"

That was a good question. One she didn't have an answer for yet. "I don't know. But Deke assured me it wasn't drugs."

"I don't think we can trust Deke's assurances." Samantha sighed and spilled the rest of what she knew.

While Samantha spoke, Rose paced the small room. *Where is the fuse box?*

When she couldn't find it, she returned to the screen. Kade hadn't arrived in the fighting ring. Maybe he'd changed his mind.

When Samantha finished her tell-all, Calum looked at Rose. "Deke promised you could earn money by delivering a box? A box your mother hid at the Savannah Preservation Office and that was recently stolen. A box with unknown contents—"

"Not drugs," Rose said.

"Hopefully not," Calum said. "Except Deke disappeared, and now you need to find this box and deliver it to a man named Hezekiah Usher?"

"Yes." On-screen, Magnus was showing off his backflips, and she prayed he'd break his neck.

She really was a terrible person.

"And this money?" Calum touched her arm. "You need it to pay your brother's medical bills?"

When Magnus started doing handstands for the crowd, Rose shifted her prayers from Magnus's death and dismemberment to his ultimate defeat at Kade's hands. "Yes."

"Rose?" Calum tapped her shoulder until she met his gaze. "If you're Magnus's cousin, does that mean you're the daughter of Dr. Thomas Guthrie and Violet Levaux Guthrie? The same couple killed in a car crash ten years ago?"

Rose raised her chin. "How could you know that?"

The lines around Calum's eyes softened. "I met your father a few times. He was my father's colleague."

"My father was a surgeon." She considered what little she knew of Calum Prioleau's family. Other than the fact they owned most of the city. "Wasn't your dad a lawyer?"

Calum gave her a wry smile. "Our fathers ran in the same circles."

It took her a moment to realize what Calum was saying. "My father was a member of Doom?"

"In his younger years—before you were born—he was a fighter. Once he became an established physician, he graduated to sponsor. Of course, your mother never knew about Doom. After his death, your uncle Isaac took over the sponsorship. Then, after Isaac's death—"

"My cousin Magnus became a sponsor."

"Yes," Calum said.

Rose's knees melted, and she sank into a folding chair. "My father would never—"

Calum held up a hand. "This place is run by men who would *never*."

Still, her father had fought in this human cock-fighting pit? And he'd been a sponsor? Of all the memories she had of her father, she'd never once heard him raise his voice or act in any kind of violent or angry way. He'd loved and protected her until his death.

She took a few deep breaths and brushed stray hairs off her cheek. It was possible she never knew her parents at all. And that realization made Rose feel even more alone.

Samantha stood behind Rose and squeezed her shoulder. "Calum, do you have any idea where Deke would've hidden an eighteenth-century box?"

"No," Calum said. "A year ago, Deke asked to fight. When the sponsors said no, he left Doom in a sulk and never returned. But Rage of Angels was his life. If he hid a box, it would've been at the club."

"I searched the club already." Rose took off her sweatshirt and tied the arms around her waist. The heat and humidity were building up in the small room. "I also went through his apartment. I did find an article about the box tucked into a book, *The Complete Works of Shakespeare.* Deke used the article to bookmark Sonnet 116."

Calum frowned and stared at the monitor. Kade still hadn't appeared, but Magnus, with all his antics, didn't seem to mind. "'Love alters not with his brief hours and weeks, but bears it out even to the edge of doom.' This club's name comes from that verse."

Rose stood and paced the room. "Doesn't that mean the box has to be here? Maybe in one of the storage rooms? Or maybe Deke asked someone to hide it here for him?

"The box isn't here," Calum said. "Deke didn't have access to Doom on his own, and there's no way he could've come in without anyone knowing. As far as asking a member to hide it, almost everyone hated Deke. No one would risk their Doom membership doing a favor for him."

"That box has to be somewhere." Rose rubbed her temples to ward off a rising headache. "But right now, I need to get Kade out of that fight."

"You can't." Calum checked his watch. "The best thing you can do for Kade is to go home and wait for him."

The door opened, and Vane came in, carrying his gym bag and a water bottle. He'd showered and wore sweats topped with a black long-sleeved T-shirt. He'd cleaned his face, and butterfly Band-Aids lined his forehead. Bruises covered his cheeks, and his lower lip was swollen.

He walked with a slight limp and winced when Samantha touched his arm. "Are you okay, Vane?"

"Sure." Vane's deep voice cracked.

"You got my message?" Calum asked Vane.

"Yes. I'd like to take Samantha home." Vane coughed and took a drink from his water bottle.

Calum shared a glance with Samantha before saying, "Good idea. You two can talk about your cover story."

Vane took another long drink, finished his bottle, and tossed it into the trash can. "When can I—"

"Fight again?" Calum said. "Considering your performance tonight, you'll be on the roster for the next fight night. Although I have no idea how you're going to hide this extracurricular activity from your buddies at Iron Rack's Gym."

"I'll think of something."

Calum nodded. "I don't schedule the fight nights. That's the manager's job. He'll be in touch."

The door opened, and a teenage boy came in with a manila envelope. After handing it to Calum, the boy paused near Vane and said breathlessly, "Great fight, man."

Vane barely looked at the boy. "Thanks."

Once the boy left, Calum handed the envelope to Vane. "You didn't win, but you stayed in longer than expected. This is your base fighter pay plus a small bonus."

Vane shoved the money into his gym bag and looked at Samantha. "Ready?"

Vane really was a man of few words.

"Vane?" Calum asked. "Does anyone at Iron Rack's know about this?"

"*No.*"

Calum held up a hand. "I promise we won't say a word."

Samantha kissed Calum's cheek and said, "I'm sorry." When she passed Rose, she whispered, "I'll call you tomorrow. Until then, don't do anything rash."

Before Rose could answer, Samantha and Vane disappeared. That's when Rose turned on Calum. He was texting again. "Mr. Prioleau, is Arragon a Fianna warrior like Leonato?"

Calum glanced at her. "How do you—"

"It's a long story. I don't know much—most of it from a Wikipedia article. I'm just wondering what two Fianna warriors are doing here."

Calum finished texting. Once he put his phone on the table, he paused as if weighing his words. "Leonato has fought in Doom before, but I didn't know until recently what he was or that he worked for the Prince. Samantha and I met Arragon last week. We were sworn to secrecy, so I won't say any more. Just stay away from them. Don't talk to them or about them."

A light-headedness came over Rose, and she sat in the chair again. Part of her had hoped that Kade's stories about the Prince and Fianna warriors were fairy tales. "The Prince wants my box."

"Let the box go, Rose. I'm serious. Walk away while you still can."

"If I do that, my brother will die."

"*Rose.*" Calum's exasperation shone on that single word, reminding her of her father. He'd often fussed about her stubbornness and inability to follow the rules. "I—"

The door opened, and a man in a black suit entered. "I'm parked outside, Mr. Prioleau."

"Thank you, Ivers."

"I don't need a ride—"

"Ivers will escort you out and take you home." Calum's tone told her there'd be no more argument.

She sighed. Although she didn't want to be beholden to anyone, the heat, humidity, and stench of male violence had left her nauseated enough to appreciate the ride.

She took Kade's truck keys out of her pocket and handed them to Calum. "Can you give these to Kade?"

"Of course." Calum placed the keys on the table and

nodded toward the monitor. Kade had just entered the pit. Even with the sound muted, the crowd moved as one mass—like a giant, undulating wave—with fists in the air. "There's one more thing you should know. I endorsed this fight tonight. Without my signature, the fight wouldn't have happened."

She frowned. "Why would you do that?"

"Because Magnus threatened to call CPS on you. I'm not sure what that's about, but I'm not stupid." He moved in close enough for her to see the silver flecks in his blue eyes. "Rose, I own Rage of Angels. I know you work there under the assumed name of Lily Levaux. Which, to be honest, wasn't the best choice since Levaux was your mother's maiden name. A lot of people in town knew her. Including Magnus."

She rubbed her forehead with her fist. "I was in a rush to get out of my interview with Deke, and it was the first name I could make up." She'd regretted it immediately. The name had made it easy for Magnus to discover her secret.

"If Magnus calls CPS—"

"They'll take Timmy away, and I may never be able to win guardianship." She clenched her fists. "Why are you telling me this?"

Calum shifted his focus to the monitor. "I know you think you're alone and have no one to trust, but that's not true."

She didn't agree, but now was not the time to argue. Especially since her throat closed up, preventing her from speaking.

Ivers touched her shoulder. "Ma'am?"

She left the room only to be assaulted by even louder sounds and more revolting smells. From this angle, she couldn't see into the pit. The men's shouts fought for dominance over the ear-splitting rock music. She swallowed and, for a moment, considered forcing her way through the crowd, jumping into the pit, and dragging Kade out of there. Vane had looked awful after his fight, and her stomach revolted. Is that what would happen to Kade?

"Ma'am." This time, Ivers didn't ask. He ordered. "This way."

She wiped her cheeks with her fingers, took a deep breath to kick back the dry heaves, and followed Ivers out of Doom.

All of this was her fault. And she swore she'd find a way to make everything right.

CHAPTER 11

*K*ade entered the pit and pumped his fists in time to the death-metal beat.

Men screamed his name, and he smiled. While Magnus gathered support from the middle, Kade walked the perimeter. He flexed and waved, giving the crowd what they wanted because he needed time to shift his mind-set.

He didn't want to be here. Yet here he was.

Hell, he'd spent five minutes in the Fighter's Hole trying to remember the combination to his locker. That's how long it'd been since he'd fought. Random sparring matches with Nate in Iron Rack's ring didn't count.

Although Kade had sworn that last time in the pit would be his final fight, he'd stashed a pair of black shorts in his locker. Maybe he'd jinxed himself.

Now, as he mentally prepared, he couldn't help but work through the steps that'd brought him to this moment. He'd known there'd be consequences for hitting Antoine. Still, any man who hit a woman deserved a beatdown. If this was the price, Kade would pay it.

But he didn't have to be happy about it.

He finished his crowd walk and moved toward the center, where Magnus was showing off with handstands and back-flips. Kade's last fight with Magnus had been outside of Rage of Angels, eight months ago. But this was the first time in Doom's history that the referee and a sponsor were fighting each other. So Kade understood the frenzy of the men.

They expected blood. Maybe worse.

He inhaled, exhaled, and faced his opponent. Magnus pointed at Kade as if daring him to attack.

The shouting and music suddenly stopped, leaving a hollow silence in its place. Then someone with a love of old-school industrial rock shifted the playlist and turned up the volume until Kade couldn't hear his own heartbeat. When the announcement came through that there would be no referee, the onlookers screamed.

That meant one thing. No rules. *Fuck.*

Magnus moved first, taking Kade to the floor. His head hit the ground, and everything went blurry. He blinked a few times and jumped to his feet, fists flying.

Thank you, Ranger School.

His fist caught Magnus's jaw. Kade's second swing slammed into Magnus's stomach. The third was a left hook straight to the nose.

Magnus fell on his ass, and the crowd exploded.

Kade backed away, hands in the air surrender-style. He barely noticed the roar of men around him. Barely noticed the pain in his rapidly swelling knuckles. Barely noticed the crowd's chant of, *"Kade! Kade! Kade!"* All he focused on was the way Magnus moved. How Magnus rested his weight on his heels. How he pulled one shoulder down before he swung.

Magnus popped up and leveled a right hook. The pain exploded through Kade's face. But it was worth sacrificing a cheekbone to get to know his opponent. Magnus threw another punch aimed at Kade's nose. Kade ducked until

Magnus's roundhouse kick caught Kade's side. It drove the breath from his lungs but wasn't enough to knock him down. Magnus kept hitting and kicking while Kade dodged and evaluated.

Magnus moved fast, but his hits were filled with more force than precision. This was no strategic attack. It was more of a full-on steam-driven fight meant to maim, hopefully kill. Kade had to keep some clarity in the moment. Only a perfectly aimed hit could take down a man so enraged.

At the right moment, Kade hit Magnus in the jaw. Kade's knuckles ached like they'd all been dislocated. Magnus stumbled back, and Kade kicked Magnus's stomach. He fell to his knees, and Kade took advantage. He threw himself on top of him, bringing them both to the sandy dirt. They rolled until Kade ended up on top, fists flying. Cuts and bruises made Magnus's swollen face look like it'd been trampled by a horse.

Magnus gripped Kade's neck and squeezed. Magnus was shorter and stockier, but tonight he was stronger than a boar in rut. Instead of trying to rip off Magnus's fingers, Kade hit Magnus's face. *Left, right, left, right.* Kade attacked regardless of the agony shooting from his wrists to his shoulders. He kept hitting regardless of the numbness of his swollen fists, regardless of Magnus's tight hold that made Kade see alternating flashes of lights and stars.

Somehow, Magnus got in a right hook. The kind that struck the perfect location with perfect timing.

Kade fell over, and he dragged in oxygen. His chest felt like it had caved in on itself. Magnus released an unholy yell, and his foot found Kade's kidney.

Instinctively, Kade curled up and used his arms to protect his head.

Magnus screamed and kicked and screamed and kicked, again and again and again. Pain hijacked Kade's body, leaving him breathless and blinking.

When the assault stopped, Kade shifted and saw the glint of a knife's blade. He blocked the hit with one arm, grabbed Magnus's wrist, and twisted the knife out of his grasp. Kade tossed it into the crowd, but not fast enough to roll away from Magnus's foot.

A moment later, everything went black.

KADE WOKE SLOWLY.

When he rolled over, he found himself on the cot in the corner of the Fighter's Hole. He pulled up one knee to stabilize his aching ribs and leaned against the wall. The cool, smooth stones behind his back eased his hot, pain-infused torso. He didn't appear to have broken bones, but the swelling throughout his body attested to soft-tissue damage. He closed his eyes and listened to the hum of the metal fan in the corner. At least the room was empty.

He had to count his blessings when they came along.

A few minutes later, he heard a man clear his throat and opened his eyes.

Calum leaned against a locker, arms crossed. He'd taken off his suit jacket and laid it on a bench. His shirt had so much starch it didn't show a single crease or sweat stain.

A lecture was the last thing Kade needed. "How long have I been out?"

Calum checked his watch. "Twenty minutes. I gave everyone a recess after you lost."

Kade flexed his bruised hands. The knuckles were stiff, and he needed to move them if he didn't want to end up with clawed fingers.

"Losing wasn't your fault." Calum spoke in a low voice, as if he was afraid of who might be listening.

Kade lifted an eyebrow. "I'm not even sure what happened."

He'd seen a knife. Of course, his entire body hurt, so it could be possible… He pulled the elastic waistband away from his taut stomach and checked the situation down below. He whistled in relief.

"I can't throw Magnus out," Calum said. "He's a sponsor."

Kade lifted his head. Had he missed part of the conversation? "Excuse me?"

Calum sighed loudly. "Magnus drew a knife."

Kade shrugged. "It was a no-rules fight."

"Still, all weapons have to be approved by the sponsors. We did not approve any weapons." Calum took a water bottle off of the first aid table and carried it over to Kade. "It turns out Magnus is on illegal steroids."

Whoa. Kade opened the water, wincing at the pain in his hands, and drank half the bottle in one gulp. "Are you sure?"

Calum sat in a nearby metal folding chair. "Magnus admitted it."

"I don't understand." Kade finished the bottle and tossed it into a nearby trash bin. "What happened after I passed out?"

"The manager jumped into the ring, but Magnus hit him."

Magnus hit the manager? "That's a violation of the rules." Doom didn't have many rules, but no one touched the sponsors or the manager.

"Yes, it is," Calum said. "It took ten patrons to get Magnus to the ground. A few of the patrons brought you in here to recover, while Magnus was thrown into the office to cool off with one of our patron doctors. The doc diagnosed a classic case of 'roid rage."

Kade swung his legs off the cot and stood. Although wobbly, he stabilized himself. He needed a shower and a hundred ibuprofens before his body stiffened, and he was unable to move. "Thanks for the save."

He wasn't too proud to admit to being saved. Being saved was better than being dead.

"You're welcome."

Kade took off his shorts and tossed them into the trash. Stark naked, he headed for his locker. But Calum's silent regard was loaded with unspoken warnings. "*What?*"

"I can't get rid of Magnus."

Kade spun the lock. "You said that already."

Calum frowned, probably because he wasn't used to people correcting him. Or maybe it was the blatant male nudity. Either way, Kade didn't give a fuck. He was a soldier. Modesty hadn't been an issue for him since basic training.

"Magnus is dangerous," Calum said. "Especially hopped up on illegal steroids."

Kade opened his locker and yanked out his gym bag. Then he headed for the open shower stalls on the far side of the room. He turned on the nozzle and waited for the water to shift from frigid to freezing. "I don't care."

He stepped beneath the water and raised his face to the spray. He used the bottle of generic liquid soap on the shower shelf and rinsed off. When he was done, Calum took a dry towel from a nearby rack and tossed it to Kade.

"You should care." Calum paced the area that consisted of a wall of lockers, a self-serve first aid station, and a middle bench with a stack of water bottles on top. "And"—he nodded to the wound on Kade's shoulder—"you're bleeding."

So Magnus had found flesh with his knife.

"Shit." Kade wrapped the towel around his waist and headed for the first aid station. His shoulder could probably use a few stitches. Except he wasn't about to go to the hospital. After pouring a hefty dose of hydrogen peroxide diluted with sterile water on the cut, and cursing liberally, he used butterfly Band-Aids. Not well, apparently, since Calum came to help.

"Magnus is a problem." Calum's whisper made it sound like he was planning a covert op or plotting an insurrection. Considering the size of his fortune, probably both. "Magnus hates Rose."

Kade hissed when Calum wrapped gauze around his shoulder to keep the smaller bandages in place. Kade, unsure how much Calum knew about Magnus and Rose's relationship, kept his next question vague. "How do you know that?"

Calum taped the gauze into place. "Earlier tonight, Magnus threatened to call CPS about Timmy Guthrie."

"Because Rose worked at Rage of Angels as a stripper?"

"Yes. Although, technically, the club is still closed and Rose isn't Timmy's guardian." Calum wiped his hands on a towel and tossed it into a laundry bin. "After Isaac died, a judge transferred temporary guardianship to Magnus."

Shit. Kade hadn't realized that. "How the fuck did that happen?"

"I suspect a lot of money and a corrupt judge. Rose is only twenty two, and Magnus is older by seven years. He also has money and a job, while she couldn't even hire a lawyer to represent her in court. What I didn't understand, until tonight, is why Magnus filed a petition with the court for custody of Timmy. Especially since he allows Timmy to live with Rose. Magnus doesn't care about either of his cousins."

Kade ran a hand over his wet hair.

Calum threw away the bandage packaging. "Rose told me about Deke and the box. Well, technically, Samantha told me, and Rose confirmed. Are you helping her find this box?"

"Yes." Kade hesitated, not sure how much information he should offer Calum. Except he already knew a hell of a lot. "Isaac knew about the box, even before her parents died. So it makes sense that Magnus not only knows about the box as well, but believes one of his cousins can lead him to the location of the box. A box worth two hundred thousand dollars."

"Exactly." Calum put the gauze and tape back into the first aid box. He seemed unfazed by the amount of money Rose would get for the box. Then again, maybe it wasn't that much money to him. "You have to finish the night. We still need a referee for the next six fights."

Kade closed his eyes and fought back a wave of exhaustion. He wanted to walk away and never return. He wanted to check on Rose. Except he'd signed a contract for tonight's fights. A contract that Calum—the lawyer who'd written the damn thing—would never release Kade from.

After dropping the towel, he pulled on a clean pair of gym shorts he'd found in his gym bag. He winced because his raw knuckles ached like they'd been shoved in a blender with sandpaper. Unfortunately, he didn't have another clean shirt. "I'll be out in a minute."

"Here." Calum took a white T-shirt from a lost-and-found basket in the corner and threw it. "It's clean."

Kade caught it and held it up. The shirt would barely fit Rose. "It's too small. I have an Iron Rack's T-shirt in my truck."

"We don't have time." Calum checked his watch. "Five minutes, Kade. After the final fight, meet me in the office. I'll give you your paycheck."

"And Magnus?" Kade slipped the tee over his head, surprised the seams didn't rip.

"Selah, along with a few patrons, has escorted Magnus out of the club." Calum picked up his suit jacket. "I know this isn't the best timing, but you need to know that I'm aware of the Fianna and the Prince and your situation with them."

Kade tugged the shirt down until he gave up and took it off. He'd just work without a shirt. "Who told you?"

"Arragon." Calum put on his jacket and buttoned all three

buttons. "And that's all I'm going to say about it."

Kade sighed, not at all surprised. Arragon, the most senior warrior, often contacted the rich and powerful in the cities where the Fianna was running operations. "Just be careful, Calum. Arragon is a straight-up killer."

Calum nodded. "I have seen that truth for myself."

Using the mirror, Kade evaluated the facial-laceration situation. Magnus had gotten in a few good hits. He'd not broken any skin, but there'd be some nice bruises tomorrow.

A low rumble began outside the walls. The patrons were getting antsy.

Kade flexed his fingers, trying to ease the stiffness. "What about Rose?"

"Ivers drove her home.

"Thank you." Kade shut his locker and smoothed back his wet hair so it plastered against his head. "I just wish I knew what happened to Deke."

That was something Kade hadn't cared about in his pre-Rose days.

Calum headed toward the exit but paused in the doorway. "Deke isn't coming back."

Kade glanced at Calum. Maybe it was the way Calum's voice cracked on the last word. Or how he ran a hand through his perfectly coiffed hair. But Kade's stomach clenched and dived until it reached his knees. "How do you know that?"

"The same way I learned about the Fianna's existence." Calum straightened his shoulders and met Kade's gaze. "Last week, there was a situation with a Fianna warrior named Balthasar that ensured Deke will never be a problem for anyone ever again."

Kade sat on the bench and inhaled deeply. "You're sure?"

"Yes." The crowd's roar got louder, and Calum glanced toward the pit before adding, "I knew Rose's father. Thomas Guthrie was a renowned surgeon in Savannah and a sponsor of Doom until he and his wife died in a car accident years ago. Isaac Guthrie inherited Thomas' Doom sponsorship."

Kade hadn't heard that gossip. "Does Rose know?"

"I told her tonight." Calum moved into the room again. "Did you know Rose's brother has ventricular septal defect?"

Kade snorted. "Does HIPAA not apply to you?"

Calum shrugged. "One of Timmy's doctors was here tonight. We spoke in the briefest terms after he checked on Magnus. Timmy's situation is serious. He needs a heart transplant, but his chances of getting one are slim."

"Because of money?"

"It's not just about money. A potential pediatric heart transplant patient must have a certain type of health insurance that pays for the entire procedure as well as the anti-rejection drugs. While the surgery could run over a million dollars, the anti-rejection drugs can be over three thousand dollars per month. No hospital will give a child a heart—especially a smaller-sized heart that is so hard to find—if the family can't afford to keep it beating."

Kade whistled low. That seemed harsh and cruel. "What about fundraisers?" He didn't want to ask outright why Calum couldn't pay for the surgery.

"I can't give Rose the money, if that's what you're asking. It doesn't work that way. And I can't raise it with a fundraiser."

"Why not?"

"Because of the desperate nature of pediatric heart diseases, and the potential for abusing the transplant list system, pediatric hearts are handled differently than other transplant surgeries. Every step is monitored and controlled. But those controls also put limitations on what parents can do to save their children. The rules aren't there to be cruel. They are there to make things equal for every child. Yet, at the same time, those rules make it nearly impossible to get a heart. Less than thirty percent of children who need a heart will ever get one."

"That's so... *sad*." Knowing he'd do *anything* to save a child he loved, he wasn't surprised that the government established rules to protect the process.

"Yes, it is terribly sad." Calum sighed and leaned a shoulder against the wall. "In the case of pediatric hearts specifically, giving money to a patient for any reason violates complicated organ anti-trafficking regulations. To get Timmy on the transplant list, Rose must pay her medical debt, purchase a private, approved health insurance policy, and prove that for the rest of Timmy's life she and her insurance company can pay for his anti-rejection medications.

"Drugs which will end up costing millions if Timmy lives until he's an adult. Her only other option is to get him into an approved experimental drug or treatment study. That's how most children get their surgeries because very few families can afford to buy the insurance and dig their way out of debt. Unfortunately, getting on the list or in an approved study is the easy part."

"What does that mean?"

"Pediatric heart availability is the biggest barrier."

Kade swallowed. He was a complete ass. He'd never even considered that another child would have to die for Timmy to get a new heart. Sometimes Kade needed a kick in the balls to remind himself that others had far worse problems than he did. "What is Timmy's prognosis?"

"Not good." Calum headed for the exit again, moving closer to the loud chanting that now shook the walls. "Timmy's future rests on Rose finding and delivering that box. It won't give her all the money she needs, but it's a start. Otherwise, she has no chance of making Timmy an eligible transplant patient. A situation that guarantees her brother's certain and early death."

CHAPTER 12

Hours later, Kade parked his truck across the street from Rose's apartment. After finding an old Iron Rack's T-shirt in the back seat, he slipped it on and shoved his Fianna phone in the glove box.

Shadows cast by the spotlights illuminating the cathedral's bell towers danced around him. He rolled down the windows to catch the breeze from another incoming storm and rested his head against the steering wheel. He'd left the club after refereeing six more fights, with the last one drawing so much blood they'd sent a fighter to the ER.

But that was the sponsors' problem.

The digital church bells rang twice, signaling the early morning time. He was exhausted, and his entire body ached like he'd been dropped out of a Black Hawk helicopter and run over by an M1 tank.

When he heard an evil hiss, he opened his eyes. King George emerged from the bushes surrounding the bell tower and sat on the sidewalk. Kade glanced at Rose's house. Light leaked out of the windows, and he hoped she hadn't stayed awake for his sake.

King George ran across the street and stood guard in front of the door.

Being mauled by a feral white cat was the absolute last thing he needed tonight.

In the few minutes it had taken to walk here, his legs had cramped, and he limped across the street. He tried to stretch his arms, but his shoulder muscles constricted.

Once he reached the bottom step, King George extended his front claws.

"Look, buddy"—Kade adjusted his bag, which felt like he'd stuffed it with bricks—"let me pass, and I'll feed you."

The cat sneered.

"Fine." He dug through his bag, sifting through books of matches, guitar picks, old condoms, and loose change until finding a dried-up protein bar. He'd no idea if cats even liked protein bars, but he had nothing to lose. He broke off a bit and tossed it onto the porch. The cat shifted and watched the piece land near a rocking chair with missing back slats.

Finally, on the fourth piece, the cat moved, and Kade made it to the front door. He was about to knock when he noticed something through the window—Rose pacing the living room, arms waving as she talked to a man dressed in black.

Leonato.

ROSE TOOK off her sweatshirt and threw it on the loveseat. Then she turned away from Leonato and headed for the kitchen. The church bells had rung twice, and she needed a cup of tea.

No, first she needed to see Kade. Then she needed to find her box, deliver it, and get paid.

And where was King George?

Leonato followed her into the kitchen, carrying her sweatshirt. He'd cleaned himself up after the fight and now wore black combat pants and a black T-shirt. Except for the white tape across the bridge of his nose that matched his white eye patch and some cuts and bruises on his cheeks, he looked surprisingly unhurt.

He'd not fought with his eyepatch on, but she didn't have the nerve to ask him if he could see out of that eye. If he couldn't, it would make his win over Vane that much more impressive... and terrifying.

He draped her sweatshirt over a chair, and her cell phone fell out. He picked it up, saying, "My lady—"

"I know, Leonato." She filled the teapot, placed it on the burner, and turned on the gas. At this moment, she was grateful to Kade for telling her about the Fianna, including the strange way they spoke, their eerie walk, and Leonato's role at the hospital weeks ago. Now she didn't feel like she was stumbling around in complete darkness. "You've said it three times. I need to find that box and give it to you."

Leonato still held her phone. "Aye."

"Why doesn't the Prince make you look for it?"

"'Tis not I who seeks forgiveness. 'Tis not I who must learn to trust."

Well, that wasn't helpful. She took out *one* mug and tossed in a chamomile tea bag. "I need to find the box by Sunday?"

Now he moved toward the counter and placed her phone on the charger. "Aye."

Again with the old-fashioned way of talking. "Except the man to whom I'm supposed to take the box may pay me two hundred thousand dollars. I need that money. That is why I agreed to be Deke's courier, despite the fact he was a disgusting excuse for a man."

"The Prince may offer some recompense."

"Can you be more specific?"

Leonato frowned as if annoyed at having to deal with her.

Well, she wasn't thrilled with him either. Especially since he'd killed that man at the hospital and beaten up Vane at Doom. But Leonato had been waiting for her when she'd arrived home and had insisted on coming in to talk to her. Although she remembered what Kade had said about the Fianna, she couldn't just walk away from the money she could make—money that could save Timmy's life—by delivering the box to the right person.

Unfortunately, King George hadn't been around to defend her.

She poured boiling water over the tea bag. "No answer?"

Leonato held out both hands, palms up, as if that would solve everything.

"Nice." She added sugar and looked out the window toward the lit-up church across the street. The last thing she wanted to do tonight was climb the bell tower and rescue the cat. "I believe I was supposed to deliver the box to a man named Hezekiah Usher." She glanced at Leonato. "Is that true?"

Leonato nodded.

Wow. Leonato spoke even fewer words than Vane.

She inhaled the soothing scent of heated chamomile and met Leonato's dark gaze. "Do you know how to contact Hezekiah Usher?"

Leonato looked away. "No."

She snorted. She could spot a liar in the dark across a crowded, noisy strip club. "If the Prince won't pay me, you can tell him to go to—"

"That's enough, Rose." Kade appeared in the doorway, holding his gym bag.

The harshness of his voice stopped her argument with Leonato, but she wasn't happy about it. She sat at the table and cradled her hot mug between her hands. Kade had cleaned up and now wore jeans with a faded Iron Rack's T-shirt. He had bruises and cuts on his face, and a bandage on one arm peeked out from his T-shirt sleeve. "The Prince wants my box but doesn't want to pay me."

"I'm not surprised." Kade came into the kitchen. "What are you doing here, Leonato?"

"Explaining the terms of the search to Lady Tempest."

She threw up her hands. "My name is *Rose.*"

Kade sent her an exasperated glare.

She went back to staring into her mug. She wanted Leonato to go away and her cat to return home.

Leonato spoke to Kade. "Have you found the box?"

Kade tossed his gym bag onto the floor near the table. "Fuck you, Leo."

Leonato frowned, and Rose sipped her tea to hide her smile. Did Leonato not appreciate the cussing or the nickname?

Kade went to the sink, took a glass from the cabinet, and filled it with tap water. "I've spent the last six hours in that fucking pit. I'm tired. Pissed off. And close to the point where I no longer give a shit about what you or the Prince want."

Kade raised his water glass as if toasting Leonato and drank the contents in three big gulps.

Leonato's eyes narrowed into black slits.

Rose watched both men as they faced off in a private battle. They studied each other as if considering—what? If they could take each other in a fight? Outwit each other in some game of the Prince's choosing? Stare at each other until one of them blinked?

She pushed her mug away and dropped her head in her hands. A headache threatened behind her eyes.

Kade came over and placed a hand on her shoulder. "Are you okay?"

"Yes." She raised her head and met his worried gaze. "Do we even know for sure if Deke had the box before he died?"

"Aye." Leonato took a folded-up photo from beneath a strawberry magnet stuck on the refrigerator door. "He stole it and hid it."

"We've searched the club and Deke's apartment," she said. "It's not there."

Leonato opened up the photo and laid it on the table. "'Tis a pity."

Kade refilled his glass with water. "I scoured Doom after everyone left tonight. I have no idea where else to look."

Leonato raised an eyebrow. "'Tis a quandary."

"In about one second," Rose said to the warrior, "I'm going to throw something at you. I don't care how scary you're supposed to be."

Leonato smiled, and chills scurried down her spine. His smile didn't represent happiness or joy. His smile was meant to intimidate. Maybe even destroy. "Do you trust in love, my lady? Do you trust anyone or anything?"

She stood and held on to the edges of the table to hide her shaky hands. "It's time to leave."

Leonato moved closer until Kade pulled her back and stepped between them. "Go, Leo. Now."

"My lady?" Leonato fixed his brown gaze on her. "If love looks on tempests, is it never shaken?"

She shared a glance with Kade. He'd told her earlier that the Fianna required all warriors to memorize poetry and be able to communicate by using Shakespearean verses. A form of extreme self-discipline, apparently. But from Kade's frown, he didn't know what was going on either.

Leonato continued, "Is love the star to every wander'ng bark, whose worth's unknown?" Now he paused to give Kade a full once-over. "Although his height be taken?"

"What the hell?" Kade spat the words.

"Or"—Leonato smiled at them as if they were children to be protected and pitied—"is love an error, an impediment, a sickness that causes a man to lose in Doom? A sickness that imprisons them in hell forever?"

The shakiness traveled to her legs, and she sat again.

"Fuck you." Kade grabbed Leonato's arm and dragged him out of the room.

She wasn't sure what Leonato's message meant, but the harshness of his voice and the way he'd studied Kade with so much animosity told her it was a threat. A threat she couldn't decipher. A threat that settled on her heart. A threat warning her that she and Kade were in grave danger.

She heard loud male voices, and then the front door shut.

King George appeared first, his dirty white fur announcing his time in the bell tower. When Kade's boots echoed in the hallway, she held her breath until he appeared.

His blue eyes glittered, and his rapid breaths made his chest move with such force she could almost hear his heart rate.

King George checked his bowl, scowled at her, and jumped over Kade's boots. Once the cat disappeared through the kitty door leading to the backyard, Kade sank into a chair, closed his eyes, and sighed.

Now that they were alone, she found her voice. Something in Leonato's strange message had resonated. "Kade? Did you lose your fight to Magnus?"

CHAPTER 13

Rose sipped her tea and waited for Kade to respond. Since Leonato's threat, her breaths had become short and stuttered. Like she was incapable of taking in enough oxygen. She wanted answers and action. But when Kade clasped his hands on the table and closed his eyes, she asked in her softest voice, "Are you hungry?"

The way he hung his head reminded her of her brother after two days of cardiac testing. A true study in exhaustion and despair.

"No." His voice, lower than a whisper, reeked of defeat.

She noticed lines around his eyes and mouth that hadn't been there yesterday, and her heart ached for him. "I'm sorry for the trouble I've caused."

"Rose..." He shook his head. "None of this is your fault."

"How can you say that?" She stood and went to the fridge. She was restless and needed to keep moving. After the night they'd had, there was no way he wasn't hungry. But first, his hands needed care. "I asked Antoine for information about Deke and found my way into Doom. Both actions led to you having to fight Magnus tonight. Now you're stuck helping me—"

"I'm not stuck." Kade flexed his fingers, showing off his swollen, bruised hands covered with cuts. "I'm done."

She filled a bowl with ice cubes and placed it on the table in front of him, along with a clean dish towel. "What does that mean?"

Gently, he placed both hands in the ice bath and sighed. "I've been playing this game with the Fianna for too long."

She didn't say anything. It was a tack she took with Timmy when his moods shifted between upbeat kid and pensive preteen. Kade would speak when the words came to him. In the meantime, she took out a package of cheese and the last of the ham slices.

"Rose?" He looked at her with half-shut eyes that held emotions she couldn't begin to decipher. "I'm tired."

"I'm not surprised." Not sure what else to say, she did the next best thing. She turned on the gas stove and found the cast-iron skillet. After adding a dollop of butter, she used a spatula to spread the melting butter around the pan. Then she started buttering bread slices. "Once you eat, we need to get you to bed."

Had she actually said that? She grimaced as she layered cheese and ham and bread until she had two sandwiches. Then she glanced at him. Luckily, he'd had no reaction. He sat with his hands in the bowl with his eyes closed.

She laid the sandwiches into the pan and watched them sizzle. The scent of toasted bread and melted cheese filled the room. "It never occurred to me that you'd lose."

"Magnus." Kade cleared his throat. "Your cousin is taking illegal steroids. He had a knife."

She spun around, still holding the spatula. "A knife?"

Kade opened his eyes and wrinkled his nose. "Is something burning?"

She went back to the grilled cheese, lifting the edges to make sure they weren't scorched. "I don't understand."

"Magnus, in a classic case of steroid-induced rage, beat me. End of story."

"Is that allowed? The steroids or the weapon?"

"Steroids, no. Weapons, sometimes. If approved."

She swallowed, grateful she hadn't had to watch the fight. But also sad that Kade had had to deal with Magnus alone. She breathed in the familiar smell of grilled ham and cheese, and a sudden sadness flowed through her. Then she remembered why she rarely made it.

She used her arm to wipe away a tear.

"Hey." Kade moved until he stood behind her, drying his hands on the towel.

He didn't touch her, but she felt his warmth. "It's nothing."

"I don't believe you," he whispered. "What's wrong?"

"Could you please get me two plates out of the cupboard?"

"Okay."

When he handed her the plates, she slid the sandwiches onto one. Then she grabbed a few peanut butter cookies from the cookie jar and put them on the second plate. "I know you said you're not hungry, but I think you were lying. Probably because you're worried about eating my food."

He held both plates and smiled at her. "I am worried about that. Yet you still insist on feeding me."

"Cooking relieves my anxiety." She grabbed a napkin. "Don't worry. I have food. And this is the least I can do considering it's my fault you had to fight tonight."

"I told you it's not your fault." Kade sat and accepted the napkin. "Thank you for making this. I am hungry."

"You're welcome." She moved the pan off the burner. "Do you want some coffee?"

"No." He took a bite and mumbled, "Thank you."

The formalness between them added to the tension. But she wasn't sure how to fix that. She poured him a glass of milk and sat on the opposite side of the table. He ate in silence while she sipped her now-cold tea.

She stared out the dark kitchen window over the sink. Her yard backed up to the tall iron fencing that encircled Colonial Park Cemetery. Lights attached to the highest branches in the sweeping oak trees highlighted the centuries-old tombs. She wasn't sure what else to say about tonight's ordeal, or Leonato's strange warning, so she did something she never did. She brought up the past. "This was my father's favorite meal."

Kade wiped his mouth and drank his milk. "Grilled cheese?"

"Yes." She pulled a clean napkin from the holder to blow her nose. "My parents had a beach house on Tybee Island. Whenever we were there, usually on the weekends, my dad made us grilled cheese for breakfast. Even though my mother insisted it wasn't proper breakfast food."

He looked at her with an apology etched in his blue eyes. "Calum told me that Isaac and Magnus inherited your father's Doom sponsorship. He also explained your brother's congenital heart defect."

She nodded, but stayed silent. The irony was that there was a ton to say. Since she didn't know where to start, she sipped her tea.

When had the silence between them eased from tense to comforting?

"I don't talk to any of my brothers anymore." Kade's low voice filled the emptiness of the small room.

Without leaving her seat, she tossed her napkin into the nearby garbage can. "May I ask why?"

"An argument over a woman."

She took a cookie and savored the sweetness, trying not to

appear too interested. Although it was hard to hide the flush of jealousy that rose from her neck to her cheeks. "The five of you fought over the same woman?"

"My grandmother Nin." He took another bite of his second sandwich.

Relief rushed through her body, and she exhaled silently.

He finished off the last bite and grabbed three cookies. "My father owned a horse farm, and my mother died when I was six. After her death, Nin moved in and raised us. She also took care of my dad when he got sick. After my dad died from cancer a few years ago, none of my brothers wanted to take Nin into their homes. They put her in a nursing home, where she died. I grew up in the Blue Ridge Mountains north of Atlanta, but my brothers buried her on Isle of Grace, where she'd been born and raised."

"My parents are buried behind the small church on the Isle of Grace. My father used to have extended family on the isle—the Tobans—but I didn't know anyone lived out there anymore." She hadn't been there in ten years, since the night her parents had died.

"A few families still live there, including my aunt." After he finished his cookies and milk, he eased his hands back into the melting ice bath. "When I found out my brothers abandoned Nin, I was furious. But I was also angry with myself because I'd been in no position to care for her. I'd once had a dream of owning my own horse farm and having a house large enough for both of us to live in."

"That is a lovely dream." She took a cookie and broke it in half. She wasn't hungry but needed to keep her hands busy. Otherwise, she'd leave her seat, slip onto his lap, and run her fingers through his hair until the pain in his eyes receded. "My dream is to one day go to college and become a pediatric nurse."

"You'll make a great nurse."

She smiled, pretending to agree. While she did think she'd love nursing, there was no way she'd ever have the money or freedom to go to school. Besides, no nursing school would want a woman who'd barely graduated from high school and been a stripper.

Instead of talking about her crash-and-burned dreams, she asked, "Did you not know at first that your brothers put Nin into a home?"

"Not until it was too late." Kade drank some more milk and took another cookie. "I was an active-duty Army Ranger. And, as a bachelor, I had no home for her. By the time I found out what happened, Nin was dead and buried."

She remembered the Army Ranger tattoo on his back. She'd seen it the night he'd fought Magnus at Rage of Angels. "Where were you stationed at the time?"

He sighed and looked up at the stained ceiling. "I wasn't stationed anywhere. Like Leonato implied earlier, I was imprisoned."

A sickness that imprisons them in hell forever. Leonato's message reverberated through her limbs, leaving behind a tingling mess.

She kept her voice steady and low. "I don't understand."

"I was in prison, serving a life sentence for treason and espionage." When he met her gaze, his blue eyes carried so much pain she wondered how he didn't crumble under the weight. "I'm a traitor."

KADE HELD his breath while Rose cradled her mug and stared at the plate of peanut butter cookies.

He hadn't told her the entire truth about his imprisonment. He'd just wanted to share something about himself to ease her sadness. He'd recognized her grief and understood her struggle to talk about losing her parents. But withholding information regarding his conviction hadn't been a deliberate attempt to lie to her. There just wasn't much else to say that would help them in this situation. Besides, he was more interested in deciphering Leonato's threat than expounding on the past.

While Kade hadn't understood all of Leonato's speech, Kade had gotten the most important part. His powerful emotional connection with Rose was going to get them both killed.

The other thing that kept his mind running in circles was the idea that once he joined the Fianna, he'd have to learn to speak like Leonato. While many in the world might find the Fianna's language requirement strange or quaint, Kade understood the purpose. It was another form of intense penance, extreme self-discipline, and focused self-control. For one purpose. To marry emotional pain with physical aggression in order to follow orders—and kill—without question or hesitation. Without compassion or empathy. Without mercy or remorse.

After a deep exhale, he withdrew his hands from the ice bath and wiped them on the towel. Then he took his dishes to the sink. He stood before the open window, allowing the night's breeze to cool his heated body. He understood that running the AC cost money she didn't have, but the humidity threatened to drown him.

As he considered what to say next, lightning flashed outside the window, followed by a large clap of thunder. The tombstones in Colonial Park Cemetery shimmered in the scattered beams of random security lights placed high up in the sweeping branches of ancient oak trees. The rising breeze was bringing in another summer storm.

He was in a hell of a quandary. If they found the box and gave it to the Prince, he'd be free of the Fianna. If they found the box, and he allowed Rose to sell it to the reclusive Hezekiah Usher, Kade would have to join the Fianna on Sunday. If he didn't find the box, or ran away with the box, they'd both be killed. Or, the more likely scenario, the Fianna would make Kade kill Rose before they executed him.

The Fianna enjoyed those types of psychological games.

"Kade?" Her voice sounded quiet and hesitant, as if she, too, was searching for words in the midst of their rubble-filled lives.

He sat down and flexed his fingers. The ice had helped, but now his joints were stiffening again. "Yes?"

She raised her head and, instead of seeing anger or fear in her now-green eyes, he found concern. He took a few more deep breaths to release the ache in his chest.

He couldn't remember the last time anyone had shown concern for him.

She touched his wrist, as if knowing his fingers couldn't take the pressure. "What happened?"

He stared at her smaller fingers on his darker skin. Her unexpected response made his heart clench and his lower half harden. He shifted to alleviate the ache in his groin. "All inmates say this, but I'm innocent. I didn't betray my country."

Yet it destroyed him every time he thought that his country believed he was guilty.

King George's nose appeared through the kitty door. He hissed and disappeared. That white cat had to be the crankiest animal Kade had ever met.

Rose gently squeezed his arm. "Don't mind King George."

Kade stared out the kitchen door window that offered a view of the church's lit-up bell tower. He made sure not to move his arm. He needed the pressure of her presence, the possibility of her acceptance if he was going to confess all. "I was on a three-man patrol in the Middle East—I can't tell you where. There was an ambush and a firefight. When it was over, I'd lost two team members, and four nearby civilians had been killed, including a child. I was the only survivor."

She bit her bottom lip but didn't ask any questions.

He shifted in his seat. "There was an inquiry. Then an investigation. Turns out, one of my buddies with me that night was working undercover with the local militia. This guy had given them intel so they knew when and where to find us, and the militia placed the civilians there because they were family members of the militia's enemies.

"My so-called buddy—the real traitor—was killed. The militia leader was apprehended. During his interrogation, he named me as the one who'd given them the intel. I have no idea why he named me, but the authorities believed it. Since the rest of my team was dead, all I had in my defense was my word. Which, apparently, wasn't worth much since I was tried, convicted, and sent to Leavenworth for life."

"Life." She shook her head. "But you were innocent."

The fact her sentence was a statement and not a question made him want to kiss her until she swooned in his arms. Instead, he shrugged.

He *was* innocent. But he'd learned the hard way that in the real world the truth didn't matter. The perception of truth was what drove governments, financial markets, and armies.

Even families.

He took her hand off his arm, kissed her palm, and then picked up the photo Leonato had placed on the table earlier. It was folded to show a beautiful woman holding the hand of a distinguished man. They stood in a garden with a fountain behind them.

"Kade"—she clasped her fingers in her lap—"how did you get out of Leavenworth? Did they discover the truth? That you weren't the traitor?"

He leaned forward until his forearms rested on the table.

The fan above their heads pushed the warm air around, but cooler air came in through the open window. "Three years ago, I was in my cell, contemplating my life, when the warden appeared. The charges against me had been vacated. I was free, and two men were waiting outside to bring me home."

"Your brothers?"

"No. Two Fianna warriors. Leonato and Sampson."

Rose's eyes widened. "The Fianna got you out of prison."

"Yes." Kade's voice sounded dry, and he cleared his throat. "Leonato told me I was free to leave Leavenworth as long as I agreed to move to Savannah, work at Rage of Angels, and fight at Doom. My job was to let them know about certain activities. If I didn't agree, the charges would be unvacated and I'd have to return to prison. I'm not sure how the Fianna has so much power, but they do."

Rose got up to pour a glass of water and handed it to him. "You were their informant?"

"I *am* their informant." Kade took a few sips, appreciating the cold against his parched throat. He was still dehydrated from the fight. "When I started fighting at Doom, they wanted information on the fighters. It's how they identify potential recruits."

"Did they try to recruit you?"

Now that was a question he didn't dare answer. Instead, he pointed to the folded photo of the lovely couple. "Are these your parents?"

"Yes." She unfolded the photo and smoothed it out on the table. Her parents stood next to two men. On the other side of the men, but a few feet away, a young Rose sat on a bench holding a baby. "One of those two men next to my parents is my uncle Isaac."

Yeah. Kade recognized that dark-haired asshole. "And the fourth man wearing the bow tie and seersucker suit and twenty extra pounds?"

"Harry." She ran her finger over her mother's face, and her voice softened. "My parents met Harry at Yale. Harry was my dad's roommate. All three of them were great friends."

From her slight smile, it seemed like she was remembering happier times. "Are you still in touch with Harry?"

"Sometimes. He lives in New York and Boston, but travels a lot." She glanced at Kade and shrugged. "He was devastated by my parents' deaths. After Timmy and I went to live with Isaac, Harry would randomly visit, bringing us presents. Until one visit when he and Isaac had a huge argument. I heard loud voices but didn't understand what they were saying. Harry stormed out, and I've not seen him since."

Her voice trembled, and she cleared her throat. "A few years ago, he tracked me down and began sending me checks."

"He sends you money?"

"Not a lot. The checks are random in amount and timing. And there's never any money for Timmy's hospital bills. But the checks always seem to come when I have no money for food or rent." She folded the photo again until it only showed her parents. "Even though I hate seeing Isaac's face, this is the only photo I have of me and Timmy with our parents."

Kade took the photo from her. "Who snapped this?"

"Magnus. A few months before my parents died."

Kade got up and positioned the folded photo beneath a strawberry magnet on the refrigerator.

"Kade?" She came over and took his arm. "What would it take for you to be free of the Fianna?"

Kade focused on her eyes, which had shifted from green back to hazel. Her slightly crooked, yet adorable nose. Her lush lips. Her honeysuckle scent. Her messy red hair that was falling out of her ponytail. She still held his arm, and his body hardened even more. "I don't know."

It was a flat-out lie. But there was no way he would admit

that his freedom depended on her finding that box. Or that she would die if she didn't.

"I wish I could help you."

He closed his eyes, not sure how to respond. The fact that this woman who had more troubles than anyone he'd ever known, a woman who struggled with trusting others, wanted to help him almost made him crumble. She humbled him. Her kindness and stubbornness and fierceness. Her passion to protect those she loved made him feel like he'd failed her in some way. Even though he hardly knew her.

"Kade?"

Her whisper swept over him, and he shivered before opening his eyes. "Yes?"

"Why are you helping me?"

He took her face between his palms and met her gaze. Although he was lying to her about almost everything in his life, he couldn't fake his feelings. Not with the way his entire body reacted to her scent, her kindness, her gentle, feminine beauty. "Because I'm falling in love with you."

CHAPTER 14

ose closed her eyes, and heat rushed through her with a speed that took away her breath.

Kade just admitted he was falling in love with her, yet she couldn't form any words. While she was seriously attracted to him, and had to admit to the deep, underlying connection between them, she couldn't help holding back emotionally. Yes, she wanted him. Yes, she craved his touch. Yes, she was worried about him getting hurt while he protected her. But she was scared. He kept secrets and fought in a dark world she didn't understand. And she wasn't sure what to do—or feel— about that.

Love required trust. And trusting others had always been her biggest fear.

Luckily, she didn't have to think about it at that moment. He held her face so gently she barely felt his fingers against her skin. His masculine scent turned her legs into cookie dough.

She remembered all the things he'd done for her since she'd met him. Not to mention what he'd endured since her run-in with Antoine.

Kade moved slowly. Although she thought she was ready

for his kiss, when his mouth tested her lips, she moaned and encircled his waist with her arms. His hands found her hips, and he dropped butterfly kisses all over her face. The heat from his larger body, his murmurs of pleasure when she wrapped her arms around his neck, and his sudden inhale when she surrendered to the kiss, changed everything.

His lips became hot, and he tilted to deepen the kiss. No one had—ever—kissed her like this. Never with so much passion. Never with so much force. Never with so much demand. Yet he tempered his insistence with a gentleness that melted the icy facade she worked so hard to maintain.

Kade's kiss was the most erotic moment she'd ever experienced.

When he raised his head, she opened her eyes to see his glittering blue gaze. "I swear to you that I'll protect you and Timmy."

"We have to find that box, Kade. It is the only way to set us free."

His eyes darkened, almost as if he wanted to contradict her. Instead, he said, "I know." His lips brushed hers again just as the church bells rang, and he added, "But not right now."

"No," she whispered as his lips moved down her neck. "Not right now."

He pulled her in close, crushing her breasts against his chest. She tightened her arms, and a growl came from the back of his throat. She smiled inside and ran her fingernails down the back of his neck.

He swung her up in his arms without breaking their kiss and left the kitchen.

He was limping, and she pulled away. "You don't have to carry me."

He paused at the open doorway to her bedroom and met her gaze. "I want to carry you."

He spoke with such intensity her lower stomach

contracted, and she traced the abrasions on his forehead. "You have to be exhausted and in so much pain."

He shrugged. Then winced. "I'm fine."

With one arm around his neck, she pressed her head against his shoulder to hide her smile. "I admire your determination and your strength."

He adjusted her in his arms and blinked a few times. Instead of letting her go, he said, "I want this, Rose. I need to be with you."

She recognized the hidden question within his statement and rested her fingers against his mouth. "I want this as well." She whispered so she wouldn't break the erotic spell around them. "Although I know what you think you saw between me and Deke that night—"

"I don't give a fuck about that," he said gruffly.

"I do." When she squirmed, he lowered her to her feet, still keeping her within the circle of his arms. "Although I danced at the club, I wasn't one of Deke's women."

She didn't want to use any disparaging words against the dancers who had been Deke's women—they all had had their reasons. Mostly sadness and desperation.

He kissed her forehead. "I wish I could forget what I saw. And I know that makes me an asshole. Every time I think of you sitting on Deke's lap, I want to run him over with my truck and then use him for target practice."

She rested her head against Kade's chest and felt the force of his rapid heartbeat. "I was making a deal with Deke to get the courier job. What you saw was all that happened."

Kade pressed kisses to her hair. "I'm sorry for being such a fucking hypocrite."

She raised her head to meet his gaze. "Why are you a hypocrite?"

"Well"—he kissed the tip of her nose—"I'm not a virgin."

The way he said it, with the seriousness of a mortician,

made her laugh out loud. "I never would've known."

He frowned until she rested her lips against his. "I'm teasing."

He smiled and swung her up in his arms again. Except now his limp was even more pronounced. "If you set aside my inglorious, reckless, and unmonitored youth, you might be surprised to discover I've spent much of my adult life living in forced celibacy." He placed her on the bed. "I'll be right back."

He disappeared and a moment later returned with… condoms?

"Where did you get those?"

He lay down next to her. "Sampson gave them to me years ago, after I was released from prison. I threw them in my gym bag and forgot about them. But I don't want to talk about the Fianna or prison anymore."

Before he kissed her again, she added, "Since we're telling all, my youthful transgressions were few. Nothing turns a girl off of men faster than working at a strip club, especially one like Rage of Angels."

His chest rumbled with soft laughter. "That doesn't surprise me at all."

She lifted her arms so he could strip off her shirt. "No?"

Kade stood over her and yanked off his T-shirt. "Your name is Tempest, isn't it?"

"You were never supposed to know that." She shimmied out of her jeans. "You have a bandage on your arm."

"It's nothing," he said as he dropped his own pants.

He didn't wear any underwear and was fully erect. Yet the bruises covering his torso and legs attested to the fight he'd endured earlier.

She swallowed while he studied her. She lay on the bed wearing her pink lace bra and matching panties. Although she worked as a stripper, she felt more vulnerable than she'd ever experienced while dancing in a cage.

Kade's hooded gaze took in every inch of her body. From the size of his erection, which he now held in one hand, she knew he found her desirable.

But was that enough for her? Was it enough for him?

Then again, in this moment, did it matter? Kade was the epitome of male perfection. Roughened skin lightly covered with hair was pulled tight over defined muscles. Every indentation on his body looked as if it had been cut with a sculptor's knife. No softness. No weakness. He would give no quarter. And she remembered what she'd seen in the fighting pit, the powerful masculinity she'd witnessed between Vane and Leonato.

Was that what Kade had looked like in the pit? So fierce and deadly?

"Kade, your bruises—"

"Are fine."

She wasn't sure if she believed him but lost that thought when he lay on top of her, using his massive arms to hold his weight above her. "I swear I will never hurt you."

Her exhale sounded unsteady, and she was surprised to realize she'd been holding her breath.

Her lingering worries didn't matter. Right now, all she cared about was her physical connection with Kade. "I know."

He lowered his lips to her ear. "Are you sure?"

"Yes." She took his face in her hands and said, "Please, Kade. I need this too."

It'd been years since she'd had physical contact with anyone. And none of it had held any meaning. But her feelings for Kade transcended anything else she'd ever experienced. She just didn't know what to do with it all. She had no adult experience with sharing emotions or expressing feelings. And she had made it a mission in her life never to trust others. Both those things terrified her almost as much as her growing connection with Kade.

Kade closed his eyes and lowered his head to kiss her. Once his lips met hers, he growled, and she wrapped her arms around his body to pull him closer. She loved his heat, his scent, and the promise of his weight on top of her.

As if reading her mind, he pressed his much larger body onto hers. She inhaled sharply at the heat that rushed through her. The scratchy hair on his legs moved against her smooth skin, his hard chest against her soft breasts. Still, he deepened the kiss even more, until she was sure she would drown beneath the pressure of all of these new sensations.

His erection, hot and hard, pressed against her stomach. One of Kade's legs separated hers until his thigh moved against her feminine core.

She bucked, tightening her hold, and he laughed. Lifting his head slightly, he kissed her nose and then her cheeks. He moved against her, and she raised her hips. As his lips traveled down her neck, her nipples hardened even more.

With one leg still between her thighs, his kisses traced her collarbone.

"Kade." Her voice sounded gravelly. "I don't want to hurt you. Your bruises—"

"Are fine."

She laughed, and a moment later, his mouth found her nipple. She arched her back, surprised she didn't throw him off the bed. She bit her lower lip and grabbed the sheets on either side of her hips. His leg moved in a rhythm that matched the way his tongue caressed her breast. Licking, sucking, and playing with a gentle roughness that sent her heart racing and her mind spinning.

When he raised his head to watch her, he said in a gruff voice, "You are so damn beautiful."

She touched his shorn dark blond hair but was unable to form words. He made her feel beautiful.

As if knowing she couldn't respond, he smiled and moved

lower to kiss her stomach. His warm lips against her tummy sent fire through her body. She suddenly felt hot and restless, as if a thousand fireflies were zipping through her veins. When one palm planted on the bed next to her waist, he shifted so both of his thighs pushed between hers. She closed her eyes, and his kisses along her hip bones drove away all other thoughts.

She barely heard the tear of the foil packet.

When he raised her hips, he said harshly, "Look at me, Rose."

She opened her eyes, transfixed by the view. Kade, with his bulging muscles and the skin pulled tight over his face, stared at her with dark blue eyes partially concealed by his hooded eyelids. He was everything she'd dreamed of in a man, and he wanted her. That truth sent a rush of desire straight to the very center of her body, and her voice cracked under the stress of her own need. "Please, Kade. I can't wait any longer."

He bared his teeth, held on to her waist, and entered her. The initial sensation made her gasp as he thrust into her with a powerful grace that both filled and consumed her. His body was asking and taking at the same time, and she clung to his shoulders as he possessed her with a fierceness she'd never experienced. A possessiveness that made her want to stop time and stay locked with him forever.

KADE HELD his breath and drove into Rose with a force he couldn't control.

Despite his aching muscles and the sensitive bruises, heat shot through his body, from his toes, through his cock, and straight to his head. Sweat beaded his skin, and his arm muscles ached in a good way. A deeply satisfying way. In a way that meant he was holding most of his weight so he wouldn't crush Rose.

Rose.

He opened his eyes and stared down at the woman beneath him, her long red hair strewn across the white pillow. Her eyes were closed, and she was now grabbing his ass, as if asking him to increase the tempo and pressure. A request he obliged. He used his thighs to force her legs apart even farther so he could move deeper. Her body clenched around him, as if not wanting to let him go. The pressure in his balls increased, and his breath shortened. He was moments from exploding, but he didn't want to leave her behind.

He might be a brute, but he could be a gentleman.

Her nails dug into his ass, and she wrapped her legs around his hips. As he pistoned in even deeper, she threw back her head and cried out, "*Kade.*"

A moment later, he lost all control. It was as if his cock had taken control of the situation and decided he'd grab everything she had to give him. When her legs tightened even more around him, he closed his eyes and allowed his body to take over. He drove and drove and drove until an explosion of pleasure forced the air from his lungs and all thoughts from his mind. A white-hot heat swept through him with a fury that both surprised and shocked him. Yet his body wouldn't let up. He kept driving and forcing and demanding until that final moment when he offered everything he had, everything he was, everything he would ever be.

It took a long moment before he could unclench his teeth, lower his head, and kiss her. Gently at first. Then a bit harder, until he collapsed on top of her. She'd done what Doom's pit had never been able to do. She'd drained him of strength, breath, and all thought except for one.

The one he was afraid to even consider.

He kissed her once more before rolling onto his back and

discarding the protection. He quickly returned to her side and tucked her into his embrace. It was only then that his aches and pains resurfaced.

"Kade?"

She shifted, and he stifled a moan. "Yes?"

No matter how *not fine* his body felt, especially his shoulder wound, he'd endure ten times the pain if it meant he could hold her like this forever.

"Thank you." She kissed his chest and pressed her palm against the spot she'd kissed. "That was incredible."

He held back her long hair with both hands so he could study her face. No, memorize everything about her. "I should be thanking you."

Seriously, even though she'd not admitted her love for him, she'd given him everything tonight. Hell, she'd even fed him when she probably didn't have enough money to keep the lights on.

King George hissed from the doorway, and he threw a pillow at the cat. "Will my being here be a problem for his royal highness?"

"No." She snuggled closer and laid her head on his shoulder. Luckily, it was the one without the throbbing knife wound. "King George has a bed on the floor near the bathroom. I leave the door open because when Timmy isn't home, King George likes to come and go all night long."

"Wonderful."

She chuckled at his obvious lack of enthusiasm, and he smoothed her silky hair so it covered his chest, hiding his bruises. He held her close and let his breath find a new rhythm, somewhere between labored and erratic. Not that he minded. Beyond the physical pain, his entire body felt weak. Weak in a good way. A manly way. A way that told him that he was screwed.

A way that told him if he wanted to win his freedom, he'd

have to betray Rose and leave her behind.

A LOUD BOOM WOKE ROSE, and she blinked, trying to figure out where the noise had come from. Her room was dark, and another loud rumble startled her. *Thunder.*

The storm had arrived, and rain pounded on the roof.

Lightning flashed outside the window, followed by another hit of thunder. King George purred in his bed on the floor, and she shifted until something around her tightened —Kade's arm.

She was lying on the bed. Naked. *With Kade.* He'd admitted he was falling in love with her, and they'd made love. Something she'd dreamed about since first meeting him, but also something she'd never expected to happen. Especially since she wasn't sure about her own feelings. She definitely cared for him. Admired him. Worried about him.

Yet, in spite of all his wonderful qualities, he held secrets. She suspected from her brief conversation with Leonato that Kade hadn't told her the entire truth about his relationship with the Fianna. If he couldn't share everything with her, she couldn't offer him her heart.

A flash of lightning brightened the room before plunging her back into darkness.

If she couldn't trust him, she couldn't love him.

Or maybe she was just overthinking everything. These emotions were so new, so raw, she didn't know how to process them all. The only thing she knew for sure, though, was that Kade made her feel like the most beautiful, most desired woman in the entire world. That was a gift she'd never be able to thank him for. Although she hoped it was a gift she'd be able to reciprocate.

She touched his hair and smiled. His soft snoring told her

he was sound asleep. Not even the next crack of thunder broke through his slumber. The room seemed unusually dark, and she didn't hear the hum of the overhead fan. Even with the window open, the room was hot and stuffy. She glanced at the bedside table. The clock was off as well.

When had the power gone out?

Gently, she moved out of Kade's embrace and found the flashlight in her nightstand. She'd started keeping a flashlight in every room because power outages in the historic district were becoming more common.

In the bathroom, she washed her face and changed into a lightweight cotton chemise. She also braided her long hair to keep it off her back.

"That's better." She grabbed a towel and went to the window.

Although it was still pouring, it was too hot to close the window. She lowered the sash until a few inches remained open and placed the towel on the floor to catch stray raindrops. A breeze wandered in. It wasn't as cool as she'd like, but circulating air was worth the risk of getting the floor wet.

Suddenly, the power returned. The clock blinked, and the overhead fan began to spin again. The lights in the cemetery behind her house popped on, adding an eerie glow to the room. King George rolled over and, when another combo of thunder and lightning struck, he jumped from his bed and left the room, probably headed for the kitty door in the kitchen.

She was about to turn back to the bed when she noticed something glowing in the shadows behind her house. Someone stood beneath an ancient oak tree near the iron gates separating her yard from Colonial Park Cemetery. He held a lit cigarette in one hand. His other hand held a weapon pointed toward the ground. When the smoker inhaled, the small end of the cigarette glowed again, exposing the outline of the shadowed watcher. *Magnus.*

CHAPTER 15

*K*ade stretched his aching arms over his head and rolled over. When his head hit another soft pillow, he embraced the comfort—until he realized he wasn't where he was supposed to be. This pillow was soft and smelled like lavender, unlike his scratchy linen that smelled like bleach.

After checking the clock on the bedside table and discovering it was eight a.m., he sat up and took in the empty, unfamiliar room. He lay on top of the covers with a throw blanket over his naked body. Memories of what had happened last night fell into place in his mind. He'd lost a fight to Magnus, which explained why every one of Kade's muscles protested when he moved. He'd argued with Leonato, who'd responded with a cryptic threat. And he'd made love to Rose. An act that would eventually destroy him.

He scrubbed his eyes with his fists. He wanted to say that what they'd done, including when he'd admitted his feelings for her, had been due to the stress they'd been under. Except he'd wanted Rose from the first moment he'd met her, and that desire had only increased with every interaction. Despite the fact he belonged to the Fianna, he'd sought her out at Rage of Angels, at the hotel where they had once worked, and at the hospital the night Leonato had killed a man in front of them.

Hell, he'd even fought Magnus at the club to protect her and willingly gone to jail. Where he'd probably still be if Sampson and Leonato hadn't bailed him out the next day.

Kade pressed his head against the rickety headboard and closed his eyes.

Shit. Shit. Shit. What a fatal mistake. Eight months ago, his fight with Magnus had revealed his attraction to Rose to the Fianna. Revealed the truth before he'd even understood it himself.

And that was probably why the Prince had set up this no-win situation. Fianna warriors were supposed to be dead to the world. No families. No lovers. No emotional ties whatsoever. Yet his fight with Magnus had shone a giant spotlight on Kade's one weakness—his growing feelings for Rose. And, because rumors about the Prince's lack of mercy were true, the Fianna ruthlessly exploited Kade's weakness.

He rubbed his forehead with his fist. How could he have made such a terrible mistake?

Since meeting Rose, he'd been unable to stay away from her, even when he'd barely known her. And now that they'd made love, he wasn't sure he could leave her.

Yet, while he'd admitted his growing love for Rose, he'd also left out the most important details of his life. And Rose wasn't stupid. She had to suspect he was hiding things. It was probably why, despite the passion she'd shown in his arms, she hadn't spoken her own feelings aloud.

He couldn't blame her. He was neither a prince nor charming. He was a man in an impossible situation. A man in love with a woman who had trust issues. A man who rarely asked for help because it made one beholden to others. A man about to commit the rest of his life to a murderous cult that dated back centuries.

He opened his eyes, determined to crush his pity party. Rose needed him, and they still had work to do. They had twenty-eight hours to meet the Prince's deadline, and they still had no idea where to find that box.

When he saw the cup of hot coffee on his bedside table, his throat closed up. He'd never get enough of her sexually, but her inherent thoughtfulness was what made his heart brim with other unfamiliar emotions. Emotions he struggled to understand, much less define.

Yes, he loved her. But his feelings for her were so much more intense than he'd expected. Then again, other than Nin and his mother, he had little experience in loving women. Infrequent sex with random females from the club didn't count.

He swung his legs over the edge of the bed and moved slowly, testing each tight muscle group before standing upright. Unfortunately, King George, who'd been guarding the bathroom door, decided Kade had committed an Act of Aggression. The cat bared his teeth.

Kade held out his hands and backed up. "Whoa, kitty."

He hit the edge of the bed and fell onto his naked ass. The pillow flew across the room, and King George pounced after it. A moment later, Rose emerged from the bathroom with a towel wrapped around her body. Wet strands of hair hung past her shoulders.

He drew the throw blanket over his lap and tried not to stare at her bare thighs. The towel acted more like a short, strapless dress, exposing way too much soft, bare skin.

The cat hissed at him again, and she shooed him away. "King George, be nice!"

The cat left the room with his back arched and his tail high in the air. As if to say to Kade, *kiss this.*

"I'm sorry." Rose clutched the towel, keeping it tight

around herself. "I'd like to say King George isn't normally this nasty in the morning, but that would be a lie."

Actually, Kade wasn't thinking about the cat at all. He was too distracted by the drops of water that rolled down the curve of her neck and slipped between her breasts. His body hardened with one part in particular becoming almost painful. Needing a distraction, he took the mug and inhaled the scent of roasted beans. "I don't mind King George. Nin had a cat like that once. It took a while, but I eventually won her over."

She took a step forward. "How long is 'a while'?"

He sipped his coffee and sighed. It was perfect. Hot, black, and not too bitter. "Seven years."

She laughed and shifted awkwardly, her hands grasping the towel. "You don't give up, do you?"

"Nope." He drank again, unsure of what to do or say next. She hadn't moved, and he wasn't about to stand up and expose his very nude *issue*. Although, after what they'd shared in her bed, he wasn't sure where this morning-after awkwardness came from.

"Your arm." She pointed to the bandage that covered the knife wound. "You were hurt last night."

He glanced at his arm. The cut had bled through the bandage, turning the white gauze pink. "I'll be fine."

"Enough with the fine!" She went into the bathroom. A moment later she returned, wearing a robe and carrying a first aid kit. "Let me change the bandage."

Before he could say no, she sat next to him and took off the old gauze.

While she worked, he said, "Thanks for the coffee. And the place to crash."

That's the best I can do?

A flush colored her cheeks. Was she embarrassed?

He cleared his throat. "How did you sleep?"

She replaced the butterfly Band-Aids and rewrapped his arm in clean gauze. "A thunderstorm woke me."

"I didn't hear it."

She put away the first aid kit and threw out the old bandages. Then she picked up a towel from the floor beneath the window and tossed it into a corner hamper. "You were asleep."

He looked around for his pants. If she was this skittish, he didn't want to prance around naked.

"He was here." She paused to look out a window. "At least, I think it was him."

Kade found his jeans, slipped them on, and moved until he stood behind her. He placed his hands on her shoulders, and her floral scent filled his lungs. "Who was where?"

She pointed toward an enormous oak tree on the cemetery's perimeter. It was the kind of tree that would remember tricorn hats and Sherman's soldiers.

"Last night. During the storm. I saw a man beneath the tree, smoking." She tightened the robe's belt, and a drop of water dripped down her neck. But she didn't throw off his touch. "I think it was Magnus. Although it was dark and rainy and hard to see."

"Magnus?" A low hum began in Kade's head, and he drew her away from the window. He took her place, making sure she stayed behind him, and scanned the backyard. The cemetery lay behind the iron fence and thick foliage. Nothing seemed disturbed. "Are you sure?"

"Yes." She touched his back, and Kade shivered. "He had a gun."

"Fuck." Kade shut the window and yanked down the blind. He found his burner phone on the floor where it had landed when he'd stripped off his pants. He had two text messages. One from Nate about coming into work, and a message from Vane thanking Kade for last night.

He closed his eyes and sighed. What had he been thinking? Getting involved with anyone right now—especially Rose—was a bad idea. As in a horrible, disastrous, no-good idea that could get them both killed.

There was no way in hell that he'd ever hurt her. If the Fianna went so far as to force him to assassinate her, he'd take his own life before he touched hers. That meant this entire situation was beyond dangerous. Beyond screwed. Almost beyond fucked up. The problem was he'd never had a mission go beyond the *fucked-up* stage, so he had no idea what lay beyond it.

He sank onto the edge of the bed. He had no idea what to do next.

"Kade?" Rose sat next to him and touched his arm. "What's wrong?"

He shook his head. It was time to move past worry and fear. It was time for action. "First—"

"I forgot!" She ran out of the room. "I have something in the oven."

He got up, hating how his body ached, and headed for the bathroom. By the time he showered and dressed again, texted Nate that he wasn't coming into work today, and made it to the kitchen with his empty coffee mug, the aroma of cinnamon and blueberries had taken over the house.

Rose was setting the table. While he'd showered, she'd changed into a blue sundress and had braided her damp hair. This morning, she seemed younger. More vulnerable.

"Sit." She lit a jar candle and went back to the counter. The smell of lavender added to the warmth in the air. "I hope you like blueberries and eggs."

"I do." *Who didn't?* He poured them each a glass of orange juice from a pitcher on the table. He also refilled his mug from the coffeemaker. "Although I've never eaten them together."

She laughed and brought over two plates of cheesy scrambled eggs. He took them from her and laid them on the table while she hurried to the oven. After donning oven mitts, she pulled out a coffee cake. Another wave of cinnamon and blueberries hit him, and he groaned. "That smells amazing."

"It's my favorite blueberry coffee cake." She placed it on the table, and they sat across from each other. "I only make it when Timmy is around because I do not need to eat an entire cake by myself."

He drank his coffee, appreciating the fact it was freshly brewed and hot. "Sometimes I wish I could eat like a teenager again."

She laughed and glanced at his arms. "At least you don't have the metabolism of a zombie."

"One of the benefits of working at a gym." He waited until she'd served him a piece of coffee cake before asking, "Have you talked to Timmy today?"

It seemed ordinary. She clearly didn't want to talk about what had happened between them last night, but she'd gone to a hell of a lot of work to make him an amazing breakfast.

"I texted Timmy this morning," she said between sips of orange juice. "He wants to come home. But he still has a fever, so he's stuck there for another day."

"Timmy has a cell phone?"

"Just an inexpensive prepaid phone, similar to the one I had before you bought me a new one yesterday. It only makes calls and sends texts." She smiled over her coffee mug. "While I could call him on the phone in his hospital room, he's a typical kid who prefers to text. When he has to leave his room for tests, he hides the phone in Teddy Hawkins—his stuffed bear. The technicians don't want kids carrying phones around, but they don't mind if they bring their stuffed animals. Timmy feels better knowing he could contact me at any moment."

"Smart. Especially with all the power outages lately.

Although that building is so old, I wouldn't be surprised if the hospital is still using copper phone lines."

She nodded. "I have a landline here in the house as well. My landlord gives us weak Wi-Fi, but the phone lines were probably installed right after World War II.

Kade laughed and took another deep draw of coffee. While he was worried they were running out of time, he forced himself to appreciate this moment of sitting with Rose, talking about little things, and eating breakfast as if they were a regular couple in a happy relationship. "I'm glad Timmy is feeling well enough that he wants to come home."

She nodded and bit into her cake.

Kade ate his piece in four bites and then dug into the eggs. He was hungrier than he'd realized and decided that no matter what else happened that day, he was buying her groceries. Once he cut a second slice of cake and poured another cup of coffee, he realized she'd barely touched her breakfast.

Was he supposed to make conversation? He was used to living alone. It'd also been a long time since he'd woken up with a woman, so he wasn't sure what to do. He wiped his lips with a napkin and studied her while he savored the cake, which, really, was one of the best things he'd ever eaten.

Finally, he broke the silence. "Are you okay?"

She put her fork down, sipped her coffee, and shrugged. She kept her gaze on the flickering candle in the center of the table.

Damn. *Please don't cry.* "In the bedroom..." He cleared his throat. "I started to say we need to come up with a plan to find that box."

She nodded. "I'm not sure what to do next."

She hadn't mentioned what had happened between them, so he didn't bring it up.

Although he wanted to.

She stood to grab more napkins from the pantry and

returned to the table. "All I do know is that I'm going to find that box and deliver it to someone who will pay me."

"Rose." He took another bite of eggs and tried not to moan. They were that good. "I know it's none of my business, but Calum filled me in on Timmy's situation. Including the complicated rules regarding pediatric heart transplants."

"It is complicated." She shoved the napkins into the holder. "I just hope the two hundred thousand I might make by delivering that box will cover Timmy's outstanding bills and the initial monthly payments for the insurance he needs."

Her phone rang, and she said, "Excuse me." She grabbed her phone and headed toward the living room. "I have to take this."

He nodded and continued eating. But being the ass he was, he stood with his plate so he could eat and hear her conversation at the same time.

"Yes, Doctor. I'm so glad you received my new phone number." She stood near the window of the small living room. "Is this a possible course of action for Timmy?" After a long pause, she said, "If Timmy is approved for that study, I'll figure out the money, permissions, and get him to Virginia. Thank you, Doctor."

By the time she returned, he had the sink full of sudsy water and was halfway through the dishes. He kept his gaze on the window, watching the tree where Magnus had set up his stakeout the night before.

Magnus. Although Rose wasn't sure if the stalker had been her cousin, Kade had no doubt. And that was another issue that had to be handled sooner rather than later.

"You don't have to do the dishes." She grabbed an apron from a wall hook next to the church door key and slipped it on. "You're my guest."

He nodded to the dish towel on the counter. "You can dry while we talk through what we should do next."

After she finished clearing the table and putting the food away, she stood next to him and started drying. "That phone call... It was from UVA's University Hospital. About Timmy."

"Is Timmy seeing a doctor at the University of Virginia?"

"Not yet." She blew stray hairs out of her eyes. "Dr. Singh is a pediatric cardiologist who is pioneering a new drug protocol that improves the chances of survival for pediatric heart transplants—maybe into adulthood. Her research is being funded by multiple sources, all of which have rules and limits on how the research is to be done."

"Take their money, take their bullshit—sorry. That's what my dad used to say."

"Your dad wasn't wrong." She took a wet dish from him, dried it, and put it away. "Because of Tommy's rare blood type and the fact his condition is congenital, he's made it onto the short list of potential subjects." She sighed heavily. "It might mean I wouldn't have to worry about getting private insurance."

He handed her a clean mug. "Okay." For some reason, she wasn't smiling. "What's wrong?"

"I am still required to pay Timmy's outstanding hospital bills." She dried as she added, "Dr. Singh just received FDA approval for her drug protocol that could improve Timmy's heart which makes him a better candidate for transplant surgery. Or, in the best case, not need surgery at all. If Timmy is approved for the study, he will become one of her patients."

"Rose, that's wonderful news."

She gave him a weak smile. "The drug protocol is great news. Except, if it doesn't work, another child has to die for Timmy to survive until adulthood." She wiped her forehead with her arm. "That's how pediatric transplants work. That's why there are so many rules about how they are paid for and who receives them."

He paused to watch her eyes shift from hazel to green.

He'd spent so much time with her now, he was learning green eyes meant she was feeling intense emotions. "If it's a research study, is there a cost?"

She stacked the rest of the dry dishes and put them away. "After paying off Timmy's hospital bill—which is a requirement of the study—I'll have to get both of us up to Virginia within hours of receiving the notification. I'll also need to find a place to live and work so I can cover my living expenses."

"Still"—he bumped her shoulder with his—"good news."

"I'm trying to be optimistic, but I don't have the money required to relocate." She took the sponge to wipe the kitchen table. "I still owe the hospital here in Savannah more money than I could ever make. And I don't have a car to drive to Virginia. Then there is the other thing."

He took the sponge from her and rinsed it before laying it next to the faucet. "Other thing?"

"Permission." She took off her apron and hung it on the hook near the door. "I'm not Timmy's legal guardian. I can't sign any paperwork allowing this drug study or any surgeries on Timmy's behalf."

Kade drained the sink and folded the dish towel over the sink's edge. There was something so soothing, so normal and monotonous, about doing dishes that he almost enjoyed it. "Calum told me Magnus is Timmy's guardian."

"Yep." Rose blew out the candle on the table. "When my parents died, Isaac became our guardian. He moved himself and Magnus into my parents' home."

Kade snorted. Isaac had been one of the cruelest men Kade had ever known. And the last person anyone would want as a parent or a guardian. While Kade hated Magnus, it was no surprise he'd turned out to be a bastard. His father had seen to that. "That must have been awful."

"It was horrible." She took her blue sweatshirt off of a chair and hung it on a hook near her apron. "When living in my parents' home with Magnus and Isaac became intolerable, I ran away. I was sixteen and had to leave Timmy behind. My plan was to find a new living situation quickly and then take Timmy with me. I was so naïve."

"You were sixteen. You were a child with no idea how the world works."

"I have to be honest." Even though the napkin holder was full, she stacked and straightened them. Apparently, if she couldn't bake or cook her way out of a stressful situation, she organized things.

"Honest about what?"

"Even if I'd understood the impossibility of my plan, I would have left anyway. I had to get away from Magnus and Isaac. They weren't sexually or physically abusive, but they were emotionally destructive."

Kade didn't say anything because he knew she wasn't looking for sympathy. She was seeking a witness.

Done with the napkins, she rearranged the salt and pepper shakers around the candle. "Nine months ago, after my uncle died, I turned twenty-two and had saved enough to rent this house. Harry even sent me some money for the security deposit. But despite having a safe place to live, Magnus asked the court for guardianship of Timmy and won, probably due to his power and money."

Kade leaned his ass against the counter and crossed his arms. "Why does Magnus allow Timmy to live with you?"

She sat and glanced at him. "I don't know why. Maybe because Magnus can't be bothered to care for Timmy."

"Magnus mentioned that guy Remiel Marigny who wanted this box, and Magnus sounded stressed about not having it." Kade tapped his foot on the floor. "Rose, is it possible Magnus wanted guardianship because he believes you know the location of the box and was hoping to use Timmy's guardianship as leverage?"

"I never thought of that." She shifted her gaze to the floor. "Except selling the box for two hundred thousand is nothing to Magnus. He has plenty of money. So much so that—as Timmy's guardian—he could pay off Timmy's debt and get him the insurance he needs."

Kade shook his head. Magnus was such an asshole. "Remember what Magnus said on the phone yesterday? If he didn't give the box to Remiel Marigny, he could end up dead."

"You're right." She met his gaze. "Maybe the box is worth more than we think it is."

"I think we should consider the possibility."

She placed her elbows on the table and held her head in her hands. "I assumed Magnus asked for guardianship to get his hands on the trust my parents had put aside for us."

If money was involved, she was probably correct. Except Kade didn't want to say that part out loud. "What was in this trust?"

She sighed, lifted her head, and met his gaze. "My parents' house, their Tybee Island beach cottage, and the money they'd saved. I was to receive everything on my twenty-third birthday. Except, after Isaac's death, Magnus sold my parents' house and everything in it.

"And before you ask me if I fought all of this, I tried. I just didn't have the money to hire a lawyer who was willing to go against one of the most vicious lawyers in the city. Magnus has power and clout. He threatened every lawyer I contacted until no one would take my case. I even went to city hall, but no one would listen to me."

Kade studied her profile while she fussed with the salt and pepper shakers again. A low, tight feeling in his gut grew until it almost choked him. What she didn't say, what he was now understanding, was that every adult she'd ever loved and believed in had betrayed her. Including people who should've been looking out for her, like social workers, judges, and prosecutors. No wonder she didn't trust anyone. Even this mysterious Harry, who knew her situation and wasn't consistent with his help.

Although Kade hated paranoia, a terrible thought was building in his mind.

He turned to stare at the cemetery behind her house. The white mausoleums glittered in the sunlight. "How was Magnus able to sell your property without your consent?"

"I don't know." Her voice lowered, and he glanced at her.

She sat so still, he could barely see her breasts moving with each breath. He wanted to go to her but had the distinct feeling she needed to do this—remember this and say this—alone.

"At first, I didn't even know it was happening until I saw the SOLD sign on the house here in town. Only one local lawyer would talk to me, and he was the one who discovered that the money in my parents' estate accounts had disappeared." She watched Kade with shiny eyes. "Unless I could afford to file a lawsuit, there wasn't anything I could do."

Kade knelt in front of her and took her hands. They were ice cold, and he rubbed them between his palms. Although his knuckles were swollen and achy, holding her fingers soothed his own. "Where was your parents' home?"

She sniffled. "Pulaski Square."

He whistled low and gently squeezed her hands. "One of those historic mansions?"

Those homes were worth millions.

"Yes." She withdrew her hands and wiped her face with her fingers. "My mother restored the property and the gardens. It was beautiful."

Kade stood to pace the room. As she brought the brutality of her uncle's betrayal into greater focus, Kade's suspicions increased. "Your father was a surgeon with a million-dollar historic home, a beach house, and was one of Doom's sponsors—which costs a ton of money."

"My mother was also from a wealthy family in New Orleans."

His heart rate increased as he paced. "You were to inherit everything when you turned twenty-three? Except Isaac died after your twenty-second birthday?"

She nodded.

"Do you think it's possible..." he paused near the sink. He hated voicing this idea out loud, but it had to be said.

"Think what is possible?"

He clasped his hands behind his neck and exhaled. "Could Magnus have killed Isaac before your twenty-third birthday, so he could steal your inheritance?"

CHAPTER 16

Rose stood and gripped the back of the chair to steady her shaky legs. When that didn't help, she sat again. Not only was the thought of Magnus being a murderer a horrible one, the realization that it could be true was even worse.

"Oh, Kade." Her voice sounded breathy, as if filled with the tears she was blinking away. "You could be right. I just can't believe I didn't think of it myself."

He knelt in front of her and took her hands. "Even though Magnus is an ass, he's still your last living relative, other than Timmy. It's not easy for good people to think bad things about someone they've lived with. Someone they wanted to love even if that person made it impossible."

She wiped away tears with her fingers. "Magnus accused me, in public, of causing Isaac's death and stealing something from him."

"The night that Magnus came to the club and attacked you?"

"Yes." The cathedral bell struck nine times, signaling that time was passing by, and she closed her eyes.

Unfortunately, that night had become a permanent, humiliating memory. Magnus, who'd been very drunk, had pulled her out of the cage she'd been dancing in and thrown her on the floor. Then, despite the fact she'd been topless, he hit her. An action that caused Kade to grab Magnus and toss him out. An action that led to a brutal fight outside the club. An action that ended up with police sirens, Kade in handcuffs, and Magnus—as usual—walking away as the victim. "The night you fought Magnus, broke his wrist, and were arrested."

"Magnus may have been projecting his guilt on to you."

She opened her eyes. "And taken his self-hatred out on you."

"If Magnus sold your homes and everything inside, and still thought you'd stolen something from him, I bet he was talking about that box."

"I agree." Her phone rang, and the caller ID popped up as the Savannah Preservation Office. She showed the phone to Kade before answering on speaker so he could hear as well. "Hello?"

"Hi," a cheery female voice said. "This is Sarah Munro from the Savannah Preservation Office. May I speak to Rose Guthrie?"

"This is Rose. Thank you for calling back."

"My assistant told me about your interest in the puzzle box that was stolen from the SPO a few months ago." Sarah paused, and Rose heard the sounds of horns and traffic in the background. "I was wondering if you could you meet me at Nectar of Gods. It's the new coffee shop on the corner of East Harris and Abercorn, across from Lafayette Park. I'm on my way to work and need to pick up an order for a meeting. We could talk there, in person. I would prefer not to speak on the phone."

Rose glanced at Kade who nodded. That coffee shop was a

short walk from her house. "We can meet you there in twenty minutes. Would that work?"

"Perfect. See you then."

FIFTEEN MINUTES LATER, Rose and Kade entered Nectar of Gods Café. Kade had insisted they leave their new cell phones at home. He'd also mentioned he'd locked his Fianna phone—the one Leonato and Sampson had given him years ago—in his truck. The same truck he'd moved to a parking lot a few blocks away from her house. "Tell me again why we left our phones behind? We used them last night."

"Because I'm paranoid." Kade took her hand and led her to a table in the corner. "If we don't need them, I don't want to carry them."

She wasn't normally a paranoid person, but she'd also had no idea that the Fianna even existed. Although she was worried Timmy might contact her and she wouldn't be there to pick up.

"This shop smells amazing." She dropped her pink backpack onto the table and slipped on her sweatshirt. Since she lived without AC, she tended to get cold in places that were kept at arctic temps, like most of the stores and restaurants in Savannah.

"I agree." Kade rearranged the chairs so his back was against the wall and took out his wallet. He wore his jeans and his Iron Rack's T-shirt as well as a black leather jacket he'd had in his truck. It hadn't taken her long to realize that the coat, despite the heat, covered the weapon he had in his back waistband.

She'd quickly come to realize that no matter the space they were in, Kade was always scanning his surroundings. Always watching. Always waiting. Always armed.

"Buying you coffee is the least I can do." Kade handed her a twenty-dollar bill. "I'll have whatever drink smells like Heaven and chocolate are on their honeymoon and making babies."

She laughed and went to stand in line. Because there were a few people ahead of her, she studied the room. All the tables were taken, and the café was filled with people drinking coffee topped with whipped cream in glass mugs.

"Rose?" a soft female voice asked.

She lifted her head. She was the next in line and recognized the pretty barista behind the register. "Bianca?"

Bianca Legare came around the counter, and they hugged each other. Not only had Bianca been a waitress at Rage of Angels, they'd known each other since grade school. Unfortunately, Bianca's life story was almost as sad as Rose's. They'd spent hours commiserating over the fickleness of the Fates and what they'd do if they ever met those three evil sisters.

"I haven't seen you since the club closed." Bianca hurried back to the register and tightened her black and gold apron with the NOG logo. It made a striking contrast with her white-blonde hair. "How have you been?"

"I'm okay." Rose waved a hand around the cozy coffee shop. "Like you, I had to get another job."

Bianca lowered her voice and checked behind her as if making sure no one was paying attention. "And Timmy?"

Rose shrugged. "The same."

Bianca nodded. "Well, I have something that will cheer you up. At least temporarily." Bianca pointed to a glass on the counter filled with a dark coffee drink topped with cream. "It's called a Bicerin. It's from Turin, Italy. It's made with melted chocolate, espresso, and warm whipped cream."

"Sounds delicious. I'll take three." Since they weren't that expensive, Rose figured she'd buy one for Sarah since she was going out of her way to meet them.

"Here." Bianca took two warm chocolate croissants out of the small oven behind her and slipped them onto a plate. "They're on the house. And they're amazing."

"Thank you." Rose took the plate and paid for the drinks. "It's so good to see you again, Bianca."

Rose was just beginning to realize how lonely she'd been since the club shut down.

Bianca handed her back some change, but her face had changed slightly. She looked tired and... sad. "Rose, have you seen Deke lately?"

Rose swallowed. She wasn't sure what to say. As far as Rose knew, Bianca wasn't involved with Deke's other businesses. Yet Rose hadn't been either—until she'd agreed to be his courier. "I haven't seen Deke since the night of Sally's murder." That, at least, was the truth. "Why?"

Bianca tilted her head to see behind Rose, and then she whispered, "My brother Aemon is missing. And the last time I spoke with him, he was on his way to meet Deke."

"I thought Aemon moved to New Orleans?"

"He returned months ago. Never even told me he was coming home. He just appeared one day, saying that he hated working for the law firm. Then, a few weeks ago, he disappeared."

"I'm so sorry. Have you contacted the police?"

"No." She shrugged. "Aemon wasn't always on the right side of the law. If he's just hiding out, I don't want to get him in more trouble. I even checked the cathedral's bell towers, wondering if he'd taken over Timmy's old hiding spot."

Rose offered a small smile and touched Bianca's arm. "If I hear anything, I'll let you know."

"Thanks." Bianca brushed away strands of hair from her face. "I'll bring the drinks over when they're ready."

"Thanks." Rose pointed toward the table where Kade waited. "I'm over there."

Bianca's eyes widened. "Is that..." she lowered her voice. "Kade Dolan?"

Rose nodded. Before she could respond, a brunette woman walked in carrying a large straw bag. She walked with purpose in her low-heeled sandals and pink sundress. She'd twisted her hair into a bun and held her cell phone in her other hand. It was obvious from the way the woman held herself that she wasn't just beautiful, but confident and kind as well.

The type of woman Rose hoped to become one day.

Rose looked back at Bianca. "Thank you for the croissants. Hopefully, soon, I'll fill you in on the Kade situation."

Bianca winked. "I can't wait."

Rose met Sarah in the middle of the shop. She recognized the historian from her photo in the journal article. "Sarah?"

Sarah smiled and nodded. "Rose?"

"Yes." Rose led Sarah to the table. "I ordered you a Bicerin, and my girlfriend gave us two free chocolate croissants."

"How wonderful."

After introducing Kade, and taking the drinks and napkins from Bianca, they settled into their seats.

Kade pushed the plate of croissants between Rose and Sarah. "Please eat these. I had way too much blueberry coffee cake this morning."

"Thanks." Sarah took a napkin and placed it on her lap. "My assistant said you had questions about the puzzle box that was stolen a few months ago."

Rose finished a bite of her croissant and said, "I believe that box belonged to my mother, Violet Levaux Guthrie."

"How interesting." Sarah held her Bicerin glass with both hands. "I found the puzzle box hidden in a room on the third floor."

"That was my mother's office, before she died. I was wondering about the box itself. Any idea why someone would steal it?"

"The box itself isn't unusual for the time period. One thing might make it worth quite a bit of money. The initials engraved on one of the silver panels along the side of the box read 'EG, All My Love, BG. 1776.'"

"That wasn't in the article we read," Kade said.

"I left those details out of the article." Sarah broke off a piece of her croissant and ate it. "Detective Garza of the Savannah Police Department, who investigated the theft, believes the thief might have known more about the box than I'd discussed in the article."

Rose shared a knowing look with Kade who'd already finished most of his Bicerin. Detective Garza had come to the hospital the night Leonato killed a man. And had also questioned them after Sally's murder at the club.

The power blinked on and off, and Sarah ate another piece of her croissant. "I love this city, but the crazy power outages and violent crimes seem to be increasing."

Rose agreed. "Sarah, what else did Detective Garza say?"

"The detective believed the thief was waiting for the box to be found. And once he discovered where it had been hidden, he stole it."

Kade leaned forward and clasped his hands on the table. "Why would the detective think that?"

"Because that box was the only thing stolen. There are a lot of antiques in the SPO building that would fetch a high price on the antiquities black market. Since I didn't talk about the engravings on the box in the article, Detective Garza believes the thief knew about the engravings before he even stole the box."

Rose sipped her Bicerin. "Why would that detail on the box increase the value?"

"Because the initials EG and BG may stand for Elizabeth Gwinnett and Button Gwinnett."

Kade frowned. "You mean the patriot, Button Gwinnett, who was one of the founding fathers from Georgia?"

"Yes. He also signed the Declaration of Independence." Sarah pulled out her phone, searched for an image, and placed it on the table between them.

Rose squinted at the image of the Declaration on the small screen. "I see John Hancock's signature."

Sarah pointed to the left of Hancock's signature. "See this large and loopy signature?"

"Button Gwinnett." Rose took another sip of her drink and used the napkin to wipe the whipped cream off her lips. She felt like a child, but she didn't care. The drink was worth giving up all of her dignity for. "Did the man who owned my mother's box sign the Declaration of Independence?"

"I believe so." Sarah slipped the phone back into her bag. "Button Gwinnett was a grocer who came to Savannah from England. After losing his business, he discovered a talent for rhetoric and politics and became entrenched in Savannah's society. Then he joined the Sons of Liberty, attended the First Continental Congress in Philadelphia, and signed the Declaration of Independence in 1776.

"When Button Gwinnett returned to Savannah, he read the Declaration aloud to the Sons of Liberty in the Declaration's first known public reading. Many historians believe he read it aloud in a room below Tondee's Tavern—the original one, not the current bar on East Bay Street. Unfortunately, after Button Gwinnett's death, the box disappeared until your mother found it."

"My mother purchased it in an antique shop in New Orleans."

"Do you know which shop?" Sarah took a small notepad and a pen out of her bag and began writing. "It would be great if we had a receipt. Then again, the box is missing, so it probably doesn't matter."

"I'm sorry," Rose said. "I don't remember the name of the antique shop. I just know it was in the French Quarter."

Sarah wrote for another minute, closed the notebook, and took another bite of her pastry.

"Sarah," Kade asked. "If we find the box, how much would it be worth?"

"Without proof of ownership"—Sarah tapped the notebook with her pen—"but with the possibility that Button Gwinnett was the owner, I'd place the auction value at three hundred thousand. Double that if one can prove Button Gwinnett was the original owner. Triple that if you can prove provenance, a chain of ownership custody, that includes a receipt of your mother's legal purchase."

Kade whistled low and pushed his chair onto the back two legs.

Wow. That was a lot of money. Money she could use right now.

She shared a glance with Kade and knew he was thinking the same thing. Deke had only offered her two hundred thousand. Then again, even if she found the box she had no way to prove anything close to a chain of custody.

She finished the last of her croissant and wiped her fingers on her napkin. She was surprised she'd eaten the entire thing. But that was the thing when one was worried about buying groceries. If free food came along, you ate it all even if you didn't need it. "How could one prove that BG stands for Button Gwinnett?"

"A receipt from 1776 showing that Button requested the box to be made for his wife, Elizabeth, would help. On the bottom of the box, there's an engraving with the initials JL inside a lily. I believe this refers to Joshua Linguard, a famous metalworker in Charleston. Although Joshua disappeared in the early eighteenth century, his workshop remained open through the nineteenth century.

"I've already checked the Charleston archives, though, and wasn't able to find any records from Joshua Linguard's workshop dating back to the eighteenth century. Apparently, there'd been a fire that destroyed the workshop and all the records inside."

"Could something in the box prove who commissioned it?"

"Maybe," Sarah said. "It's too bad the box was stolen before I was able to figure out how to open it. I'd love to know what it contained."

Kade clasped his hands behind his neck. "Have you ever heard of a man named Hezekiah Usher?"

Sarah nodded. "Hezekiah Usher was the first publisher in the Massachusetts Bay Colony in 1647. He printed and sold books out of his Boston store."

"Do you know if he has any current-day ancestors?" he asked.

Sarah tilted her head and stared at Kade for a moment. A moment that turned into a long minute. A moment that made Rose wonder what Sarah knew and didn't want to tell them. Or was afraid to tell them. "Why are you asking?"

Kade and Rose glanced at each other again. From the low tone in Sarah's voice, it was obvious she didn't want to talk about this.

"We," Kade nodded at Rose, "came across a business card with the name Hezekiah Usher printed on the front, along with a Boston area phone number that doesn't work. But there was no other information about how to contact him."

Sarah tossed her notebook and pen into her bag and then glanced out the window facing the street, as if making sure the tourists outside weren't listening. "Stay away from Hezekiah Usher."

"Why?" Rose asked.

Sarah didn't answer. She just stood and hiked her straw

bag on her shoulder. "I'm sorry I have to leave, but I have a meeting in less than an hour. It was nice meeting you both."

Kade rose as Sarah left the table and headed for the counter. After speaking with Bianca, and retrieving a large brown bag, probably filled with pastries, Sarah left the coffee shop.

Rose looked up at Kade. He'd tracked Sarah's exit and seemed fixated on something outside. Rose wasn't sure where to start with all the revelations. So she began with the most surprising one. "Kade? Is it possible that Button Gwinnett once read the Declaration of Independence aloud to the Sons of Liberty at your fight club?"

Kade sighed, sat, and took her hand. His warm fingers squeezed her cold ones. "Yes, it's possible. I've been hearing that rumor for years." He continued to stare out the window with a view of Lafayette Park across the street. "Why would this current-day Hezekiah Usher, and the Prince, want this box?"

His voice sounded so low, she wasn't sure if he was asking her or himself.

"I wish I knew." She kissed his hand and stood. "I need to use the restroom. I'll be right back."

He stood and began clearing the table. "When you get back, we'll figure out what to do next."

"I just want to find this box so this nightmare will end."

"Rose." Kade paused until she met his gaze that drew her in, making her feel like she was drowning in a deep blue sea of unfamiliar emotions. "We will find the box."

In spite of how hard she fought to tamp down her worries, her voice sounded shaky. "How can you promise that?"

He lowered his lips until they hovered over hers. "Because we have nothing left to lose."

She kissed him quickly and hurried to the ladies' room. His words—both a warning and a truth—resonated. He was right. At this point, the only things she had to lose were those she loved. Which meant the stakes couldn't get any higher.

Once she used the ladies' room, she bumped into Bianca on her way out. From Bianca's red, puffy eyes, it was obvious she'd been crying.

"Bianca?" Rose touched her arm. "Are you all right?"

Bianca nodded and wiped her face with her hands. "I'm just worried about my brother."

Rose hugged her and said, "It was so good to see you again." And she meant it. She'd been so focused on her own troubles, she'd forgotten other people had problems as well. And didn't that make her feel like a selfish cow?

Bianca hugged Rose back and whispered, "I heard you asking about Hezekiah Usher. Don't look for him or the Usher Society. I once knew someone in that group, and now he's dead. The Usher Society is dangerous."

Before Rose could respond, Bianca ran into the ladies' room.

When Rose returned to the table, she found Kade near the front door. His focus was still on something across the street. His tight lips, flared nostrils, and the way he fisted his hands told her something was wrong.

She adjusted her backpack on her shoulder and followed his line of sight. In the park across the street, a man leaned against a tree with his arms crossed. Tall, black hair, and dark skin, he wore jeans and a navy T-shirt. Although he stood in the shade, he had on a navy hat embroidered with the white logo for the New York Yankees. He appeared to be staring directly at Kade.

She touched his arm. Despite wearing a leather jacket, she felt the muscles shift beneath her fingers. "Kade?"

He took her hand and kissed the palm. "We're leaving now. Don't let go of my hand and follow my lead." He opened the door and left first, keeping her behind him. Then he hurried down the street, and she struggled to keep up since she was wearing sandals.

From now on, she was only wearing running away shoes.

A moment later, Kade glanced back at her. His blue eyes darkened and he ordered, *"Run."*

CHAPTER 17

It took Kade thirty minutes to get Rose back home safely.

They'd not taken the straightest path. Instead, he'd led them both through alleys, a parking garage, and abandoned building lots. He'd forced them to take every twist and turn he could find, and he was grateful she'd kept up without asking questions. That alone implied that while she didn't trust him completely, she was willing to let him protect her despite knowing he held secrets.

In their current fucked-up situation, that was a huge step forward in their relationship.

Once inside, Kade tossed off his jacket and locked the door. Then he checked all the other doors and windows. It didn't take long because her house was so small.

When he was sure the house was secure, he found Rose in her bedroom, taking off her sandals. "Are you okay?"

"Yes." She met his gaze, one sandal dangling from her fingers. "What just happened?"

He placed his weapon on the bedside table, sat on the bed

next to her, and ran a hand over his head. "We were being followed."

The sandal dropped to the floor with a low thud. "By Leonato?"

"No. By his buddy Sampson." Kade lay back on the bed and stared at the ceiling. "Fianna warriors always hang out in pairs. Maybe Leonato was busy."

"How did they find us at NOG? We left our phones here." She lay down next to him, and then shifted until her head rested on his chest.

"I have no idea." He wrapped his arm around her shoulder and held her close. He loved feeling her heart beat against body.

"Why did we have to run in circles to get home? If Leonato knows where I live, so does Sampson."

"Because I want Sampson to think we went someplace else first. I have no doubt that one of them will eventually show up here again, but for now they'll be running around town looking for us." It was one of the reasons he'd moved his truck, with his Fianna phone, before they'd gone to NOG. He wanted to keep the warriors guessing about his whereabouts for a little while longer.

She lifted her head to meet his gaze. "We threw Sampson off our trail just to annoy him?"

"Yep." Yes, it was petty. But Kade was tired of being followed and tracked all the time. If today's stunt forced Sampson to wander around the hot city for an hour, it was worth the effort. "I wonder what Sarah knows about Hezekiah Usher that she didn't want to say?"

"I wish I knew. I saw Bianca in the bathroom." Rose rested her head on his chest again and draped an arm across his stomach. "She'd overheard our conversation and told me to stay away from Hezekiah Usher and the Usher Society. She said she knew someone who'd been involved with them, and that person died. She said they were dangerous."

He grabbed his burner phone from the charger next to the bed. "What is the Usher Society?"

"I don't know."

With one hand, he searched for the Usher Society on his phone. "I'm not finding anything about them."

"You can search the internet on that cheap phone?"

"Yes, but it's slow and I have very limited data. I could use my Fianna phone, but I know they monitor that one."

"I'm not surprised you can't find anything." She snuggled in closer, and he tightened his hold. "So far, none of our clues have given us anything."

"What else did Bianca say?"

"Just that her brother Aemon went missing, over a week ago, the same day he was supposed to meet Deke."

"I remember Aemon." Kade tossed the phone onto the bed and closed his eyes. "Aemon made a ton of money gaming online. He was a brilliant computer kid who dropped out of college and moved to New Orleans."

"He worked for a law firm but came home a few months ago."

Kade opened his eyes. "Did Bianca say which law firm?"

Rose raised up on an elbow and met his gaze. "No."

"Is it possible Aemon worked for Beaumont, Barclay and Bray?"

"Possibly." Rose sat up. "I can text Bianca and ask."

Rose grabbed her phone from the kitchen and returned to the bedroom. She held Deke's planner and was texting.

Kade slipped his free hand behind his head and stared at the ceiling again. Water stains had dried in swirling concentric circles. This whole city always felt humid and dank, and carried an overwhelming scent of mold and decay. Since he was used to it, he normally didn't care. But since saving Rose from

Antoine the other night, he'd begun to hate everything about Savannah. If he were in charge of his own fate, he'd take Rose and Timmy and leave for another state. Maybe even another country. As long as where they landed kept them safe and together.

Rose sat on the edge of the bed, still texting. "Bianca says Aemon worked for Beaumont, Barclay, and Bray. She even sent me his phone number at the firm, except she said it was disconnected."

Rose showed him the phone's screen. Then she opened Deke's planner to the phone number Deke had written next to the initials A.L. *Fuck.* "The phone numbers are the same. And I bet A.L. stands for Aemon Legare."

"At least we know who Deke was calling at the law firm."

Kade got up to pace the room. "So Aemon and Deke were working together, and now they're both... *missing.*"

"Kade? What are you not telling me?"

"Last night Calum confirmed Deke's death."

She sighed heavily. "I'm not surprised. And, I have to be honest, I don't care other than the fact it makes our search harder."

"I feel the same way." Kade flexed his hands and moved to the window overlooking the backyard. "My guess is that Aemon helped Deke set up the website that took the extra bets for Doom." Kade glanced back at Rose to find her still texting. "Did Bianca say anything else?"

"I asked her what else she knew about the Usher Society." Rose tossed the phone aside and met him at the window. She wrapped her arms around her waist and shivered despite the fact she still wore her sweatshirt. Despite the fact the room, without AC, felt warmer inside than out. "Bianca said the Usher Society was made up of powerful, rich people who bought and sold priceless manuscripts on the black market. And that we should stay away from them. She said these people were no better than drug dealers and murderers. Which was something I really didn't need to hear right now."

He took Rose in his arms. Once she wrapped her arms around his waist, he rested his chin on her head. "So what does a black-market manuscript dealer want with your puzzle box?"

"Maybe there's a priceless document in the box. That could be why Magnus, and the Prince, are so determined to find it."

"At this point, I'd believe anything." He closed his eyes and breathed in her honeysuckle scent. Being with her, like this, eased the constant restlessness he'd been living with since leaving prison.

When King George appeared behind them and hissed, Kade opened his eyes and rejoined the real world.

"I need to feed him." Rose kissed Kade's chin and left his embrace to deal with the tyrannical feline.

After using the bathroom, he splashed cold water on his face to force away the funk of his impending failure. When he returned to the bedroom, his phone buzzed on the bed.

He recognized the caller ID and answered, "What do you need, Calum?"

"You know I've been renovating the club while it's been closed due to...uh..."

"Sally's murder investigation?" Kade rubbed his forehead with his fist. He'd been the one to find the young stripper's body in the alley behind Rage of Angels.

"Yes," Calum said. "I just received a call from the foreman inspecting the water-damaged floors in the office. He found a key chain hidden behind the couch. It has an old key to the club's front door and a fob for a Harley Sportster, circa 2012. Are they yours?"

Rose returned, and Kade put the phone on speaker so she could hear. "Those are Deke's keys. Is there anything else on the chain?"

Rose bit her lower lip but stayed quiet.

"A brass tag engraved with J1999."

Kade dropped onto the edge of the bed, and Rose sat next to him. He made sure their thighs touched. He needed to be near her to feel grounded. "Does the tag have a screw hole in both ends, like it might have come off a locker?"

"Yes."

"It could be from Iron Rack's Gym. The old man who owned the place got lockers from an abandoned high school. We ended up not using them because we had only a master key, and they were all locked. The old man was too cheap to re-key free lockers."

"Are the lockers still there?" Calum asked.

Kade placed his hand on her thigh. He felt the heat of her skin through the dress's thin cotton, and his body responded appropriately despite the terrible timing. "It's possible they're still in the back storage room."

"The one with the rats?"

Rose wrinkled her nose.

Kade felt the same way. "Yes."

"Could the box be in that locker?" Calum asked.

"Deke hardly ever came to the gym except…" Kade paused and leaned forward, pressing his elbow into his thigh. "Six weeks ago, the old-man owner and Deke were arguing in the office. I don't know what Deke said, but the old man threw him out and told him never to come back."

"Maybe the old man found Deke in the back room."

"It's possible. Even if that locker is still there, I don't know if I can find the master key. Unfortunately, I can't just show up at the gym with a blowtorch without answering awkward questions."

"That locker may contain what you're looking for. Although, if you can't find the key, call me. We'll figure something out."

"I'll go to the gym now." Kade swallowed and thought of something else. "Calum, do you know anything about the Usher Society?"

A long silence preceded Calum's answer. "Why?"

Since they had nothing to lose by asking, Kade said, "I think Rose was supposed to deliver the box to a man named Hezekiah Usher."

"Yes." Calum offered another long pause. "Rose confirmed that last night at Doom."

"Well, this man may run the Usher Society."

Calum muttered a curse beneath this breath. "Kade, once you search the gym, meet me at Prideaux House. It's not far from the gym. We'll talk about this there. I don't want to do it over the phone."

Kade knew the historic property. Although *property* was a generous term since both the enormous house and garden were in the last stages of decay. The only things that lived there were ghosts and vermin. "Don't tell me you bought that place as well as Iron Rack's Gym."

"Collecting old properties is a hobby of mine. Besides, it was once owned by my family before they changed their name from Prideaux to Prioleau."

Rose frowned and pointed to the phone, and he asked the question he knew she wanted to know the answer to.

"Calum, what interest do you have in this box?"

"None. I just hate what Isaac and Magnus did to Rose and her brother."

Kade wasn't sure if he believed Calum or not, but they had no other allies. "See you soon." He hung up and stood. "No, Rose."

She stood. "I'm coming with you."

"You're not." He shoved his phone in his back pocket. "I'm going to drop you at the hospital so you can see Timmy."

"Kade—"

"I'm not doing this because I don't think you can handle yourself." He grabbed his weapon, left the bedroom, and found his gym bag in the living room. He'd have to carry his weapon in his bag because it was too damn hot to wear his jacket, and he didn't have his leg holster. "I'm doing this because you're being followed. Magnus. Sampson. And who the hell knows where Leonato is right now."

She stood in front of him, her hands on her hips. "I don't understand."

Kade slipped the clip out of the gun, checked to make sure it was fully loaded, and slammed it back in. "First rule once you realize you're being followed? Never change your routine."

"Otherwise, they'll know we have a clue."

"Yes."

Her only response was to leave the living room.

He grabbed his bag and followed her into the bedroom, where he found her opening a dresser drawer and pulling out jeans and a white top. When she yanked open another drawer to find a pair of socks, a silver sequined bra fell out and landed on the floor.

He shoved the weapon into his back waistband, stole the socks from her, and tossed them onto the bed. "Why are you changing?"

"I need to put on running-away clothes. Because I'm going with you."

He took her arms and made her sit on the edge of the bed. "I just told you—"

"I don't care." She waved to the jeans on the floor. "I'm supposed to see Timmy while you get the key to this locker, find the box, and meet Calum at Prideaux House?"

He knelt before her, and she looked away. What he was asking of her required a huge amount of trust. She was putting her future in his hands.

"Rose?" He touched her cheek. "I promise I won't betray you."

She nodded, but still wouldn't look at him. "I don't have any choice, do I?"

"It's safer this way."

She faced him, her eyes a darker green than he'd ever seen. "How do I know I can trust you?"

He hid his broken heart behind a steady smile. The fact that they'd made love a few hours ago and she still didn't trust him cut deeply. So deeply he wasn't sure if his heart would ever recover. "I give you my word."

The only thing he had left in the world to offer her.

Her shoulders trembled, but she kept her focus on his face as if trying to figure out all his hidden secrets. "The last man I trusted took everything from me. He was a violent bastard, and so is his son. I had to run away to survive. I barely finished high school and was homeless for weeks. If my school counselor hadn't taken me in, I never would have graduated. After that, I was on my own."

He moved his hands to her shoulders so she'd keep his gaze. "I know what it's like to be betrayed. Found guilty of something you didn't do. Left behind. Forgotten by friends and family. And I sure as hell know how hard it can be to ask for help when all you know is dishonesty and treachery. All I can do is promise not to do the same to you."

She wiped away a tear.

"What can I do to reassure you?" *Other than taking you back to bed?*

"I don't know." She pushed his hands off her shoulders and paced the room. "That is the problem, Kade. I don't know you. All I do know is that you've been in prison and are involved with the Fianna. The same group of men who want my box and don't want to pay me."

He stood and grabbed her hands, forcing her to stop. "Do

you remember when I told you about my maternal grandmother?"

She nodded.

"I was Nin's favorite." Kade cleared his throat. "I knew—in that way a kid knows—that my brothers resented me. Years later, when I was twelve and most of my brothers were preoccupied with being teenagers, Nin gave me something. My brothers never forgave her. I think it was why they treated Nin so horribly after my father's death."

He inhaled until his lungs hurt, and he blinked a few times.

Rose squeezed his hands. "What did Nin give you?"

He reluctantly released her hands and opened his gym bag on the floor near the bed. After unzipping an inside pocket, he found his most-valued possession.

He held out his palm to show her. "A silver pocket compass watch. It's a Mercer family heirloom. Apparently, one of our female ancestors gave it to her husband as a wedding present. It was the only thing of value she had, and her husband promised he'd carry it until he claimed his beloved's last kiss."

"That makes me want to cry." Rose took the silver compass watch and opened it. "It's heavier than it looks. And the watch doesn't work."

"It's eighteenth century. I can't afford to get it fixed."

She read the engraving on the inside lid aloud. "'Love's not Time's fool.'"

"I never knew what that meant." Kade ran a hand over his head. "Until recently."

She looked up at him. "What does it mean?"

"Time can't change the essence of love because true love doesn't change over days or weeks or years. True love lasts until the end of time. True love remains steady no matter the storm winds that batter it. No matter how far away the lover goes, or how age changes their appearance, true love will always be what it claims to be. True. Honest. Forever. Love is the most important thing to believe in. The most important thing to trust."

She swallowed, and he held his breath until their gazes met. He hated the tears swimming in her eyes, yet was also grateful. Her sadness could be a way to tie her to him, even if only temporarily.

He was so not a prince.

"That's beautiful," she whispered.

"I know." He took her hand that held his compass watch. "I want you to keep this."

Her eyes widened, and she shook her head. "No—"

"Yes." He wrapped her fingers around the compass watch. "This is my promise to you. Whether I find that box or not, I will return to you. And I will never leave you without love's last kiss."

ROSE SAT on the edge of the bed, closed her eyes, and clenched her fist until the silver compass watch warmed in her hand.

How could she trust Kade when she hardly knew him?

How could she be falling in love with him when she wasn't sure she could trust him?

He moved, and she opened her eyes, surprised to see he'd picked up the silver bra. It'd been part of her most popular costume at Rage of Angels.

When its sequins sparkled in the sunlight, he said, "This was the costume you wore the night we met."

She looked away but couldn't stop the warm flush that traveled up her neck to her cheeks. She remembered that night. She'd been dancing in a cage that hung from the ceiling and had felt his stare from near the stage, where he'd broken up a fight.

The first time she'd met his blue gaze, something inside her had shifted. He hadn't looked at her with disdain or disgust or desire. He'd just regarded her as if he understood—she was simply a woman in a cage. A woman in a desperate situation. A woman with no other options.

In that moment, the iron straps around her heart loosened the smallest bit.

"I know the truth, Rose." He laid the bra across her knees and sat next to her. "That night, I saw it in your eyes. The woman who wore this was a character in a story. A wandering ship in a storm." He paused when the church's bells rang eleven a.m. "You pretended to be empty—like a bell tower without a bell. Until we spoke."

How did he have the words to describe how she'd felt in that cage? Seen as an object, unseen as a woman. A woman with her own desires and fears and dreams. "After my set, I was walking back to the locker room, and you offered me a glass of water."

His smile brightened his face. "Do you remember what you said to me?"

She shook her head.

"You told me you didn't date bouncers or bartenders." He laughed beneath his breath. "Then you walked away."

"That was rude." She placed the compass watch on the bed. The stream of sunshine highlighted the etching of an eight-pointed star on the silver cover.

"No." He took her hands and squeezed. "I recognized it for what it was—self-protection. I understood then, and I understand now. You have no reason to trust me. I'm an ex-con, Army Ranger, Doom referee and fighter, gym employee, and my life is owned by the Fianna."

"Surely you've paid them back for releasing you from prison."

"Rose"—he kissed the back of one hand and then the other—"it doesn't work that way. I belong to them until they decide I don't."

She pulled her hands out of his grasp and stood quickly. "What does that mean?"

He stood as well but didn't approach her. "I can't tell you."

Her cheeks burned, and she moved toward the window. Outside, the oak tree separating her from the dead appeared so strong and steady. Especially compared to the fact that her world felt like it was falling off its axis. "You ask me to trust you, yet you admit you're keeping secrets."

He came up behind her and touched her shoulders. "I'm sorry."

She turned halfway to see his profile. He didn't meet her gaze. His sight was fixed on the tree where Magnus had stood.

"Kade," she asked softly, "are you going to give the Fianna my box?"

"*No.*" He turned her until they faced each other. His lips lowered until they hovered over hers. "Like I said last night, I'm in love with you."

"That's not possible." She backed away, and he dropped his hands. "We hardly know each other. I've caused you nothing but problems. And you're keeping secrets."

He moved forward with determination, and she retreated until her back hit the wall. His gaze darkened, making his eyes appear more black than blue. He took her shoulders and drew her against him. "I promise you, Tempest Rose Guthrie, I will return."

His lips met hers in a firestorm of need and want and desire. He held her so close, every inch of her soft body was up against hard muscles. The kiss started out demanding, as if daring her to object. But when she relaxed against him and wrapped her arms around his neck, he deepened the kiss until she melted into his embrace. His distinctive scent filled her nose, sending flames of heat down her back. She stood on her toes and tilted her head. He followed the motion, pulling her up even higher until her breasts were crushed against his chest. When his lips broke from hers, he trailed kisses down her neck.

He nibbled the delicate skin beneath her ear. "*Rose.*"

She shivered from the tingles that started in her lower stomach and spread throughout her body. "Yes?"

"Do you trust me?"

She lowered her feet to the floor and opened her eyes to meet his gaze. "I honestly don't know." She licked her lips, and his breath shortened into bursts. "But I can try. I want to."

He dropped kisses on her nose, both of her cheeks, and a final kiss on her lips. "That's all I need."

He held her close again, this time resting his chin on her head.

"Kade? Don't get killed. Don't end up in another forced fight. And don't lose that box."

He chuckled, and she felt the rumbles in his chest. "In that order?"

"Yes." She snuggled closer into his embrace and used her most serious voice. "And return to me unharmed. If you don't, I'll sic King George on you. He's not as nice as I am."

Kade kissed her head. "I promise."

CHAPTER 18

Kade parked his truck around the corner from Iron Rack's Gym and shoved his Fianna phone and his burner phone into his back pockets. It hadn't taken long to take Rose to the hospital and then check his Fianna phone messages. He'd even held his breath until seeing the empty notifications screen.

When this was all over, he was never going to carry a damn cell phone again. He needed his burner phone to contact Calum, but he couldn't abandon his Fianna phone. If he missed a message from Leonato or Sampson, they'd know Kade wasn't where he was supposed to be. So he had to walk a thin wire between planting his Fianna phone where the warriors thought he'd be while he was off doing something else.

Sometimes he really hated technology.

After locking the truck, he scanned the area to make sure he wasn't being followed. Then he crossed the street and hurried through an empty lot covered with broken concrete interspersed with knee-high weeds.

It was time to put his risky-as-hell plan into motion. The

risky-as-hell plan that would allow Rose and Timmy to live the rest of their lives together in peace. With all the interest in the thing, it was possible the box was worth far more than two hundred thousand dollars. Maybe worth enough to change Rose and Timmy's lives forever.

The first step in his plan? Finding that damn box.

Normally the gym opened at five a.m., except Nate had recently changed that to noon on the weekends. While the new hours weren't great for business, today Kade was grateful.

He turned into a narrow alley. Dark, with a slimy brick walkway that saw little sun, it dumped him into the gym's yard, consisting of a broken concrete patio, a thin palmetto, and straggly pink azaleas. He pushed open the back entrance that led into the storage room. The door should've been secure, but the lock hadn't worked in years. Luckily, the rats that lived in the back room were as effective as the fiercest guard dog.

Since the lights didn't work, he used the flashlight app on his phone. It only took a minute to find a row of old lockers in the back corner, behind stacks of rotted gym mats. Eleven of the twelve lockers had brass tags at the top of the doors. The last one, next to J1998, had no tag. And it was locked.

"Fuck."

Now he had to find that master key. There were only two places to look. The reception desk or the main office desk. He made his way through the junk and debris to head into the main gym. He slammed the door shut before the stench of mold, as well as any rats, could escape. Luckily, the lights and the ear-blasting music hadn't been turned on because no one was here yet.

He slipped behind shelving units that held free weights and studied the area. He heard noises upstairs, where Nate and his men lived.

The shrieking phone at the front desk startled him, and he moved closer to the boxing ring.

When the phone went silent and the stomping noises upstairs abated, he ran to the desk. Luckily, Luke—one of Nate and Pete's buddies who acted as office manager—hadn't locked the drawers. Probably because the key to the desk had been lost as well.

Kade quietly rummaged through the drawers. He found rusted binder clips and carbon paper, but no key.

Voices from the second floor sent Kade running toward the broom closet beneath the stairs. He tried to breathe evenly as two men descended. If they found him there, he'd just say he'd decided to come into work. So he wasn't sure why he was being so cloak-and-daggery. Maybe because he didn't want anything to distract him from his plan—or ask any questions he didn't want to answer right now.

"Nate." Pete White Horse's voice sounded clipped. "Stop being so fucking annoying. Buying coffee at Screamin' Perks isn't going to bankrupt us."

"Why isn't the coffee Luke bought good enough?" Nate asked.

"It tastes like horse piss."

"Lovely." Nate's boots hit the first-floor landing, and he unlocked the manager's office. "I still think, while we're in this start-up phase with no money or capital, we shouldn't splurge on lattes."

Both men entered the office. A moment later, they emerged with Nate clutching dollar bills. He'd hit the petty cash box.

He paused near the desk. "Who filled up the box? Last night, we had less than fifty bucks. Now there are hundreds of dollars in there."

Had Vane filled up the petty cash box with his fighter's fee from Doom?

"Who the fuck cares," Pete said. "Just go with it."

Nate frowned. "I think we need a financial audit of this place."

"You know what?" Pete unlocked the gym's front door and opened it.

Nate passed Pete and gave him an annoyed look. "I'm not interested in what you know."

"You can be so fucking annoying." Pete let the door slam shut.

Kade watched and waited until both men crossed the street and turned toward the coffee shop. He had less than ten minutes before they'd return. At least they'd left the main office open.

Kade passed the stairs, slipped into the office, and closed the door. Despite having new owners, the place was still a wreck, filled with cheap furniture and bowing bookcases. A filing cabinet in one corner held a printer. A credenza behind the desk was piled high with file folders—old and new. The huge picture window that overlooked the street was still partially covered by an enormous Jolly Roger flag.

The one new thing, though, was the map of Afghanistan and Pakistan that took up an entire wall.

Fascinated, Kade studied the red glass-headed pins stuck in clusters around the Pamir River Valley. Yellow pins covered the Wakhan mountain range. Ten orange pins were stuck in Islamabad. And a single gray pin stabbed the Hindu Kush.

A crash came from the second floor, followed by a male curse. No time for curiosity. He went for the filing cabinet first, knowing it wouldn't be locked because nothing in the run-down gym had ever been locked. Except for the one locker he needed to get into, of course.

Nate and his men hadn't even started going through the contents, because it still held all the old man's files, filled with advertisements and receipts. Once assured the master key wasn't there, he went for the desk. It didn't take long to check the side drawers. The main drawer, however, was so swollen from the humidity that it wouldn't open.

He glanced out the window and saw Nate and Pete slowly walking back, holding trays of coffee cups.

Kade yanked the drawer until it loosened. Unfortunately, it came out with such a clatter, he was sure the entire block had heard the noise. Quickly, he sorted through the drawer's junk only to find nothing he needed. He shoved the drawer back in, except now it wouldn't close all the way. After another minute of fighting the drawer, he said, "Fuck it."

He planted his fists on the desk and drew in a few deep breaths. *Where is that damn key?*

Boxes of new metal shelving, along with plastic bags from the local hardware store, were stacked in a corner near the window. Besides a few folding chairs and a small refrigerator, there was no obvious place to hide anything. And he didn't have time to tear the room apart.

He stared at the desk. Receipts, pens, legal pads. Nothing unusual...except for a tomato soup can being used as a pencil holder. "That's new."

Through the window, he saw Nate and Pete coming closer. "Shit."

He moved quickly. In his haste, he knocked over the soup can. Pens and pencils rolled everywhere, and he grabbed the can before it could fall off the desk. As he returned it, he heard something rattling in the bottom. He turned it over and dumped a small key into his hand.

"Find what you're looking for?" Vane said from the doorway.

This morning, Vane wore black combat pants, boots, and a faded olive drab T-shirt. His long brown hair hung loose around his shoulders, which had to be deliberate since it cast enough shadows to hide the worst bruises on his face. He still had white tape on his nose. But other than a bandage peeking out from beneath his T-shirt sleeve, he didn't look nearly as beaten up as one would expect after fighting at Doom. And he could easily blame his bruises on the classes he'd been teaching.

"Just searching for a pencil." Kade refilled the can with the pens and pencils that had fallen out. In the process, he slipped the key into his back pocket. That's when he noticed a hand-written notebook page peeking out of a manila folder. Across the top, someone had written *LMCF* and, below that, *Jack Keeley and Tank Wofford 3C-116.*

Kade blinked to make sure he wasn't hallucinating the names. Then he remembered the other night, while they'd been doing laundry, that Vane had called his boss Kells.

Kade glanced at the map. The page. Then at Vane, who stood with his arms crossed.

Vane had also mentioned Cain's wife was still living in North Carolina.

How could I have been so stupid?

"*Kade?*" Vane cleared his throat. "Nate said you weren't coming in today."

Kade kept his voice bored and noncommittal despite his sudden trembling. "I'm checking on the schedule for the rest of the week."

Vane scoffed. "I don't think so."

"What is your problem?" Kade motioned toward the open door that showed Pete and Nate putting the trays of coffee on the front desk. "Your buddies figure out where you were last night?"

Vane's nostrils flared, and his eyes narrowed. "You promised—"

"Yes, Vane, I did. And I intend to keep that promise." Kade took the *LMCF* page out of the folder, held it up, and nodded toward the map on the wall. As he suspected, there were more names on the page. "A long time ago, I was an

Army Ranger trained by an officer named Jack Keeley. And I just figured out the identity of your boss—Colonel Kells Torridan. But I won't say a word about it if you don't say a word about me being in the office or the back room. Because that's where I'm going next."

"You don't have a fucking clue what's going on." Vane moved closer, hands fisted. "I can't let you go until I know you're not a threat to me or my men."

Kade slipped the page back into the folder. "You have nothing to fear from me."

"Vane." Pete popped his head into the room. "Nate bought coffee—hey, Kade. I thought you weren't coming in today."

"I'm not. I forgot something in the back room but wanted to ask permission before searching."

Pete grimaced. "Search away."

"Thanks." Kade smiled widely, like the request was no big deal. "Once I grab it, I'll let myself out the back door."

"No prob. Take some of those damn rats with you when you leave." Pete went back to the reception desk and found his coffee.

Kade crossed his arms and continued his face-off with Vane. "I'm going to find what I need and leave. And"—he glanced at the map on the wall—"I won't tell a soul that two Green Beret A-teams in your unit were accused and convicted of the Wakhan Corridor Massacre."

"We're innocent."

"Aren't we all." Kade left the room just as Samantha came into the gym and kissed Pete.

When she spotted Kade, her eyes widened.

He continued, nodding at Nate and Pete along the way. Luckily, Nate had a mouthful of donut, so he just waved.

Once in the back room, Kade hurried to the locker. The key turned quietly, and he opened the door. Lying on the locker's top shelf, he found a black drawstring bag. He loosened the drawstrings and took out a wooden box decorated with silver edges. Just like the one in the photo with the journal article. Except it was heavier and more ornate than he'd expected.

He returned the box to the bag and shut the locker door.

A rat ran over his boot, and he hustled out the door leading to the patio. It was only when his vision starred that he realized he'd been holding his breath.

"Kade?"

Kade looked up as Samantha hurried out of the gym and met him near the entrance to the alley. She wore black leggings, an oversized purple T-shirt, and black combat boots. With her hair in a messy bun, she sent him a glare that reminded him of Rose. "Where is Rose?"

"She's at the hospital with Timmy."

"Oh." Samantha stared at a pink azalea bush with only two blooms. "What do you know about Nate and Pete and the rest of the men?"

They were part of an infamous Green Beret unit that had been dishonorably discharged and imprisoned for coordinating the Wakhan Corridor Massacre, an event the U.N. had classified as one of the most brutal crimes against humanity ever perpetrated. "Not much. And I have no reason to tell anyone what little I do know."

She nodded but refused to meet his gaze. "Thank you."

Before he could respond, his Fianna phone buzzed with a text from Leonato.

Lady Rose needs help.

Kade blinked and read the message twice just as Vane came out the back door.

When Vane saw Samantha, he stopped.

Before he could say anything, Kade addressed Vane directly. "I'm worried about Rose. Would you go to the children's hospital and take her back home? I'll meet you there."

Hidden within the request was a promise. *Do me this favor, and I'll keep your secret.*

Vane studied Kade for a long moment before nodding. "Where is the children's hospital?"

That's right, Vane was new to Savannah.

"I'll take you," Samantha said. "If you don't mind driving. I don't have a car."

"Will Nate mind if you take one of the cars?" Kade knew that Vane and his men had two cars and a motorcycle between them.

"Nate won't notice." Vane glanced at Samantha. "Are you ready?"

"I'll grab my purse and meet you out front." Samantha ran inside, leaving the men alone.

Vane motioned to the bag Kade carried. "Where are you going?"

"An errand."

Vane cleared his throat. "After getting Rose, I'll drive the women to Rose's house and wait with them until you get there."

"Thank you." Kade hesitated before adding, "Watch your back. Someone may be following Rose."

Vane nodded, and the silence strung out between them.

Kade tilted his head and studied Vane. Was Vane playing games? Or building relationships? After all, building relationships was a Green Beret specialty.

Once Vane left the patio, Kade exhaled and headed down the alley. He hated asking anyone for help. Especially a man he barely knew and wasn't sure he could trust. But, considering what Kade now knew about Vane and his men, Kade had the upper hand in all of this. As much as Kade hated admitting it, he'd do anything—including betraying what was left of Colonel Kells Torridan's once formidable 7th Special Forces Group—to save Rose.

ROSE SAT on the edge of the hospital bed while Timmy finished his ice cream.

She hadn't heard from Kade. Just as she'd done earlier that morning, she'd left her phone at the house in case it was being tracked. She had no idea how long it would take to find the box. If he found it at all.

Before leaving for the hospital, she had changed into running away clothes and braided her hair again. Then she'd done a quick online search about selling eighteenth-century artifacts, proving Sarah's assessment. The box could be worth far more than the payout Deke had mentioned she'd receive, but it wouldn't matter if they didn't have supporting paper-work. She'd be lucky to sell it elsewhere for half of what Hezekiah was supposedly offering.

Not that any of her mental gymnastics mattered since they still didn't have the box.

Timmy licked the plastic spoon. "How's King George?"

She took his cup and spoon and tossed them into the trash. "Spending too much time in the bell tower."

"He misses me." Timmy wiped his face with a napkin. "I wish you could bring him here. He'd like the hospital. There are lots of places to hide and people to hiss at."

"I have no doubt." She picked up Teddy Hawkins and held him against her chest. For some reason, she needed the strength that came from the worn-out stuffed animal. "I talked to Dr. Singh. She's considering your case for the new drug protocol study."

"I don't want to leave Savannah. It's our home." Timmy dumped the bag with the Attacktix figures Kade had brought weeks ago onto his lap and lined them up, making battle sounds.

"Magnus sold our home. Remember?"

Timmy didn't respond. His usual reaction whenever she spoke about Uncle Isaac or Magnus or their parents' house.

She sighed and placed Teddy Hawkins on the pillow behind Timmy's head. She didn't blame him for not wanting to talk about those things. Still, she knew in her heart it was time for both of them to move on. Her growing relationship with Kade had taught her that. "Besides, it's been years since we lived there."

"I had every right to sell the mansion." Magnus stood in the doorway, arms crossed. He wore a black leather jacket over dark jeans and motorcycle boots. His black T-shirt matched his hair, and his bitter scowl complemented the purple and blue swelling on his face.

She smiled at the truth that Kade had given Magnus those bruises.

She stood and moved in front of Timmy. The possibility that Magnus may have killed his own father left her disgusted, angry, and even more protective of Timmy. "What are you doing here?"

"I'm on official business." Magnus stepped aside for a woman in a sensible green pantsuit and white blouse. Her tight bun and manila file folder reeked of *social worker*.

Since her parents' deaths, Rose had met so many social workers she could spot them a mile away at midnight during a hurricane.

The woman held out her hand. "I'm Miss Carter. I'm a social worker with Savannah's Child Protective Services."

Rose shook quickly and nodded. "What is this about?"

Miss Carter offered a patronizing smile. "I'm here about Timmy."

"I'm fine!" Timmy said from his bed, still playing with his battle figures. "I just had ice cream, and I might go home tonight. King George needs me."

Miss Carter waved at Timmy, but when she moved toward

the bed, Rose stepped in her way.

"What about Timmy?" Rose demanded.

"I'm reviewing his case." Miss Carter pressed the file against her chest. "I need to ensure that Timmy is in the best possible situation. Mr. Guthrie, Timmy's guardian, believes that the stress of his career doesn't allow him to offer Timmy the day-to-day care that a child needs. So Timmy lives with you. Correct?"

"Yes." Rose's clipped tone sounded harsh even to her. But she didn't care. "Timmy and I live in a safe, clean home. He goes to school, where he's a good student, and after school he takes art classes."

"I don't like art class." Timmy followed that statement with more battle sounds.

"He also swims, when the doctors allow it," Rose added. "I cook all of his meals and, when he's sick, I bring him to the hospital."

"I'm not concerned about his physical care." Miss Carter opened the file and tapped a page with one finger. "Your employment situation is incomplete. It says here that you worked as a waitress and at a club. Can you tell me, exactly, what you do at this club?"

"Does it matter?"

Miss Carter's tight smile left wrinkles around her mouth. "Your employment situation could determine whether or not we place Timmy in a temporary foster home until Mr. Guthrie can work out a better living situation."

Heat burned through Rose, and she glared at her cousin.

Magnus smiled like he'd just won a sweepstake that included expensive cars, beautiful women, and tons of money.

"Excuse me, Miss Carter." Rose grabbed Magnus's arm and dragged him away. "We'll be right back."

Once in the hallway, she closed the door to Timmy's room. She hated leaving her brother alone with Miss Carter, but Rose didn't have a choice. Not if she wanted to confront —and maybe kill—Magnus. "What are you doing?"

"Destroying your life." Magnus leaned against the concrete wall, and his brown gaze pierced hers. "But I can make this all go away if you give me the box."

"The box that belonged to my mother? The box Deke stole from the Savannah Preservation Office and attempted to sell to Hezekiah Usher behind your back?"

"Yes." Magnus leaned in closer. "I know you and Dolan are looking for it."

"I don't have it. If I did, I wouldn't be in this situation." She waved toward the door window that showed Miss Carter talking to Timmy. Luckily, he was more interested in his toys than her.

"I don't believe you."

"I don't give a—"

Magnus held up a hand. "Do you know who once owned that box? And what's in it?"

She had no idea what was inside. Still, she raised her chin. "Of course. But I still don't have it."

"Rose." Magnus stared at his boots, but his voice came out deep and hard, as if he was promising all sorts of punishments for disobeying him. "If you sell that box to Hezekiah, I'll hand you over to Remiel Marigny's men who aren't as nice as I am. Then I'll make sure Timmy ends up in some crummy foster care home."

She crossed her arms and stood as tall as she could in her sneakers. "First of all, I have no idea who Remiel Marigny is, so your threat means nothing to me. Second, this isn't the eighteenth century. I am not your property to 'hand over'. Third, I will fight you every step of the way before I allow you to put Timmy in a foster home."

He smiled as if mildly amused by her defiance. "Do you have the money to hire a lawyer?"

No. And he knew that. She looked down the hallway, toward the spot where Leonato had killed that other man weeks ago. The corridor was empty, probably because Timmy was one of the few patients on the floor today and the nursing staff was always short on the weekends.

Magnus chuckled in that knowing way she despised. "If you had the means, you would have hired a lawyer years ago to contest the will that left my father in charge of your parents' trust."

She closed her eyes. That had been the problem all along. She had no money. No power. No way to prove what her uncle had done. Years ago, she'd gone to a social worker, the police, and the district attorney, but no one had cared. Except for Harry and his random checks, and the school counselor who'd taken her in during her senior year in high school, no other adult had helped her. Since her parents' deaths, she and Timmy had been on their own in the world.

"I want that box, Rose."

"I don't have it, Magnus." She opened her eyes and moved close enough to see the black rims around his brown eyes. Close enough to smell the sweet tobacco smoke unique to his brand of cigarettes. "Even if I did, I wouldn't give it to you."

"So you'd offer it to your lover?"

She turned away. "Get out."

He gripped her arm and hissed, "Did Kade tell you he's an ex-con and a murderer?"

Murderer?

She threw Magnus off and brushed strands of hair away from her face. "You have no idea what you're talking about."

"Kade was imprisoned for murder until the Prince released him. In return, Kade must eventually become a full-fledged Fianna warrior. From what I've heard that time is approaching quickly."

Magnus knew about the Fianna? So much for the super-secret club. "Kade is *not* a warrior."

"Don't be naïve. The Prince doesn't free men from prison —especially murderers—unless he's recruiting them. Your lover is a Fianna assassin-in-training. And he wants your box as much as you do. My guess is that the Prince is making the box part of Kade's tithe."

She waved a hand around. "Ridiculous."

Although she had read on the Fianna Wikipedia page about the tithes recruits had to offer the Prince. The tithe had to be something that tied the warrior to the world.

Yet, according to Kade, he owned nothing of value. Except for the compass watch he'd given her.

Magnus laughed in his knowing way that made her want to scratch out his eyes. "So Kade isn't planning on finding the box and giving it to the Fianna instead of you?"

She gritted her teeth. "Go away."

She took the doorknob just as Magnus hooked his arm around her neck, forcing her back against his chest. "I'd love to know what you promised Deke in return for delivering that box and receiving two hundred grand."

She clutched his arm, but he was too strong for her. "Let go!"

"*I knew it.*" Magnus's lips touched her ear, and she gagged on the stink of his expensive cigarettes. "You let him fuck you."

"*No.*" She kicked Magnus until he tightened his hold around her neck, and a dizziness rushed over her. Since they were alone in the hallway, she pushed the door, trying to get the social worker's attention. Magnus spun her around and threw her against the wall. Then he used his arm against her throat to pin her. She couldn't scream, and her hits and kicks didn't deter him.

The light-headedness made Rose nauseated, and her vision dimmed.

"Hey!" The male voice echoed in the corridor.

Magnus released her, and she dropped to the floor.

"Rose!" Samantha knelt on the linoleum and took Rose into her arms. "Are you all right?"

She curled up, dragged in air, and coughed.

A loud grunt made Rose look up. Vane had Magnus in a headlock and dragged him down the hallway, into the darker shadows away from the nurse's station. Magnus worked his way free and slammed his fist into Vane's stomach. But Vane retaliated with a right hook.

"What's going on?" Miss Carter appeared, shutting Timmy's door behind her. Despite her quiet demeanor, her voice had an edge like sharpened steel.

The men separated. Their chests heaved with exertion, and their red faces dripped with sweat. Although Vane appeared more fierce than normal in black combat pants, boots, and a green T-shirt.

Samantha helped Rose stand. She wasn't sure what to say, because the truth could cost her whatever rights she had to see Timmy.

"Everything is okay, ma'am." Vane shoved his hands in his pockets. "Just sparring."

Magnus, obviously not willing to admit to the fight, pointed at Vane. "See, Miss Carter? These are the kinds of people Rose hangs out with."

"Miss Carter." Rose cleared her throat because it still hurt. "I—"

"Enough." Miss Carter held up a hand. "After hearing about Timmy's forays into an abandoned bell tower, his stories about aliens, and his obsession with King George the Third, I'm considering opening a CPS case. In the meantime" —she looked at Rose—"I rang for a nurse. Timmy threw up the ice cream you brought him. I believe he has a fever."

"That's why he was admitted," Rose snapped. "Because he

has a fever."

"Don't antagonize her," Samantha whispered.

Rose released a deep breath and glared at Magnus. The worst part about this situation was that she had no legal rights to Timmy. The court hadn't placed Timmy in her care. Magnus had allowed Timmy to live with her because he couldn't be bothered. If he wanted Timmy, Magnus could just take him.

Unless, of course, this entire situation was, truly, about extortion. If she didn't give Magnus the box, he'd make sure Timmy went into foster care.

At that moment, she hated her cousin.

A nurse came around the corner and stopped when she saw everyone in the hallway. "How did you all get up here? There is a visitor limit."

"Ma'am." Samantha held up her hands, palms out. With her messy bun and oversized purple T-shirt over black leggings, she didn't look much older than Timmy. "There was no one at the desk."

"It's Saturday, and we're short-staffed. Still"—the nurse pointed at the men—"you need to leave, or I'll call security. You can wait for Miss Guthrie and Miss Carter outside."

The nurse headed into Timmy's room, and Miss Carter followed.

Samantha touched Rose's arm. "Vane and I will wait downstairs to take you home."

Rose nodded. She didn't want to say anything else in front of Magnus, who was still growling at Vane.

Vane fisted his hands at his sides. After a staring contest with Magnus, Vane took Samantha's hand, and they left.

Once they disappeared, Rose pointed toward the exit sign and said to Magnus, "Get. Out."

Then she went into Timmy's room, wishing she could slam the door.

Kade paced around the attic of Prideaux House, kicking away the yellow police tape he'd torn down to get inside.

A week earlier, the house had been taken over by police looking for a man who'd blown up the city's power grid. Kade had no idea if they ever caught the guy, but since the police had thoroughly searched the place and were now dealing with the city's heroin issue, no one would be paying attention to the comings and goings at the abandoned mansion.

Calum had been right to choose this place. Prideaux House was a perfect clandestine meeting spot.

Kade paused near the only window that wasn't boarded up. The stained-glass design showcased a skeletal hand gripping the blade of a cutlass. Blood dripped down, the drops forming the words: *Sans Pitié.*

No Mercy. No matter where he went in this city, he couldn't get away from its pirate past.

Where the house was in such a state of ruin and decay that it should be condemned, the garden below was even worse. Broken statuary, empty fountains, and overgrown trees made it a Gothic nightmare. He'd bet money he didn't have that the place was haunted.

He rubbed his forehead. All of this pondering was just a distraction. Now that he had the box, he was playing a dangerous game with the Prince. Kade just hoped it didn't end with his and Rose's violent deaths.

"Did you find the box?" Calum stood in the hallway door, his pressed tan suit and blue silk tie a sharp comparison to Kade's worn jeans and dusty combat boots.

"Yes." He nodded to the drawstring bag he'd tossed onto the grungy couch in the corner. "Now I need to find Hezekiah."

Calum joined Kade at the window. There was nothing to see in the garden below, but this seemed less awkward than staring at each other.

"Were you followed here?"

"No. I left my official Fianna phone in my truck near Iron Rack's. I'll retrieve my truck when we leave." But that meant he didn't have much time. If Leonato was tracking Rose, he'd see Vane and Samantha taking Rose home instead of Kade.

"That's smart," Calum said. "I'm sure the Fianna have tracking devices on their phones."

Kade nodded. The Fianna's technical capabilities were as good, if not better, than most intelligence agencies. "Now we just have to deliver the box in a way that gets Rose her money and me my freedom."

Calum leaned his shoulder against the wall and met Kade's gaze. "I'm not sure I understand."

Kade wasn't sure if he should trust Calum, but right now he had few options. "If I give the box to the Prince tomorrow, I will not have to join the Fianna. But that will leave Rose with nothing. If I give the box to Rose, and she sells it to Hezekiah —or anyone else—I have to join the Fianna immediately. And I'm sure one of my first assignments will be to assassinate

Rose. Because mentally destroying their recruits is their version of fun and games."

Calum didn't act surprised or concerned by Kade's admission. Then again, Calum always held his cards close. "And if you both run away—"

"We'll be dead by the end of the month." Of that fact, he had no doubt.

Calum shifted his gaze back to the ruined garden below. "What are you going to do?"

"I have a plan. But I need your help." Kade stared into the garden and lowered his voice. "I have to admit that I'm not great at asking for favors."

He'd never felt more powerless or alone in the world than at that moment.

"I understand. No man wants to be beholden to another." Calum kept his voice matter-of-fact. "You need to contact Hezekiah Usher."

"Among other things, yes." Kade glanced at Calum. "What do you know about him?"

"Hezekiah is president of the Usher Society, a shadowy group that buys and sells antiquities, especially books and documents. Some of his business is legitimate, most is not. And, like most illegal activities, this group attracts not just rich, bored collectors but people who need to launder money."

"Drug dealers and other criminals?"

"Yes, as well as gun runners, corrupt governments, and terrorists."

Great. Kade sighed and pinched the bridge of his nose with two fingers to help ward off an incoming headache. "Can you contact him?"

"I already did."

Kade lowered his hand and watched Calum carefully. His perfectly coiffed, Ivy League demeanor seemed at odds with the harshness in his tone. Despite his always impeccable appearance, Kade had witnessed Calum in enough verbal throwdowns at Doom to know that the richest man in Savannah—and possibly the entire South—should never be underestimated. "And?"

Calum cleared his throat. "Hezekiah knows that the Prince wants you to retrieve that box and hand it to the Fianna. That means Hezekiah must also know about the Prince's offer to release you from your obligation in return for the box."

Kade inhaled and watched a raven land in the broken pond. It drank from a small pool of dirty water left by last night's rain. "How the hell does Hezekiah know about my relationship with the Fianna?"

"I suspect that Hezekiah and the Prince have a tit-for-tat working relationship. The kind where they take turns owing each other."

"Owing each other what? The Prince doesn't need money."

"Information." Calum took out his phone and began texting. "But if Hezekiah is aware of your situation, that means your tiny circle of trust has gotten that much smaller."

"Fuck."

"It's also possible the Prince wants to make a side deal with Hezekiah, in case Rose sells the box to him."

Kade focused on the dusty black drawstring bag sitting on the dingy couch. Calum's assumption was probably correct. If the box was so important, the Prince would never leave its acquisition up to chance. Would never leave it up to the decisions of a condemned man.

Calum released a long breath. "What will you do?"

"I don't want to join the Fianna." Kade's throat closed up on the words. He'd never actually said them before, mostly because he figured he still had six months to figure out an escape. But now he knew the truth. There was no escape. Not from his past. Not from his present. Not from any of his choices. That meant he didn't have a future. "The only thing I am sure of is that I can't let Rose die by my hand or Timmy die due to a lack of money. If the world loses one, it loses the other as well."

"A hell of a situation." Calum spoke softly, as if not to disturb the cobwebs around the window.

Kade closed his eyes. "My only chance is Hezekiah Usher. If Rose gives him the box and receives her money—before the Prince finds out—I may be able to get Rose and Timmy out of town without anyone getting hurt."

"Your plan has less than a ten percent chance of working."

Kade opened his eyes and smiled grimly. "I figured five percent."

Calum shrugged. "I'm a natural optimist."

Kade chuckled. Not because it was funny. More because it was tragically true. "Did you find anything on Deke's cell phone?"

Kade changed the subject to break the desperate mood. The fear was choking him.

"Yes. And you were correct. Deke was running illegal bets off the books through a secret website on the dark web."

Kade told Calum about Aemon Legare, who was missing, who might've been involved with building the website.

"That doesn't surprise me," Calum said. "I tried to hire Aemon myself because my law firm could always do with a genius programmer. Instead, he turned us down and left for New Orleans. I was unaware he was working for Beaumont, Barclay, and Bray, which means he was probably working dark. If that's the case, he was most likely involved with nefarious things."

"Like infiltrating Doom?"

Calum nodded. "Deke was allowing much higher credit

than normal with the requisite higher interest rate. He also had a much higher default rate than Doom."

Because most of the men who threw down at Doom were average guys who couldn't afford outrageous bets at higher interest rates. Hence Doom's overly strict and conservative betting policy. "Was Deke funding the bets?"

"No. I wasn't able to track the funding source. But since we know that Deke worked for Magnus, I bet he funded it—along with Beaumont, Barclay, and Bray."

"Why do you say that?"

Calum held up his phone with the law firm's website. "Look who just merged his own law firm with Beaumont, Barclay, and Bray. That move gives the New Orleans firm a Savannah office."

Kade took the phone and scowled at Magnus's ugly face. It was a typical corporate head shot with styled hair, a dark suit, and a red tie. "Corruption all around."

"I'm sure Magnus set up the betting scheme, paid Aemon to build the infrastructure, got Deke to run it, and funded it with the law firm's money. There's no way Deke was smart enough to manage a betting book that large all by himself." Calum put the phone back into his pocket. "I'll let the other sponsors know. Now we have to decide what to do about your situation."

Loud footsteps sounded, and they both turned toward the door.

A large man entered, wearing jeans, a white dress shirt, and a shoulder holster. Detective Jorge Garza.

Kade immediately bristled. He didn't know the detective well. Garza had interviewed Kade after Sally's murder a week ago and tried to talk to him the night Leonato killed that man at the hospital. The detective had also recently shown up at Iron Rack's Gym to hang out. Kade figured the cop was friends with Nate and Pete.

"Hey." Detective Garza nodded at Calum. "Got your message. Hell of a place to meet."

"That's why I chose it." After making sure Kade and the detective knew each other, Calum continued, "Now, Detective Garza, tell Kade what you told me earlier today."

Kade crossed his arms and waited for the bad news. Because, with the way things were going, it could only be bad news.

Detective Garza leaned his ass against a wooden table pushed against the wall and gripped the edge with his palms. "Yesterday, we pulled a body out of the river near that run-down motel by the train tracks. He'd been dead at least six weeks."

Kade swallowed, hating where this might go. "What does that have to do with me?"

"I reread the police report Rose Guthrie filed six weeks ago. There are similarities between her story at the children's hospital and the man we found. Rose mentioned you were there that night, Mr. Dolan, but we never got your statement."

Kade straightened his shoulders. He didn't like being set up and was surprised by Calum's tactic. "It must have slipped my mind."

"Uh-huh." Garza's eyes narrowed. "The victim was wearing a black T-shirt with a Rage of Angels logo on the back. The same kind the club's bouncers and bartenders used to wear. The same kind I saw you wear the night I broke up a fight between you and Magnus Guthrie. The night I arrested you."

"I was released the next day," Kade reminded him.

"I remember." Garza stared at his shoes for a long moment. "The victim we pulled from the river had a small hole at the base of his neck. A hole caused, I believe, by a misericord."

Shit. Detective Garza also knew about the Fianna.

"I also believe"—Garza took his phone out of his back pocket and laid it on the table— "the victim was killed by a Fianna warrior. From Miss Guthrie's report, it's possible you and Miss Guthrie witnessed this man's murder."

As if reading Kade's mind, Calum said, "When I told you, Kade, that I knew about the Fianna, I forgot to mention that Detective Garza is aware as well."

Fabulous. "Am I a suspect?" Kade asked Garza.

Garza raised an eyebrow. "Should you be?"

"No." Kade wasn't a warrior. Yet.

Garza held up his phone. "This is the victim's photo. Do you recognize him?"

Despite the bloated, fish-eaten face, Kade recognized the victim. "His name is Banjo."

Garza took notes on his phone. "First or last name?"

"Both. Deke hired him as a bartender a week before his death. I never worked with him, and I don't know why the Fianna would kill him."

"Do you believe he was a threat to Rose Guthrie?"

"No. I'm not sure they ever met or worked together. Like I said, he was a recent hire."

"Any idea where I can find employment records on this man? I'd like to notify his next of kin."

"At the club." Kade glanced at Calum. "The employment records are in a filing cabinet in the security office."

"I had the cabinet moved before renovations began." Calum turned to Garza and added, "I'll have the records sent to the station."

"Thank you." Garza paused in his note-taking and placed his phone on the table. "Mr. Dolan, can you think of any reason why Banjo came after Rose six weeks ago? Or why a Fianna warrior killed him and allowed his body to be found? As far as I know, warriors only leave dead bodies around to send a message."

"No."

"A message?" Calum asked Garza. "To whom?"

"Miss Guthrie," Garza said. "Or Mr. Dolan."

When Garza and Calum stared at Kade, he shoved his hands in his back pockets and said, "Like I said, I don't know why the warrior who killed Banjo would do so to save Rose."

The Fianna rarely went out of their way to save anybody.

The attic door opened, hitting the wall with a loud thud. Nate Walker and Pete White Horse appeared dressed in jeans, black T-shirts, and combat boots. Nate wore a motorcycle jacket while Pete had on a gray hoodie. No matter how hard they tried to blend in, to look like regular tourists, their sheer height, massive width, and don't-screw-with-me demeanor gave them away. Both men carried themselves with the strength and self-confidence that came with knowing they could take on—and take down—any evil fuck who got in their way.

Kade glared at Calum. "What the fuck is this?"

"You said you needed help." Calum waved a hand toward the former Green Berets. "We all have our secrets, and in the case of Nate and Pete, their secrets are intertwined with yours."

"I don't understand."

"The Fianna," Detective Garza said. "You, and your woman, aren't the only people the Fianna have fucked with." He came over and squeezed Kade's shoulder. "I know you don't know us, but you *can* trust us."

Kade shook his head. "You don't understand—"

"Except we do." Pete sat on the table and it sagged beneath his weight. Weight that, Kade knew, came from solid muscle. "Calum filled us in on the basic details. You're in deep with the Fianna. May even be forced to become a warrior?"

Kade gave a reluctant nod and sent another glare at Calum.

"Okay." Pete nodded toward Nate. "You're not the only potential recruit in the room."

Nate looked away, toward a box of trash in the corner. After a long, awkward moment, he met Kade's gaze. "Yep."

Whoa. Kade ran a hand over his head and paced the room. That was the last thing he'd expected to hear today. "Did Calum fill you in on Rose and her box?"

"Yes," Pete said. "Garza, Nate, and I are up to speed."

Kade shifted his attention back to Calum. "I still don't understand why you brought these men in. They're in more danger now—"

Calum held up a hand. "Don't assume you're the only one in a no-win situation. The truth is that earlier, when you told me you needed help, I texted Nate and Pete to meet us here. I'd already told Garza the story, and he filled Nate and Pete in on the situation while they were on their way over."

Wow. Calum must've texted Nate and Pete while they'd been talking. "You don't even know what kind of help I need."

"I know"—Calum nodded toward the three other men—"that whatever you want to do, you can't do it alone. So let's hear the plan."

Kade exhaled and stared at the ceiling. With these men on board, he might be able to pull this off. And at that moment, it didn't matter that he didn't know them well. At least not well enough to trust them entirely. His ass was against the wall, and he no longer had the luxury of making choices.

"To start with, I'm always being tracked by the warriors Leonato and Sampson. They make me carry a cell phone so they don't physically have to follow me everywhere."

He quickly described the warriors and filled in a few details about his and Rose's situation, including the issue with Timmy being in the hospital. "If I can get Rose into a meeting with Hezekiah Usher, before the Fianna find out, she can exchange the box for the money."

"Can you arrange this meeting?" Garza asked Calum.

Calum looked up from texting. "I'm negotiating the details with Hezekiah now. Rose can meet him at ten p.m. tonight."

"Good." Kade leaned a shoulder against the window frame and focused on the outside world again. "In the meantime, I have to throw off the warriors. They may be watching Rose. But, for the rest of the day, I need to make them think I'm still looking for the box. Then, once Rose meets Hezekiah, I have to smuggle her and her brother out of town."

"*Okaaaay*." Pete grimaced before asking. "How can we help?"

A bird landed in the center of the broken concrete pond, and Kade sighed. "I need someone to drive my truck, with my cell phone, around Savannah as if I'm searching for the box. Go to Tybee Island, where Rose's parents had a summer house. Then head to the Isle of Grace. Her parents are buried behind the small church out there."

"The driver could also visit the golf club on the Isle of Hope," Calum said. "Her father was a member and rented a locker. Those errands would take the rest of the day."

"I can drive." Pete glanced at Nate. "Will you cover for me at the gym?"

Nate nodded. "What do you want me to do?"

Calum spoke before Kade. "Samantha and Rose are at Rose's house. If Leonato is watching Rose, we need a diversion so Samantha can get Rose out of the house and over to the apartment above Juliet's Lily boutique."

"That landscape architecture firm in St. Julian's alley?" Kade had walked by it a few times. It was a beautiful, secluded sanctuary in the middle of the city.

"Yes." Calum began texting again. "There's a tunnel entrance near Rose's house and an exit about a block away from Juliet's Lily. If we can get you and Rose to the apartment, without any warriors seeing you, it's a safe place to stay until your meeting with Hezekiah."

Nate threw a smile at Garza. "You up for some public disturbances. Without real bullets, of course."

"*Shit.*" Garza's hands landed on his hips. "I have firecrackers in the car that I confiscated from some teenage graffiti artists earlier today. I suppose I could turn in two firecrackers instead of twenty. I haven't written the report yet."

"Perfect." Nate looked at Calum. "Now. How are we getting everyone out of town, after the exchange, before the Fianna rain down hell?"

"We can use the Juliet's Lily truck," Calum said. "Kade, do you know where you want to take Rose?"

"The Isle of Grace," Kade said. "My Aunt Mamie owns Mamie's Café, the only store on the Isle. Since she and my cousin are out of town, and I have a key for emergencies, I'll stash Rose there. Then I'll return to town to get Timmy."

"Not a great plan," Pete said.

Calum put his phone away. "The getaway part does need work. But let's focus on diverting the warriors, getting Pete to your truck, and moving you and Rose to the safe house."

"I agree," Garza said. "This situation is fluid. A lot could change between now and tonight."

Calum held out his hand to Kade. "Truck keys?"

Kade handed them to Calum, with directions to where he had parked. "My Fianna cell is in the glove box."

Calum gave the keys to Pete. "If you need more driving time later today, go to my cottage on the Isle of Hope. I'll send you the address and will make sure there's a meal waiting for you."

"Great." A moment later, Pete left with promises to check in.

When Calum and Garza moved to the corner to talk quietly, Nate came over and gripped Kade's shoulder. He still smelled like a breath mint and, from the way he fisted and unfisted his other hand, seemed restless. But his intelligence and strength of will were apparent in his sharp gaze and strong grasp. "Don't worry. We'll save you and Rose. Everything will work out."

"Thanks."

"Come on, Nate." Garza appeared next to them. "Calum will text Samantha and tell her the situation. And he'll take you, Kade, to the apartment where you can wait for them."

Although he appreciated the help, he preferred action to waiting. "I'd rather get Rose myself."

"We know," Nate said with so much understanding in his voice that Kade wondered what had happened to the brother. "But it's better this way."

Unfortunately, Nate was correct.

Once Nate and Garza left, Kade exhaled loudly. He felt like he'd been carrying a howitzer on his back. "You should know, Calum, that Vane is with the women at Rose's house. I asked him to drive them there."

"I know. I just sent him the plan and didn't tell the other men." When Calum was done texting—something he always seemed to be doing—he looked at Kade. "When Nate and Garza set their diversion, all three of them will leave. Vane said he'll stay with the women until they get safely to the apartment. But don't text Rose. We can't be sure the Fianna aren't tracking your burner phones."

"Thank you."

"*Soooo,*" Calum slipped his cell into his jacket pocket and his gaze bounced around the room. "You and Rose will meet Hezekiah at ten p.m. at Doom."

"That's a strange place to meet. What's the catch?"

Life, and the Fates, had taught him there was always a catch.

"In order to win an audience, you must fight someone. To the death."

Kade laughed because, really, why not? "Who?"

"Magnus."

The room went silent, like those moments after a grenade went off and deadened the sound within the blast radius. "Calum, I'm not sure if you're aware of my past—"

"That you were accused of treason *and* murder?"

"I'm innocent of both." Kade swallowed and returned to the window. "I've never killed anyone outside of a combat situation."

And his number of kills—at least those he knew of—had been small compared to other soldiers he'd fought with.

Calum cleared his throat before saying, "Do you think you can do this?"

Kade scoffed. "It's hard to kill a man with your bare hands. It's not like in the movies." Never mind the irony of becoming the kind of man his accusers thought he was. "Who knew that men who buy old documents would be so bloodthirsty."

"Hezekiah, and men like the Prince, inhabit a world where nothing is as it seems." Calum came over and gripped Kade's shoulder. "You can always back down. I can get you and Rose out of town—"

"The Fianna would kill you and Rose in the space of a heartbeat." Kade sighed and crossed his arms over his chest. "I would never put you or Rose in that kind of danger."

While he hated Magnus, Kade wasn't sure he'd be able to murder a man in a fighting ring. Unless that man was determined to murder him.

How had he ended up in these no-win, fucked-up situations? First it had been Leavenworth. Then the Fianna. And now Magnus.

"What do you want me to say to Hezekiah?" Calum asked.

"I'll do it." Kade nodded toward the garden below. "I have no choice if I'm going to save Rose."

Calum moved until he could look out the window.

Below, in the garden, a crumbling statue of some Greek goddess—probably one of the fucking Fates—held a set of scales. Nearby, a man in jeans and a black T-shirt stood beneath an oak tree, texting.

Leonato.

CHAPTER 20

Rose filled the teapot, placed it on the stove, and watched Vane through her kitchen window. He paced along the cemetery fence line, his cell phone pressed to his ear. The moment they'd returned, King George had taken off. Probably to find a nice mouse and drag it back to his lair in the bell tower.

Samantha slipped her cell phone into the back pocket of her jeans and brought a plate of peanut butter cookies to the table. "How are you feeling?"

"Angry. Confused. Worried." Rose turned on the burner. "Strangely detached."

Samantha took a cookie and broke it in half. "Detachment is a normal reaction to traumatic events."

"I guess." Rose still couldn't believe Magnus had attacked her. At the time, she'd been too shocked to be afraid. But now she was more concerned about Timmy. Magnus was dangerous. And his behavior today proved to her that he could have been responsible for Isaac's death. Believing someone was capable of murder was a terrifying thought.

Maybe that's why she couldn't get Magnus's accusation about Kade out of her mind.

On the drive home, not wanting to talk about the attack or think about the possibility that Kade was a murderer and a Fianna recruit, she told Vane and Samantha about Magnus's plan to send Timmy into the foster care system if she didn't give up the box. She had no idea if Magnus could even do that, but she couldn't risk losing Timmy.

Samantha finished her cookie and wiped her hands on a napkin. "Your cousin is horrible. I remember when Magnus attacked you in the club, and how Kade broke his wrist."

"Magnus fights with everyone who doesn't indulge his every whim."

"Magnus is an entitled, self-centered ass."

"Yes, he is." Once the water boiled, Rose poured it into two teacups. Then she asked the question that had been bothering her since last night. "Samantha, how do you know Calum and Vane?"

"I've known Calum for years, ever since I moved to Savannah." Samantha came over to grab her cup. "If I tell you about Vane, you have to keep it a secret."

Rose tilted her head. "Secret like the Fianna?"

"Yes." Samantha sipped her tea and added sugar from the bowl next to the sink. "You remember Nate and Pete?"

"The bouncers at Rage of Angels who now manage Iron Rack's Gym." Kade had mentioned their new jobs. Rose sat with her mug. "Isn't Pete your boyfriend?"

"Yes." Samantha joined her at the table. "Nate and Pete, along with a few other men including Vane, were once part of the 7th Special Forces Group under the command of Colonel Kells Torridan. They're former Green Berets hiding here in Savannah."

Rose wasn't surprised to learn that Nate and Pete were ex-military. When they'd worked at Rage of Angels, they'd looked and acted like soldiers. Vane simply oozed the part. "Hiding from what?"

"An enemy who destroyed their careers and their honor." Samantha blew on her hot tea. "It's a long story, but Calum is helping them establish themselves here in Savannah. I'm sorry I can't say anymore. And please don't tell anyone. I'm only telling you now because, not long ago, I ended up in danger from not knowing the truth."

"I promise I won't say a word." Rose touched her friend's hand. "Thank you for trusting me."

Vane came in through the kitchen door, his chest heaving as if he'd just run a mile. "Rose, how quickly can you put together an overnight bag?"

Rose stood, unsure if she was more surprised or confused. "About ten minutes."

"Good." Vane left the kitchen and headed for the living room. "Leave your cell phone behind."

Once Vane disappeared, Rose looked at Samantha. "Why do I need to pack anything?"

"Because"—Samantha stood as well—"we're taking you to a safe house. I just didn't realize it would happen so quickly."

"I don't—"

Samantha took Rose's arm and led her into the bedroom. "I'll explain while you pack."

Ten minutes later, Rose carried her pink backpack into the kitchen. After placing her cell phone on the charger near the sink, she shoved her mother's Yale sweatshirt into the backpack. She hadn't packed much because she wasn't sure what she'd need or how long she'd be gone. It hadn't helped that Vane had said nothing about what was going on. Most of his conversation was made up of orders like 'hurry up' and 'let's go'.

Except now that Rose was ready, Vane had disappeared.

She found Samantha in the living room, peering out the living room window. "Why are we going to a safe house?"

Samantha replaced the curtain and faced her. "So you and Kade can hang out, without any warriors watching, until you meet with Hezekiah tonight."

"I have a meeting with Hezekiah?"

Samantha sat on the couch, her hands tucked between her knees. "I think so."

The kitchen door opened, and shut, and Vane stomped into the living room. "We have a problem."

With his long hair pulled back behind his neck, and his features that seemed to be cut from granite, he appeared fearsome and potentially violent. Then she remembered his fight the night before and felt less stressed. At least she wasn't alone in this.

"I know." Samantha pointed toward the window. "One of Magnus's thugs is outside. The one with only one ear. I recognize him from the club. But usually there are two of them."

Rose hurried to the window and moved the curtain an inch. A tall, beefy man stood across the street, near the cathedral, in the shade of a pink crepe myrtle tree. Nearby, King George lay on the grass in front of the bell tower in full sunshine. "That's Magnus's driver. I call him One Ear. His brother, the one with the scarred face, is Magnus's bodyguard."

"Then we'll leave through the kitchen." Vane pulled his weapon from his back waistband and slipped out the clip. Once he checked it, he slammed it back in. "We'll go when we get the signal."

Rose sat on the couch next to Samantha. Why was waiting for something to begin always the worst part? "What signal?"

"Nate and Garza will set a diversion." Vane paced the room, flexing and unflexing his fingers, and told them about Pete's plan to drive around Savannah.

When Vane finished, Rose asked, "Why are Nate, Pete, and Detective Garza helping me?"

"You'll have to ask them," Vane said as he continued to stomp across the room. "Samantha, what have you told Rose?"

Samantha took Rose's hand and squeezed.

"Not much," Samantha said. "Just that you and your men were once Green Berets who are now in an unprovoked war with a terrible enemy."

Vane shifted his gaze to Rose. "You can't—"

"I won't." She held a hand over her heart. "I promise."

Vane checked his watch and disappeared into the kitchen. He returned with the plate of peanut butter cookies, some napkins, and placed them on the rickety coffee table.

"I spoke to Luke, one of my buddies at the gym." Vane ate a cookie in one bite. "Last week, when we took over Iron Rack's, Luke started a background check on all the employees, including Kade."

"I know Kade was imprisoned at Leavenworth," Rose said. "For treason."

"And for murder," Vane said.

Rose removed her hand from Samantha's grasp and clasped them in her lap. So Magnus hadn't been lying.

Samantha took a cookie. "There's no way Kade is a murderer."

Vane frowned. "We don't know anything about Kade."

"That's ridiculous." Samantha said firmly. "I know for sure that if Kade was a horrible or dangerous person, Nate and Pete wouldn't be helping him out."

"Maybe," Vane said. "Maybe not."

"Doesn't the army execute treasonous murderers?" Rose was sure she'd read that somewhere.

"Everything I thought I knew about military justice was

recently proven wrong," Vane said. "So I don't know the answer to that question."

"Still," Samantha said. "I know that if Pete trusts Kade, he's a good guy."

While Rose appreciated Samantha's endorsement, she hated these doubts that crept into her heart and mind.

"Vane, are you aware the Fianna released Kade from prison?" Rose knew she shouldn't be sharing information about Kade's life, but she had no one else to talk to about it. Besides, if Vane wanted her to keep his secrets, hopefully he'd keep hers.

"No." Vane checked his watch again. "Nothing surprises me anymore."

"Wait." Samantha stood and grabbed Vane's arm, forcing him to stop moving. "You know about the Fianna?"

"Only the same rumors every soldier has heard." He stared at Samantha's hand on his arm until she released him. "The Fianna date back to the Druid priests of ancient Ireland." Vane took another cookie but stared at it instead of eating it. "They were pagan warriors who fought off the Romans, the Britons, the Vikings, and everyone else who came to their shores. The Fianna were fierce fighters known for their brutal recruitment training that had a fifty percent death rate."

"Surely they are more civilized now." Rose stood and returned to the window. Magnus's driver was still there, staring at his phone.

"Not by much." Vane ate his cookie and wiped his hands on a napkin. "Their training, even today, is legendary. It's all about self-mortification and the harshest discipline. They train naked in the woods, speak in Shakespearean verse, hunt each other to the death for sport—"

"I don't think that last one is true." Samantha smiled at Rose, as if comforting a child.

Vane took the last cookie and shrugged. "The gauntlet is true."

Rose noticed another man near the bell tower. In jeans, blue T-shirt, and a New York Yankees hat, he was on one knee petting King George. Was that Sampson? Leonato's buddy?

She was about to say something when Sampson stood and walked behind the church. She squinted against the sunlight. Maybe she'd been wrong.

She released the curtain and shook out her arms. "What's the gauntlet?"

"A corridor of seasoned warriors." Vane popped the cookie into his mouth. "Forty on each side, each one holding a weapon. As the recruit walks through, each warrior strikes him. If the recruit survives, which is rare, he offers a tithe and becomes a full-fledged warrior."

Rose sank onto the couch. "That's barbaric."

"Yep," Vane said. "It's also deadly. But that's the point. Only the strongest survive."

Before Rose could respond, a series of loud popping sounds came from the backyard. It almost sounded like... *gunshots.*

Vane nodded at Samantha, then Rose. "Time to go."

KADE WAS A PRISONER.

As he paced the attic of Prideaux House, he forced himself not to scream. Leonato was still outside, while Kade was stuck inside the hot, stuffy room where all the heat from the day had risen and settled.

And, since the building should've been condemned decades ago, there was no AC.

His burner phone rang, and he answered with a tentative, "Hello?"

"It's Calum. What's the situation?"

Kade neared the window and spotted Leonato sitting on a broken stone bench in the shade, staring at his phone. He looked up when Sampson appeared in his New York Yankees baseball cap. Sampson leaned against a tree, with arms crossed, and said something that made Leonato frown.

Despite the fact they both wore jeans and T-shirts, their size and the way they walked gave away their warrior status. "Now both Sampson and Leonato are outside."

"I thought my ploy would work."

"So did I," Kade said.

Calum had left thirty minutes ago, hoping that when Leonato saw Ivers drive up in the Bentley to pick up Calum, Leonato would leave. Since Calum owned Prideaux House, he had every right and reason to inspect the property.

"The thing is, Calum, I don't think they're waiting for me. I'm not sure they even know I'm here. Since you left, Leonato has had his eyeballs glued to that phone."

"It's possible they're tracking Pete."

"So why stay in the garden?

"I don't know. Maybe, because of all the police tape around the property, they think it will be private."

"That would make sense."

"Kade, I wanted to tell you that I confirmed the plan with Vane. He'll get the women to Juliet's Lily safely. I don't want you to don't freak out."

"Army Rangers don't freak out."

"So you're not pacing the room like a caged ex-convict?"

"Maybe a little." He closed his eyes and leaned against the wall. "Thank you, Calum. I just wish I could help. I feel so powerless and useless."

"Because you're a man of action, Kade. But sometimes letting others help is the right thing to do."

Kade opened his eyes. "Have you ever considered hosting a daytime talk show?"

Calum laughed. "Just let me know when they leave. The warriors can't stay there all day. I'm sure they have things to do."

Kade stood off to the side of the window and peered out again. "You may be right. Sampson is walking away, as if in a huff. A quarrel, perhaps?"

"Who knows—"

"Hold up." Kade moved closer to see the new man who'd entered the garden. "Someone is here. A man in a three-piece suit."

"Do you recognize him?"

"No. His face was shaded when he came in, and now I see his back. But, from his waving hands, he seems to be arguing with Leonato."

"Does your burner phone take photos?"

"No." Kade squinted to get a more focused view. Not only was he high up on the top floor, the stained-glass windows only had a few clear panes. "The man is leaving now."

As the man crossed the garden, moving in and out of the sunlight, something about him seemed familiar, but Kade couldn't place the memory.

"What is Leonato doing?" Calum asked.

"Texting." Kade snorted. "Leonato reminds me of you."

"Thanks." Calum paused. "Just so we're on the same page, I told Vane that you found the box. But he won't tell Rose. I figured you'd want to do that yourself."

"I appreciate it." Kade ended the phone call and prayed that Leonato would do something normal, like hit the bathroom or grab a sandwich. Extreme self-discipline and patience were Fianna virtues. But those virtues were also fucking annoying.

Kade dragged a folding chair near the window so he could

sit while he waited for Leonato to do something other than text. While Leonato studied his phone, Kade leaned his chair back, stacked his feet on a nearby table, and closed his eyes.

Slowly and carefully, he compiled a mental inventory of every moment he'd spent with Rose. He wanted to get every memory correct, down to the color of her hairbands, because if he had to join the Fianna, memories of her were the only things he'd have left.

Suddenly, he let the front chair legs hit the floor and opened his eyes. He'd just remembered where he'd seen that man in the garden before. He was the man from Rose's refrigerator photograph.

He was her family friend, Harry.

CHAPTER 21

Rose picked up her pink backpack from the kitchen table while Samantha drank a glass of water. Vane had ordered them to wait here while he'd gone outside.

Whatever those loud noises had been, the city had responded quickly. Helicopters whirred overhead and sirens sounded like they were coming from around the city.

Through the kitchen window, she noticed people in the cemetery clustered in groups behind large oak trees and mausoleums. Yet Rose felt strangely calm. Not because she wasn't worried. It was more of a stillness before a storm, like those strange, gray hours before hurricane winds began. When the radar showed an incoming storm, and the air was stagnant, damp, and charged with static electricity. Charged with anticipation. Charged with fear.

She inhaled deeply and then exhaled. "What are we waiting for?"

"I don't know. But I trust Calum, Vane, and Kade." Samantha handed a glass to Rose. "Drink up. It's hot and we have at least a thirty-minute hike through the tunnels."

Rose put down her backpack, finished her water in one

gulp, and placed the glass in the sink. She envied Samantha's ability to trust men she hardly knew.

"Do you have a flashlight?"

"Yes. And there may be some more batteries in the drawer next to the fridge." Rose took the flashlight out of a cabinet and handed it to Samantha. While she tested the batteries, Rose checked to make sure Kade's compass watch was securely tucked into her backpack.

Last night. Had it only been last night that Kade had fought at Doom and then, early this morning, they'd made love? She rubbed her forehead and stared at her cell phone on the counter. She'd made love to a man she hardly knew, who might be a murderer and a potential Fianna warrior.

Yet, in all the time she'd known Kade, he'd never been anything but kind and protective. She hated that she was now doubting him. Hated that she couldn't let Magnus's words go. Hated that she wasn't able to talk to Kade.

While Samantha rummaged through the drawer, Rose picked up her phone and stared at the blank screen. Vane had told them that Kade wouldn't call because he was worried about the security of her home and cell phones. Still, she needed to hear his voice to alleviate her anxiety. She could only assume, since they were both headed to a safe house before meeting Hezekiah, that Kade had found her box.

If she could just talk to Kade, she'd feel so much better.

Then there was the issue of Timmy. If he called, she needed to be there for him. He would worry and fuss if she didn't answer.

"Come on." Samantha touched Rose's arm. "It's time."

Vane opened the kitchen door and was motioning to them. She grabbed her backpack off the table and slipped the straps over her shoulders.

Samantha headed out first and pulled Vane aside to say something. While they were both distracted, Rose turned off her phone and zipped it into the side pocket of her backpack. Then she left her home, not sure when—or if—she'd ever return.

A few minutes later, after racing through her neighbor's backyards, they ended up at the corner of Abercorn Street and East Perry Lane. Tourists filled the sidewalks and street, only moving when police cars zoomed by.

Pop, pop, pop, pop.

People screamed and moved in frantic circles. Some headed toward the cemetery, others toward the cathedral. Luckily, Vane was so tall it was easy to follow him in the crowd. Samantha took Rose's hand and they hurried across the street, dodging cruisers and police officers on bicycles.

Once they made it to West Perry Lane, she glanced toward the iron gates that guarded the cemetery. A crowd surrounded two large men who were yelling and pointing at each other. *Detective Garza and Nate?*

Then she noticed Magnus's driver, One Ear, across the street, scanning the crowd.

"Come on!" Samantha dragged Rose down the sidewalk and they ran into a narrow, dark alley that was closed at the other end. There was no escape other than returning the way they'd come.

Vane led the way until he stopped, about halfway down, near a rusted iron door. Nearby, someone had painted an image of a white skeletal hand gripping the blade of a cutlass. Below, in red, were the words *Sans Pitié*.

Rose rested against the moldy brick wall. Her breaths were loud and erratic. Samantha stood next to her, as if trying to blend into the wall.

Vane pulled the door handle, and it barely budged. After a few more tugs, he got it open about a third of the way. Enough space for Rose and Samantha, but there was no possibility of Vane getting through.

"Can you open it any farther?" Samantha asked.

"I'll try." Vane yanked the door, his arm muscles contracting with the effort.

Rose took a few more deep breaths when she noticed a shadow at the end of the alley. Magnus's driver. His back was towards them... for now.

She touched Vane's arm and motioned toward the other end.

Vane moved quickly until he stood between One Ear and Rose and Samantha. "Samantha, take Rose through the door. I'll close it after you."

"No." Rose said. "He'll see you, and there's no way for you to escape."

Vane glanced at her, his eyes dark and narrow. "Go. *Now.*"

Samantha squeezed through the door, disappearing into the darkness.

Vane pushed her towards the small entrance. "Don't worry, Rose. Men like me and Kade are really hard to kill."

"But—"

One Ear turned and hurried in their direction.

Vane nudged her again, and she fell into the dark space. She tripped over a pile of bricks and found Samantha with her back against the wall, fumbling with the flashlight. Once it came on, the light seemed dim in the midst of blackness.

A loud scraping sound filled the space, and the door to the outside world shut them in. And the space got even darker. Rose couldn't hear any noise coming from the other side of the door. She worried about Vane.

She adjusted the straps of her backpack and nodded at Samantha. Since Vane was willing to fight on their behalf, yet didn't want his buddies knowing he was involved, the only way to repay him was to be brave. "Do you know the way?"

"Not really." Samantha moved ahead and shone the light around the small room. Besides the door Vane closed behind them, the only other way out was forward, through a small hallway. "But this is our only option."

Once they moved through the hallway, they found stairs that headed down. The deeper they descended, the more foul the air became.

Rose's eyes watered. "Will Vane be okay?"

She still couldn't believe what he'd done for them. The sacrifice he'd made for two women he barely knew.

"Yes," Samantha's voice echoed around the narrow stairway. "He was right. He and his men are hard to kill. You saw him fight last night in Doom. One Ear doesn't have a chance."

Rose prayed that was true.

A few minutes later, they reached the end of the stairway and had a choice to make. The tunnel off to the right versus the one to the left.

Samantha's face was barely visible within the shadows cast by the flashlight's beam. "We're going left. Are you ready? There may be..." she wrinkled her nose, "rats."

Rose figured as much. But, again, if Kade and Vane could fight their enemies with courage and strength, then so could she. "Lead the way."

Three words she'd never said to anyone in her life.

Forty minutes later, Rose and Samantha emerged from the stairs and found themselves in a parking garage stairwell. They'd climbed out of the tunnel at such a steep angle, Rose's calves and upper thighs burned.

She took her backpack off her shoulders, dropped it onto the stained concrete landing, and leaned against the wall. Her back ached, and she took in deep breaths of fresh air. Although this alcove reeked of urine and tobacco smoke, it was still better than the disgusting stench in the hot tunnel.

She glanced at Samantha who stood nearby, also against the wall, with her eyes closed. Her long hair had come loose from a messy bun and hung around her shoulders in a mass of blonde curls. "I can't believe you give tours of these tunnels."

Samantha's laugh sounded like a gruff cough. "Not these tunnels. The tunnels that the tour company uses are clean and ventilated and safe." She opened her eyes and met Rose's gaze. "The tunnels we went just through must have been built in the fourth level of Hell. I think those rats were descended from hellhounds."

"That is a perfect description." Rose laughed despite of the grossness they'd just endured. "Now what?"

"To Juliet's Lily. It's only a block away." Samantha used her palms to push against the wall and stand straight. Smudges on her nose and cheeks looked like bruises, and her black leggings were filthy. One might think she'd fought her way out of a lion's cage.

Rose had no doubt she looked the same. "Will we have to dodge rats?"

Samantha snorted as she headed down the stairs and onto a gravel path that led toward the street. "If we do, I'm leaving Savannah tonight. And I will never return."

"Timmy and I will go with you." Rose picked up her backpack and followed her friend into the sunshine. Then she promised herself she'd never take fresh air for granted again.

A few minutes later, they crossed a street and saw Vane near the entrance to an alley. Except this alleyway had a lovely arch across the top and potted flowers protecting the opening. Creeping fig and purple clematis vines covered the brick walls around the opening.

Unlike the previous alleys they'd survived, this one looked like a photo from a Savannah tourist magazine. It was beautiful, welcoming, and charming. Except for the fact that Vane, with his ripped T-shirt, long brown hair hanging around his shoulders, and crossed arms over a massive chest, guarded it with a fierceness usually found on prison guards and airport security.

When he saw them, he lowered his arms and nodded. As soon as they reached him, he motioned for them to go first. He followed, and when she glanced back, she noticed he held his weapon.

They passed Juliet's Lily storefront, and she found herself in the loveliest courtyard she'd ever seen in Savannah. It was surrounded by two historic buildings, Juliet's Lily and Dessie's Couture Dress Shop, both with small apartments above them. A fountain in the middle added a calming sound, and pots of brightly colored flowers and vines filled the space. In one corner, garden statuary stood as if on display for sale. It was the kind of space that promised peace and beauty and love.

"Kade is upstairs." Vane took her backpack and went up a nearby staircase. The apartment, above Juliet's Lily, had a small balcony lined with flower boxes. When he entered the building, he left the door open.

Even from here, she could smell the lavender and gardenias growing in the flower boxes.

Samantha sank onto the edge of the raised pond, closed her eyes, and allowed the mist to soak her back.

Rose sat next to Samantha. While she wanted to see Kade, she needed a moment to gather her thoughts and calm her mind. She hated complainers, but it had been a hell of a trip through the tunnels. Not just from the physical hardship, and the rats, but because her mind couldn't shut off the idea that Kade had been convicted of murder and might one day become a Fianna warrior.

They were worries she couldn't let go of. If both situations were true, why hadn't he told her? After everything they'd shared, why would he keep such terrible secrets? At the same time, he'd admitted his love for her and she'd not given an answer in return. She'd given him no reason to trust her, yet had demanded he make promises he might not be able to keep.

All of her emotions were so muddled. No wonder she craved the courtyard's temporary peace. The mist felt cool and refreshing on the back of her arms and neck. "It's beautiful here."

"I know. I'm hoping to move into this apartment soon since the owner just got married."

It would be a lovely place to live. "We should go upstairs."

Samantha sighed. "I know. I just wish...." She sighed again.

Rose glanced at her friend's profile. Damp curls lay against the curve of her neck. "Wish what?"

Samantha shook her head and opened her eyes. "I wish that life wasn't so complicated."

"I agree." Rose looked up at the apartment balcony again, at the door which would lead her back into Kade's arms. If she decided that's where she wanted to be. "Do you ever question your decisions?"

Samantha's laugh echoed around the courtyard. "Every day." She pointed to the four-foot-tall concrete statue in the corner. A woman in an ancient Roman dress holding up scales. "And every day I curse the Fates for the bad things that have happened to me, and then ask them to help me. It makes sense the Fates, and I, are all confused."

Rose stood and found her sweatshirt. "I'm confused too."

Samantha smiled at Rose. "The one thing I have learned, just within the past few weeks, is that making decisions out of fear or anger or hatred will only make you miserable."

"Fear is a tough emotion to shake off."

"I know." Samantha stood and took Rose's hand. "But you know what's on the other side of those emotions?"

Rose shook her head.

Samantha whispered, "Love." She squeezed Rose's hand. "Now let's go find Kade so you can win your happy ending."

CHAPTER 22

What was taking Rose so long?

Kade paced the apartment above Juliet's Lily that had no AC and was even smaller than Rose's. With a galley kitchen on one end, and a living area with a round table and loveseat at the other, he could walk the space in less than ten strides.

At least it was cozy, with throw blankets and a soft area rug. Even the tiny bedroom had a queen-sized bed piled high with white pillows. Potted ferns and gardenias made the space feel safe and protected. With picture windows overlooking the courtyard, he felt like he'd stepped into a separate reality.

He normally didn't notice things like interior design. Normally didn't care about décor or color or plants. But he was trying to see the space through Rose's eyes. He had no idea what the rest of this day, or the mission tonight, would bring. But, since he'd escaped the attic, he'd decided that the only thing that mattered in this fucked-up situation was Rose's safety and happiness.

Even if that meant killing Magnus in the pit. Or joining the Fianna so she and Timmy could live their lives in peace.

Kade fisted his hands so he wouldn't hit the wall. His restless anger didn't just come from being in these boxed-in situations that he dreaded. It also came from the fact that Vane was the one helping the women. Vane was the one protecting them and making sure they arrived safely.

Kade wasn't jealous of the brother, just frustrated that he'd been stuck in a fucking attic while Leonato met with a man who might be Rose's family friend, Harry.

Except Kade had no way of proving that. Since he'd not had a great view, and wasn't sure about the man's identity, he'd decided not to mention it to Rose. There was no point in worrying or upsetting her. They had enough real things to be worried and upset about.

Two knocks sounded on the front door. Once Kade ID'd Vane, he let the man in. "Where is Rose?"

Vane pointed into the courtyard. Rose and Samantha were sitting on the edge of the pond, talking.

"What are they—"

Vane pressed a hand on Kade's chest and pushed him back into the apartment. "They need a few minutes. From their appearances, the tunnels were rough."

"You weren't in the tunnels with them?"

"No." Vane went to the sink, found a glass, and filled it with water. "I had to let them go without me."

As he drank, he told Kade the story about the door not opening and the subsequent fight with Magnus's driver. Then Vane backtracked, and Kade learned about what Magnus had done to Rose at the hospital. Vane also had to tell Kade—*twice*—about Magnus's threat to send Timmy to foster care if Rose didn't hand over the box.

Kade began to pace the room again. His body had heated up, and his heart rate revved. Although, a few minutes before, Kade had been concerned about having to fight Magnus again, now Kade craved the upcoming battle.

Tonight there would be a reckoning on Rose's behalf.

"Shit." He ran both hands over his head as he stomped around the room. "Magnus physically attacked Rose and is having her followed. And he's using Timmy as leverage to get the box. I should've seen this coming."

"Probably." Vane poured more water and drank deeply.

"Are you sure the women weren't tailed here?"

Vane nodded and sat in one of the wooden chairs around the table. "Is it true you have a meeting tonight with Hezekiah Usher?" Vane held up both hands. "Calum told me."

"Yes." Kade paused near the kitchen window and leaned his ass against the counter. "And I need another favor."

"I'll be your second."

Kade tilted his head.

Vane shrugged. "Calum. Remember?"

"Right." Although he barely knew the brother, he was grateful for the support of a man strong enough to protect Rose and Timmy. While that might be an old-fashioned senti-ment, Kade didn't care. Once Leonato figured out Kade's plans, they'd all be in danger. "I don't want to tell Rose about the fight yet."

"I agree. We shouldn't tell Samantha either." Vane clasped his hands on the table. "It's not easy to kill a man in the pit. You sure you're up for that?"

Kade fisted his hands and took a few deep inhales to regu-late his breathing. "After hearing what Magnus did to Rose today, I can't wait."

"Good. You're going to need that anger tonight."

No kidding, brother.

Vane pointed to the drawstring bag on the table. "Is that the box?"

"Yes." Kade moved to the open door that gave him a view of the women sitting on the edge of the fountain. "I found it one of the lockers in the back room of Iron Rack's Gym."

Vane scoffed. "How ironic to find a box worth thousands of dollars in a pirate-themed gym that is probably worth more as ashes."

"Such are the Fates."

"I hate those bitches."

"Me too," Kade's chuckle sounded grim. "Vane? I get why you don't want your men to know about your fight at Doom. But why don't you want them to know you're helping me?"

Vane got up and stood next to Kade near the front door. It was still open from earlier, and the breeze filled the room with warm, gardenia-scented air. "I know you've only known us for a short time—"

"I've known Nate and Pete for weeks."

Vane nodded. Now it was his turn to pace the room. He moved with long, powerful strides and flexed his hands, as if battling with himself.

Too bad male restlessness couldn't be bottled and sold. Otherwise, Kade could buy his way out of his problems.

"My men and I... we've been in some intense situations."

"You're Green Berets. That's not surprising."

Vane curled his hands into fists, and his knuckles turned white. "I would give my life for my friends."

Kade didn't respond. Vane had mentioned that the other night at the gym. But it was as if he was reminding himself of that fact instead of stating it.

"I respect them, and they respect me," Vane said.

"Makes sense." Kade wasn't sure what to say, but felt the need to speak as a witness. "So, why are you lying to them?"

"Because they don't like me."

That was not at all what Kade expected to hear. "That can't be true."

Vane glanced at Kade with narrow eyes. "They think I'm a know-it-all. I'm also one of Kells's trusted advisors because I've known him the longest. I never asked for that position. It just happened."

"Does Kells understand the position he's put you in with the other men?"

Vane shook his head. "Kells has enough to worry about."

Rose and Samantha appeared on the balcony. Before Kade could move, Rose flung herself into his arms.

A few minutes later, after the women had used the bathroom to clean up and eaten the snacks he'd found, everyone was settled at the table with glasses of water and napkins. He'd just finished explaining how Calum, Nate, and Pete were helping them out.

Rose had also mentioned that Sampson, as well as One Ear, had been watching her house.

"Rose." Kade reached for her hand. "Are you sure Sampson didn't follow you?"

She nodded and reclaimed her hand to tuck stray hairs behind her ear. "I never saw him again. And, like Leonato, Sampson doesn't really blend in."

"I haven't seen Sampson either." Vane leaned back in the chair, and Kade hoped it wouldn't break under the weight of the large man.

Samantha held her glass of water between both hands and stared at the bags of pretzels and chips on the table.

Rose's bare feet were on the bottom run of the chair, and she was now tearing a paper napkin into strips.

In the short time since she'd been there, she'd barely looked at him. Yes, she'd hugged him as soon as she'd come inside. But when he'd kissed her forehead, he'd felt her internal flinch. There was a distance about her that he didn't understand.

So what the hell had happened while they'd been separated?

Had it been her interaction with Magnus?

That thought shot adrenaline through every one of Kade's large muscle groups. He had no idea when Magnus would be notified about the fight tonight, but Rose didn't mention it. And Kade was sure that if Magnus had known when he'd attacked Rose in the hospital, he would've bragged about it.

Maybe she'd detected that Kade was lying by omission. Since he didn't want to worry her even more, he got up and found the black drawstring bag on the loveseat. Then he handed it to her. "This is for you."

She glanced at him with a wary gaze, unzipped the bag, and pulled out a rectangular wooden box. She inhaled sharply as she ran her fingers over the etched silver plates attached to the top and sides. "I can't believe you found my box."

Without warning, she stood and wrapped her arms around his waist. "Thank you so much!"

He held her close and breathed in her fresh scent of honeysuckles and sunshine. He had to believe that this wasn't the last night they were ever going to see each other. He had to believe that he and Rose deserved their happily ever after. He had to believe that his plan would work.

Because if he failed, he wasn't sure he'd survive.

ROSE RELEASED Kade and ran her hands over the ingrained wood covered with etched siler panels. Kade had found her mother's box. And given it to her. How could she have doubted him?

Samantha got up, found a pitcher in the cabinet, and filled it with tap water and ice from the freezer. "Rose? Do you know how to open it?"

"No." Rose sat and turned the box over. "Puzzle boxes were popular in the seventeenth and eighteenth centuries, but most of those had keys. My mother found this one in an antique shop in New Orleans, without a key, and she was never able to open it.

Vane touched the silver top decorated with an etching of an eight-pointed star. "It's beautiful."

Samantha began refilling all the glasses with water.

Rose was appreciative since she was still thirsty from the tunnel adventure. It didn't help that this apartment, as lovely as it was, didn't have AC. "Some puzzle boxes have a secret panel that can be pulled out to open it. Or a hidden latch. But, like I said, my mother couldn't figure out the secret."

Or, if she had, she'd never told anyone.

"So what's the plan," Samantha said. "Calum mentioned that he made contact with Hezekiah on Rose's behalf."

"The plan is," Kade said around a handful of pretzels, "Rose and I are meeting Hezekiah tonight. Once we trade the box for Rose's money, I am going to smuggle Rose and Timmy out of town before the Fianna realize what we've done."

Rose coughed on her water. This wasn't at all what she'd expected.

Vane snorted. "That's a terrible plan."

Kade glared at the other man. "Do you have a better one?"

"Let's not argue." Samantha grabbed a bag of cheese crackers and brought it back to the table. Because junk food was the solution to this nightmare.

"Can someone lay out the details of this plan?" Rose asked.

Samantha took a handful of crackers and placed them on a napkin. "For the first part, you and Kade will stay here in this apartment until your meeting with Hezekiah. If Leonato doesn't find you here, you should be able to get to the meeting without the Fianna finding out."

Vane took a handful of crackers for himself. "The part

where, after the meeting, Kade smuggles Rose and Timmy out of town is what needs work."

"After Rose gets her money," Kade said, "I'll drive her to the Isle of Grace and stash her at Mamie's Café. Then I'll return to the city to get Timmy."

Rose shook her head. "I'm not leaving without Timmy, and we're not being stashed anywhere. I'm also worried about Timmy's health. I can't move him if he has a fever."

"Rose is correct." Vane crossed his arms. "We need help."

Samantha pulled out her phone and began texting. "I'll ask Calum to get Doc Bennett to help us. Maybe the doctor can meet us on the isle to check Timmy out and make sure he's okay to travel."

"Who is Doctor Bennett?" Rose asked.

"A doctor Calum knows." Samantha placed her phone on the table. "He's a great doctor who sometimes helps Calum with off-the-books kinds of things."

That sounded sketchy. "I don't know—"

Samantha took Rose's hand and squeezed. "I promise you, Doc Bennett is a great guy. Last week, he saved both me and my friend Juliet." Samantha used her free hand to motion to the apartment. "This is her place. And if it weren't for Doc Bennett, she wouldn't be on her honeymoon right now."

Rose released a deep breath. "All right. Except the Fianna may be watching Timmy. If we're going to do this, we all leave Savannah at the same time."

"Rose?" Kade checked his watch. "What time does the hospital close to visitors?"

"Eight p.m. But I can get in after hours. The nurses don't pay attention to me."

"Would the nurses pay attention to me?" Samantha asked. "I've visited Timmy before. Maybe, if I can get inside, I can smuggle him out. I'll take the Juliet's Lily truck, grab him and wait for you both someplace in town. We'd just have to get word to Timmy so he goes along with the plan. Then, once we're all together, we'll drive out to the Isle of Grace."

Rose nodded and chewed her bottom lip. "That could work."

Kade and Vane stared at each other for a long moment before Kade nodded. "This plan might succeed after all."

Samantha pointed to a landline phone on a table near the loveseat. "You can use that phone to call Timmy." Then she said to Vane, "Will you come with me, in the Juliet's Lily van, to my apartment before you head back to the gym?"

Vane stood. "Of course." He looked at Kade. "For now, I'll leave my vehicle near Rose's house, just in case someone is watching. What time do you want me and Samantha back here?"

"Not here." Kade stood as well. "Meet us in Johnson Square. Nine-thirty. Samantha, park the truck in the empty lot across from the coffee shop. There are no cameras on that side of the square, and you can walk to the children's hospital from there. Once Rose and I get out of our meeting, we'll meet you at the truck and leave town together."

"Samantha?" Vane's voice sounded strained, and he stared at the floor instead of her. "Are you okay keeping secrets from Pete?"

"No. But I don't have a choice."

When Samantha rose, Rose did as well. She was overwhelmed by the speed with which everything was falling into place. It was as if everyone in the room, except for her, was used to these kinds of missions.

Samantha's phone buzzed, and she read the text. "Calum said that Doc Bennett will meet us tonight once we give him the signal."

Rose swallowed, and her eyes burned with unshed tears. She wasn't even sure why she'd teared up. Or why her hands had started to tremble.

Samantha gave Rose a hug and whispered, "Don't worry. Call Timmy. Tell him it's a huge adventure, and everything will be okay. This nightmare will be over soon."

"Okay." Rose released her friend and exhaled so loudly it felt like she was expelling a thousand breaths.

Once she and Kade were alone in the small, intimate apartment, she gathered the glasses and napkins and brought everything to the sink. She needed to stay busy in order to prevent a panic attack.

"Hey." Kade took her arm and spun her around. "I know this is a lot."

She brushed stray hairs out of her face. "This is more than a lot. It's a *ton*. And I don't even know how to process everything that just happened, including the fact that so many people are putting themselves in danger to help us."

He kissed her nose. "This isn't a perfect plan, but it is a good one. And I've done a hell of a lot of mission planning."

She nodded and allowed him to take her in his arms. She still had lingering doubts about so many things, including Timmy's health and meeting Hezekiah. But there was one thing she needed clarity on before they put everything in motion. "Kade?"

"Hmm?" He tightened his hold, and she rested her head against his chest. "A few things I'm not sure about. How long are we staying on the isle? When do we get to come home?"

She felt his body tense against hers. Then he sighed, and his breath shifted her hair. "If you succeed in selling your box to Hezekiah, and if I can get you and Timmy out of town safely, the Fianna will hunt you for the rest of your life. If we do this, you can never go home again."

CHAPTER 23

$\mathcal{E}$ven though they had a plan that could work, Kade could tell from the way Rose had handled her call with Timmy, from her jerky movements around the kitchen as she put away the snacks and wiped the counter, that she hated it. That she blamed herself for this mess.

Yet all of these problems were his fault. His fault because, years ago, he'd been so fucking tired of prison he'd agreed to become a warrior. The fact he hadn't truly understood what he'd agreed to didn't matter. The Fianna had made him an offer, and he'd taken it. Now, over two years in, he realized his utter foolishness.

Another truth he needed to face? If he had followed the Fianna's rules and not visited Rose and Timmy that night in the hospital... No, if he'd not saved Rose from Antoine... No, if he'd not fought Magnus when he'd attacked Rose at Rage of Angels... Who the fuck did Kade think he was kidding? Since the first night he'd seen Rose at the club, experienced the sorrow and pride that shone through her hazel eyes, he'd been doomed. In both the literal and fight-club sense.

"Kade?" Rose finally dropped the dish towel and came over to take his hand. "I'm sorry."

He covered her hand with his and met her worried gaze. "Whatever for?"

"When I got here, I was preoccupied."

Now he squeezed her fingers. He didn't want to admit he'd been hurt by her distance. "Was there a reason?"

She swallowed and looked away. "Magnus told me you were charged with murder. And Vane confirmed it."

Kade kissed her knuckles, one by one. "I—"

"It's okay." She pressed two fingers against his mouth and met his gaze. "Even if you were charged, I don't believe it."

Kade nodded, not sure what else to say. He was humbled by her trust, and his heart shattered with what he knew would happen should he fail her.

"Magnus also said that the Fianna wanted you to become a warrior."

He backed away and ran a hand through his hair. "Why would Magnus say that?"

She sat on the loveseat and wrapped her arms around herself. "Magnus thinks that finding the box and giving it to the Prince is part of your tithe."

Fuck. He sank into the seat next to her.

She touched his shoulder, but he couldn't meet her questioning gaze. "What is your relationship with the Fianna?"

He swallowed hard and rubbed his forehead with his fist. "It's complicated." There was so much more that he wanted to say, but he couldn't. He didn't want her to worry, but he also didn't want to give the Fianna any more reasons to hurt her. "If I could tell you more than that, I would. But anything I say would put you in danger. And I'd never do that to you or Timmy."

She rested her head against his shoulder, as if silently

expressing her understanding. "I'm scared we're going to lose each other."

He leaned back into the cushions and wrapped an arm around her shoulder. "So am I." That was the first time, in his entire life, he'd admitted his fear out loud.

"Kade?" Her voice came out throaty and tight, as if she was holding in tears. "I'm afraid to trust people I barely know. I'm afraid I'll lose Timmy to a sudden heart attack during the escape. And I'm afraid the Fianna will find you and take you away from me."

He shifted on the couch so he could kiss her softly. After a few long minutes, he whispered against her lips, "I promise to protect you and Timmy to the best of my ability."

"Promise you won't leave us. That you won't let the Fianna take you away from me."

He stood, pulling her up with him, then gently held her upper arms. "I won't make a promise I might not be able to keep. But I do promise this, Tempest Rose Guthrie. I promise that I will never leave you without love's last kiss."

She met his gaze directly, her eyes now a deep, dark green. "I want more than that. We both deserve more than that."

His words got tangled in the back of his throat. He'd never felt closer to anyone in his entire life. In a few short days, she'd *become* his entire life. Yet all he could offer her were half-truths and promises he might have to break. "I want more than that too, Rose. I'm just praying our plan works."

A stray tear rolled down her cheek. She clasped her arms around his neck and pressed her body against his. "Do you have any idea how we should pass the time until we meet Hezekiah?"

The heat from her body penetrated Kade's clothes through to his bare skin. His body reacted immediately, and he fixed his gaze on her pink lips, hazel eyes, the strands of red hair that had escaped her high ponytail.

"Maybe." He touched her cheek with the backs of his fingers.

Nearby church bells struck three times. How had it gotten so late so quickly?

She stood on her toes so her lips could trace his. Her mouth moved as if she wanted to memorize them. "What if Hezekiah—"

"Let's not talk about this right now."

Although they should be working out every detail of their plan to meet Hezekiah, all Kade could focus on was how hot and hard his body had become, especially now that her breasts were pressed against his chest.

She blew in Kade's ear, and his erection jumped inside his tight jeans. "Where is your gym bag?"

He tucked stray hairs behind her ear and kissed her neck. "In the bedroom."

She released him and disappeared into the bedroom.

Before he followed, he locked the door and windows and pulled all the blinds.

Her laughter drew him after her, and he shed his clothes along the way. By the time he entered the bedroom, she was naked, waiting for him with a foil packet in her hand.

Thank goodness she'd closed the curtains because he wasn't sure if he'd bother.

He pulled her in for a hard kiss. An angry kiss. A terrified kiss.

She clung to his neck and returned his passion. Her body, curvy and soft, melted against his muscular frame. While a part of him wanted to take his time, the other, more desperate side of him took over. After opening the foil packet, he moved her against the wall and lifted her so she could loop her legs around his waist. Then he entered her.

She gasped, and he held her higher as she rode him. Her hooded lids, as well as her slick feminine core, told him everything he needed to know. She needed him as much as he needed her. He hardened even more, and nothing mattered except the incredible sensation of her up-and-down movements.

On every powerful descent, she took all of him inside of her. Every time he lifted her, his arm muscles contracted. Sweat dripped down his neck, and his biceps cramped. Still, he kept up a hard and fast motion with his hips, drilling into her at a rate that could stop his heart.

He closed his eyes to manage all the sensations exploding through his body.

When Rose called out his name, he gave her one, two, three, four more thrusts. But it was the fifth one that sent him over the edge of all feeling, all physical sensation, into a place of such intense pleasure he actually felt pain. When she tightened around his cock again, he slammed her down three more times before letting her collapse in his arms.

Holding her tightly, he felt his legs give way, and they sank to the floor. He sat against the wall, his legs splayed, his cock still partially hard, as if it wasn't sure things had ended. Rose, on the other hand, curled up on his lap, her knees pressed against his chest. He hadn't known it was possible for someone to draw in on themselves so completely.

He hadn't known it was possible to love someone so completely.

He hadn't known it was possible to love someone so completely and still plan to betray them.

～

CHURCH BELLS WOKE UP ROSE, and she stretched beneath the bedsheets.

They'd made love two more times, and she felt sore in ways that were unusual for her. A good kind of pain, though. The kind she'd tuck away in her heart and remember forever.

After their adventure against the wall, they'd moved to the shower. Then back to the bed.

She smiled and touched Kade's head. He lay next to her, naked on top of the sheets, sound asleep. Just thinking about what they'd shared sent a hot flush up from her toes to her cheeks. Especially the shower where Kade had proven that his strength was eclipsed only by his inventiveness.

She rolled to her side and watched him breathe, his chest rising and falling with a power and grace she envied. Time was speeding by, yet she wanted to stop it completely. When the clock confirmed it was five p.m., she glanced out the window. The room was dark, making it seem later.

Carefully, so she wouldn't wake Kade, she slipped out of the bed and found a robe on a hook in the bathroom. She just hoped the owner wouldn't mind her borrowing the bed or clothes. In bare feet, she padded into the kitchen. After making a pot of coffee, she sat at the table and ran her hands over her mother's box. They'd left a box worth a small fortune sitting out in the open, as if they hadn't just gone through hell to find it.

Tears pricked her eyes. The last time she'd seen this box, her mother had been holding it in her father's office. Sometimes Rose still struggled with the fact they were gone. And now she was running away from Savannah and all the memories she had of her family.

Was she really leaving home tonight? Never to return?

She didn't have many possessions, but she'd have to leave behind what little she owned. Although they hadn't talked about the logistics of what would happen after tonight's escape, she needed some answers on how to collect the few things she did have.

Her talk with Timmy earlier had gone surprisingly well.

Luckily, he had the clothes he'd been admitted in stored in the closet. And he'd been excited about the upcoming adventure and seeing King George again. She'd not mentioned they were leaving the cat behind.

She pushed her hair behind her ears. She'd left it undone, and it hung in messy waves over her shoulders and down her back.

King George was another issue that needed to be handled. As she listened to the coffee gurgle, she realized she had more ties to her home than she'd believed and would be sad to leave.

When the coffee finished, she got up and poured herself a cup. Then she found a package of cookies in the cabinet and put them on the table. She felt like she was moving through a muddy swamp in the fog at night. None of this seemed real. Was she really leaving town with what was in her backpack?

If she'd realized, she would've packed more clothes and left their clues behind.

She grabbed her backpack near the loveseat and took out Deke's planner and Shakespeare book. While the Shakespeare book wasn't really a clue, it reminded her of what had happened in Deke's closet.

She smiled. *Their first kiss.*

Then she found Kade's compass watch. She traced the etching on the outside lid and opened it. She loved the story of his ancestors who'd promised they wouldn't leave each other without a last kiss. But the real worry pressing on her heart was Kade's commitment to the Fianna.

He'd not admitted that the Fianna wanted him to join their ranks, but she wasn't stupid. Kade was a strong, fierce soldier who owed them for getting him out of prison. Of course they would want to recruit him. The thing that annoyed her the most was that she hadn't thought of it before Magnus mentioned the possibility.

This situation with Kade and the Fianna was far more

serious than he'd let on. She understood Kade's reluctance to talk about his situation, and she feared the Fianna's claim to Kade was stronger than her claim.

Then again, she'd not made a claim on Kade's heart.

Yes, they'd made love in the most passionate way possible. But she'd not admitted her love for him. She was so racked with self-doubt about her ability to trust—and love—that she wasn't sure if she knew how to be the lover Kade deserved.

And wasn't that a pathetic state of affairs?

She rubbed the back of her neck. That just meant tonight's plan had to work out perfectly. Because one thing she knew for sure—she wasn't leaving Savannah without him. She'd take on Leonato and Sampson and whoever else showed up before she'd let them have Kade.

She returned the compass watch to her backpack. Then, to distract herself, she read Deke's planner while she finished her coffee. Like last time, she didn't find anything that looked like a clue. Until she turned the last page. On the back side of December's calendar page, that had been folded down, Deke had made a list beneath the title CLUES. Four phrases separated by periods.

Sebastian. Key. Sugar. Remiel Marigny.

She traced the name 'Remiel Marigny'. Magnus had mentioned this person twice now. Once on the phone with Antoine, and then again in the hospital earlier that day. But with no other information, it was as useless as the other phrases.

With a disgusted sigh, she put the planner and Shakespeare book back into her backpack.

Kade appeared in his jeans, carrying his burner phone, and nothing else. His sheer masculinity stole her breath, and she got up to pour him a cup of coffee.

I am such a coward.

"Rose." Kade laid his phone on the table and sat. He

grimaced, as if sore as well. "We need to talk about a few things."

"I know." She placed his mug on the table, near her mother's box, and sat across from him. "Let's start with an easy one. King George. I'm assuming we can't take him with us."

"No." Kade drank his coffee and sighed deeply. "I just spoke with Calum. I wanted to confirm that Doc Bennett will check on Timmy if we need him. Calum also said that once we leave town, and things settle down, he'll have your household packed up and sent to you. Including the cat, if you can take him."

She nodded and stared into her mug. She hadn't given any thought to where they might end up or how they'd get there. "Can you tell me again why we can't go home once we sell the box to Hezekiah?"

"Because, if we do this, the Fianna will *never* stop looking for us."

She exhaled and nodded. He'd said that earlier, but she'd needed to know for sure.

"Would the church take the cat back?" Kade took two cookies from the package on the table and handed her one. As if a cookie would stop her from noticing that he'd changed the subject. "I'd think a feral cat would be a great mouser."

"I doubt it." She ate the cookie and then got up to reheat her mug in the microwave. "King George bit a parishioner."

Why were they discussing cats and mice and churches? Maybe because it was easier than facing what loomed ahead.

The microwave dinged. With her mug, she sat down again and tucked her feet up on the chair's rungs.

If one didn't want to talk about animals, what did a woman say to the man she'd just spent hours in bed with? A man she was terrified she'd lose?

She shifted her gaze again to the window over the sink. The blinds were closed. Yet some light made its way into the kitchen. "Kade, why is Calum Prioleau helping us? As the richest man in the state, doesn't he have more important things to do?"

"If you're asking me if I trust him, the answer is yes." Kade leaned forward, his strong fingers clutching his mug. "Did you know that besides having the most important and powerful clients in the South, Calum's law firm also has more pro bono clients than any firm on the East Coast?"

She glanced at him and sipped the hot coffee. "No, I didn't know that."

"I think it's because Calum carries a strong sense of fairness and justice, especially when it comes to those who have no power when pitted against the system. Whether that system is an insurance company, a huge corporation, or even the government."

"So he's not acting out of pity?"

"I don't believe so. Calum, despite his wealth, has had his own share of sufferings. I believe his generosity is born of empathy, not a need to improve his reputation or standing in the community."

She ran a finger over her mother's box again. The wood felt warm, while the silver plates decorating the sides and top were cold. A beautiful series of swirls and loops had been etched in the metal. She turned the box to see the engraving of 'EG, All My Love, BG. 1776.'

"I wish we could open this and see what's inside."

"All that matters is that Hezekiah gives you money for it." Kade covered her hand on the box. His hand felt warm and strong and safe. "Rose, you have to hide your mother's box. We can't meet Hezekiah with our only leverage."

She wrinkled her nose. "Do you think tonight's meeting could be a setup?"

"I'm not sure. But we'll be in trouble if Hezekiah has

armed guards who take the box and then kill us because we know about it."

"Oh." She'd honestly never thought about that.

Kade reached out to touch her cheek. "And you can't tell me where you hid it."

"Why not?"

"Because if they torture me, I don't want to be able to give away the location."

She closed her eyes. What a mess she'd gotten them into.

"I have something else to tell you."

She opened her eyes as Kade rose and brought his cup to the sink. Instead of coming back, he lifted the blind an inch to look out the window.

"What's wrong?"

He faced her, his hips leaning against the counter. "I saw Detective Garza earlier and learned the identity of the man Leonato killed at the hospital six weeks ago. A man named Banjo who'd been a trainee bartender at the club, working for Deke. Then, while we were *napping*—"

"Napping?" A hot flush rushed up her neck to her face. "That's an interesting spin on what we were doing."

Kade winked at her. "Anyway, while we were *distracted*, Calum left me a message. According to his contacts, Banjo was in debt to Deke and Magnus because of a bad bet at Doom."

She stood and met Kade near the sink. "I never met Banjo. Why would he want to hurt me that night at the hospital? Or was he after you?"

"I'm not sure." Kade took a curl of her hair and spun it around his fingers. "Calum discovered that, two days before Banjo died, he received money from RM Financial, a European banking firm. He received enough money to pay off his debts and allow him to live anywhere he wanted in complete comfort and safety."

"So?"

"Rose, RM Financial is owned by the Fianna. The Fianna paid off Banjo's debts. That means Banjo owed the Fianna."

"Why would Leonato kill Banjo if they both work for the Prince?"

"The Prince bought Banjo's loyalty by paying off his debts. In return, Banjo probably agreed to work the mission at the hospital." Kade released her hair and lifted the blind again to peer out the window. "It's possible this had nothing to do with you at all. It's possible the Prince ordered Leonato to kill Banjo in order to send me a message."

"What?" Rose wrinkled her nose. "The Prince killed his own messenger?"

"Leonato may have killed Banjo to keep me in line. As a warning that if I don't continue doing what they ask of me, they'll kill me too."

"That's..." She couldn't even think of an appropriate word. Brutal? Insane? "Terrifying."

"Yes, it is." He dropped the blind and sighed. "This is how the Fianna operates. Manipulation. Bribery. Torture."

She shivered and wrapped her arms around herself. "Why do the Fianna want the box now? They could've taken it from Deke after he stole it from the Savannah Preservation Office and left me out of this."

"I'm not sure." Kade leaned his hip against the counter and ran a hand through his hair. "Regardless of the reason, one thing I am sure of is that the Prince and his Fianna army are masters at making people do what they want for reasons they never share. Ultimately, everything the Prince does is for the benefit of the Fianna. No one else."

She sat, placed her elbows on the table, and dropped her head into her hands. "Kade? When I give the box to Hezekiah, how angry will the Prince be?"

"Very."

She closed her eyes. "Magnus wants the box too. He

threatened me and Timmy if I give the box to the Prince or sell it to Hezekiah."

"Rose?" The harshness in Kade's voice made her open her eyes. He knelt in front of her and held both of her hands. "What if we grab Timmy now and leave town? Screw the box. Screw the money. Just pick up and run."

"I need that money." She hated the desperation in her voice. "If I run away and don't pay that hospital bill, I'll never be able to get Timmy the proper medical care he requires, no matter where I run to. And what about you? The Fianna will hunt us down. And when they find us, they won't be merciful."

He nodded as if defeated. "So you trade the box for the money. Then Samantha and Vane will drive you and Timmy to the Isle of Grace."

"With you." She tapped Kade's knee. "Right?"

"Of course." He cleared his throat before meeting her gaze. "It's getting late. We should clean up and get dressed." He stood. "And you need to decide where you want to hide your mother's box."

"Are you sure we shouldn't bring it with us?"

"Yes. If things go sideways, you're going to need that leverage, or else Hezekiah has no reason to let you walk out of there alive."

She stood and clutched Kade's arm, forcing him to meet her gaze. "What do you mean if things go sideways?"

His blue eyes darkened. "If something happens to me, you'll have to deal with Hezekiah, and maybe the Prince, alone."

She rested her head against his bare chest, and he stroked her hair. "Any suggestions where I should hide my mother's box?"

"Somewhere no one would think of looking."

That wasn't any help. "What if Hezekiah doesn't believe I even have the box?"

"I showed the box to Calum, and he took a photo with his phone. So he is our witness. Now, get dressed and I'll make us something to eat and figure out how to handle our newest problem."

She raised her head to meet his blue eyes. "What newest problem?"

Kade took her arm, led her to the kitchen window, and lifted the blind an inch. Outside, beneath a tree on the edge of a narrow parking lot, a man within the shadows checked his phone.

Leonato.

CHAPTER 24

At six p.m., Kade finished drying the ramen soup bowls and hung the towel over the faucet.

So much for best laid plans. He had no idea how Leonato had found them. But, then again, the Fianna were expert trackers. Hunters had to be in order to catch their prey.

Kade wasn't even sure if Leonato knew he was in the apartment with Rose. It's possible Sampson and Leonato still thought Kade was searching for the box and Rose was here alone.

A text hummed on Kade's phone and he picked it up as he peeked around the edge of the blind. The sun was slipping behind the surrounding buildings. Yet Leonato remained beneath his tree, arms crossed. While normal men would have fidgeted or sat on the ground, Leonato kept still because extreme self-discipline was what set a regular soldier apart from a Fianna warrior.

Rose touched his back. "I'm ready. All of my things are packed into my backpack."

He turned in sucked in his breath. She'd put on her jeans, white T-shirt, and blue sweatshirt. She wore her hair in a long braid, and he inhaled her scent until his lungs ached. "Have you chosen a hiding spot?"

"Yes." She looked around, as if searching for a sniper.

"Rose." He used one finger to tilt up her chin. "Don't worry."

Her smile reeked of resignation. "How are you going to distract Leonato so I can get away?"

Kade held up the phone with the text from Calum that he'd just received. "We have a plan."

She touched his lips, and he kissed her. It wasn't the most passionate kiss, but it was sweet and gentle and lingering. He didn't want to let her go. Ever. And the thought of sending her out into the world alone to hide her box filled him with a dread that stole his breath and threatened his sanity. Yet it was the only way to protect her. To save her.

He released her and nodded to the drawstring bag on the table that held the box. "When we get word, you'll go out the way you came in. Head toward the courtyard while Leonato is busy in the parking lot. Then run through the alley and turn right. From there you'll have to make it to the hiding spot on your own, on foot."

She took a deep breath and exhaled loudly. "Then I meet you at Johnson Square?"

"Yes. Try to get there before ten p.m." He kissed her forehead. He'd already given her pointers on how to backtrack and other tricks to prevent herself from being followed. "Will that give you enough time?"

"Yes." She stood on her toes to give him one more kiss. Then she pointed to her white sneakers. "I even have my running-away shoes on."

Please, God, don't let her need running-away shoes.

He helped her slip the straps of the drawstring bag over her shoulders and walked her to the front door. Then he grabbed the deadbolt. "You know where you're going?"

"Yes." She touched his arm and smiled at him. "Try not to worry. I know this city well. I'll be fine, and I'll meet you before ten."

"Good." He hated the fact she'd have to walk alone in the dark.

She kissed him again until his phone buzzed with a text from Calum.

Go.

Kade unlocked the door and breathed in the fresh, humid air laced with the scents of gardenias and boxwood. Since it was summer, they had at least another two hours of sunlight.

She touched his cheek and disappeared down the stairs.

Exhaling like a wounded beast, he closed the door and went back to the kitchen window. Outside, he saw Leonato talking to... *Nate?*

Nate and Leonato spoke, with raised voices, for six minutes. Then, with a dismissive wave, Nate walked away.

Kade checked the new text from Calum.

SHE'S GONE.

AT NINE P.M., Rose slipped through the back door into her kitchen. She was grateful that she hadn't had time to lock the door when they'd left earlier.

She'd hidden her box in a place where no one would ever find it. And since she had a bit of time before meeting Kade, she'd hurried home to feed King George.

On the table, she found her mother's sweatshirt. She'd come home before hiding the box to make sure Timmy hadn't left her a message on the house phone. It had been so hot, she'd taken off the jacket and forgotten to grab it when she left.

The sun had set, but the light from the cemetery allowed

her to move around without turning on any lamps. As soon as she filled the bowl with cat food, King George appeared through the kitty door. His white fur was dirty, and she wished she had time to wash him. No, she wished she could bring the cat with her. Having King George would go a long way to settling Timmy down once he realized they were leaving town.

She snagged the photo off her fridge and slipped it into her back pocket when the house phone rang with an unknown ID. She didn't answer it until she heard a familiar voice on the answering machine.

She picked up the receiver and said, "Harry?"

"Rose." Harry's firm voice carried through the line. "I just spoke with Timmy, and he says you're going on a grand adventure tonight. Is everything okay?"

She almost laughed at that statement. But sometimes the irony was just too painful. "Everything is fine." She crossed her fingers. "Timmy is being released tonight. He's just excited."

"I see." Harry paused, and she heard his heavy breaths, as if he was walking quickly. "How is Magnus? Has he been bothering you?"

She glanced at the clock. She had forty minutes before meeting Kade and needed to get going. "He's always bothering me. But it's nothing I can't handle."

She prayed that would be the truth once she exchanged the box for the money.

"All right." Harry sighed. "I'll be in touch."

"Thank you, Harry." She squeezed the phone because she realized this might be the last time she'd speak to him. She and Kade hadn't discussed all the details, but her new life might include leaving Harry—the only person who'd ever cared for her—behind. Tears welled, and she stared at her dingy kitchen with her second-hand apron, tote bag filled with bills, and King George who snarled at her because he hated phones.

Everything was happening so quickly, she'd hardly had time to think through all the ramifications of what she was about to do. "Harry, I don't know if you know this, but I appreciate everything you've done for me and Timmy. I honestly don't know how we would've survived without you."

"It's going to be okay, Rose." Harry cleared his throat. "I need to go. I'll see you soon."

Although she knew that wasn't true, she said, "I hope so."

Once she hung up, and checked King George's water bowl for the last time, she slipped out of the kitchen door. She debated locking it but didn't want to make things more difficult for Calum. If someone wanted to steal her bills or the costumes she wore at the club, they were welcome to them. Besides, everyone she loved was waiting for her elsewhere.

The sun had set, and the clouds hid the moon, making her surroundings appear bleak. Thunder rolled in the distance, and the smell of ozone filled the air.

Once she checked her perimeter and decided no one was following her, she took off.

She ran, as fast as she could through the city she'd once loved, toward Kade.

She ran as fast as she could toward the man she loved.

"Is Rose here yet?" Kade dug through his gym bag, grateful that the Fighter's Hole was empty. Except for Vane, who leaned against a locker, arms crossed.

"No."

Kade glanced at the clock on the wall, then at her pink backpack on the ground. "She's late."

"Don't worry. She'll be here."

"You don't have to do this, Vane." Kade pulled out a clean tank top and yanked it on over his gym pants.

Once Leonato had left the parking lot behind Juliet's Lily, Kade had run to his apartment and gathered everything he needed—which wasn't much since he had to carry whatever he packed along with Rose's backpack. When he'd met Vane and Calum in Johnson Square, they'd made a few changes to the plan. Changes that Kade agreed with, but changes that meant they needed more help than he'd originally thought.

Kade had never been great about asking for help and was even worse at showing gratitude. It wasn't that he didn't want to or wasn't grateful. He just hated owing others, and he was tired of being a pawn in other men's chess games. Then there was the fact that he never knew how to say thank you. Tonight, hopefully, he'd find the words.

"I know I don't have to do this," Vane said. "Just like Nate and Pete didn't have to help either."

"Your buddies still don't know about your part in this play?"

"No. And—"

"I know." Kade tucked his street clothes into his gym bag. "You'd like to keep it that way."

Vane ran a fist over his chin. "Rose doesn't even know about the fight. She will not be happy when she finds out."

"I couldn't tell her." Because Kade hadn't wanted to ruin their afternoon. If his plan tonight didn't work, those hours might be the last they'd ever have together.

"This is so fucked up," Vane said with a sigh.

"Yep." Even though Kade would do anything to help Rose exchange that box, the moment Magnus touched Rose in the hospital he'd sealed his fate.

There was no way Kade could allow Magnus to hurt Rose without retribution. "I need to stay focused on the plan. Win this fight. Grab Rose's money. Get her and Timmy out of town. Without the Fianna finding out."

A simple plan with lots of opportunities for error. The story of his life.

Vane dropped onto the bench in the middle of the room. "Will Hezekiah give Rose the money and let her go?"

Kade picked up his weapon from the bench, slipped out the clip to make sure it was full, and slammed it back into the gun. Of course the magazine was full. He'd just needed to triple-check. Since this was a private fight, they didn't have to worry about metal detectors or security guards or weapons checks.

He handed the weapon to Vane. The brother would hold it until after the fight. "Maybe."

Vane snorted. "And if Hezekiah betrays Rose? Will you kill him too?"

Kade started taping his hands. "If I have to."

With his mood tonight, he'd kill every man in that room who threatened the plan.

"According to Calum, Magnus has been taking steroids." Vane leaned forward, his elbows digging into his thighs. "Magnus will come after you with everything he's got, if for no other reason than his pride. We both know what wounded pride does to a man."

Yeah. Kade knew all about the danger of men with vulnerable egos. He finished taping his hands. "Let's get this done."

Vane shoved Kade's weapon into his back waistband and slipped on his black field jacket that matched his black combat pants and T-shirt. Kade had to give the brother credit. With his long brown hair tied behind his neck, Vane looked like a badass Green Beret.

Kade shook out his arms and left the room. It was time to take care of Magnus.

It was time to save Rose.

Rose entered Johnson Square and collapsed on a bench beneath a gas lamp. Her lungs hurt and her calves ached. When this was over, she needed to hit the gym.

She took a few deep breaths and checked her watch. She was late. It had taken longer than expected to run to Johnson Square. She'd spent so much time looking over her shoulder, worried about being followed, she'd even knocked over a trash can.

The street lights threw shadows everywhere, and she inhaled deep breaths of humid air that reeked of mildew. Thunder rocked the sky and a raindrop hit her cheek.

Please don't be an omen.

"Rose." A man's voice came behind her.

She turned to see Nate Walker coming toward her. She took a step back. Kade had told her about the help Nate and Pete had given them. Despite having worked with Nate at the club, she didn't know him that well.

Nate stood a few feet away and shoved his hands in the front pockets of his jeans. He'd secured his long blond hair behind his neck and wore a black motorcycle jacket over a black T-shirt. He seemed larger than she remembered. Tall, muscular, and intimidating. Just like Kade and Vane, Nate filled the space in front of her with his enormous physical presence. "It's okay." He took his hands out and held them up, surrender-style. "Calum asked me to meet you here."

"Where's Kade?" She hated the tightness in her voice. But something felt... *off.*

"He's waiting for you."

"Where?"

"Across the street." Nate pointed toward the iron gate that protected Doom's alley. "Calum asked me to meet you here and take you to him."

"Kade never mentioned this." She shivered and wrapped her arms around herself. "Okay." She sighed. "I'll go with you. But if anything seems hinky, I'm running. Got it?"

He smiled, and his green eyes glittered in the lamplight. "I wouldn't have it any other way."

He turned and walked through the garden square, and she followed. When they reached the street, he offered his arm and she took it. They crossed the street, and he waved to the horse-drawn-carriage driver who glared at them. Once on the sidewalk, they headed toward the iron gate.

Nearby, Calum Prioleau, in a blue seersucker suit, texted on his cell phone.

When he saw them, he slipped his phone into his jacket pocket. "Thank you, Nate."

"You're welcome, Calum. Call me if you need anything else."

"I will."

"Good luck, Rose." Nate nodded at Calum and then walked back toward the garden square.

Once Nate disappeared, Calum said, "Nate doesn't know about Doom or Vane's involvement."

"I won't say anything." Besides, she was probably never

going to see Nate again. "Calum, why are the plans changing? I don't like change."

"I know. But you're going to have to trust me." Calum gave her a small smile. "Now, did you hide the box?"

"Yes." She paused as the church bells rang, signaling ten p.m. "Where is Kade?"

"In Doom." Calum led them through the alley Rose had exited from the night before.

"I don't understand. I thought we were meeting in Johnson Square." She looked around the alley as she thought of something else. "Where is Samantha?"

"Samantha is parked near the children's hospital." Calum opened the door, and they went down a set of stairs. As they descended, the air got cooler and danker. "I have Ivers waiting to take you and Kade to the Isle of Grace as soon as you make your trade."

"But Timmy—"

"Kade and I decided it would be better for you two to make a quicker getaway. Samantha will take Timmy out to the Isle to meet you. Once you leave, I'll text Doc Bennett and he'll head to Mamie's Café. I promise you that we will keep Timmy's health a priority as we figure this all out."

"Thank you. I've been very worried about that." She sighed in relief. The realization that she was losing control of this situation was making her anxious and irritable. Yet, at this point, her only choice was to go along. "I hope Timmy doesn't get upset. He's expecting me to be with there with Samantha."

"Samantha will take care of him. I trust her completely."

Once they went through the metal detector, which wasn't turned on, they entered the large, empty space. Without the spectators, Rose had a better view of the area.

The floor had old planking around the perimeter, but the center consisted of packed dirt and sand. Random lightbulbs hung from rafters above them. The walls appeared to be original rough-hewn beams and stone. Eighteenth century, if not earlier.

Calum turned on a spotlight that illuminated the pit, and she inhaled deeply. The other night, she'd not noticed the floor-to-ceiling frescoes on the walls. Although chipped and stained with mold, the designs peeked through. A Liberty Tree on one wall. On another, two sentences from Shakespeare's Sonnet 116.

LOVE ALTERS NOT WITH HIS BRIEF HOURS AND WEEKS, BUT BEARS IT OUT EVEN TO THE EDGE OF DOOM.

"Wow." She walked to the wall and ran her fingers over the painted word *Doom*. "Who did this?"

"The Sons of Liberty." Calum turned on another spotlight that wiped out the lingering shadows. "The original Tondee's Tavern, owned by Peter and Lucy Tondee, was once above us until it burned down. The Sons of Liberty met here in secret. British soldiers above ground, rebels below."

She moved around the room to see a faded image of an early colonial flag with vertical red and white stripes and a blue field with eight-pointed white stars. She knew, thanks to her mother, that this was a rare design of the Rebellious Flag.

She breathed in the stale air and met Calum near the fourth fresco, where someone had painted AUGUST 10, 1774.

"In 1774," Calum said, "the royal governor, James Wright, issued a proclamation forbidding the citizens of Georgia to gather and openly talk about their grievances. On August tenth, thirty men met secretly in this room and adopted eight resolutions affirming their loyalty to the king but also demanding their rights as British citizens.

"They also condemned the Intolerable Acts the king

placed on Massachusetts. These men sent these resolutions to the other colonies. Eventually, as things worsened between the Crown and her colonies, these men—still meeting here in secret, along with the Sons of Liberty—elected delegates to the First Continental Congress. In 1776, they held the first public reading of the Declaration of Independence."

She traced the date with a finger. "That happened in this room?"

"Yes." Calum went to an electrical panel on the wall and flipped a switch. A horrendous screech filled the room.

She held her hands over her ears. "I'm sure the Sons of Liberty didn't listen to music that made their eyeballs bleed and burst their eardrums."

He smiled and flipped the switch again. The deafening death-metal music turned off, leaving the room in a heavy silence.

"Calum?" She moved to the center of the pit and did a slow circle. "Where is Kade?"

"Preparing, I hope." A round, bald man in a tan suit came through the metal detector, followed by a thuggish man wearing a dark suit. They both stayed in the shadows near the edge of the pit.

Calum came forward and held out his hand. "Welcome to Doom, Hezekiah."

They shook hands and separated. But when Calum and Hezekiah came toward her, all the air rushed out of her lungs. "*Harry?*"

Harry, the man she'd known all of her life, bowed his head. "It's so good to see you again, Rose."

His familiar voice sounded sincere, almost regretful. So much so that she had to rub her eyes before asking, "What is going on?"

Harry gave her a small smile. "It's a long, tragic story. A

story I worked hard to keep you out of... until your cousin Magnus made that impossible."

She looked around the room, almost expecting to see her parents and Isaac, until Harry touched her arm. "Rose? Are you alright?"

She couldn't answer because she'd lost the ability to form words.

"I know this is confusing." Harry took her wrist. "But I swear to you, I did this to protect you and Timmy."

Hearing Timmy's name shook her out of her stupor. She yanked her wrist from Harry's grasp and rubbed the skin that his warm fingers had touched. "I don't understand. Why are you here?"

Before Harry could respond, Kade appeared from one of the alcoves.

"Rose?" He dropped his gym bag and her pink backpack near a wall and hurried over to her. He'd changed into gym pants and a tank. "Are you alright?"

She gripped his arm. "This man is Harry. But he's also Hezekiah Usher."

Kade's gaze narrowed on the Harry. "What the fuck is happening?"

"A long-awaited reckoning." After that simple statement, Harry stared at Rose for a moment. A moment that stretched out like the time it would take for all the stars to die and fall to Earth. Finally, he said, "Every time I see you, Rose, you look more like your mother. Although you have your father's hazel eyes."

She gritted her teeth. How could Harry—her parents' best friend—be Hezekiah Usher?

Kade gently removed her fingers from his arm and held her hand, almost as if worried she was going to launch herself at Harry. Which was a distinct possibility.

Harry continued speaking, as if completely unaware of the

emotional bomb that had sucked the air out of the underground room. "I met your parents while attending Yale. The three of us remained friends until their deaths. That's why I'm here. To make things right." He checked the clock on the wall and asked Calum, "Where is Magnus?"

"Late," Calum said.

Harry whispered to his thug, and the larger man left Doom through the metal detector. Once he disappeared, Harry shifted his gaze back to Rose.

That *off* feeling she'd had earlier with Nate returned, and it wasn't just because her family friend turned out to be some kind of eccentric antiques dealer.

She glanced at Kade because she needed something true and solid to focus on. "Why would Magnus be coming?"

Kade sighed heavily and squeezed her hand. "I need to tell you something."

She took a step back, but he refused to release her hand. "Why are you wearing gym clothes?"

"Rose." Harry cleared his throat and crossed his arms over his chest. "I know you have a lot of questions. But since we are short on time," he glanced at the clock again, "I'm going to lay this out for you. I asked Kade and Magnus to come tonight. They will fight here in the pit. Once Kade kills Magnus, I will pay you for the box."

"Rose?" Kade said softly. "I—"

"No." She pulled out of his grasp. Kade and Calum had known about this situation and not told her. When Vane appeared from the small hallway leading to an alcove, she realized he'd known all along as well.

As if understanding the fact she could barely form words, Calum took over the situation. "Just so we're clear, Hezekiah. Rose has the box but did not bring it with her tonight. Once Kade wins the fight and the box is retrieved, you will pay her."

Harry clucked in a disapproving way. "Rose is so much

like her mother. Unfortunately, hiding that box was the mistake that cost Rose's parents their lives."

Listening to Harry speak about her parents helped her find her voice. "What do you know about my parents' deaths?"

Harry held out his hands, palms up. "Isaac killed your parents before I could retrieve the box. Then Magnus killed Isaac to take over your inheritance."

"Those are serious allegations," Calum said. "Can you prove any of this?"

"Of course," Harry said. "I have Isaac's confession on tape and correspondence with Magnus."

Calum muttered a low curse. "Then why didn't you go to the authorities?"

Harry scoffed. "You mean the authorities in this city where Isaac Guthrie had paid off every politician, judge, and anyone else who had any kind of power? Then his son did the same? Even with my evidence, no one would listen to me. Not the Chief of Police or the D.A. Not even the mayor.

"Isaac Guthrie was a manipulative, greedy bastard who had so much dirt on the movers and shakers in this town that no one would go against him. He knew what the box was worth, and he wanted it. After his death, Magnus stepped into his father's expensive shoes and took up the blackmail schemes his father had started. Magnus even had the audacity to threaten me."

Harry's long pause reeked of annoyance rather than empathy. "When Violet refused to give the box to Isaac, he killed her and your father. Isaac believed she'd stored the box in a safe-deposit box. No one knew, at the time, that Violet had hidden it at the Savannah Preservation Office." Hezekiah glanced at Calum. "You should've seen Isaac's face after he realized Violet had tricked him and he ended up stuck with two kids he didn't want. I don't think I've ever seen a man so angry."

Calum crossed his arms and frowned.

Rose took in deep breaths to prevent herself from hyperventilating. Kade stood next to her now but didn't touch her. Although she'd already considered that Isaac and Magnus were murderers, hearing that it was true was a totally different thing.

"That's the reason for this match?" Kade's low voice held a tremor she'd never heard before. "Magnus is blackmailing you, and you want me to get rid of him?"

"Trying to blackmail me. But after tonight, all this nonsense will be over." Hezekiah checked the clock for the third time. "Once I sell that box and pay Rose, she and Timmy will be set with money forever."

"If you care about Timmy and Rose," Kade said harshly, "why don't you just give them money? Why go through all the effort to buy this box from Rose?"

Hezekiah shook his head as if that was the silliest question ever. "I buy and sell antiquities with a constant movement of money. I don't just have piles of cash in a bank. And I certainly don't have the kind of readily available funds it takes to get a kid a heart transplant. To give Rose any substantial amount of money, I need to sell something she owns. Such as that damn box. In this case, with the Prince's interest in the box, I need something in return. A commission, if you will."

"My getting Magnus out of the way?" Kade asked.

"Yes." Hezekiah studied Kade as one would review a famous sculpture. "Mr. Dolan, can you beat Magnus?"

Kade moved in front of her, as if protecting her from everyone in the room. "Yes."

Except winning meant Kade had to kill another man. He had to kill Magnus.

She felt light-headed and dizzy. Isaac had murdered his own brother and sister-in-law for a stupid box. Magnus had killed his own father for her inheritance. And her family friend, the man who'd helped feed her and Timmy when they were at their most desperate, was a criminal named Hezekiah Usher. A criminal who expected two men to fight to the death.

She clutched Kade's bare arm, shocked at the warmth of his skin. "Kade, please don't do this. I can't lose you."

"Well, isn't that sweet." Magnus came through the metal detector, wearing black gym pants and a tank.

Harry frowned. "You're late, Magnus."

"I don't give a shit, Hezekiah." Magnus chuckled low and glanced at her. "Or should I call you Harry?"

"Please stop talking." Harry pointed to the clock. "It's time."

"What?" Magnus held out his arms as if offering Harry a hug. "No goodbye?"

Harry scoffed. "How about good riddance."

She swallowed, tasting a bitterness that made her gag. How could she be related to Magnus?

Calum moved to the center of the room and did a slow circle so he could meet the gazes of everyone there. "According to Hezekiah, there are no rules to this fight. No referee. This fight ends when one man dies. If Kade wins, Hezekiah will pay Rose for the box."

"Although," Harry added, "I will have to hold her hostage until it is brought to me."

Calum nodded, as if in agreement.

Magnus clapped his hands together and moved into the center of the room. "When I win, I get the box and can do whatever the fuck I want with it."

"Wait," she said to Calum. "That wasn't the deal."

"If Kade loses"—Calum spoke in a clipped voice—"Rose can sell that box to anyone."

Harry fixed his gaze on her. "No one will buy that box from you, Rose. Every dealer in the world knows the Prince wants that box."

"I am not giving my box to Magnus. And if he tries to take it, I'll beat him with it."

Magnus snarled at Rose, "*Try it.*"

"Enough." Calum went toward the control box on the wall, held the switch, and said, "Let's get this fight started."

CHAPTER 26

A hot rush flooded Kade's body, and he nodded at Vane. There was so much emotional shit to process at the moment. But until he fought Magnus—and won—Kade had to keep those emotions buried. He needed that underground well of unprocessed feelings to fuel his rising aggression.

Killing a man was hard work. It required anger, righteousness, and stamina. And if the killing wasn't going to be a crime of passion, or committed during a moment of terror, all of that energy had to come from a secret place deep inside of himself. A dark place where he remembered, over and over again, how Magnus had threatened Rose.

Vane took Rose's arm and guided her toward the metal detector. Kade needed to be sure she could make a quick getaway if things didn't go as planned.

He clapped his taped hands together and began to circle Magnus. Now was the time to fight and win and get the hell away from these people. Away from this world of violence and betrayals. Away from the round, balding man in the tan suit and a pink bow tie who'd been lying to Rose her entire life.

That revelation just added another layer of emotional stress to this shitshow.

Vane positioned himself near Rose and Hezekiah. Magnus stood in the center of the pit, watching Kade as he walked around the perimeter.

"Gentlemen"—Calum's hand rested on the switch—"let the fight begin."

The sudden music blasted Kade's eardrums, and he motioned to turn up the thrash metal.

Magnus smiled while Kade watched and waited. From his dilated pupils and the way Magnus bounced on his toes, he had to be high.

Magnus came in fast. He grabbed Kade around the knees and they hit the ground. Kade's breath rushed from his lungs, but he wrapped his legs around the other man and rolled. Three hits to Magnus's face drove pain up from Kade's wrist to his elbow.

Magnus got in a hard left hook, and Kade's world darkened.

Magnus took advantage and threw off Kade.

He landed on his back. The moment his vision recovered, he rolled to his knees. Magnus sent a roundhouse kick to Kade's face, but he ducked and rolled again. His breaths sounded hoarse and ragged. He planted his fists against the dirt floor as leverage to stand.

Magnus circled again, as if taunting Kade to attack. Sweat poured down Kade's face and back, and his face swelled from that last hit. Still, he got to his feet and stepped back. Now they faced each other, two feet apart. Magnus's chest moved in and out freight-train fast, and he fisted and unfisted his hands. Kade waited for Magnus's right shoulder to drop. The moment Magnus swung a kick toward Kade's stomach, he grabbed Magnus's ankle and twisted, flipping Magnus onto the ground.

Kade tried to stomp on Magnus's balls, but Magnus recovered quickly. His foot connected with Kade's gut, and he fell to his knees. The pain in Kade's stomach made him blink, and he held his breath for a long moment until the agony passed.

Magnus did a crazy wrestling leap onto Kade's head. Kade moved away. Magnus hit the ground and Kade straddled him, throwing hits into Magnus's face before he could recover. One, two, three—

"No!" Rose yelled.

Kade looked up just as Magnus slammed his fist into Kade's nose.

Pain splintered his vision, but he blocked the next hit. Then, without warning, the music stopped, leaving a heavy silence behind.

He moved off and backed away, fists ready. Magnus got to his feet, shaking his head as if to clear his vision. Except it was Kade who wasn't sure if what he saw in front of him was real.

A large, one-eared man that Kade recognized from the club as one of Magnus's goons pressed a nine-mil against Vane's head.

That fucker Antoine held Rose around the waist. Against her throat, he pressed a hunting knife.

ROSE GRABBED onto Antoine's wrist and tried to pull the knife away from her neck. His other arm, around her waist, squeezed so hard she was beginning to feel faint. "*Let. Go.*"

Antoine chuckled in her ear. "Make me."

Kade moved toward her, his body covered in sweat, his eyes wide with fear—until Antoine said, "One more step, and she's dead."

Magnus coughed, and then spat on the dirt ground as he

headed toward Vane. "It's about fucking time you got here. Where is your brother?"

One Ear shook his head. "Not here yet."

"Where is my man?" Harry had moved closer to Calum. "My driver was watching the entrance."

"Dead," One Ear said. "I'd apologize but I don't give a fuck."

"This is not acceptable, Magnus," Harry said sharply. "Not acceptable at all."

Did Harry think that scolding the armed man was going to work?

Magnus's laugh sounded deep and menacing. His face was swelling with bruises, and his nose leaked blood. He wiped his face with his forearm, blood smearing on his arm. Then he pointed at Vane. "On your knees, or Antoine kills Rose."

Vane's face held a thunderous anger. For a moment it seemed like he was going to wrestle One Ear for the gun until Kade nodded at him.

Vane cursed and dropped to his knees. Magnus pulled two weapons out of Vane's back waistband and shoved them into the waistband of his gym pants. Then Magnus took plastic zip ties out of One Ear's back pocket. After securing Vane's wrists and ankles, Magnus pointed Vane's weapon at her. "I want the box, Rose. Or your friend dies."

"Rose?" Kade stood a few yards away, his hands out as if pleading, his chest heaving. "Don't say a word."

She swallowed, except she choked on her own saliva. She couldn't let anyone else get hurt. There was no path out of this. Except for one.

"Don't do it, Rose." Vane's eyes glittered with intent. "Magnus will kill you once he gets that box."

Antoine shifted the knife, and she felt a twinge as the blade's edge moved against her neck. "I'll take you to the box."

"Dammit!" Kade came toward her until Magnus held the gun's barrel an inch from her forehead.

"On your knees, Dolan."

"Fuck you," Kade spat.

Magnus nodded at One Ear who went over to Calum and, with a weapon aimed at his chest, forced him to his knees. Once Calum's hands and ankles were tied with zip ties, One Ear did the same to Hezekiah.

When One Ear got to Kade, he roared like a bull. "*Fuck you.*"

Magnus pressed the weapon to her head until she could feel the edges of the barrel's metal tube. "I'm going to count to three. One. Two—"

Kade's knees hit the dirt. One Ear bound Kade's wrists and then knocked him over to bind his ankles.

"I promise you, Magnus." Kade's voice held a fierceness that made her tremble. "When I find you, I will not be merciful."

Magnus smiled, as if enjoying the game. "Rose, be a good girl and put your hands behind your back."

"Rose!" Kade yelled from his position on his side with his hands tied. "Don't do it."

Magnus used a zip tie to bind her wrists together, and she almost gagged on his stench of male sweat and sweet tobacco. Then he took a weapon out of his waistband and handed it to One Ear. So now the goon had two guns. "No one moves until I return. Got it?"

One Ear focused a weapon on Vane, and the other on Kade. "Yes, sir."

She met Kade's gaze. While she was terrified, the anger in his stare made him appear as if he could destroy an entire nation without any remorse. Without any thought to the innocents who would die as well.

Magnus took her upper arm and dragged her toward the exit. "Don't try anything stupid."

As she walked through the metal detector, the lights went out and she stumbled.

Red emergency lights pulsed on with a loud hum, and Magnus pushed her forward. "If you give me that box, you'll save the others. If you don't, I'll kill all of you."

The force in his voice told her he wasn't kidding.

The last thing she heard as she left Doom was Kade yelling, "Don't listen to him, Rose."

She knew Kade was right, but right now she had no choice. This was her only chance to save everyone she loved.

A FEW MINUTES LATER, she sat in the backseat of a black Mercedes with her hands bound behind her back. Magnus, next to her, pointed the gun in her direction while Antoine turned on the car.

The power in the entire city appeared to be out. In response, drivers were running lights and stop signs and causing gridlock around the garden square.

Antoine turned on the headlights. "Where are we goin', boss?"

Magnus glared at her until she croaked out, "St. John the Baptist Cathedral."

As Antoine pulled into the traffic, she saw a man in a black sweatshirt standing in Johnson Square, near a closed-up coffee cart. The deep hood hid his face, and he stood with his legs spread and arms crossed. His posture appeared so still that Rose shivered under his regard. Next to him, another man wearing a baseball cap leaned against a tree. When the headlights passed by, she saw his cap's white logo signifying the New York Yankees.

Leonato and Sampson.

"Fucking Fianna." Magnus hit the seat in front of him with his fist.

Antoine glanced in the rearview mirror as they inched forward in traffic. "How did they find us?"

"Who the fuck knows." Magnus turned to look out the back window. "They may be tracking Rose."

Her throat was so dry she could barely speak, and she bit her lower lip. She'd forgotten that her phone was still in her backpack inside of Doom. "My burner phone is turned off. So they can't be tracking me. Maybe they're tracking you."

"You are an idiot." Magnus scoffed and faced forward again. "The Fianna can track any phone. Including turned-off burner phones."

She closed her eyes and took a deep breath. Was that how Leonato tracked her to the apartment over Juliet's Lily, and then to Doom? Had she betrayed everyone she cared about, including Harry, because—for the briefest moment—she'd been afraid to trust Kade completely?

When they turned a corner, she opened her eyes and glanced toward Johnson Square. Both of the warriors had disappeared.

While that was scary and strange, she had another, larger problem.

She'd not told Kade where she'd hidden the box. Although he'd asked her not to tell him, she should have trusted that he'd never betray her, even if he didn't believe it himself. And that decision, most likely, was going to get her killed.

CHAPTER 27

Kade was so angry with himself, he could kill something. Except the something he wanted to kill had kidnapped the woman he loved while he was bound, waiting to be saved.

The red emergency lights buzzed, sending eerie shadows throughout the room.

One Ear, Magnus's guard, walked around with both weapons drawn.

Kade whispered, "Vane—"

"Shut the fuck up!" One Ear kicked Kade, and he rolled away to protect himself.

He had to figure a way out of this before Magnus hurt Rose. Because Kade had no doubt that once Rose handed over that fucking box, Magnus would shoot her.

When One Ear moved toward Calum and Hezekiah, Kade shimmied in Vane's direction.

Vane shifted his large body, also bound at the wrists and ankles, just as a loud gunshot blew through the room.

One Ear screamed and fell to the floor with a huge thud. He'd been shot in the leg and now clutched his thigh as he yelled like a stuck pig. The gunman ran into the room, hurried over to One Ear, and pistol-whipped him until he blacked out.

When the gunman straightened, he scanned the room with his weapon ready, and said, "Calum? What the fuck happened?"

Kade blew out a breath, closed his eyes, and said a silent prayer. *Thank you, Nate Walker.*

ROSE SHIFTED to look through the car's back window.

The city was still blacked out, and traffic was terrible. Despite the late hour, cars and trucks sped through intersections without working traffic lights. They'd even had a few scary incidents where Antoine had had to hit the gas to avoid getting T-boned.

She took a few deep breaths to even out her beating heart and sat forward again. The passing city appeared dark despite the number of cars on the road. Because the power hadn't come back on yet, the city's police helicopters had been deployed. They hovered overhead with their searchlights bouncing off the shiny streets. It had rained while they'd been in Doom and was still drizzling.

Hopefully the electricity would be fixed quickly, before the looting began. Unlike that night, over a week ago, when the power had been out for over twelve hours and criminals had taken over the streets.

She closed her eyes and made sure to breathe through her mouth so she wouldn't have to smell Magnus's sweet tobacco stench. So many questions swirled in her head, but one stood out. "Magnus, when did you learn that Harry was Hezekiah Usher?"

"After your parents' deaths."

She opened her eyes and glanced at him.

Magnus's dark gaze glittered in the passing headlights. "Isaac introduced me to Hezekiah at your parents' funerals. Hezekiah was your father's college roommate and best friend." Magnus shifted in his seat and checked his watch. "Hezekiah is from seriously old money, but he was never popular—until he met your father. Your father, captain of Yale's rowing team, gave Hezekiah the social clout his money couldn't buy."

She moved her shoulder to wipe her damp cheek. "Did you know Isaac killed my parents?"

"Not until my father's death nine months ago when I went through his papers. I did discover, though, that your mother wasn't supposed to be in the car that night." Magnus glanced at her. "I found correspondence between Hezekiah and Isaac that made it sound as if killing your father was Hezekiah's idea."

The blood rushed to her heart, and she felt faint. "That's not what Harry said."

Magnus chuckled under his breath. "Everyone lies, Rose. Including your lover, Kade. Or haven't you figured that out yet?"

"Harry—I mean Hezekiah—wouldn't kill my father. My parents were going to give him the box."

"Not exactly. Your mother believed the box belonged to Button Gwinnett and hoped that Hezekiah could help her open it. But she wasn't just going to give it to him."

Rose stared out the window again. She didn't remember that, but she'd also been a teenager who'd paid little attention to what the adults around her were doing. "So the box can be opened?"

"It's a puzzle box." The irritation in his voice matched his eye roll. "It can be opened if you know how to solve the puzzle."

Antoine slammed on the brakes to avoid hitting another car going through an intersection. Without stoplights, driving had become a free-for-all. Suddenly, three police cars drove by and parked in the center of the road. "The cops are setting up roadblocks."

Magnus hit the seat in front of him. "Hurry up!"

"Yes, boss." Antoine made a right turn and had to swerve out of the way of a stalled utility truck.

She wriggled her hands, trying to force blood to flow to stop the tingling. "Magnus, do you know what is in the box?"

Magnus rubbed his forehead and sighed, as if annoyed. "Isaac believed the box held Button Gwinnett's will. Since Hezekiah was in love with your mother, the plan was to kill your father so Hezekiah could win your mother for himself. Then, once Hezekiah got the box and sold the will, he'd split the proceeds with Isaac. Hezekiah and Isaac would end up with more money than they could ever spend, and Hezekiah would secure your mother's love."

Rose scoffed. "My mother never would have married Harry—I mean Hezekiah."

Magnus nodded. "I agree. Hezekiah was delusional if he believed your mother would run into his arms after the death of her husband."

Antoine paused at a four-way stop and glanced in the rear-view mirror. From the red and blue flashing lights coming from every direction, it appeared as if the authorities were shutting down all the main roads throughout the city. "Since when is someone's will worth money?"

"Since the signature on the will is worth almost as much Julius Caesar's, and even more than William Shakespeare's." Magnus pointed left. "Go around the square. We'll have to take one-way alleys."

She inhaled sharply. She'd never heard that story and wasn't sure she believed it. After all, Magnus was a brilliant liar.

As Antoine turned left, she tried to move her arms. They

were going numb, and a cramp was forming between her shoulder blades. Since asking questions helped keep her focused, she said, "Why is Button Gwinnett's signature worth so much money?"

Magnus shook his head as if she were a toddler. "It's worth a fortune because there are only fifty-one of his signatures in circulation. So people who like to collect the signatures of every man who signed the Declaration of Independence will pay an exorbitant fee for Gwinnett's signature to complete their sets."

"*Whoa.*" Antoine pulled to the side of the road to let two fire trucks pass by. "And I've never heard of this Gwinnett guy."

"That does not surprise me," Magnus muttered beneath his breath. "I just wish Deke had been as ignorant."

She blew stray hairs out of her face. "Why did Deke betray you?"

"Because he was a greedy fucker." Magnus hit the seat in front of him again. "Deke was supposed to bring me the box after he stole it from the Savannah Preservation Office. Except he figured out the situation and contacted Hezekiah on his own."

"So you killed him?"

"Nope." Magnus checked his cell phone, cursed, and then shoved it into his back pocket. Cell service was probably still down. "Deke got himself killed all on his own."

She shifted in her seat again and turned toward the window. Had her mother really believed that the box held Gwinnett's signature? If so, it would explain why so many people wanted the box. And why her parents had been murdered.

Antoine turned into a narrow alley, despite the fact they were going against the one-way sign. When they emerged, the cathedral stood a hundred yards away, its white bell towers disappearing into the dark, cloudy sky. From the helicopters circling overhead, and the sirens echoing throughout the area, she doubted the power would return tonight.

"Magnus?" She coughed to clear her throat. "Why did Deke want me to be the box's courier?"

Magnus turned to look through the back window. Red and blue lights pulsed at the end of the alley, and he let a few curses fly before saying, "Because Hezekiah required a courier, and Deke wanted to fuck you. It's as simple as that."

She frowned and leaned her head against the glass. "And the fight between you and Kade? Was that Hezekiah's doing?"

She suddenly realized she'd stopped thinking about him as Harry. It was as if her family friend had never truly existed.

Antoine laughed out loud. "Hezekiah wanted Magnus dead because he was blackmailing him."

"Shut the fuck up and find us a place to park," Magnus snarled. "Someplace the cops won't notice."

She looked at Magnus. Although Hezekiah had admitted his plan back at Doom, she needed to be sure of the details. "You're blackmailing Hezekiah because you have proof he was involved in my parents' deaths. So Hezekiah decided to have Kade kill you in a death match?"

"Yes. That was Hezekiah's plan." Magnus shrugged. "So I changed it."

"You ended the fight early because..." She lowered her voice to whisper, "you were afraid you were going to lose?"

Magnus growled and swung his hand holding the gun. Before she could move, he hit her forehead. Pain exploded behind her eyes, and everything went black.

KADE TOOK in deep breaths until he centered his breathing and could evaluate the situation.

Nate had cut Kade's zip ties first. Then, while Kade freed Vane, Calum, and Hezekiah, Nate grabbed the first aid kit from the Fighter's Hole. Nate seemed concerned about keeping One Ear alive and was wrapping up his leg. The bullet had only grazed the guard, but Nate said he didn't want to take chances.

Although Nate did talk while he played nurse. "Once I left Rose with you, Calum, I headed toward the gym. But as I crossed the street, I noticed an SUV driven by one of the thugs who used to frequent the club. He had a jagged scar over his left eye and was watching Rose."

"One Ear's brother," Kade said as he helped Calum up.

Calum said to Nate, "They both work for a local criminal named Magnus Guthrie."

Nate frowned as he cleaned up the bloody bandages. "I followed this man on my bike for a few blocks and watched him park behind the Juliet's Lily truck. I was surprised when he got out of his vehicle carrying a weapon. And even more surprised when I saw Samantha sitting in the truck."

Vane collected the two weapons that One Ear had dropped after being shot. "Is Samantha alright?"

"Yes." Nate stood, holding a small trash bag filled with used medical supplies. One Ear lay on the floor, not moving due to the beating Nate had given him. At least he wasn't going to bleed out on the pit's floor. "For the moment."

Vane checked the clips of both weapons and emptied the chambers. "What does that mean?"

"It means, brother, that I had to knock out the scarred guy and lock him in the trunk of his own SUV before he hurt Samantha. Then, when I confronted Samantha, she told me *everything* that has been going on for the past few days. She drove me here and showed me how to get into this place. Now she's safe in the Juliet's Lily truck, parked nearby, and tending to another man who'd been knocked out near the entrance."

"My driver." Hezekiah straightened his suit jacket. "He's not dead?"

"Not yet," Nate said.

"Nate." Kade cleared his voice. "Did you see two men take Rose? They may have put her in a car and driven away."

Nate shook his head. "But with the entire city's power and cell service down, the craziness is picking up outside."

Shit. Kade hadn't realized that the power was out everywhere. "We need to find Rose before she gives Magnus that box. Once Magnus has what he wants, he will kill her."

"Do you have any idea where she hid the box?" Calum asked.

"No." Kade ran his hands over his head and clasped them behind his neck. "I don't even know where to begin."

Vane reloaded the weapons. "I'll search Rage of Angels."

"Thanks." Kade inhaled deeply and grabbed control of his emotions. "Calum, can you take Samantha, Hezekiah, and his driver to Prideaux House?"

Calum nodded. "We'll wait for you and Rose there."

"My driver may need medical attention," Hezekiah said.

Calum took some water bottles from a case on the floor near the metal detector. As he handed everyone a bottle, he said, "I'll call Doc Bennett. He'll check out anyone who needs help."

"Nate?" Kade asked. "I know you're not a part of this, but someone needs to stay here with One Ear. And we can't leave his brother in the trunk of his SUV forever. We can deal with them once I find Rose."

Because Kade was going to find Rose. And then destroy Magnus.

"Actually," Nate glanced at Calum. "Before the city's power went out, I spoke with Detective Garza. He'll be here soon. He'll help with his mess." Nate waved an arm toward One Ear who'd begun to moan and roll around.

Fuck. Kade squeezed the bridge of his nose. "You called a cop?"

"Don't worry, Kade." Calum came over and touched his shoulder. "I'll tell Garza and Nate what I can. Garza will know what to do and how to keep this quiet. Can you trust us?"

It wasn't so much a matter of trust as it was asking for help. Could Kade ask these men to help him in this situation? Especially when the Fianna were involved?

Hell, the last time he'd accepted anyone's help he'd ended up swearing the rest of his life to an ancient cult of hardcore assassins.

He dropped his hand and nodded. "Tell Garza and Nate whatever you think is necessary." Kade found his gym bag against the wall and grabbed a T-shirt. After stripping off his tank, he pulled the shirt over his head. Then he stripped off his shorts and yanked on his jeans.

Fuck modesty.

Vane shoved his weapon in his back waistband and covered it with his jacket. "Where are you going to search?"

Kade tugged on his socks and boots and tied them. "I'm going to Rose's house. She may have left a clue there."

When he was ready, Vane handed him the other loaded weapon. He slipped it into his back waistband. Then he took the knife out of his bag and shoved it into his boot. He always felt so much more at ease when he was armed.

Vane gripped Kade's shoulder. "After checking the club, I'll meet you at Rose's house."

"Thanks."

Once all the men knew what to do, Kade and Vane left Doom. Nate followed them outside to wait for Detective Garza.

Kade wished he had a vehicle until he saw the chaos in the streets. Roadblocks had been set up, cars were snarled in gridlock, and helicopters with searchlights whirred overhead.

Nate handed him a small key. "My bike is locked up across the street."

"Thanks." Kade slipped the key into his pocket. He'd heard gossip around the gym that Nate didn't drive, but since the brother didn't volunteer why, Kade didn't ask. Yet, he was grateful. A bike would get him across town in a third of the time, even with the roadblocks. Except even he wasn't going anywhere until the fire trucks, with blaring sirens, could make it down the traffic-clogged street.

"I'll check on Samantha," Nate said to Vane. "She's parked near where I'm meeting Garza. I'll make sure Calum gets her home safely."

"Thanks," Vane said.

Kade fisted and unfisted his hands. He was relieved Samantha was okay. It had never occurred to him that Magnus would target her. But after the incident at the hospital earlier that day, Kade should have realized. Another epic failure.

Nate turned to leave when he stopped, turned back, and said, "Vane. I know what you've been doing."

Vane shrugged and stared at the ground.

"I'm still our unit's Executive Officer," Nate said. "Since part of my job is to protect you and the other men, I'm not going to say anything to anyone about your extracurricular activities. Including Kells."

Vane looked up, his eyes wide.

"As long as you tell me the entire truth." Nate nodded at Kade. "Once this is over, of course." Without waiting for a response, Nate headed for the corner to wait for Garza.

"Kade, I'll meet you at Rose's as soon as I can." Vane turned and ran in the opposite direction from Nate.

The moment the fire trucks broke free, Kade hurried across the street and unlocked the bike. The humid air tinged with the scents of rain, gardenias, and mold smelled like failure. No, it smelled like death.

CHAPTER 28

Rose stumbled on the curb near the side entrance to the cathedral, across the street from her house. The traffic in this part of the city had lessened, possibly due to all the roadblocks being set up. Sirens rang in the distance, and lights from the circling helicopters spun around her.

Her head ached, and her vision blurred. Magnus had woken her up by pouring water on her face and slapping her. Now he yanked her arm as he dragged her toward the side entrance of the church. The pain in her shoulder brought tears to her eyes, and she tried to wipe her face on her arm.

Antoine, who'd walked ahead, grabbed the doorknob. "It's locked."

"There's also an alarm and security cameras." She didn't mention they wouldn't work during a blackout.

"The city's power is down, so the alarms and cameras are off as well." Magnus pressed his weapon against her side. "How do we get in?"

She nodded to the planting beds showcasing thorny roses, gardenias, and pots of wild lavender. "There's a path behind those rose and honeysuckle bushes. It takes you to the bell tower's utility door."

Each bell tower had a disguised door for workmen to use so they wouldn't have to tramp through the church.

"Hold her," Magnus ordered Antoine.

Antoine took her arm while Magnus pushed his way through the bushes toward a narrow path that led to a door. "Fuck."

She smiled, grateful for the lack of light. "Watch out for rose thorns."

Antoine slammed a fist into her stomach. She landed on her knees, where she fell forward until her forehead hit the sidewalk. Every breath hurt, and the tears she'd been holding back flowed down her cheeks.

"Rose?" Magnus said from behind the plants. "Where is the fucking key?"

The spasms throughout her body came in waves, and she couldn't form words.

Antoine squeezed her arm and dragged her to her feet. "Where is the key?"

She whimpered and closed her eyes. Shallow breaths helped with the pain but made her light-headed. "Around my neck."

She'd taken it from her house before hiding the box.

Antoine pulled the cord from beneath her T-shirt and over her head. "Got it," he said in a louder voice so Magnus could hear.

"Bring her here."

Antoine pushed Rose, and she opened her eyes before she fell again. A minute later, she stood in between the men and the door to the bell tower. She nodded at the ornamental molding of stars and roses around the doorframe. Most of the stars had six points, but one had eight. "The keyhole is behind the eight-pointed star."

Magnus shoved his weapon in his waistband, unlocked the latch, and the door swung open on creaky hinges. "How did you figure this out?"

"It's a long story." She had no intention of telling him it was how Timmy had slipped in and out of the church unnoticed for so long before getting caught.

Before she stepped into the darkness, she heard a loud *meow*.

King George ran past Magnus and disappeared beneath the rosebushes. She wasn't surprised the cat ran away. King George's abandonment was probably due to the fact she'd allowed Kade into the house.

Antoine shoved Rose into the small room and took a penlight out of his back pocket. The circular area was eight feet in diameter with a concrete floor. It still had the original wooden stairs that spiraled up to the top of the spire where the bell used to hang.

She inched her way toward the door leading into the church until Magnus threw her against the wall. Since Antoine's light wasn't powerful enough in the intense darkness, he and Antoine appeared as dangerously armed shadows.

"Where is it?" Magnus demanded.

She coughed and turned away. Unfortunately, the door to the main church was behind Magnus.

Magnus held her throat with both hands and squeezed.

She couldn't fight him because of her bound hands. Panic tightened her chest, and her vision wavered.

"She can't talk if you're choking her," Antoine said.

Magnus tossed her onto the ground and pointed his gun at her head. "If you don't help me, I'll kill you right now."

"Everyone will hear the gunshot." Her voice sounded hoarse and scratchy, and she wished she could drink some water.

Antoine handed something to Magnus. When he screwed it onto the gun's barrel, she realized it was a suppressor.

She pressed her shoulder against the wall to help herself stand. "It's upstairs. Where the bell used to be."

Both men looked up. The stairs spiraled into the black space above.

Magnus motioned to Antoine. "Use your light to lead us. I'll follow Rose. And remember"—he pointed the weapon at her face—"I don't give a shit if you live or die."

She nodded. There was nothing else to say, because he spoke the truth.

Antoine took the first step with the light, and Magnus motioned for her to go next.

"I need to hold on to the handrail," she said. "Can you unbind me?"

Magnus studied the narrow wooden staircase. Then he took out a knife and cut the plastic zip tie around her wrists.

She rubbed her wrists as the blood rushed back into her hands, leaving behind a stinging sensation. Then she zipped up her sweatshirt. She wasn't cold, she just needed the security and warmth her mother's sweatshirt offered.

"Let's go." Magnus pressed the barrel against her back. "Remember, if we don't return to Doom with that box, everyone you love will die."

She gripped the handrail and took the first step toward her own death.

Twenty minutes later, Kade parked Nate's bike behind Rose's house.

He wasn't surprised the city's power grid was still down. Although he was surprised the streets in this part of the city were quiet. He'd just dodged a gauntlet of roadblocks, police chases, and throngs of people on every corner.

Yet here, near the cathedral, things were different. It *felt* different. The quiet wasn't peaceful so much as heavy. Like this part of the city was holding its breath, waiting for some disaster to strike.

The clouds separated, allowing some moonlight to emerge. The cemetery edging her backyard looked creepier than usual. He let himself in through the unlocked kitchen door and hit the switch, forgetting for a moment that the power was out. King George hissed, and Kade stepped back. Except the cat wound around his feet instead of trying to claw out his eyes.

When he couldn't find the flashlight he'd seen earlier in a kitchen drawer, he scoured the house until finding one in a hall closet. He worked his way through the house, searching for clues. It didn't take long because she had few belongings and even fewer places to hide things. Even though he hated invading her privacy, he went through her dresser drawers and her desk in the living room.

It didn't help that the cat followed him and scratched at his heels.

He returned to the kitchen and got a glass of water. He leaned his hip against the counter while he swung the light around the room. He was looking for clues that would tell him where she'd hidden that box.

King George stood on his back legs and scratched at Kade's pants when the house phone on the kitchen counter rang. It startled him because the power was out—until he remembered it was a landline.

He picked it up on the third ring. "Yes?"

"Hello?" The young man's voice sounded wobbly, like he'd been crying. "Rose?"

"No, Timmy." Kade cleared his throat and softened his voice. "This is Kade Dolan. Are you okay?"

"Yes." Timmy sniffled. "Miss Samantha never showed up with my sister. I've been trying to call her cell phone, but it doesn't work. The power is out everywhere. I don't want her to be scared."

Although Kade didn't know a lot about kids, he remembered being one himself. And he remembered how he used to hide his fear from his brothers. "I'm looking for her too. But I'm sure she's all right. Do you have power at the hospital?"

"My machines and the phone in my room work. But the lights in the hallway are red and flashy." Timmy sniffled. "Do you know when my sister is coming to get me?"

"No." Kade sat in a kitchen chair. The cat jumped onto his lap and dug his claws into Kade's thighs. He winced. "Are you okay staying there until I can find Rose?"

"Yes. My pirate friend already checked on me. He's scary looking, but he's nice to us. He always brings all the kids our favorite flavors. Except he didn't bring ice cream this time."

"Does he wear a white eye patch?" Rose had mentioned the pirate guy who delivered ice cream to the kids, and Kade was annoyed at himself that he hadn't made the connection sooner.

"Yes." Timmy sniffled again. "He said his name is Leo. He asked me if I've seen Rose tonight, but I haven't. Then the power went out, and I got scared."

"Everything will be okay. Try not to worry."

"Do you think Magnus will come back? He scares me too."

"No." Kade moved the cat off his lap and stood. He was too restless to sit. "I'll call you once I find Rose."

"Promise?"

He was in no position to make any promises. Still, he said,

"I swear that Magnus will never hurt you again, and I will find and protect your sister."

Timmy exhaled loudly. "Okay. Make sure that Rose feeds King George on time. He gets cranky if he doesn't get fed."

King George looked up at Kade with an unwavering stare.

"I will. I think your cat has multiple personalities."

"He has three. He wants to love you, kill you, or lead you back to his home."

Kade frowned at the cat. "His home?"

"The home where I found him. The home he loves. The bell tower."

Kade turned his attention to the hooks near the back door. The church key was missing. "Thanks, Timmy. Now go back to bed, and I'll be in touch."

Kade threw food into King George's bowl and ran out.

Across the street, the cathedral's twin spires reached through the clouds into the dark sky. He focused on the bell towers. For the briefest moment, in the highest window of the left tower, he thought he saw... a light.

Someone whistled. A moment later, he met Vane on the small strip of grass next to the church.

"I found nothing at the club," Vane said.

Kade repeated his conversation with Timmy and pointed to the cathedral's bell tower.

When more splashes of light flickered, Vane let out another whistle. "You think—"

"I do." Kade took out his weapon and led the way. "Let's go."

CHAPTER 29

When Rose lost count of how many turns of the stairs she'd taken, her knees wobbled, and she rested against the wooden railing.

She was amazed that Timmy used to make this climb daily to feed King George. Except Timmy was an energetic boy when not stuck in the hospital.

Magnus poked her in the back with his weapon. "Move."

She grabbed the rail and kept going. Her eyes had adjusted to the low light that came from Antoine's penlight ahead of her. But she still had to feel her way along each step. It was probably a good thing she couldn't see to the ground. The last thing she needed was an episode of vertigo.

When she reached another landing, her breath caught in her throat. Was the air thinner up here? Or was she on the verge of a panic attack?

The gun against her back told her that neither altitude sickness nor a major freak-out would deter Magnus from claiming her box.

Finally, she found Antoine on a six-foot-square wooden landing attached to the tower on two sides. The other two sides had four-foot-long wooden railings to prevent one from falling down to the concrete floor below. Workmen had left piles of wood and bricks and other construction debris on the landing, including crates filled with tools.

Windows on all four sides offered views of the entire city, and she headed for the closest window that overlooked the river. Unfortunately, the city was still dark, and the window didn't open. She desperately needed a dose of fresh air to help clear her head. The aroma of freshly cut pine, mixed with damp and mold, irritated her nose. She sneezed. Twice.

"The city's power is still out," Antoine said to Magnus.

Magnus muttered, "Fucking Fianna."

Antoine moved next to Rose and peered out of the window. "The Fianna are responsible?" he asked.

"Yes. They've been messing with the power for weeks."

Antoine snorted. "Why?"

"It's just something they do before a big operation goes down. Like a warning shot across a bow." Magnus grabbed her shoulder and spun her around. He pressed the gun to her stomach. "Where is the box?"

Antoine gripped the window frame and closed his eyes. "I don't like heights."

Magnus cursed and placed his phone, with the flashlight app, on the floor so the light shone up on them. "Go downstairs and make sure no one comes up."

Once Antoine left, the phone's light emphasized Magnus's bone structure, giving him a skeletal look. Like a Jolly Roger pirate flag. "Where is it?"

If she told him, he'd kill her. But what would buying time get her? Everyone she loved was in danger, and she was alone in this. She'd been so afraid to trust Kade, she hadn't told him where she'd hidden the box. And she'd led the Fianna directly to Doom.

Now Kade, even if he could get away from One Ear and the Fianna, had no way to find her.

She moved toward the north window and pointed to one of the construction crates against the wall. "It's in this box."

Magnus kept his gun steady and nodded. "Give it to me."

"It's filled with tools." She bit her lower lip. "Everything in there is heavy. I can't—"

"Don't play the fucking girl card." Magnus pulled back the slide on the gun and raised it to her face. "I want it now."

She took a deep breath to steady her racing heart and knelt in front of the two-foot-high crate. Her knees ached on the plank floor. She lifted the lid, turned her head, and pretended to sneeze. As she did so, she surreptitiously lifted a hammer out and hid it behind the bin. One by one, she took out the rest of the tools and placed them on the ground between her and Magnus. She grunted and groaned with each one, although they weren't that heavy.

Once all the tools were on the floor, she said, "The box is in the bottom."

Magnus shook his head as if she were an exasperating teenager. "Get it."

She reached in, paused, and used her most dramatic, breathless voice to say, "It's not here."

Before Magnus could respond, a shot rang out downstairs.

Magnus leaned over the railing and yelled, "Antoine?"

"Rose?" Kade's voice echoed throughout the tower.

"Up here!" She grabbed the hammer and stood, keeping the tool behind her back.

Magnus stomped over and shone the light in the bin. When he saw it was empty, he pistol whipped her. Pain shot through her shoulder, and she fell to the ground. Her knees hit the hard wood, and she rolled onto her side. She curled up, making sure to keep the hammer beneath her body.

"Where is it?" His voice sounded brutal and violent and angry.

"I don't know." She tightened her grip on the handle. "It was here. I swear!"

"Bullshit." He dragged her to her feet and shook her until she opened her eyes.

Once she had a solid footing, she swung the hammer and clipped him on the shoulder.

His weapon fell to the ground. "Bitch!"

He threw her forward, and her head hit the edge of the bin. She fell onto her back, her vision splintering in the faint light. The hammer slid across the platform.

"Rose!" Kade's voice sounded closer but still so far away. "I'm coming!"

When she saw the gun near the bin, she kicked it. The weapon skidded across the floor and off the platform. A few moments later, it hit the concrete floor below. A loud clanging sound echoed throughout the bell tower.

Magnus grabbed her shirt and pulled her up. "Give me that box!"

Rose clutched his wrist, but Magnus dropped her. When her head hit the floor again, the dim light faded in and out. She tasted the tang of blood and started to gag.

Magnus picked up the hammer and held it close to her head. "Where. Is. My. Box?"

"Release her." Kade's order came from the shadows behind Magnus.

Magnus turned, and she scooted away, pressing herself against the wall.

"Rose!" Kade tossed her a flashlight and she pointed it at Magnus.

Magnus stood in front of her, still holding the hammer but facing Kade.

Kade lunged, taking Magnus down at the knees. They hit

the landing, and the wooden structure groaned in protest. The men threw fists, and their fight took up the entire space.

Keeping the light on Magnus so Kade could see, she scooted away until she reached the open edge, protected only by a wooden railing held up with intermittent posts. Beneath her free hand, she felt the board she'd loosened earlier that day.

Somehow, the men were upright. Kade threw punch after punch. Magnus dodged and swung the hammer. Finally, Kade threw himself on top of Magnus, and they rolled toward the open edge of the platform. The hammer flew off the ledge. A few seconds later, it crashed on the floor. The metal head hitting the concrete floor rang throughout the dark space.

Kade straddled Magnus, and Kade's fists cracked Magnus's jaw. But Magnus responded with a huge surge of strength and tossed Kade off.

Magnus stood near the edge, his massive chest heaving, his hands fisting. "Ready to concede, Dolan? You should do it quickly because Remiel Marigny is coming. And he will destroy you."

Kade used the railing to stand. "*Never.*"

Magnus reached behind his back and pulled his switchblade.

"He has a knife!" she yelled.

Kade took a step back, and she realized he had a knife as well.

As the men watched each other, she placed the flashlight on the floor, picked up the board, and stood in the shadows. The men were completely focused on each other. The moment Magnus moved forward with the blade, she swung the board. It hit his temple. He fell onto his back and grabbed her ankle.

She dropped the board and landed on her hip. She tried to kick him away, but he just squeezed her ankle tighter.

Kade sliced his knife across Magnus's hand that gripped

her ankle. Magnus yelled and released her. She kicked him, but he scrambled up again.

He raged toward Kade, knife out.

She found the board and swung again, hitting Magnus's legs. He tipped sideways and fell against the railing.

She heard the wood splinter before the railing broke. Magnus grabbed a broken railing post, but the force of his fall sent his legs over the edge. Now Magnus's body hung over the side while he clung with one hand to a splintered piece of pine.

Kade rolled onto his stomach and gripped Magnus's wrist. "Stop swinging your legs."

She lay next to Kade and reached down as well, except she couldn't grab Magnus's free hand. Even in the dim light, she could tell that his free hand had been badly cut by Kade's knife.

Magnus looked at her, his eyes narrow, looking almost resigned. "Kade will never belong to you. He's spoken for."

"Magnus!" Kade's arm strained against the other man's weight. "Give me your other hand."

Magnus reached up and missed Kade's grasp, leaving behind a bloody smear. On the second attempt, Magnus gripped one of the vertical posts near Rose.

"Release him." Leonato appeared on the stairs behind them.

"Help him." She pointed at Magnus. While her cousin was a monster who'd tried to kill her, she didn't want to be responsible for his death. She wasn't sure if she could live with that. Her goal in life was to heal people, not commit murder.

Magnus's hand in Kade's grip slipped a bit more, and she was sure, even in the dim light, that Magnus was crying.

Leonato stepped closer. "'Tis always unfortunate when necessary evils, from which there can be no evasion, become inevitable."

She glanced up at the warrior, who took no action to help them. "We don't need your lectures."

Especially lectures she didn't understand.

"As you wish, Lady Tempest." Leonato stepped over Rose's body and kicked Magnus's wounded hand where he clung to the vertical post.

"Ahh!" Magnus released the post and now was held by Kade's strength alone.

"Give me your other hand!" Kade ordered Magnus.

Magnus reached up just as Leonato dropped a brick on Magnus's head.

Magnus screamed and let go.

Rose covered her ears, but when she heard the body hitting the concrete below, she screamed.

CHAPTER 30

Kade had no idea how long he lay on the landing, half his body over the edge. Although he couldn't see the ground, he'd heard Magnus's body hit the stone floor.

Kade knew he should check on Magnus, to see if he was still alive and needed medical help. But Kade's gut told him Magnus was gone. No one could survive that kind of fall.

"Kade?" Rose knelt next to him and touched his shoulder. "Are you all right?"

He sat up, found his flashlight near a crate, and dragged her into his arms. Everything sounded echoey, as if he were underwater.

Of course that fucker Leonato had disappeared. Probably to clean up the Magnus mess downstairs. But right now, Kade didn't care. Didn't care about Magnus's death. Didn't care about Leonato's murderous bullshit. Didn't care that his clothes were covered in sawdust or that his mouth had filled with blood. All he cared about was holding Rose in his arms. All he cared about was that Rose was alive.

She wrapped her arms around his waist. "What did

Leonato mean when he said, "'Tis always unfortunate when necessary evils, from which there can be no evasion, become inevitable'?"

Kade shifted until his back hit the wall and they were away from the edge of the platform. A phone lay nearby, with a weak flashlight app, offering some more light. With his legs stretched out, she curled up next to him. Her erratic breathing had slowed, but her body shook from the adrenaline withdrawal. He wasn't sure of Leonato's meaning, but he could take an educated guess.

"I think Leonato was referring to murderous deeds that must be performed in order to rebalance the world. The Fianna believe their punishments are a form of justice when those in charge look the other way."

She touched his face until he met her gaze. "Leonato acted as judge and jury?"

"Essentially, yes." Kade smoothed her hair away from her face and kissed her forehead. "It also means that all of the Fianna's deeds—even their deadly ones—are performed in service of their greater goals. Whatever they may be."

She shivered, and he held her against his chest.

"Hey." Vane came onto the landing. His penlight threw shadows that obscured his lower body. "Magnus is dead."

Kade trailed his fingers up and down her back. Even through her sweatshirt, he felt her shiver. Probably a delayed reaction to the adrenaline. "Antoine?"

Vane came over and helped them stand. Then he picked up the phone and turned it off. "Antoine ran through the church and disappeared. I was going to run after him, but Leonato appeared and said Antoine wasn't worth it. At least I think that's what the warrior meant. It sounded more like the 'villain will be done for.' Or something equally strange."

Once Kade and Rose were upright, Kade shoved the

phone into the back pocket of Rose's jeans and croaked out, "Thanks. I owe you, brother."

Vane shrugged and turned away, as if not used to being thanked. His flashlight's beam landed on the space on the floor where Rose had pulled up the plank.

She retrieved the box still in the drawstring bag and held it against her chest. "What about Magnus's body?"

Kade took the drawstring bag from her so she could walk downstairs unheeded. "Leonato has backup that will take care of Magnus."

"Leonato and his buddies are downstairs now." Vane's voice carried an unusual calmness, as if the Fianna cleaning up a dead body was an everyday occurrence. While Kade didn't know what the former Green Beret had seen and done over the years, Kade could guess.

"Oh." Rose coughed. "I'm not sure I want to know what they'll do with him."

Kade brushed stray hairs behind her ear. He was clueless about what else to say, because he wasn't sure what the Prince would do with Magnus's body. Except that, even in death, Magnus would serve the Fianna's agenda.

"And your escape plan?" Vane asked.

Kade slipped the bag's strings over his shoulders. The weight of the box pressed against his back. "With Leonato on my ass, I'll have to think of something else."

"Excuse me?" Rose's eyes widened, and her glance bounced between Kade and Vane.

Kade dropped a quick kiss on her lips. "I—" A whistle from downstairs—probably from Leonato—interrupted Kade, and his body stiffened. "We need to leave before Leonato decides to recruit Vane, too."

Vane smirked and went downstairs.

Kade handed Rose his flashlight. Her hand shook, scattering light. The shadows exposed the hollows of her face and the furrows in her brow. "I'm worried about what happens next. How are we going to get away?"

"I have a plan." He took her face between his palms and kissed her deeply. When he lifted his head, he whispered, "I love you, Rose. I just need you to know that."

With her free hand, she covered his hand still pressed against her face. Her trembling lips told him she struggled with her own emotions.

That was okay with him because he knew the truth. She loved him, even if she couldn't admit it yet. "It's time to give Hezekiah the box and get your money."

Only then can I save you.

A FEW MINUTES LATER, when they reached the first floor, Kade handed Rose the drawstring bag and paused.

Leonato stood alone in the center of the area, arms crossed. The acrid smell of bleach permeated the air. Magnus's body had been removed and the concrete cleaned. One of the benefits of having a Fianna warrior—with contacts and money to make difficult situations go away—on your side. And Kade was grateful. He'd seen terrible things in combat, and those images still haunted him. He'd never want that for Rose.

Without a word, Leonato led them through the bell tower door and across the street toward Rose's house. The power was out, the streets remained empty, and the air felt still. Almost expectant, like waiting to administer a judgment.

Maybe he felt that way because he'd just fought a literal battle to the death, and there was no body. One could say that Magnus's death hadn't happened.

This was how the Fianna managed to function in secret with no ramifications or remorse. With the same ruthlessness and lack of emotion that Leonato displayed.

And Kade would have to become like Leonato to survive.

Kade clutched Rose's hand. Although he prayed he wouldn't have to become like Leonato, Kade knew the truth. The Fianna expected far more than this from their warriors. The Fianna required all a man had to give. The Fianna demanded complete obedience, including a tithe that stripped a man of his soul.

For almost three years, he'd worried and wondered about what his tithe would be and whether he had anything worth giving up. Now, as Rose squeezed his hand, he realized he had everything in the world to lose.

Something the Prince was aware of, thanks to Kade's own actions over the last few days.

Leonato paused on the sidewalk, and Kade saw at least ten warriors hiding in the shadows. One stood on the roof of a truck. Two attended Rose's porch. Another pair had stationed themselves on top of the corner grocery. The rest stood in the garden square across the street. When Leonato whistled, they all hit their chests with their fists and bowed their heads.

She clutched the drawstring bag to her chest until Kade placed a hand on her shoulder and whispered, "It'll be okay. We need to go with them."

She took Kade's hand. As they followed Leonato into the darkness, one thought crowded Kade's mind. *How am I going to leave Rose?*

AN HOUR LATER, the city's power came back on. Ten minutes after that, around two a.m., Rose followed Kade and Leonato into Prideaux House.

They were late because Rose had insisted on stopping by the hospital to see Timmy and reassure him. Although it was past regular visiting hours, the night nurse had allowed Rose's short visit while Kade and Leonato waited outside. Vane had left them to check on Samantha at her apartment and then return to Iron Rack's Gym.

On their way to Prideaux House, Kade had given Rose the details about Nate's appearance at Doom, and how King George had helped Kade find Rose in the bell tower. Then she'd told him about Hezekiah's possible involvement in her parents' deaths and Button Gwinnett's will.

She'd also mentioned seeing Leonato and Sampson outside of Doom. But, apparently, they'd not gone inside to free Kade or the other men. They'd just shown up at the bell tower in time to kill Magnus.

From Kade's frown, he was still processing everything that had happened in the past few hours.

As they made their way around the debris on the first floor, she took Kade's hand and breathed through her mouth. The mansion had fallen into ruin, and the smell of mold burned the inside of her nose. Although the sick feeling could also be attributed to the night's traumatic events.

She'd hated her cousin without apology, but no one deserved to die in such a violent way.

They walked up three flights of stairs to the attic, avoiding holes and soft spots on the landings. Leonato, who led the way, had insisted on coming with her and Kade, probably because he suspected they had an escape plan. Since she and Kade hadn't had a chance to talk about other options, her stomach had twisted into an anxious knot.

She had no idea how they were going to get away once she received her money.

Kade chose that moment to glance at her and wink. Had he sensed her unease?

She sighed and followed the men to the fourth floor. In the bell tower, Kade had asked her not to worry. Maybe she should just trust that he had a plan.

Hezekiah's driver, with a white bandage around his head, stood in front of a door at the end of the hallway. Leonato entered the room first, but before she and Kade went in, he pulled her into a different room. It was dark and dank, but for the moment, they were alone.

He took her box and placed it on the floor. Then he spun her around, and she pressed her hands on his chest. His heart beat rapidly beneath his T-shirt, and heat rolled off of him.

"Kade," she whispered, "what are you doing?"

"This." Kade dragged her into his arms and kissed her. His lips demanded entrance, and when she opened her mouth, his tongue swept in. He set up a hard, fast rhythm that made her forget everything.

She wrapped her arms around his neck, and he forced her against the wall. His larger body pressed in on hers, and she felt every hard, hot inch of his muscular, male form. Her worries evaporated, and her strength faded away.

All she could do was hold on tight and melt beneath the onslaught. Fire burned inside her veins, and her lower stomach contracted until it hurt. Still, she couldn't let go. Wouldn't let go. His kiss told her everything she needed to understand about how he felt about her and her own feelings in return.

His lips softened, and he trailed kisses down her neck. She leaned her head back and allowed him to take control. Right now, in his arms, all that mattered was they were together, and somehow they—along with Timmy—would escape this mess.

"Rose." Kade's harsh whisper made her shudder with desire. "When we go into that room, promise me you'll sell the box to Hezekiah. Do not, for any reason, give the box to the Prince. I have a plan to save you and Timmy, but you have to trust me. Can you do that?"

She held his head with her palms, kissed him, and spoke words she'd never said to another person. "Yes, Kade. I trust you."

$\mathcal{K}$ade led Rose past Hezekiah's driver and into the attic room. She clutched the drawstring bag to her chest and studied the area. It was larger than she'd expected, with a ratty couch, construction debris in the corners, and a rickety table. Someone had placed LED lanterns on the table and along the room's perimeter. It wasn't a lot of light, but enough to see the situation.

Apparently, even with the city's power back on, this dump still had no electricity.

Leonato leaned his hip against the table, arms crossed. His frown told her he wasn't happy about her and Kade's short detour. She also had the distinct impression that while Leonato was annoyed, he carried no remorse about his actions at the bell tower. He appeared unconcerned, even bored, with everything that had happened.

A man in the shadows cleared his throat. She squinted because of the low light until the man came out of the corner. Tall, dark-skinned, with a shaved head tattooed covered in Celtic designs. Arragon. The warrior she'd met with Samantha the night they'd snuck into Doom.

Kade grabbed her hand in warning. Whatever Arragon was doing here, it couldn't be good for either one of them.

Footsteps sounded behind her, and she turned to see Sampson—still wearing his New York Yankees hat—enter the room and guard the only exit.

Hezekiah, who'd been talking to Calum near the shabby couch, looked at her. Calum gave her a nod and a smile that, for some reason, calmed the butterflies in her stomach.

She wasn't sure why three Fianna warriors needed to be present, but there was a lot about the Fianna she didn't understand.

She straightened her shoulders and squeezed Kade's hand so tightly she was sure she'd cut off all circulation. But he didn't seem to mind or notice.

Hezekiah came over to her, hands out. "Do you have it?"

She handed the bag to Hezekiah. "Yes."

While Hezekiah opened the bag and took out the box, Arragon spoke in a deep voice edged with a French accent. "My lady, do you know what you do?"

She tucked a chunk of loose hair behind her ear. Half of her braid had escaped, and she'd not even realized it. "If I give the box to the Prince, will he pay me for it?"

"Nay." Arragon held out his hands, palms up. "Yet, if you allow yourself to trust the Prince, he may offer aid."

She tilted her head. "You expect me to give up thousands of dollars on the promise that the Prince—the leader of a murderous cult dating back centuries—may offer aid? After Leonato killed an innocent man at the hospital, tracked me all over town, and then murdered my cousin?"

"Aye." Arragon hit his chest with a fist and bowed his head. "For trust to be given wisely, it must first be received by the heart. 'Tis but a simple gift."

She pressed the heels of her hands into her eyes. She was

too tired to decipher the warrior's meaning. "Please stop talking."

"Rose"—Calum touched her shoulder and she dropped her hands—"I believe what Arragon is saying is that offering trust to others is a gift. But it's a gift that can only be given when a person trusts themselves first."

Now everyone was lecturing her about trusting herself?

"How does one do that, Calum?" She waved a hand around the room, encompassing all the men. "How does a person trust themselves, and trust others when they've never seen trust in action?" She stared directly at Hezekiah. "When all they know is betrayal and heartbreak?"

Hezekiah didn't even have the grace to look at her. All his attention was on the box he held.

Kade squeezed her shoulder, as if reminding her of her promise.

Calum's smile seemed so sad, so full of pity, that she turned away. Her vision went fuzzy, and the back of her throat burned.

Kade kissed the top of her head.

"Well?" Hezekiah's annoying voice cut through the tension.

She didn't know what to do. If she gave the box to the Prince—the same Prince who'd ordered Leonato to kill an innocent man and an evil man with the same amount of cruelty—she might receive some help. If she gave the box to Hezekiah, she'd receive her money, and somehow she and Timmy and Kade would get out of town.

Kade had asked her to trust his plan to save them. And of all the men in the room, he was the only one she did trust.

"Do you have the money?" she asked Hezekiah.

Hezekiah stroked the box as if it were a beloved pet. "I will wire it to your offshore account."

She shook her head. "I don't have an offshore account."

She didn't know how one went about getting an offshore account.

"You can use one of mine for the time being." Calum pulled out his phone and began texting. "I'll have one set up for you, Rose, and transfer the money. But it's Sunday and it won't happen until Monday." He glanced at her. "That is, if you trust me."

She swallowed. Calum had given her no reason not to trust him, and she did need his help.

"It'll be okay," Kade whispered as he ran his hand up and down her back.

The rhythm of his touch helped clear her head. "Thank you, Calum."

"Lady Tempest Rose," Arragon said in a strained voice, "are you sure of your own mind? Lord Usher should no more be trusted than any other man."

Hezekiah had lied to her all of her life. He may even have had something to do with her parents' deaths. But she'd promised Kade she'd sell the box to Hezekiah, so that's what she was doing. "Arragon, do you include the Prince in that statement?"

Arragon opened his mouth, but Leonato spoke first. "If Lady Tempest Rose cannot forgive herself, she cannot trust. If she cannot trust, she cannot see the truth."

"'Tis true," Sampson said in a deep voice. "Leave her be, Arragon."

She turned toward Leonato and Sampson until Kade gripped her arm. "Don't argue with them. You won't win."

Although she wanted to throw some choice words at the warriors, she said to Hezekiah, "Once the money is wired to Calum's account, you may have the box. Calum will hold on to it for now."

Hezekiah returned the box to the drawstring bag and

placed it on the couch. Then he pulled out his phone and began texting. "*Finally.*"

The awe in his voice left a sick pit in her stomach. All of this violence, all these deaths—including her parents'—had been caused by the existence of that stupid box.

Would wishing a curse on whoever originally owned the box make her a bad person?

If so, she didn't care.

"Now," Hezekiah wheezed and took a breath, "do you have the key?"

Key? "It's a puzzle box, Hezekiah. That means there's a trick to opening it. A trick I don't know." She blew stray hairs out of her eyes. "If you want to see what's in the box, break the damn thing open."

"The box is worth money on its own, so I will not destroy it." Hezekiah checked his watch. "If you find the key before I leave Savannah tomorrow night, I'll throw in a bonus." He paused to smile at Kade. "Maybe finding that key will free you from your bargain as well."

She glanced at Kade and noticed how drawn and pale his face appeared. Panic crawled up her spine, leaving her dizzy. When she wobbled, Kade pulled her into his arms again. Somehow the room had been invaded by a subtext she couldn't see and didn't understand. "What bargain?"

He whispered, "It's nothing."

"Well"—Hezekiah moved toward the door—"if you find the key, call Calum. He'll know how to get in touch with me."

A moment after Hezekiah left the room, Leonato's voice broke through the strange tension. "'Tis time."

"Aye." Sampson added a heavy sigh.

She glanced at Kade. That *off* feeling had returned. Like they all knew the punch line to a joke she didn't understand. "What's going on?"

When Kade nodded at Leonato, she touched Kade's chest.

His heart had kicked into high gear, as if he was about to run away.

"I don't understand." She tried to swallow away her scolding tone, but failed. "Time for what?"

Kade took her shoulders and forced her to meet his gaze. His blue gaze drilled into her with so much sadness that she teared up without understanding why.

"Kade?"

Instead of speaking, Kade kissed her hard. It wasn't passionate so much as resigned. Then he released her and backed up. Toward Leonato and Sampson.

"Wait." Rose took a step toward Kade until Calum grabbed her arm, forcing her to stop. "What's going on?"

Leonato whispered something into Kade's ear while Kade kept his gaze fixed on her face. The sorrow etched around his eyes, the droop of his shoulders, and the way he flexed his hands made her heart skip beats.

"Rose"—Calum's low voice sounded strained, as if he was choked up—"I'm so sorry."

She tried to throw off Calum, but he tightened his hold on her arm.

A moment later, Kade, Leonato, and Sampson left the room.

"Kade!" She rushed after him when Arragon stepped in front of her. She hit his hard chest. "Where are you taking him?"

"Your love is keeping a promise." Arragon placed his hands on her shoulders and bent in to whisper, "Always remember, this was your choice. Who you trust is always your choice. And now that you've made it, you must accept love's last kiss."

Arragon released her and left the room. She went after him until Calum moved in front of her and grabbed her wrists.

"Let me go, Calum!" She struggled, but he refused to release her. To his credit, he was far stronger than he appeared in his pressed suit and bow tie. "We had a plan. To leave town together. He made me promise to sell the box to Hezekiah. He had a plan for all of us to get away together."

"Kade never intended to go forward with that plan." Calum released her and shut the attic door. Then he stood in front of it, barring her from leaving.

She glared at Calum. "Kade told me—"

"He lied to protect you." Calum used a softer tone, as if knowing she was one step away from throwing the old bricks stacked in the corner. "After Kade saved you tonight, he knew he had no other choice. He knew, to protect you and Timmy, that he had to leave with Leonato to fulfill his obligation."

"What obligation?"

"To join the Fianna." Calum held up a hand to stop her from interrupting. "Since Kade's release from prison, he has been on borrowed time."

She covered her ears and shook her head.

Calum crossed his arms and stared at the dark window over her shoulder. "Arragon told me the Prince made a deal with Kade. If you and Kade found the box, and he gave it to the Fianna, he'd win his freedom. If you two found the box, but he allowed you to make your trade, he'd have to join the Fianna immediately. If he did neither, the Fianna would force him to kill you."

"No, no, no, no, no." The air rushed out of her lungs, and she sank to her knees. By giving the box to Hezekiah, had she condemned the man she loved?

"Rose?" Calum crouched in front of her, and she raised her head. "Are you sure you don't know where to find the box's key?"

"The man I love has just joined a murderous cult. I don't give a damn about the stupid box or the key."

"You should."

"*Why?*"

"It's leverage. If you find the key, you may be able to trade it to the Prince for Kade."

She stood and flexed her hands against her thighs. "Do you think the Prince would go for that?"

"I don't know. But as long as Hezekiah wants that key, the Prince may want it as well."

"Except I have no idea where to even look for the key. My mother and Magnus both said the box was a puzzle to be solved. And Deke never mentioned…"

She remembered Deke's planner with those phrases. *Sebastian. Key. Sugar. Remiel Marigny.*

"It's late." Calum touched her shoulder. "Let me take you —" His ringing cell phone interrupted him, and he answered with a curt, "Yes?"

After a few more yes and no responses, he hung up and looked at her. "Change of plans."

"Is it about Kade?"

"No." Calum picked up the drawstring bag from the couch, opened the attic door, and motioned for her to leave first. "That was Detective Garza. He wants to see you, and I'm not allowing you to go without your lawyer."

She pressed a hand to her stomach. It had tightened into a cramp that left her almost doubled over in pain. Kade had told her about Nate stuffing one of Magnus's goons in a trunk and shooting One Ear in the leg. "Is it about Magnus's thugs?"

"No. The police found a body."

And the nightmare continued. "Magnus."

Calum took her hand to lead her along the hallway, and then down the stairs. "I'm not sure."

"Is there any chance—"

"That you'll see Kade again?" Calum motioned for her to avoid a hole in the step below. "From what little I know about the Fianna, my best guess is no."

"I didn't get to say goodbye."

"That's the point." He waited until they reached the first floor before continuing, "The Fianna require their warriors to give up everything that means anything. They have to die to this world and leave everyone behind."

She caught a sense of sadness in his words. "It sounds like you're familiar with this process."

"I lost my best friend to the Fianna." Calum led her into the back garden that would make a perfect backdrop for a zombie movie. "Despite my parents' positive economic situation and social position, I was bullied as a child. My best friend always protected me—until the Fianna took him away."

"And this best friend?" she asked softly. "Did you ever see him again?"

"Yes." Calum sent her a wry smile. "His wife and I are living proof that there is always hope."

She wiped away a tear, not sure why this man whom she hardly knew—whom she'd trusted with her money—eased her battered heart. The low glow of streetlamps illuminated the eerie mansion that looked as ruined as her life felt.

When they reached the street, his butler, Ivers, appeared and opened the back door of the Bentley for her.

She slipped into the car and glanced back at Calum, who, for some unknown reason, was also now her lawyer. "Do you think there's hope for me?"

"I do, Miss Tempest Rose Guthrie." Calum sat next to her and shut the door. Once Ivers got in and drove them away, Calum added softly, "Because if anyone deserves a happy ending, it's you."

<h1 style="text-align:center">CHAPTER 32</h1>

Rose followed Calum into the police station.

Despite it being almost three a.m., the station was busy. Probably due to the earlier blackout.

Some officers stood around in groups looking at whiteboards, others escorted people in handcuffs, and a few hurried down hallways clutching cell phones and file folders. She wasn't sure if they were running to something or away from something.

They headed up the stairs, and Calum said softly, "Besides the crime that comes with these blackouts, there are multiple law enforcement task forces in town for this heroin epidemic and other recent violent incidents."

"Like Sally's murder at Rage of Angels."

"Yes," Calum said.

Rose would be happy if the city could help the addicts that seemed to multiply daily. Even happier if the city could find out who'd killed Sally.

Once on the second floor, Calum led her toward a tall man who stood in front of an interrogation room. Tonight Detective Garza wore a white dress shirt, jeans, and a jacket that covered his holstered weapon. He held a file folder against his chest, and his brown eyes took in everything from her dirty jeans to her half-done braid.

She touched her hair. She probably should've cleaned up before coming here to meet him.

"Calum." Detective Garza tilted his head. "Are you here as Miss Guthrie's lawyer or for moral support?"

Calum's smile appeared tight and thin. "Both."

Detective Garza's dark eyes narrowed. "Awesome."

Great. A sarcastic detective. Just what she needed tonight.

He ushered them into the interrogation room and shut the door. "I turned off the listening equipment."

Calum held out a chair for her. "Won't that be a problem for you?"

"No." After she sat, Detective Garza took the seat across from her. Calum grabbed the one next to her. "The power surges have been screwing with our equipment. I'll blame it on that."

Now that she was seated in the warm and humid room, exhaustion washed over her, and she tried to hide a yawn behind her hand.

Detective Garza opened the file. "I called you down here because a body was found thirty minutes ago on the train tracks near the River View Motel."

She held her breath deep in her chest. That hourly, cash-only hotel along the Savannah River was in one of the worst areas of town. "Have you ID'd the victim?"

"Possibly." Detective Garza handed her a photograph from the file. "This is a photo of the ID we took from the wallet we found near the body."

She read the name Magnus Guthrie next to the grainy DMV image on the license. Then she handed it to Calum.

"That is my cousin's ID. You said it was found on the body?"

"No, ma'am." Detective Garza opened the file again. "Near the body. To positively ID the victim, I need you to look at another photo. But this one is more disturbing."

"Okay."

Detective Garza placed a photo in front of her, and she covered her mouth with her hands. It was a photo of a partially severed arm with a tattoo of a raven on the bicep.

"Miss Guthrie, is this your cousin?"

She nodded and kicked back her gag reflex. She really didn't want to vomit in the interrogation room.

"Identifying a body this way"—Calum slid the photograph of the arm back toward the detective—"is not standard operating procedure."

Detective Garza clasped his hands behind his neck. "This isn't a standard death."

Calum raised an eyebrow. "Meaning?"

"Someone placed Magnus Guthrie on the train tracks so a train would run over him." Detective Garza shoved the photo back into the folder, closed it, and fixed his gaze on Rose. "I suspect Mr. Guthrie was dead before the train hit him. The coroner will confirm that if she can. It may be difficult since we only found pieces of Mr. Guthrie. There is a team down there now still combing the area for body parts."

She suddenly felt cold, as if all the blood had rushed to her heart.

Calum pointed to the folder. "Do you have more photos of the crime scene?"

"I do. But you don't want to see them." Detective Garza cleared his throat and pulled out his phone. "There's something else. I found this near the... uh... victim's head a few yards away from the tracks."

She took a few deep breaths. The Fianna had dumped her cousin's dead body on train tracks to be mutilated. And these men now had Kade.

Detective Garza scrolled through his phone and placed it on the table between them. It was a photo of words cut into the dirt.

What fates impose, that men must needs abide; It boots not to resist both wind and tide.

Calum muttered a prayer beneath his breath.

Detective Garza slipped his phone into his jacket pocket. "We're going to need more than your prayers, Calum."

"I don't understand." Both men seemed to know something she didn't. "What do those words mean?"

"It's a verse from Shakespeare's *Henry VI*," Garza said. "Essentially, it means that whatever the Fates—those vile, vindictive bitches—want, they ultimately get."

"How do you—"

"I have a Masters of Letters degree which means I can read Latin and understand Shakespeare."

Calum reached over to squeeze her hand. "This also means that when the Fianna left your cousin's body on the train tracks, along with this message, they knew Detective Garza would work the case."

She bit her lower lip. She wasn't sure what she could say in front of Detective Garza.

"It's all right, Miss Guthrie," Detective Garza said softly. "I know about the Fianna. I know this"—he tapped the file on the table—"was a Fianna kill. And when the anonymous call came in about your cousin's body, it came directly to me." Garza paused and sent a direct glare at Calum. "At the time, I was dealing with a man with one ear who'd been shot in the leg and his scarred brother who'd been stuffed in the trunk of an SUV."

Calum cleared his throat and sat back in his chair. "Interesting."

She swallowed and didn't say anything. She didn't want to put either her or Kade in a suspicious light.

Although it probably wouldn't matter for Kade.

"Why do you think the Fianna killed Magnus Guthrie and called me about it?" Detective Garza asked Calum.

"I don't know." Calum took out his phone to start texting. "But the Fianna are aware of your knowledge about them. So they—and the Prince—must believe you can cover this up. Maybe they're testing you. They tend to do that."

"I suspected as much. After I took this photo"—Detective Garza patted the pocket with his phone—"I smoothed out the words. The words weren't cut deeply, and the ground was muddy. So I was able to remove them before anyone noticed."

Calum tilted his head. "You tampered with evidence at a crime scene?"

Detective Garza glared at Calum. "I didn't want to. I had to. But that message was not meant for me." He leaned forward, his hands clasped on the table. "Do you know who the message might be for?"

"I have an idea." Calum looked at her. "Don't say anything else, Rose."

She nodded. She just wanted to go home.

Detective Garza stood and grabbed the file. "Miss Guthrie, I'll call you once everything we can find of Magnus makes it to the morgue. We may need to do an official ID using the head—"

"I'll do it." Calum stood. "I knew Magnus well enough to make a solid ID."

"I'll let the coroner know," Detective Garza said.

She stood as well, grateful for Calum's support.

"Miss Guthrie"—Detective Garza studied her with deep-brown eyes—"when did you last see Magnus Guthrie?"

She glanced at Calum. In the car on the way to the station, they'd discussed what she should and shouldn't say. When he nodded, she said, "Earlier today, I saw Magnus at the children's hospital with my younger brother, Timmy. We argued until the nurse asked him to leave."

"What did you argue about?"

"Timmy. Although Timmy lives with me, Magnus was officially Timmy's guardian. My cousin was concerned I wasn't doing enough to care for Timmy." She deliberately left out the CPS information. If Detective Garza wanted more, he could dig for it himself.

"Where were you tonight during the blackout?"

"Don't answer that, Rose," Calum said.

Sweat dripped down her neck, and a wave of dizziness came over her. She sat again and rubbed her forehead.

"Miss Guthrie is tired," Calum said in a firm, low voice. "If you need anything else, please contact me, and I'll arrange to bring Miss Guthrie back to the station. Or, if you'd prefer, we can meet at my mansion."

Detective Garza sighed and crossed his arms over his chest. "Take Miss Guthrie home, and I'll be in touch."

"Thank you." Calum touched her shoulder, and she rose. "Let's go."

She left the station with Calum. But she followed behind slowly because she knew the truth. Without Kade, she had no home.

Monday morning, at nine a.m., Rose entered the Savannah Preservation Office.

After Calum had dropped her off at her house the day before, along with her pink backpack and Kade's gym bag, she'd taken a bath and pretended to sleep. Except, the entire time, her heart had raced while her mind had rewound the past few days. She'd relived everything. Tried to remember every choice and every decision. From running after Antoine to giving Hezekiah the box. She'd held up each decision, hoping to decipher all the reasons she'd acted the way she had.

She'd spent hours tossing and turning in the bed she'd shared with Kade. She'd spent hours asking herself the same question over and over again.

If she'd given the box to the Prince, would he have let Kade go?

She'd asked Calum that question in the car on the way home from the police station. He'd hedged and said that no one ever knew what the Prince was thinking or planning. The Fianna made their own rules, had their own sense of justice and punishment, and worked toward goals that could take decades to achieve.

So, according to Calum, it was impossible to second-guess any dealings with the Fianna because no one ever knew where they stood with the Prince.

Still… if she'd made different choices, could she have saved the man she loved?

And because it was a day of regrets and self-recriminations, she was also angry at herself for not telling Kade she loved him when she'd had the chance.

Drizzle began just as she shut the door behind her. The sign said the SPO didn't open until noon on Monday, but last night she'd received a text from Sarah, the archivist they'd met at NOG, asking if Rose could meet her here this morning.

Sarah appeared from the reading room on the right. Today she wore jeans and a pink tank with a matching sweater. Her long brown hair had been brushed into a high ponytail with a pencil sticking out. She pressed an open book against her chest. "Hello, Rose. Where is Kade?"

Rose cleared her throat. "He couldn't make it today."

"I appreciate you coming so early this morning." Sarah moved toward a carved mahogany checkout desk near the stairs. The SPO was a large antebellum mansion that had been converted into a library. She dropped the book on the desk with a soft thud. "I have something for you."

While Sarah rummaged around the desk, Rose pulled Kade's compass watch out from behind her black T-shirt. She'd found a chain in her junk drawer which allowed her to wear the compass watch around her neck and keep it near her heart. She appreciated the warmth of the metal as it warmed against her skin, as well as the weight. She'd held it all night and dreamed of Kade's last kiss.

Feeling wobbly, she sat in a nearby chair, closed her eyes, and rubbed the compass.

"Rose?" Sarah touched Rose's arm, and she opened her eyes. "Are you okay?"

No. But she didn't want to be rude and cry all over Sarah. "Last night, I lost something valuable. Something I loved."

Sarah pulled an antique chair from the polished hallway and sat across from Rose. She held a brown leather portfolio in her lap. "I'm so sorry."

Rose sniffled and found a tissue in her purse. "Thank you."

Sarah handed Rose the leather portfolio. "I've been cleaning out the upstairs office, the same room where I found your mother's box, and yesterday I found this."

She opened it to find a notebook tucked inside, along with a newspaper clipping. "What is this?"

"It belonged to your mother. She was working on a churchyard restoration project on the Isle of Grace, and this was her field notebook."

Rose ran a hand over the leather edging. Although she tried hard to picture her mother writing on the white note-book pages, she couldn't. She could barely remember what her mother looked like. Ten years of grief had left her with only echoes of the past corrupted by silent screams of blame and guilt.

Blame and guilt that hadn't been Rose's to carry. The problem was that after so many years, she wasn't sure how to let all those emotions go.

Sarah lifted the newspaper article and unfolded it. "This article is about the restoration of the St. Mary of Sorrows cemetery on the Isle of Grace."

Rose squinted at the article yellowed with age. One of the newspaper photos was of a tombstone engraved with the name Mercer and the date 1774. Beneath that was an image of an eight-pointed star. "Do you think this article has anything to do with the puzzle box?"

"I don't know. They were in the same room but in different closets."

Rose scanned the article, finding nothing of interest. "I recently heard the Mercer family has lived on the Isle of Grace since before the American Revolution."

"That makes sense." Sarah pointed to the star carved on the tomb. "Most colonial-era tombs have five-pointed stars. Eight-pointed stars were rare before 1770."

Rose turned the article over only to find laundry detergent ads on the back. "Why?"

"Eight-pointed stars are one of the symbols of the Sons of Liberty." Sarah clasped her hands in her lap. "You're welcome to take the portfolio and the article. I didn't know what to do with it, but I didn't want to throw it out."

"Thank you." Rose traced the eight-pointed star on the newsprint. Something about it seemed familiar. "Sarah, what do you know about the Mercer family on the Isle of Grace?"

"Not much." Sarah went behind the registration desk and returned with an old book. "I've been studying the history of the Isle of Grace. The Mercer family is one of the isle's original inhabitants, and one of the women, Lucy Mercer, married Peter Tondee."

"The owners of the original Tondee's Tavern, where the Declaration of Independence was first read aloud?"

"Yes." Sarah opened the book and ran her finger down an index page. "The Mercers, along with the Toban, Capel, and Montfort families, arrived in the mid-1600s. A few other families came from Louisiana after the American Revolution, including the Boudreaux and Marigny families."

"The Marigny family?"

"Yes." Sarah turned a page. "The Marigny family came from New Orleans."

Rose's first instinct was to call Kade—until she remembered he was gone.

Then again, the history of these families didn't matter. The only thing that did matter was finding that key so she'd have something to trade for Kade. "Sarah, do you have any idea how one would open that box you found? The one that was stolen?"

"No."

Rose sighed and skimmed the pages in the portfolio. Most of them were notes about the church's structure and plans for restoring the churchyard.

As she read, she realized Sarah was staring at the compass watch hanging from the chain around Rose's neck. She reached for it, and Sarah shook her head as if coming out of a trance.

"Rose, where did you get that pendant?"

She unhooked the chain and handed the compass watch to Sarah. "It's a compass watch that once belonged to the Mercer family. A friend of mine gave it to me."

Sarah dropped the book onto the floor and opened the compass watch. Once she read the inscription, she closed it and said, "It's heavier than it looks."

"I thought so too."

"Hmmm." Sarah turned the compass watch over to expose the eight-pointed star sketched in silver. "That's interesting."

Rose took out the newspaper clipping again and held it next to the compass watch. "The star on the compass watch is identical to the star carved into the tomb."

Sarah held the compass watch in her palm and covered it with her other hand. Then she twisted until a small *pop* sounded. She held it up for Rose to see. The eight-pointed star was now raised above the lid about a quarter of an inch, as if it had been released by a spring beneath. "It's spring-loaded."

Rose took the compass watch, pressed down on the raised star, and twisted. The metal star reset into the cover and appeared as if it were simply an etching instead of three-dimensional. "How did you know it does that?"

"It's part of a two-piece latch used on seventeenth- and eighteenth-century sugar boxes."

Rose raised an eyebrow. "What is a sugar box?"

Sarah found her phone in her pocket and scrolled. "In the seventeenth and eighteenth centuries, sugar was more valuable than gold. In prominent homes, sugar was kept in boxes with intricate locking mechanisms."

She gave Rose the phone so she could see photos of colonial-era boxes available for auction. Wood boxes, some decorated with etched pewter or silver plates, with no obvious locks.

"Sarah, these boxes look like my puzzle box. Except mine has more decoration."

"You're right. My guess"—Sarah grabbed a magnifying glass from the desk—"is that your compass watch is the second part of a locking mechanism for a sugar box. Locks this intricate were rare and quite expensive. But if Button Gwinnett commissioned it for his wife, he would've had the money to make something so intricate."

Rose gave Sarah back her phone. Then she held out the compass watch so Sarah could study the star with the magnifying glass. "Are you saying this compass watch could open a sugar box? Maybe even my box?"

"It's possible." When Sarah turned the compass watch over, she said, "Look."

Rose peered through the glass. Flowers and swirls had been etched on the other side. In the center was a lily with the initials JL in the center.

"Like I mentioned when we met at the café"—Sarah pointed to the initials—"this is the mark of Joshua Linguard. He was a famous metalworker in Charleston who disappeared in the early eighteenth century. After his disappearance, his son took over the firm. Joshua Linguard's workshop is responsible for some of the most beautiful work with iron and other metals in Charleston and Savannah and New Orleans."

"Did his workshop make this compass watch?"

"I can't say for sure without a receipt, but it's possible. If it is a Joshua Linguard original, it's worth a lot of money."

"Just like the box that was stolen." Rose tilted her head. "Sarah, is it possible—"

"Yes." Sarah took the portfolio out of Rose's hand and brought it over to the desk. She pulled out some photos that had been tucked into the portfolio's back pocket and laid them on the desk. "Your mother must have taken these photos of the box before she hid it."

Rose hurried over, and Sarah pointed to a close-up photo of one of the box's decorative silver plates etched with flowers and swirls, similar to those on the compass watch. In another photo of the bottom of the box, she saw the logo with the lily and initials JL. "What does this mean?"

"Both your box and your compass watch may have been made by the Joshua Linguard workshop. Maybe even made for Button Gwinnett. Although I'm not sure how the Mercer family ended up with the key. Regardless of how they got separated, the box and key would both be incredibly valuable." Sarah handed Rose a photo of the box's top etched with an eight-pointed star. "See the edges around the star? Don't they look darker—or maybe deeper—than the other engravings?"

"Yes." Rose held the compass watch against the photo. The star on the box and on the compass watch appeared to be the same size.

Sarah returned the photos to the portfolio. "My guess is that the etched silver star on the top of the box is spring-loaded."

Rose held the compass watch. "And if I use this pop-up star to depress the star on the box—"

"You'll activate the locking mechanism and open the box."
Sarah smiled widely. "I just wish it hadn't been stolen."

Rose stayed silent. Sarah didn't know Kade had found the box. Or that Rose had sold it to Hezekiah. While she was cautiously excited about having—maybe—found the key, she had another concern. "Don't you think this is a huge coincidence? Someone I recently met gives me a compass watch that unlocks my mother's box? A box she hid ten years ago?"

"I don't believe in coincidences." Sarah shrugged. "And I don't believe in fate."

"What's left?"

Sarah smiled. "Logic."

That made sense, considering all of Sarah's degrees that Rose had read about on the SPO website.

"Rose, if you think through all the steps that led you here today, you may discover a series of planned events that make sense only in hindsight."

"Perhaps." She slipped the chain over her head and slid the compass watch beneath her T-shirt. It was silly, but by keeping it against her skin, she felt closer to Kade.

"Do you believe in fate?" Sarah handed Rose the portfolio. "Or are you the kind of woman who would resist both wind and tide?"

Rose bristled and held the portfolio against her chest. She wanted to ask if Sarah knew Detective Garza. Instead, she asked, "Are you a fan of Shakespeare?"

Sarah laughed and started straightening up the books on the desk. "I'm a fan of history. And no one could decipher the human psyche and its effect on historical events like William Shakespeare."

Since Rose had barely finished high school, she wouldn't know. But instead of being defensive, she could answer honestly because of the empathy Sarah exuded. "I've been resisting things my entire life, even when ordered not to."

Sarah's voice lowered, as if offering solace. "Has that worked out for you?"

Rose remembered Kade's kisses and his passion that had left her breathless and complete. "Yes." Then she remembered him walking away with Leonato and Sampson, and the horrible sinking in her stomach intensified. "And no." She cleared her throat. "It has left me unable to trust others, including myself."

She exhaled, shocked at her own admission.

"Rose—" Sarah's phone buzzed, and she pulled it out of her pocket. She stared at it for a moment and then placed it face down on the desk. "Trust is a gift. To others as well as to ourselves."

"I've never thought about it that way."

Sarah's smile brightened her brown eyes. "Do you know the source of your own mistrust?"

"Yes." The day her parents died.

"Well, whatever happened on that day, you need to forgive yourself. Once you forgive yourself, you'll be able to trust yourself. Only then can you offer that gift of trust to others."

"What if I can't do that?"

"You can do that." Sarah touched Rose's hand. "I lost my mother at a young age, so I speak from experience."

"But—"

"No buts." Now Sarah squeezed Rose's fingers. "You're a woman of courage and self-determination. Don't forget that."

"I won't." Rose turned away to hide the tears welling in her eyes. "Thank you."

Sarah had just explained, in much simpler language, Arragon's lecture.

The only problem was that it was all too late.

After Rose said goodbye, and entered the SPO's garden, her phone rang. "Hello?"

"Rose, it's Dr. Singh. My team and I have approved Timmy for my experimental drug study."

Rose's heart raced, and she sank onto an iron bench near a fountain tucked within a raised pond. The cool water misted her hot cheeks. "I... uh..." she swallowed and closed her eyes. "I mean—"

"It's okay." Dr. Singh lowered her voice. "I know this is overwhelming. I'm going into a meeting now, but I will email you the details. My assistant will also be in touch this afternoon to walk you through everything you'll need to do."

Rose opened her eyes. Small birds played in the water, and children's laughter came from the park across the street. Both the birds and the kids were oblivious to the miracle that had just fallen into her lap. "Thank you, Dr. Singh."

"You're welcome. I look forward to meeting Timmy."

Once Rose hung up, she dialed another number. The moment Calum answered, she told him about Timmy's acceptance into the drug study. She ended with, "Can you take me to see Hezekiah?"

"Why?" His voice sounded both concerned and expectant.

She raised her face to the blue, sunny sky, grateful that the rain had moved on. "I found the key."

At two p.m., Ivers opened the door to Calum's mansion and said, "Good afternoon, Miss Guthrie."

"Good afternoon." She handed Ivers her umbrella, smoothed down the skirt of her black linen dress, and hurried into the foyer.

Not long after she'd seen Timmy to tell him the good news, and gone home to talk to Dr. Singh's assistant, the rain had started. It hadn't been one of the summer storms that swept through the city swiftly. It'd been the kind that brought dark clouds and lingered for hours.

But she hadn't minded. It suited her *all-over-the-place* mood. Despite possibly having the key that Hezekiah wanted, and her happiness about Timmy, she had no guarantee that the Fianna would trade the key for Kade. So she'd spent hours in the tub, dreaming about him, before braiding her hair and putting on a black dress with black patent leather sandals that made her feel confident and determined.

"This way, Miss Guthrie." Ivers led her through the foyer that was larger than the children's hospital, filled with Greek and Roman statues that had to be originals, into a sitting room that would fit her entire house.

"You look lovely, Miss Guthrie." Calum rose from the club chair near the fireplace and came over to take her arm. "You didn't have to walk in this weather. Ivers could have picked you up."

Hezekiah, who stood near the fireplace, barely looked at her.

"Thank you for the offer." She sat on one of the loveseats and accepted a glass of water from Ivers. "But I didn't mind." She'd needed the time to clear her head.

Since last night's events, she'd felt foggy. Like she was listening to the world through a tunnel deep beneath the ocean. It was a detachment she hadn't felt since her parents' deaths. Except this time, she wasn't a child. She couldn't hide under her bed, clutching her stuffed alligator. This time, she needed to face her fate with... What was it Sarah had said? Courage and self-determination. So she could be a woman who could forgive herself and trust herself. A woman who could trust others.

She needed to remember that truth now that she was in this house with Calum and the man who'd lied to her her entire life.

She nodded at Hezekiah.

He responded by raising his glass of whiskey. From the dark circles under his eyes, she wondered if he'd gotten any sleep at all.

Calum sat on the loveseat across from her. They'd discussed how they were going to deal with Hezekiah before they set up the meeting. While she'd wanted to bring up the possibility that Hezekiah had played a part in her parents' deaths, Calum was adamant that she drop the issue for now. Without proof, it was just gossip. They also were going to wait to tell Hezekiah that she had the key. And, and in regard to everything else, she was going to follow Calum's lead.

Another lesson in trust.

"Rose," Calum said, "per your request on the phone earlier, I told Hezekiah about Timmy's acceptance into Dr. Singh's drug study."

"News I'm very happy to hear," Hezekiah said.

"Thank you." She sipped her water to prevent herself from reaching for the compass watch she wore around her neck and beneath her dress. The compass watch was the only thing she had left of Kade. Part of her hoped it wasn't the key.

Calum leaned forward, his hands clasped. Today he wore gray wool trousers, a white shirt, and a gray vest with a red tie. "Hezekiah, yesterday you made an offer to Rose. If she found the key, you'd offer her a bonus. Can you elaborate?"

Hezekiah stood straighter, his shoulders no longer slumped. "Did you find the key?"

"Answer my question first," Calum demanded.

Hezekiah wobbled and grabbed the fireplace mantel. "In exchange for the key, I will pay to move Rose and Timmy to Charlottesville. I will also find them a suitable place to live and purchase Rose a car."

She met Calum's surprised gaze. She'd not expected any of that.

"Hezekiah." Calum moved to the bar, poured himself a glass of water, and refilled Rose's glass. "How did you know there was a key to the box? That it wasn't just a puzzle box?"

Hezekiah accepted another glass of whiskey from Calum, and Rose wondered if Calum was trying to get Hezekiah drunk.

Calum confirmed her suspicions when he winked at her.

She hid her smile by drinking her water.

Hezekiah sipped his whiskey and coughed. "My family has been following this box—and the key—since 1777 when

Button Gwinnett gave the box and the key to Lucy Tondee on the eve of his fatal duel."

"Wait." She glanced at Calum. "Button Gwinnett died in a duel?"

Calum nodded. "Right here in Savannah. He's buried in Colonial Cemetery. He died during the first year of the Revolutionary War, which is why no one recognizes him as one of the Founding Fathers."

She sipped her water. What were the chances that the man who'd owned her box had been buried behind her house?

"Anyway," Hezekiah said in an annoyed voice. "My family lost track of the box during World War I. After Rose's parents died, I thought the box was lost forever until I saw Sarah Munro's article in the *Georgia Historical Journal*. Once I studied the photos, I knew it was the box my family has been looking for since the end of the Revolutionary War. Its theft only convinced me even more of its authenticity."

"Was this the same Lucy Mercer Tondee who was married to the owner of the original Tondee's Tavern?" Calum asked.

"Yes." Hezekiah smiled into his glass, as if remembering something. "Did you know that Doom was her idea? Before the British sieged Savannah, Lucy was desperate for money. So she offered the underground space for fight clubs. That made her enough money to escape the city with her daughter."

Calum glanced at Rose, confirming what they both believed. If her compass watch had come from the Mercer family, there was a good chance it was the key to Button Gwinnett's box.

"Excuse me while I retrieve the box from my safe." Calum stepped out of the room, leaving her alone with Hezekiah.

Hezekiah went to the bar and poured himself another liberal amount of whiskey.

"Hezekiah?" She softened her voice, trying to keep her disgust for the man from leaking through. "Magnus told me that you hope to find Button Gwinnett's signature inside the box."

"Yes."

"What I don't understand is"—she used her sweetest smile —"if your family has been following the box for years, have the Fianna known about it as well?"

"Of course." Hezekiah smirked. "Who do you think paid to have the box made?"

She swallowed and tasted an awful bitterness in the back of her throat. "Why did the Fianna make the box and key for Button Gwinnett?"

"No one knows except the Prince." Hezekiah stopped talking when Calum entered the room, carrying the drawstring bag.

Calum took the box out of the bag and placed it on the coffee table near Rose.

She ran her fingers over the eight-pointed star etched into the silver plate on top of the box. It seemed about the same size as Kade's compass watch. "Is there any chance the Prince will trade Kade for this key?"

"No," Hezekiah said.

"I concur," Calum said. "After I spoke with Hezekiah to set up this meeting, I contacted Arragon and offered him the key in exchange for Kade. Arragon declined."

She wasn't at all surprised. But she was grateful to Calum for asking Arragon on her behalf.

Hezekiah rubbed his hands together and came closer.

Calum went to the desk in the corner of the room and brought back a piece of paper and a pen. "Write down exactly what you're offering Rose in exchange for the key and sign it."

"You have the key?" Hezekiah's breathlessness made her ill.

Calum handed Hezekiah the pen. "Possibly."

Hezekiah wrote, while Calum suggested edits.

Then Calum brought it to her. "Read this carefully. If you want to add anything, now is the time."

She read through the words, although she barely saw them due to her blurry vision. "I want to add a clause that if whatever is in that box is valuable, I receive a percentage of the proceeds."

"Let's say fifty percent." Calum crouched next to her and added the language. "Now both of you need to sign and date the bottom."

"Wait," Hezekiah said. "I didn't agree to that."

"You will if you want the key," Calum said.

After she and Hezekiah signed the document, Calum laid it on his desk. When he returned to her, he whispered, "It's time."

She pulled the chain over her head, twisted the compass watch until the star popped up, and handed it to Calum. Her breath burned in her chest like she was handing over a piece of her heart. No, her entire heart.

Calum placed the raised relief of the star onto the etching in the silver top of the box. Gently, he pressed down, and the silver outline depressed. Calum twisted the key, and the lid sprang open.

Hezekiah inhaled sharply.

A dusty smell came from the box, and Calum lifted something out that had been wrapped in canvas yellowed with age. He placed the parcel on the table and opened the canvas. A book lay in the center of the fabric.

Hezekiah hurried to grab his briefcase from near the fireplace. He came back to the table wearing white cotton gloves and holding a wooden stick that looked like a tongue depressor. Using the stick, he opened the book.

From her vantage point, she could read the title. *Bay Psalm Book.*

"This can't be possible." Hezekiah's voice held what sounded like awe and surprise. Still using the wooden stick, he turned to the title page, where a name was signed. *Button Gwinnett.*

Hezekiah took off his glasses and wiped them with a handkerchief. He paled and sank into the loveseat across from her. "Do you know what this means?"

"If it doesn't mean I'm going to see Kade again, I don't care." She also wasn't concerned about her tone of voice or lack of politeness.

Calum tapped her arm, as if requesting she hold herself together for a few more moments. "I know this means you're a richer man than you were yesterday, Hezekiah."

Hezekiah put his glasses back on. "This original *Bay Psalm Book*, which my family published in 1640, is a metrical translation of the Psalms."

"A hymnal?" Calum said.

"Yes." Hezekiah wrapped up the book and returned it to the box. "Only eleven copies from the *Bay Psalm Book*'s original print run have been known to have survived."

She sighed loudly. She just wanted this meeting to end so she could go home and cry herself to sleep. "So?"

Hezekiah put his gloves and wooden stick away in his briefcase. "In 1640, the Usher family published The Bay Psalm psalter. It was the first book ever printed in the colonies, with eleven hundred, hand-printed copies made. This publishing milestone was a huge achievement on its own, but now that only eleven copies remain, these first editions have become quite valuable."

"How valuable?" Calum asked.

"The psalter without the signature"—Hezekiah shrugged —"is worth a minimum of forty million. With Gwinnett's signature, at least sixty."

She stood, not sure she'd heard correctly. "Excuse me?"

Calum tapped Rose's shoulder until she sat again. A good idea since she felt dizzy.

"Calum, once I sell the psalter, I'll let you know and wire the money to Rose's account."

When Hezekiah dropped the compass watch into his coat pocket, she said, "I want the compass watch back."

Hezekiah gave her a blank glare, as if surprised she was still there. "No. It's part of the box's value. For which you have already been paid."

She sank back into the chair. Although she now had more than enough money to save her brother, she had nothing left of Kade.

"Hezekiah," she asked as he retrieved the drawstring bag and slipped the box into it. "Why did my mother tell you about the box after she found it?"

"I knew your parents in college. After we graduated, I invited them to join the Usher Society."

She brushed away stray hairs that had come loose from her braid. "Your shady group of people who buy and sell old books?"

"As well as other documents and antiquities." Hezekiah stacked the drawstring bag and his briefcase on the coffee table. "When your mother found the box, she sent me photos. Suspecting this might be Button Gwinnett's box, I told her to hide it until I could get there. Unfortunately, your father was a terribly naïve man. He told his brother, Isaac. And Isaac, also a member of the Usher Society, understood the box's potential value. Wanting it for himself, he killed your parents."

"Magnus told me that Isaac only intended to kill my father."

"That's not true." Hezekiah found his whiskey glass and refilled it at the bar. "Although Magnus tried to blackmail me with correspondence he'd found that supposedly proved I was in on the murder."

"Which is why you'd hoped Kade would kill him in Doom's pit?"

Hezekiah frowned and downed his drink. "I know that's what I said last night, but that's not the entire truth."

She shared a confused glance with Calum. "I don't understand."

"While Magnus's death would have been a relief," Hezekiah said, "I set up the fight because the Prince insisted."

Heat rushed through her and she stood. "You mean the Prince wanted Magnus and Kade to fight?"

"Yes," Hezekiah said. "The fight was a test. If Kade won, he'd continue to be recruited. While Magnus—a problem for the Fianna—would be taken care of."

"And if Kade had lost?" Calum asked.

Hezekiah shrugged. "They'd lose a recruit who didn't want to join. And, I suspect, they would have killed Magnus later."

She wavered on her feet and Calum helped her sit again. Once she was on the loveseat, she realized she'd been holding her breath. So she forced herself to take deep, steady breaths.

"Hezekiah?" Calum's harsh voice rumbled through the room. "Why would you do as the Prince asked?"

"Because, Calum," Hezekiah sighed heavily, "I'm in debt and have a cash flow problem. I can't get any more loans, and all of my money is tied up in property. In return for my part in this play, the Fianna will offer me credit. Except now that I have the Bay Psalm Book, I won't have to take their money after all."

"What about Rose?" Calum asked. "Why did Deke ask her to be the courier?"

"Again," Hezekiah refilled his glass until Calum took the decanter away. "The Prince ordered Deke to ask Rose to be the courier. Deke was involved with some nefarious people—"

"Including Magnus?" she asked.

"Among others." Hezekiah carried his glass to the loveseat across from her and sat. The seat sagged beneath his weight. "Deke had secretly asked the Fianna for asylum. In return, he promised the Prince information about some rogue Fianna warriors and"—Hezekiah raised his glass in Rose's direction—"Rose had to be the courier. She is the rightful owner of the box. The Prince demanded that the transaction be as honest and clean as possible."

She rubbed her fist across her forehead. "Is that why the Fianna is interested in my life?"

"Yes," Hezekiah said. "The Fianna has been watching your family for years, hoping the box would reappear."

"Then there was Kade's concern for you." Calum gently touched her shoulder. "The Fianna used you to test his physical and emotional strength."

She swallowed and remembered that night in the hospital. Kade had been so sure that Banjo's death had been a warning not to stray from the Fianna's rules.

Hezekiah leaned back in his seat and sighed. "Everything with the Fianna is a fucking game. In fact, I'm selling the box and key to the Prince this afternoon."

She sighed and tried not to cry. All of a sudden, she was really tired. "Hezekiah?"

He leaned forward, still holding his glass with whiskey swirling in the bottom. "Yes?"

Despite Calum's warning glance, she said, "Were you in on the plan to kill my parents?"

Hezekiah stared into his glass for a long moment. The kind of silent pause that felt like years instead of moments. "You have no reason to believe this, Rose, but I loved your mother."

He raised his glass, as if offering a toast. "Your mother was the one who got away. And I hated Isaac for what he'd done."

"When you run with criminals," Calum said softly, "you compromise yourself."

Hezekiah downed his drink. Then he pressed the glass against his forehead and closed his eyes again. "Like I said last night, I couldn't convince anyone in this city that Isaac was guilty. And the day I learned that Isaac had full custody of Rose and Timmy, I had to leave town."

"Why?" Calum took Hezekiah's glass away and placed it on the bar.

When Hezekiah opened his eyes, they'd filled with tears. "Because Isaac used the kids as leverage. If I didn't keep quiet, if I didn't stay away from them, he'd make their lives even more miserable."

Calum poured a glass of water and handed it to Hezekiah. "Do you know why the Guthrie estate wasn't held in trust until Rose and Timmy became legal adults?"

"All I know is that Isaac finagled a court order allowing him to sell any and all the assets once Rose's parents were buried—which he didn't do right away. Unfortunately, that order also included Magnus upon Isaac's death."

Rose blinked away random tears. "Magnus sold what was left, including the houses, days after Isaac's death."

Calum crossed his arms. "I've been doing my research. As it turns out, my father's law firm handled the Guthrie wills."

Hezekiah raised an eyebrow. "You mean *your* law firm?"

Calum nodded. "I've looked at the original documents. Everything, after Rose's parents' deaths, was placed in a trust. So the court's judgment to allow Isaac and Magnus to sell any assets was wrong."

"Did my uncle paid off a judge?" Rose asked.

"Probably," Calum said.

"I have no doubt." Hezekiah drank his water and placed the glass on the table. "Rose, I'll have my business manager contact you. Let me know when Timmy needs to be in

Virginia, and we'll have you moved by then. Unless you have any reason to stay in Savannah?"

She shook her head. "No reason anymore."

Hezekiah stood and held out a business card to Calum. "I hope you'll accept my personal offer to join the Usher Society. You already know many of the members."

"I'm sure I do." Calum refused the card by shoving his hands in his pockets.

Hezekiah placed the card on the table, gathered his brief-case and drawstring bag, and left the room.

Alone with Calum, she said, "Is it true you looked into my parents' wills?"

"It is." Calum sat next to her, smoothing out wrinkles in his pants. "I'm sorry I wasn't here when everything happened. I would have stopped it. Except I was a college freshman at the time."

She smiled at him. "I'm sorry too."

"I also wish I could tell you that I could fix what happened. But Isaac is dead, and the houses and money are gone."

She'd figured that was the case. "Thank you for trying. I appreciate it."

Calum tilted his head. "What's wrong?"

She clasped her hands in her lap and stared at the empty coffee table. "I know I should feel something about the fact that Hezekiah is Harry, the only person who ever helped me and Timmy. But I don't. In fact, I don't feel anything. Not love or hate or worry."

"That's the way grief works," Calum said softly. "It shuts everything down so the mind can process the loss while still allowing you to function in the world. It's a safety mechanism."

"Not a very good one."

"I agree. But I don't make all the rules around here."

She laughed at the annoyed tone in his voice. "Maybe one day you will."

"Maybe." Calum sighed and sat forward, his attention also focused on the spot where the box had sat on the table. "I know this is a gruesome topic, but once I identify Magnus's body at the morgue and we get a death certificate, we'll begin the process of making you Timmy's legal guardian."

"Do you think you can make that happen?"

"I have a meeting with a family judge later today. After I show the judge the original wills, I believe we will prevail. My firm will also deal with the CPS situation. I don't know how far that has gone, but now that Magnus is dead, I'm sure I can convince the judge that living with you in Virginia, and having Timmy enrolled in that drug study, is the best possible solution."

She exhaled and savored the relief that rushed through her body. "I have something for you." She took a cell phone out of her dress pocket. "This is Magnus's cell phone. I found it last night after... you know. I thought it might help you with your betting problem at Doom."

Calum took it and smiled at her. "Thank you. This might be exactly what I need to shut that betting book down."

Calum stood, slipped the phone into his jacket pocket, and held out his hand for her. "Let's feed you and make a plan."

She took his hand and stood as well. "A plan for what?"

"A plan to begin your new life in Charlottesville, Virginia." Calum led her out of the sitting room and toward the dining room. "A plan to move you and Timmy to your new home."

She offered a pretend smile filled with sunshine and roses. But the truth was her heart was broken. She'd lost the only man she'd ever loved, and no amount of money could ever bring him back.

CHAPTER 35

The next day, Rose entered the kitchen dressed in jeans and a pink T-shirt. It'd taken all of her energy to get dressed, so she'd just braided her wet hair and hadn't bothered with lipstick or mascara.

As she poured herself a mug of coffee, she was shocked to hear the cathedral bells ring eleven a.m. Apparently, she was slipping into some strange time/space continuum where the hours passed at warp speed.

Samantha opened the kitchen door to let in a breeze, and King George ran out. He'd been particularly difficult since the night Kade had joined the Fianna. Rose had barely seen the cat, and he only appeared for food.

Samantha placed a plate on the table and filled it with four blueberry muffins from the bakery bag she'd carried in. "I got the muffins from Screamin' Perks. I know they're your favorite."

Rose sat, broke the pastry apart, and ate a bite. It stuck in her throat, but she forced it down. "Thank you."

Samantha went to the coffee pot, filled with yesterday's

brew, and frowned. Then she dumped the pot, along with Rose's mug, into the sink and began boiling water for tea.

"While you were sleeping"—Samantha place tea bags into two mugs—"I spoke with Calum. He's on his way over with some paperwork. He finalized the setup of your offshore accounts, as well as a bank account in Charlottesville. Hezekiah's money should be deposited soon."

Rose smiled. She was grateful for the cash, and so happy she never had to work at Rage of Angels again. But her heart hurt, as if it was encased in an iron band. She hated what this money—and the freedom it bought her—had cost. A lifetime of true love. Kade's life and freedom.

She still couldn't comprehend what he'd given up for her and Timmy. She swallowed another piece of muffin. Calum had told her that the more she kept doing normal things, the easier they would become.

"I also talked to the movers that Hezekiah hired." Samantha poured boiling water over the tea bags and carried the cups to the table. Then she sat across from Rose. "They'll be here tomorrow. Since you don't have much, it won't take long to pack everything up."

She glanced at the tote bag, filled with hospital documents, that hung off the back of the chair. She had an appointment later that day with the children's hospital to make sure all of Timmy's outstanding bills were paid before they left Savannah. Calum had insisted that she take one of his lawyers with her, a specialist who dealt with medical debt, to make sure there'd been no fraudulent charges. Then she was meeting with her landlord to pay off what remained of her lease.

One of the biggest things she'd learned in the past few days was that lots of money could buy excellent legal help. Another thing for which she was grateful.

She sipped her hot tea and attempted another bite of

muffin. Although she still disliked Harry, he'd arranged for private medical transport for Timmy from the children's hospital directly to the Charlottesville hospital. Luckily, she could travel with Timmy since he was nervous about all of these fast-moving changes.

She hadn't said anything to Timmy about Harry's other life. Because Timmy trusted so few people, she'd called Harry last night and they'd come to an agreement. Harry would still have a small place in their lives, on the periphery. Harry and Timmy could call each other as long as she was in the room. When Timmy was old enough, she'd explain the situation and allow him to decide who he wanted in his life.

Harry had not only agreed, he'd thanked her. Then he'd told her he'd found them a place to live in Charlottesville. It wasn't fancy, but it was furnished and safe and near the hospital. And a small-yet-safe car would be waiting for her as well.

While she'd probably never trust Harry again, she'd come to the realization that he'd also been a victim of the Prince's mind games. Albeit a willing victim who might still be involved with the Fianna. Hence her boundaries regarding his relationship with Timmy.

She pushed the plate away and noticed taped boxes near the kitchen door. "Did you pack up the kitchen?"

"Vane and I did that together early this morning while you were sleeping." Samantha blew on her tea. "I worked in the kitchen while Vane did the books."

"Thank you." Rose wasn't sure what else to say. Just breathing caused a heavy numbness. Like slogging through molasses and sand at midnight.

"But," Samantha continued, "you can't tell Vane's buddies that he helped me. Except for Nate, Vane's men don't know about his involvement with any of this. Nate told everyone that Vane is clearing tunnels today."

There were so many people Rose needed to thank, and she

wasn't sure she'd get a chance. "I promise not to say a word. Besides, I may never see any of them again."

For some reason, that knowledge hurt her heart as well. She was leaving her entire life behind. Both her past with her parents and the future she thought she'd have with Kade.

"We'll stay in touch." Samantha took Rose's hand and squeezed. "I promise."

Rose squeezed back. For the past twenty-four hours, all she'd done—besides sleep and cry—was discuss with Samantha everything that had happened. Rose had needed to talk out the details with the hope she could find a way to save Kade. Except they'd come up with no answers. "Everything has been about me lately. What's going on with you?"

Samantha shrugged. "The club reopens tomorrow, and I'm going back to work. It's either that or get a roommate to help with expenses."

Samantha talked about her boyfriend, Pete, and Rose tried to listen. She even nodded when appropriate and smiled when required. She'd already offered Samantha a huge amount of money. But Samantha—while grateful—had turned it down. She said she had personal reasons for not accepting it, and Rose had to honor that.

Loud male voices came from the backyard, and she turned toward the open kitchen door. Calum and Nate stood near the doorway, both wearing frowns.

"I'm serious, Calum," Nate said in a strained voice. "You should've told me about Doom, as well as the fact that Iron Rack's helps to run it."

"You had enough to deal with." Calum's voice sounded more controlled, almost bored. "It's not a big deal. Besides, after what happened at the last fight, we won't be scheduling any more for a while. Not until I can make sure the illegal betting has stopped."

"I don't like being lied to," Nate said. "And lies by omission count."

"Fine." Calum's tone now sounded strained, and he pointed to something behind the house. "Your bike is over there. It may have gotten rained on."

"Screw you, Calum." Nate disappeared and reappeared, wheeling the bicycle past the door. "Tell Vane I'll cover his absence for whatever time he needs. But no more fucking lies."

"Got it." Calum, in a pale blue suit and navy tie, came in with a tray of takeaway coffees in one hand and a file folder under his arm. Once he placed everything on the table, he exhaled and offered them a tight smile. The shadows beneath his eyes proved that Rose wasn't the only one having a difficult time with everything that had happened.

"How are two of my favorite women?" he asked.

"Adjusting." Samantha glanced at Rose. "At least I think we are."

"Good." Calum undid the lowest button on his suit and sat next to Rose. He placed his cell phone on top of the file folder.

While Samantha handed out the fresh coffees, Vane knocked on the door jamb. He held a small gym bag, similar to Kade's. "Hey. Did I just see Nate leave on his bike?"

"Yes." Calum stood and brought a coffee to Vane who dropped his bag by the table and took up a position near the sink. "Nate said he'll cover for you for as long as you need. We just can't lie to him anymore."

"Right." Vane nodded and took the takeaway cup. "Thanks for the coffee."

"For the record," Samantha said to Calum and Vane, "we should never lie to Nate. He saved my life and would give up everything for his men."

Calum and Vane nodded, glanced at each other, and then looked at the floor.

Rose wasn't sure what Samantha's scolding was all about, but it seemed private. So Rose didn't want to ask.

Vane's face reddened and, from the way he scanned the area, he seemed to be watching the backyard, the back door, and the doorway leading to the front of the house. Like Nate, Vane wore jeans and a black T-shirt. Both Nate and Vane reminded her so much of Kade that her chest tightened until it hurt.

She sipped the very hot coffee, hoping the burn in her throat would pull her out of this emotional morass.

"I'm happy to see you awake, Rose." Calum drank his coffee and took a napkin from the holder. While he wore an easygoing smile, the shadows in his ice-blue eyes held a warning. Not for her, but for those who would oppose him. Maybe this was how one family maintained their position as the richest in the South for over three hundred years. "We have things to discuss."

"What things?" Rose asked.

"By three p.m. today, I will receive a wire transfer in your name for forty million, two hundred thousand dollars. The *Bay Psalm Book* sold for more than Hezekiah expected. I'll have the money direct-deposited into your offshore account."

Rose opened and closed her mouth a few times. Although she'd heard Hezekiah's estimate, she'd assumed he was exaggerating. "Wow. Thank you." That sounded so lame, but she wasn't sure what else to say.

Vane whistled low and drank more coffee.

Samantha frowned. "The reptile should give her back the key."

"While I agree," Calum said, sipping his coffee, "I don't have any more leverage."

Rose tilted her head. "Leverage?"

Calum's tight smile did nothing to soften the hardness in his gaze. "It's a saying."

Samantha brought her teacup to the sink and poured it out. "Everything in this world is about leverage."

"Isn't that the truth." Vane spoke so softly Rose almost missed it.

But she didn't miss the long glance that Vane and Samantha shared.

What is that about?

"Rose?" Calum touched her hand. "Are you okay with all this?"

She nodded and forced a smile. "I'm more than okay." She covered his fingers with her hand, surprised at how warm he felt. "I will never be able to thank you for all you've done for me."

"It's been my pleasure. Now"—Calum withdrew his hand to open the file folder—"we have documents to sign."

"What about the CPS situation?" Vane asked.

"I spoke with a judge yesterday, and she dismissed the CPS case due to lack of evidence and standing. The judge also awarded Rose temporary custody of Timmy so they can move to Virginia for Timmy's treatment. I'm sure they will award Rose full custody within a few months."

Relief washed through her, leaving behind a hollow, echoey feeling in her chest. "Thank you, Calum."

"You're welcome." Calum tapped his phone with two fingers. "Rose, have you thought about what to do about Magnus? Do you want a funeral?"

She held her takeaway cup with both hands, astonished that she hadn't thought about that either. "I don't know what to do. Isaac and my parents are buried in a family crypt on the Isle of Grace. Magnus should probably be buried there too. But I have to be honest, I don't want to host a wake or a funeral. Does that make me a terrible person?"

"No." Samantha sat, took Rose's hand again, and squeezed. "It's okay just to bury him."

"I agree," Vane said.

"As do I," Calum said. "I'll leave you the name of a funeral home that can make the arrangements. I'll also have my assistant send out an obituary to the newspaper. We'll just say that he requested a private burial. That should keep any interested people, including the press, away."

"Thank you." She'd forgotten that Magnus was well-known in this city, both as a lawyer and a playboy, and that some people might be upset at his passing. Although she had no idea who those people might be or why they'd miss him.

Calum opened the file and laid out papers with colored page flags. "The coroner can't determine if Magnus was dead or alive when he was on those tracks. But since the investigators found a suicide note in Magnus's home, I suspect that later this week, his death will be deemed a suicide."

Rose released a deep sigh and started signing pages that Calum had flagged. "What about Magnus's estate?"

"Unfortunately, there's nothing left. Magnus gambled away what was left of your parents' estate, and he leveraged all of his other assets when he merged his law firm with Beaumont, Barclay, and Bray."

"I'm not surprised." She continued signing papers, not sure what they were. While she knew better than to sign things she hadn't read, she trusted Calum. Like she trusted Samantha and Vane. Like she'd trusted Kade.

And trusting others was something that, a week ago, she wouldn't have been able to say about anyone.

Once all the papers were signed, she placed them in the folder and slid it toward Calum. "Thank you so—"

He held up a hand. "Not necessary. But I do feel I need to say something to the room."

He cleared his throat and stood, making sure he met the gazes of Rose, Samantha, and Vane. "I spoke briefly with Arragon. He reminded me that none of us can speak of what happened with Kade or Hezekiah Usher or Leonato. For our safety as well as Kade's."

They all nodded, and Calum picked up the file and his cell phone. "Good. Rose, once the wire transfer is complete, I'll let you know. Are you packed for the movers tomorrow?"

Rose stood and gripped the edge of the table. "I don't have much to pack. And Samantha and Vane are helping me today."

"Then"—Calum took her hand and squeezed—"once you're done, the three of you should spend the day as tourists in Savannah. Eat ice cream. Take a carriage tour. Smell the gardenias. Enjoy the sunshine." He scrunched his face as if leaving Savannah was the worst fate he could imagine. "Do anything you think you might miss after you move to Charlottesville."

For the first time in days, she smiled. "I'm moving to Virginia. I think they have flowers and sun there, too."

"Let's hope so, but I doubt they will be the same." He kissed her on the cheek. "I'll come around tomorrow to make sure all goes well. And I believe Hezekiah is providing transportation for you and Timmy?"

She nodded. "Calum, there is something else. One of the last things Magnus said to me was 'Remiel Marigny is coming'. Magnus also mentioned that name in the hospital, when he threatened me, and Deke wrote that name in his planner. Do you know what that name means?"

Calum, Vane, and Samantha stared at her as if her ears had doubled in size. Then they all glanced at each other before Calum said, "Remiel Marigny is dangerous. If he ever contacts you, call me. Promise me?"

Rose wrapped her arms around herself. "I promise."

Calum said goodbye and left, shutting the door behind him.

As Samantha bustled around the kitchen, she accidentally knocked Rose's cell phone off the charger.

Guilt swelled up and almost choked her.

Vane gently touched Rose's arm. "What's wrong?"

Her breathing felt erratic and sweat beaded her brow. She sank into her seat and focused on her breaths so she wouldn't hyperventilate. As hard as she'd tried to forget, her lack of trust had ruined her life as well as Kade's.

Samantha sat next to her and held her hand. "Rose?"

"It's all my fault," she said in a breathy voice. "I made a mistake, and now Kade is gone."

Samantha and Vane shared a confused look.

Rose shook her head to clear her blurry vision. "When we left the house to go to the apartment above Juliet's Lily, I took my cell phone." She took another deep breath and then her words came out in a rush. "It was turned off. I don't even know why I took it. I was afraid to miss a call from Timmy. Even though he often calls the house phone. I was worried Kade was a murderer. I was terrified I was making a mistake by trusting people I didn't know."

She stopped rambling because she was out of breath. Then she tasted salt. She was crying and dry heaving at the same time.

"After that night at Doom, when Vane fought Leonato, the warrior came to my house. He was super annoying. But I remember he held my phone. I think he may have put a tracking device in it or something. I don't know how these things work."

"It's okay." Samantha knelt next to Rose and held her close. "It's not your fault."

She rested her head on Samantha's shoulder, hating that she'd turned into a sniveling, soggy mess. "I'm so sorry. I put everyone in danger. And I lost Kade."

"Samantha is right. None of this is your fault." Vane went

to his gym bag and rummaged through it. When he turned around, he held a device that looked like a penlight. "Nate just bought these for all of us at the gym. He wants us to swap out our burner phones once a month. But, every few days or so, we're supposed to sweep our own electronics and other areas around the gym for tracking devices, listening devices, cameras, or anything else that emits radio waves."

"It's small." Samantha stood and took the detector from Vane. "Does it work?"

"Yes. A few days ago, Nate found hidden cameras in the men's bathroom at Rage of Angels."

Rose and Samantha shared a long look. Deke had probably been keeping track of his prostitutes who took men to the bathroom to have sex.

"Deke," Samantha muttered as she handed Vane the detector. "That's gross even for him."

"I never met the dude, but he sounds gross." Vane looked at Rose. "Can you turn off your Wi-Fi?"

"Of course." She grabbed a tissue from the counter to wipe her eyes and blow her nose. Then she went into the living room and unplugged the modem. When she returned to the kitchen, she found Vane scanning her phone with the detector.

"There's no tracking device on the phone." He began to sweep the kitchen with the device. Then he moved into the living room and her bedroom. A few minutes later, he returned to the kitchen and swept the pantry. "There's nothing here—"

"Wait." Rose glanced at Samantha. "Do you hear that?"

They ran into the pantry. A low buzzing sound came from the laundry closet. Vane opened the doors to expose the stacked washer and dryer. There wasn't much room to hang anything, and she'd laid her blue sweatshirt to dry on top of the washer. As Vane ran the detector over the machine, the detector's indicator light lit up three of five bars. When he swept the detector over her sweatshirt, the indicator lit up all five bars.

My mother's sweatshirt?

Samantha grabbed the sweatshirt and they returned to the kitchen.

Rose didn't say anything while Samantha placed the sweatshirt on the table and began to examine the seams and hems.

When she reached one of the pockets, she said, "I feel something."

Rose grabbed the sweatshirt and turned the pocket inside out. Within in the pocket seam, a small, raised area looked like someone had sewn a piece of matching blue fabric along the seam allowance.

Vane took out his pocket knife and cut round the raised area until a tiny, square device fell onto the table. He used his knife's handle to hit the device until it broke. Then he tossed the pieces into the sink and ran the disposal for a long minute.

Rose sank into her seat and stared at Samantha. "The Fianna put a tracking device into my sweatshirt?"

"Apparently so." Samantha sat next to her. "I thought those things only happened in spy novels."

"That was a nano tracker. Very expensive." Vane returned to the table and slipped his knife into his back pocket. "Although I'm surprised it still worked after you washed the sweatshirt."

"I only spot washed it." Rose tucked stray hairs behind her ear. "I don't machine wash it too often because it belonged to my mother. I'm afraid of wearing it out."

"At least I can tell Nate that his toy works." Vane put his detector into his gym bag and zipped it up. "Rose, do you have any idea how the Fianna was able to place that tracker in your sweatshirt? It was sewn in carefully. Someone even made sure to match the fabric and thread so you wouldn't notice. That had to take some time."

She clasped her hands behind her neck and closed her eyes. "I remember Leonato coming into the kitchen with my phone and sweatshirt..." she opened her eyes and said in breathless voice, "The hospital."

After telling them the story of what happened the night that Leonato killed Banjo, she finished with, "I left my sweatshirt in Timmy's room after I finished giving my statement. I didn't get it back from Lost and Found until six weeks later."

Samantha glanced at Vane. "Is it possible that Leonato took Rose's sweatshirt that night, had a tracker sewn in, and then returned it weeks later?"

"We'll never know for sure," Vane said. "But I think it's a definite possibility."

Rose released a deep breath and looked at Samantha. "I wore that sweatshirt the night we got caught at Doom. I bet that's how Arragon found us in that alcove."

"Where else did you wear the sweatshirt?" Samantha asked.

"To meet Sarah at Nectar of Gods café—Sampson tracked us there. Then to the hospital where I ran into Magnus."

Vane frowned. "Kade got a text from Leonato saying you were in trouble at the hospital. That's how Kade knew to send me and Samantha to get you. So Leonato tracked you there and was watching you."

Samantha stood and brought her takeaway coffee cup to the microwave to reheat it. "Rose wore the sweatshirt again when we ran through the tunnels to the other apartment."

"Where Leonato found us. Again." Rose bit her lip and mentally went through her actions that night. "I didn't wear it when I hid the box in the bell tower, but I did put it on when I went to Doom." She told them about seeing the warriors in the garden square when she'd left with Magnus and finished with, "I wore it into the bell tower with Magnus."

Vane gripped the back of a kitchen chair. "That's how Leonato and the other warriors were able to find you at the tower."

Samantha came over and touched Rose's shoulder. "Like I said before, this wasn't your fault. And it had nothing to do with your phone."

"Not necessarily." Vane went to the counter and took her phone off the charger. "They still could've been monitoring calls and messages."

"Isn't that illegal without a warrant?" Rose asked.

"The Fianna does whatever the hell it wants." Vane held up her phone. "Do you mind if I take this? My buddy Luke can figure out if it was being monitored. When we go out later, I'll get you another burner phone for your trip."

She nodded. "Thank you." She hadn't used the phone much, but she hated the idea that anyone would've been reading her texts or listening to her calls.

Vane slipped the phone into his gym bag. "In the meantime, Rose, why don't you rest? You've already packed your clothes, and Samantha and I can finish what little is left. Then we can do as Calum suggested. After you meet your landlord and pay the hospital bill, we'll eat ice cream and play tourist until you leave."

She almost declined his offer, but an invisible weight landed on her shoulders. Once she arrived in Virginia, she'd be a single parent in a new city. And one thing she'd learned this week? Accept help when it was genuinely offered. "Thanks. I will lie down for a bit."

Samantha took her hand and led her to the bedroom. "You sleep. We're also going out to dinner tonight. Calum made us reservations at one of the best restaurants in town. It won't be a goodbye dinner, but a meal to celebrate your new life."

Rose crawled into the bed she'd shared with Kade and sighed when her head hit the pillow. "That sounds lovely."

Once Samantha closed the blinds and left the room, Rose rolled over until she lay on Kade's side of the bed. She should be happy. In a few days, she and Timmy would be settled. He'd be in an experimental, medically supervised program that wouldn't leave them in medical debt. And now that she was a millionaire—an event that still hadn't truly hit her—she'd never have to worry about paying her bills again. Although she'd be leaving behind friends, she had no doubt they'd stay in touch. She was even beginning to think of Calum, Vane, and Samantha as family. That still left one huge gaping hole in her life. In her mind. In her heart.

That gaping hole was now a truth that haunted her days and her dreams.

She was alone. Kade was gone. Forever.

CHAPTER 36

Four weeks later, while sitting at the kitchen table in her and Timmy's Charlottesville apartment, Rose finished texting Vane. He'd wanted to let her know that —according to his buddy Luke—no one had been monitoring her burner phone. And she was so relieved.

She'd also been texting Samantha and Bianca. After feeling so alone for so long, she was determined to keep the few relationships she had no matter where she lived.

She closed Deke's copy of *The Complete Works of Shakespeare* and tossed it onto the coffee table. She'd found Deke's book in a box that Vane had packed, and she'd been trying to understand why so many pages were marked with paper clips. While the knowledge wouldn't change the world, maybe Deke's paper-clipped pages would help her figure out a way to save Kade.

Although a long shot, she had no other ideas.

Her only remaining clue was the last word in Deke's planner that didn't make sense. The words *sugar* and *key* had worked out beautifully for her. *Remiel Marigny* was to be avoided. But she had no idea know what *Sebastian* meant.

She stood and ignored King George's sharp hiss. He'd been sleeping near her feet and obviously resented her moving away. The cat resented everything about the new apartment, including the stay-inside rules.

"Hey, Timmy." She stretched her arms over her head. "Ready for dinner?"

Timmy popped his head up over the couch, game remote clutched in his hands. "What are we having?"

"Wings from Asados Grill." She winked at him. "Your favorite."

"Woo-hoo!" He slid back into his gaming position and started another round of hunting zombies.

When they'd moved in, someone had already set up the television with a gaming system. Calum wouldn't say who'd done it, but she suspected he was the culprit. While she was grateful, she hadn't had the nerve to admit she couldn't turn it all on. She'd just given the Ethernet cords and Roku sticks to Timmy.

Their move to Charlottesville had been easy—thanks to Hezekiah's business manager—and now they were settled into a routine. Since she didn't have to work, she was taking online classes at UVA, hoping to get into the nursing school eventually. She had a ton of school time to make up for, but the flexible class schedule allowed her to take Timmy to all of his appointments and meetings.

Now that she had money—Calum had set up a monthly transfer between her accounts in the Cayman Islands and her local bank—that deep pit of anxiety in her chest had eased. The money would give her more than enough time to get a degree and fulfill her dream of becoming a pediatric nurse.

But the best thing about the move was that Timmy seemed healthier. He spent four days a week at the hospital, where the new therapies were strengthening his weak heart. And she was truly grateful. As much as she wanted him to have a new, healthy heart, she hated the thought of another child losing their life.

So, for now, she was... at ease.

She went to the galley kitchen to heat up the oven and saw something outside her kitchen window. A black man with a shaved head wearing a black leather jacket.

Arragon?

"Timmy?" She grabbed her keys and slipped on her shoes. "Will you be okay alone for a few minutes? I need to go out."

"I'm good!" he said as he fired at zombies.

She hurried to meet Arragon, locking the door behind her. *Please don't leave.*

By the time she got to the street, Arragon had disappeared. She ran down a block and saw him turn the corner. It would be hard to miss the fluidness of his gait. She followed him all the way to the white rotunda that dominated UVA's Lawn. For a moment, she thought she'd lost him, only to see him slip into one of the hidden gardens the university was known for. She followed him, and the scents of roses and boxwood filled her lungs.

Although it was after seven p.m., the sun had yet to set.

A moment later, she found herself in a private, walled garden. Arragon sat on a bench in the shade, contemplating the fountain in the center. He'd taken off his jacket and wore black leather pants with a black T-shirt. Up close, she saw swirling Celtic tattoos on his shaved head. Physically, he was extremely muscular and handsome, but his complete stillness still terrified her. She almost left until she saw what lay on the bench next to him.

Kade's compass watch.

After taking two deep breaths to gather her courage, she sat next to him. "May I see Kade?"

"No." Arragon sighed as if annoyed. "'Tis forbidden."

The fountain spray cooled her face. "Why are you here?"

"By the law, I am not."

It took her a minute to realize that he meant he wasn't supposed to be here.

He was staring at the marble female goddess who rose out of the fountain in front of them. She wore a Greek tunic and was blindfolded. In one hand, she held a sword pointed into the water, and the other hand held up scales. "Will you get in trouble for being here?"

He turned toward her, and his dark green eyes held a fierceness that made her hold her breath. "Only if thou speakest."

Meaning if she didn't tell, he wouldn't either. "I won't. I promise."

He nodded. "Lady Tempest Rose, are you familiar with the Moirai?"

"They were Greek goddesses. Sisters, I believe."

"Aye." Arragon tilted his head. Was that approval in his eyes? "The three sisters who spin the webs of fate."

She scoffed. "One day, I'm going to have a serious discussion with those spinners of fate."

Arragon smiled and pointed to the goddess in the fountain. "Themis, mother of the Moirai, represents the personification of divine order, fairness, and natural law. Themis is the mother of justice."

Rose scoffed. "Themis deserves to be fired."

"Why dost thou say so?"

She frowned. "You're asking me that question? You? A Fianna warrior whose job is, supposedly, to seek retribution for those who are denied justice?" When he started to speak, she waved at him to be quiet. She didn't care if he was a big, scary Fianna warrior. She was angry and lonely and completely powerless. "We both know there's no justice in this world. If there was, my parents' murderer would be in jail instead of dead. My brother and I wouldn't have lost our entire inheritance, and I'm not just talking about money. We lost our home, our belongings, even our photos. Our memories were stolen as surely as our parents' lives."

"Was Magnus's demise just?"

She glanced at Arragon, and his level gaze fixed on hers. "Magnus was going to kill me. Besides, Leonato made that final decision."

Arragon gave her a single nod. "You offered my brother Leonato no choice."

She clasped her hands in her lap. "This is all my fault?"

Arragon shrugged. "Is that what you believe?"

"No. Of course not." She knew her words to be true, but she hated how the warrior kept confusing her. "Then there's Timmy's situation." She stood to pace around the fountain. The more she spoke, the angrier she became. "If there was any justice in the world, my brother's future wouldn't be dependent on an experimental drug or the death of another child. Even if my brother receives a transplant, he'll have to live with the knowledge that another lost his life so his could be saved."

"One life lost. One life saved. A balance must always be struck."

"And Kade's sacrifice?" She threw up her hands. "Was that a rebalancing?"

Arragon stood. "You and your brother's lives for his freedom. In the end, 'twas a simple choice."

"No. It wasn't simple." She pointed at Arragon. "Kade did nothing wrong. He was wrongfully imprisoned, and now he has to spend the rest of his life serving the Prince. What kind of justice is that?"

Arragon crossed his arms and watched her as she paced. "Your lover will now seek retribution against those who wronged him."

She turned on the fearsome warrior. "The Prince decided to release Kade from Leavenworth. The Prince offered that deal to Kade when he was vulnerable. Not the other way around."

"Yet your lover agreed." Arragon studied the fountain again, as if considering something. "First, his freedom for his service. Now, you and your brother's freedom for the same. Two freedoms for one man's oath and another man's death. 'Twas not a decision the Prince made lightly."

It took her a moment to realize whose death he referred to. "Do you mean Banjo's death?"

"Aye."

"Did Banjo know he was a pawn in the Prince's game?"

"All those who make deals with the Prince understand their part. Including your lover."

"Kade agreed to work for the Prince in return for his freedom from prison. Not to become a warrior."

"Did your lover tell you this?"

She focused on the fountain, trying to remember what Calum had told her about Kade being on borrowed time. "Are you saying that the night Kade left Leavenworth, he agreed to become a warrior in exchange for his freedom?"

"Does it matter? He belongs to us now."

"Regardless of Kade's original agreement with the Prince, I know what he wants." She turned toward Arragon and held a hand over her heart. "Kade wants a life with me. He deserves to be happy."

"Does he not also deserve justice?"

She hated these word games. "We all deserve justice."

"Yet some more than others?"

"No." She shook her head. "Maybe."

"Isaac Guthrie offered cruelty to all children, including his own. Did not Magnus deserve justice for what his father did to him?"

"You're twisting my words."

"You're twisting your logic to fit your feelings. Either justice is for all or only for those who you believe deserve it."

"That's not what I'm saying."

"There's a price for everything, my lady. Magnus's death for your life. Your lover's sacrifice, along with Banjo's offering, for your brother's freedom. Another child's heart for your brother's future. Is that not proof enough that a balance must always be met?"

She sat on the bench and dropped her head into her hands. "Arragon, if you're not here to tell me that the Prince is letting Kade go, then what does the Prince want?"

Arragon didn't respond. He just moved until she could see his black combat boots, and she looked up at him standing over her. "Why are you here?"

His wide chest heaved with each deep breath. "Time is fleeting. On the full moon, your lover will face the gauntlet. If he lives, he will make his tithe."

"That's next week." She'd read enough about the Fianna to know that once Kade tithed—if he survived the training and the gauntlet—she'd never see him again. "How do I save him?"

"Your lover's past caused his present. Yet his future can only be saved by his past."

Another riddle? "I don't understand."

Arragon shook his head, as if exasperated. Then he turned to leave.

"Wait." She stood and grabbed his arm. "All I know is that a recruit must give up all the people and possessions he loves most. He must break his own heart because it's only in suffering that he can find the will, which I assume to mean the aggression, to fulfill his duties as a warrior."

"Aye." Arragon handed her a white card with a phone number on it. "Except in rare cases, when a future is unknown in the present, a warrior may be offered a reprieve."

"For how long?"

"However long the Prince decides."

She held up the card. "I don't understand."

"I pray you will, before it's too late." He nodded to the card. "The number expires when the moon is full."

She slipped it into her back pocket. She had so many questions, but as Arragon walked away, she knew he'd offer no more answers.

Except for maybe one more.

She picked up the compass watch from the bench and ran after him, meeting him near the garden gate. "Arragon? May I keep this?"

Arragon turned to face her. Then he hit his chest with his fist and bowed his head. "'Tis yours. May you find your ever fix'd mark, my lady. May the Fates be kind. May they be just."

CHAPTER 37

A few days later, Rose turned off the ringing alarm and slipped out of bed. King George appeared in the doorway, snarled at her, and disappeared.

The cat was probably angry because breakfast was late, and Timmy had spent the night in the hospital for his weekly tests.

Although she was taking classes, every free moment she had she spent learning about the Fianna.

Unfortunately, there wasn't much to read. She had found a book in the university's Alderman Library, *David Hume's The History of England*, that had some interesting-yet-outdated information—unless recruits still ran around naked in the woods in the middle of winter while being chased by other warriors.

That seemed unnecessarily intense. Then again, so was Arragon.

After she fed King George and made coffee in the kitchen, she studied the phone number on Arragon's white card. She was no closer to figuring out his riddle and was running out of time.

So she made a call.

Calum picked up on the first ring. "Good morning, Rose."

"Did you hear from your friend? The one who you said might be able to help?" After her meeting with Arragon, she'd called Calum since he was the only person whom she could talk to.

As it turned out, Calum's best friend, Rafe, had once been a Fianna warrior. She had no idea how Rafe got away, but Calum had told her many, many sacrifices had been made in exchange for his freedom.

Not really the news she'd been looking for.

"I talked to Rafe last night. Unfortunately, he had no information to help you. He did say that the only way a recruit is freed is if he doesn't make it through the training or the gauntlet."

"Because the recruit died."

"Correct."

She leaned against the counter and, from the kitchen window, watched a woman walk by, pushing a stroller. The woman struggled to open the door of the coffee shop across the street until a stranger helped her.

What am I missing? "How can the Fianna expect a man to give up everything?"

"I suspect that most of the men who join have already lost everything. Rafe told me that most recruits had lost wives and children. They'd lost friends in combat. Their sorrow and anger led them to the Prince."

Her stomach clenched the way it did anytime she thought about losing Timmy. "That makes sense. It would be hard to be a father and leave a child."

"I can't imagine the pain of that. To sacrifice your future? Makes me doubt any of the warriors have young children."

"Thanks for checking, Calum."

"If I think of anything else, I'll let you know."

She hung up and watched as the woman with the stroller emerged, now balancing a cup of coffee. When the woman turned to the side, Rose noticed a baby bump.

Rose poured her own cup of coffee and sat at the table to open her laptop. Her browser was on the Wikipedia page for the Fianna, and she reread the entry she'd practically memorized. As she sipped, she inhaled the aroma of coffee. Her gag reflex kicked in, and she pushed the mug away. The coffee smelled bitter.

When the bile in her throat refused to subside, she dumped the coffee into the sink. Then she poured out the entire pot. After wiping down the counter, she opened the refrigerator to put the cream away, and nausea overtook her. She barely made it to the bathroom in time. Minutes later, she flushed the toilet, washed out her mouth, and looked at herself in the mirror. That's when she understood Arragon's message.

Kade's future can only be saved by his past.

She hurried back to the kitchen, dialed Calum, and said, "I have another question for Rafe."

"What is it?"

She laid out the situation, and Calum said, "I'll get back to you as soon as I know."

Once she hung up, she paced the small apartment. From the front door, through the family room/galley kitchen, into her bedroom, and then Timmy's room. Teddy Hawkins sat on Timmy's bed since he'd announced he was too old to take his teddy to the hospital. While that made her sad, she understood. She wasn't the only one who'd changed.

She grabbed Teddy Hawkins and returned to her own room to lie down. While she waited for an answer from Calum, she found Deke's Shakespeare book on her bedside table and flipped through the clipped pages. After what seemed to be hours, she noticed the front page of the book was glued to the cover.

How odd.

Using tweezers, she pulled the page off and read the owner's inscribed name. At that moment, Calum responded with a simple text.

Yes.

She ran into the kitchen, dialed the number on the white card, and prayed it wasn't too late to save Kade. Then she clutched the Shakespeare book to her chest and prayed it wasn't too late to save them all.

Kade slammed the door of the black SUV and followed Arragon across the street.

Exhaustion slowed his movements, and he didn't know the date or time. From the sun's location, it had to be six or seven p.m. He was also jet-lagged. The day before, he'd been at the Fianna training camp deep in the Northumbrian mountains until Arragon ordered Kade to drop everything and follow. Since doing anything else meant death, Kade followed.

Where am I?

It appeared they'd stopped in a university town. A large white rotunda was ahead of him. He dodged college kids talking on their phones and walking in groups, feeling lost in time and space. Out of habit, he scanned his surroundings, watching everything and everyone go by. He wasn't armed, but at this point, he'd had so much hand-to-hand combat instruction at the Fianna training camp, he *was* a weapon.

A few people watched Arragon walk in that eerie way all Fianna warriors moved. But it wasn't until the strangers watched Kade that he realized he probably walked that way too.

Arragon led the way behind a series of low buildings, past a *University of Virginia* sign, and into a secluded garden. A fountain with a marble goddess took up the center of the space, with iron benches placed around the perimeter.

"Arragon, what the—"

Arragon held up his hand. Then he pointed to a woman sitting on a bench in the shadows. A woman with long red hair, wearing a blue sundress and a white sweater.

All the breath left his chest, and his body went cold. *Rose?*

Arragon took Kade's arm. "'Tis forbidden to speak to her."

No. No. No. No. No. Seeing her was too hard, too painful. Since he'd left her, he'd forced all memories of her out of his mind. Purging her memory had been the only way to survive the brutal training. And now that he was days away from the gauntlet—a situation he wasn't sure he'd survive—he couldn't be here. Seeing her would hurt him. But holding her, smelling her hair, kissing her lips? That would destroy him in a way the gauntlet couldn't come close to doing.

When she saw them walk closer, she stood. Her green eyes were wide but completely focused on Arragon.

When they stopped a few feet away, Arragon said, "Your lord is forbidden from speaking. Do not tempt him."

"I won't," she said without even glancing at him. "I have the proof you requested."

Arragon held out his hand, and she gave him a piece of paper.

Kade stood off to the side, unsure of what to do. Arragon hadn't said anything about this meeting. But Kade knew the rules. Any contact with his former life would mean death to him and possibly to those he loved. One of the many things he'd learned in the past weeks was that the Fianna didn't threaten punishments they weren't prepared to carry out. He had a back full of scars proving that truth.

Arragon returned the paper to her. "'Tis true."

She nodded and shoved the paper into her pocket. "Does the Prince know?"

Arragon raised an eyebrow. "My lord knows of the possibility."

"So?" She still refused to look at Kade and kept her gaze on Arragon. "Call him. This ends tonight."

The only signs of her distress were how she wrapped her arms around herself and chewed her bottom lip. So similar to that night in Screamin' Perks when he'd beat up Antoine to protect her, even though she'd kept telling him she hadn't needed protection.

That seemed like a century ago.

He tried not to smile at her courage in standing up to Arragon. If she only knew—if she truly understood what Arragon was capable of—she'd run away in tears and hide. Then again, Rose had never been the run-and-hide type.

It was one of the many things he adored about her.

Correction. Used to adore. There was no more adoring or laughing or loving. That part of his life was over. He had to accept the truth that once he went through the gauntlet, he'd be a Fianna warrior for life.

Arragon took out his phone and walked to the other side of the fountain. And that's when the awkwardness kicked in.

The day after he'd left with Leonato, the warrior had filled Kade in on everything that had happened to Rose after he'd left. So Kade knew about the key, the *Bay Psalm Book*, the money, Timmy's acceptance into the drug study, and how both Hezekiah and Calum had helped her re-establish a life in the real world.

Kade wasn't at all surprised by Calum's help, but he'd been shocked by Hezekiah's. The guy didn't seem the type to show a single sign of empathy or concern, even if he had helped Rose and Timmy in the past.

Then again, if it was true Hezekiah had been in love with

Rose's mother, maybe there'd been some remorse. Or at least a shred of pity.

Kade had also confirmed a few other details. The Fianna had offered Deke asylum in exchange for information, and someone else killed him. Banjo's death had, indeed, been a message to keep Kade in line. And, after Kade left with Leonato and Sampson, the Prince had bought the box and key from Hezekiah.

Because that had been the plan all along.

To rectify the pain of the deaths of Rose's parents, the Prince had wanted Rose to sell the box to Hezekiah to receive the money. The Prince had demanded that Deke ask Rose to be the courier. The Prince had ordered Hezekiah to set up the death match between Kade and Magnus. The Prince had put the entire plan in motion as a test—to make sure Kade had the emotional fortitude to join the Fianna.

The Prince had wanted Kade to fall in love with Rose, and then give her up to become a warrior.

The most important thing he'd learned was that the Prince didn't want men who'd already lost everything. The Prince wanted warriors who had so much love in their lives that giving it up would cause immense pain. Because pain drove aggression. Pain fueled violence. Pain turned a man into a cold, ruthless killing machine.

Pain served the Fianna's purpose.

Kade exhaled and flexed his fingers. Now Rose stared at the ground, the fountain, her watch. Everywhere except at him.

He had so many questions to ask her. About her new life, Timmy's health, her unusually pale countenance. But Kade wasn't about to put either of their lives in danger. Still, he'd love to know what was going on. He desperately wanted the chance to speak to her. Hold her. Kiss her.

His arms ached from the tension of keeping them still. His

body pulsed with awareness and heat. His erection, which he hadn't considered in weeks, pressed against the zipper of his jeans. A slight breeze blew strands of hair into her face, and she brushed them away. She'd glanced at him but quickly turned away, obviously sticking to Arragon's rules.

Her hair seemed darker, for some reason. She'd also lost weight. At least ten pounds, from what he could tell beneath the loose-fitting dress. Dark circles under her eyes told him she hadn't been sleeping.

That's when a horrible thought took hold. Was she sick? Was this visit a special exemption so he could say goodbye?

He walked away until he found another shaded bench. His body felt hot, and sweat dripped down the back of his neck.

Rose was sick. Why else would he be allowed to see her this way? But if that were true, then surely he'd be allowed to speak to her. To hold her. To say goodbye.

Rose paced by the fountain, taking surreptitious glances in his direction. Within the spray, he saw a Greek goddess holding a sword and scales. He wished he could kick those damn scales out of her grasp. Except he couldn't be mad about everything the Fates had spun. He'd fallen in love with Rose. And that had been the greatest gift ever given a man.

Arragon returned and stopped a few feet away from Rose. Kade hurried over, not wanting to miss any clues about what was going on.

"This request is given rarely, if ever."

"I understand. I'm only following *your* advice."

Kade glanced at Arragon. *What advice?*

"So?" she asked in that firm, no-nonsense voice he loved. "What is the Prince's decision?"

"A temporary stay of active duty for twelve years."

"Twelve?" She waved her hand around. "It's supposed to be eighteen."

Arragon raised an eyebrow. "That is at the discretion of the Prince."

She wrinkled her nose. "There might be a new Prince in twelve years."

"Possibly, but that new Prince could require that your lover complete the gauntlet and tithe."

"What if I gave you something else? Let's call it leverage. Would that help our cause?"

"You have nothing—"

"I have two things." She picked up Deke's planner from the bench and opened it to the back page. "First, two names written in Deke's planner. Sebastian and Remiel Marigny. I don't know what they mean, but you might."

As Arragon read, his eyes narrowed. "These Fiends hold meaning to the Fianna. Pray, continue."

She placed the planner on the bench and picked up another book. The copy of *The Complete Works of Shakespeare* they'd taken from Deke's apartment. "A ton of the pages have been paper-clipped, and there are notes written throughout."

Arragon crossed his arms.

She blew stray hairs away. "Look at the inscription. I thought the book belonged to Deke. But it didn't."

Arragon took the book and opened the front cover. His frown sent shock waves through Kade. Arragon looked that way only when he was about to kill.

"So?" Rose prompted.

Arragon flipped through paper-clipped pages, and Kade noticed notes written in the margins.

"Arragon," Rose said in a steady voice, "that book once belonged to a man named Remiel Marigny. I have no idea who that is, but Magnus and Deke knew him, and Calum told me to stay away from him. It has to be worth something to the Prince."

"Agreed." Arragon shut the book and returned it to her. "I

will ask the Prince to consider offering Kade more time in exchange for the books."

She dropped the book on top of the planner and clasped her hands in front of her. "Thank you."

Arragon handed Kade a cell phone that he recognized. It was one of the high-tech burner phones all warriors carried. "Keep this with you at all times."

"Okay." Although the word sounded more like a question. Because, really, he was filled with them.

Then Arragon left the garden.

What. The. Fuck.

Kade faced Rose, and she launched herself into his arms. He held her so tightly he was afraid he'd crush her breasts against his chest. But he didn't hide any other part of his body, making sure she could feel how she affected him. Her arms nearly strangled him, and he held her tighter. He had no idea what was happening, but he closed his eyes and inhaled her honeysuckle scent.

"Oh, Kade," she whispered against his neck. "I've missed you."

She had no idea how much he'd missed her. Since he had no words, he pulled back and cupped her face in his palms. Then he kissed her. A passionate, lingering kiss filled with questions and a desperation tinged with hope.

A hope that this wasn't a last kiss, but the first kiss of many.

When he raised his head, he said gruffly, "Rose? What the hell is going on?"

She smiled at him, kissed him on the nose. "We freed you from your obligation to the Prince. For twelve years. Maybe more, if they take those books. But even if they don't, I have a plan."

"Oh, good Lord."

She traced his lips with her fingers. "If we can't come up

with a plan to free you completely in twelve years, we don't deserve our life together."

"Rose? How did you manage this miracle?"

She drew out of his embrace, took his hand, and placed it on her stomach. "Kade Dolan, you're going to be a father."

CHAPTER 38

Rose watched Kade's face carefully.

Since he'd been gone, he'd lost weight yet gained so much muscle. He seemed taller, leaner, and from what little she'd seen, he now walked like a Fianna warrior. His gait had Arragon's graceful, powerful sway. A gracefulness that had to take tremendous strength and power.

Yet, despite how sexy that was, she was more interested in his eyes. His beautiful eyes that had shifted from a hard, dull gray to that deep, saturated blue she remembered.

"Rose." He pressed his hand harder against her lower stomach. "I don't understand how..." He swallowed, and his gaze lowered to where her hand still covered his.

"Don't understand how I got pregnant, or how I got you out of the Fianna for at least twelve years?"

"I... uh...," His voice sounded breathy and low. "I know... wait... condoms?"

"Condoms have a surprisingly high failure rate." Realizing he was starting to hyperventilate, she took his wrist and dragged him to the bench in front of the fountain. "Sit."

He sat, but his breathing still sounded ragged. His eyes

had darkened again, and he kept looking around, as if checking out the shadows.

"Kade?" She sat next to him and, when he met her gaze, she used her softest, calmest voice. The one she used with Timmy before a scary doctor's appointment. "Did you know Fianna warriors can't be fathers?"

He tilted his head, and one booted foot tapped the ground.

When she'd spoken to Calum's friend, Rafe, earlier, he'd told her that Kade might be *different* when she saw him. That being pulled out of training could disorient him. That the acclimation between warrior training and the real world could be an emotional and psychological shock to the system. Similar to when POWs returned to their old lives.

She placed Kade's hand on her knee and covered it with her own. "I did some research and discovered that many warriors, after they survive the gauntlet and make their tithe, choose to be celibate."

"That's..." He paused to clear his throat. "True."

"If a warrior gets a woman pregnant, he is denied a life with the child. But the Fianna financially provides for that child."

He nodded, and now the other foot started tapping.

"Did you also know that a man who is already a father cannot be recruited until his youngest child is of a certain age? I, personally, was hoping that age would be eighteen, or even twenty-five, but in our case, the Prince said twelve."

Kade withdrew his hand and stood to pace between her and the fountain. "Are you telling me that I'm free of the Fianna?"

"For at least twelve years. But, like I said, I have a plan."

He knelt in front of her and met her gaze. "Can you explain to me, exactly, what happened?"

She smiled. "The Fianna have strict rules about fatherhood. If a fully tithed warrior gets a woman pregnant, the father is punished, but the child is cared for. The father cannot meet that child until adulthood. On the other hand, they will never recruit a man while he has a child who knows him and is financially dependent on him.

"Three years ago, when the Fianna recruited you, you were childless. But eight weeks ago, when they took you away for training, I was pregnant. Except none of us knew that then."

He stood and started pacing again. "The night Magnus died, you were already pregnant."

She stood and grabbed his wrist to make him stop moving. "Yes." Then she told him about her cryptic conversation with Arragon, who must have suspected her pregnancy was a possibility, and how she'd contacted Calum and Rafe, and then told Arragon. "Now do you understand?"

"That you and our child saved me?" For the first time since she'd seen him enter the garden, he smiled. Not an ordinary, everyday smile. But a wide grin that brightened his eyes and transformed his face. "Is this true?"

"You mean is it true that we got you away from the Fianna on a technicality?" She laughed and kissed him. "Yes!"

He grabbed her waist and swung her around and around and around. Both of them laughing and crying and kissing, all at the same time. When he finally stopped, she wobbled from dizziness. But she clung to his wide shoulders and kissed his cheek.

"Although," she said between kisses, "when I made the arrangements to meet you and Arragon, he admitted the Prince wasn't happy. That's probably why we only have twelve years instead of eighteen. Hopefully, the Shakespeare book will buy us more time."

He kissed her deeply again and, when they were done, he raised his head and said softly, "If there is a loophole, I'm sure you'll find it and exploit it."

She licked her lips and whispered," I've already considered one."

He chuckled and held her so her head rested against his chest, his chin on her head. "This plan of yours?"

"Yes. Remember, a man who already has children may not be recruited until that child is of a certain age." She paused and tapped his chest. "But that moment is determined by a man's *youngest* child."

He raised an eyebrow. "You mean—"

"You'll have to keep me pregnant, and I'll only be twenty three years old when this baby is born. By the time it takes our youngest to reach twelve, you'll be so old the Fianna won't want you anymore."

He laughed until he coughed. Then he swept her up in his arms and settled them on the bench, with her on his lap. "You, Tempest Rose Guthrie—my beautiful red-haired woman—are diabolical."

She wrapped her arms around his neck and kissed him thoroughly. When she broke away, she said, "You wouldn't have it any other way."

He kissed her nose and her cheeks. "You're right." He pressed his forehead against hers and whispered, "I wouldn't have it any other way."

She whispered, "I have something to tell you, Kade Dolan."

He chuckled. "We're having twins?"

She laughed. "No. At least I don't think so. That's not part of the plan."

He kissed her nose again. "Then what else could you possibly say to me?"

"Kade Dolan"—she held his face between her palms and placed her lips against his—"I love you."

A FEW HOURS LATER, Kade opened the door to Timmy's room in UVA's pediatric hospital.

After leaving the garden, they'd returned to her apartment, where Rose had had to explain everything again, including the concept that condoms were not foolproof. Especially three-year-old ones, like those they'd used.

He'd also found bag filled with his few belongings that Arragon must've dropped off before returning to England. Then Rose had given him more details about Timmy's new situation with the experimental drug program.

After being snubbed and hissed at by King George, Kade ate half of her groceries and promised to repay her. That's when she explained her multimillionaire status and how she wanted to get her nursing degree while he started a horse farm in the rolling hills outside of Charlottesville.

She had a plan, and he was all in. As long as he could live his life with Rose and their children, free from the Fianna, he could be happy anywhere.

But that meant something else had to happen first.

Rose hurried over to Timmy, who sat in a beanbag chair, writing in a notebook. When Timmy saw his sister, he jumped up and gave her a hug. "Did you bring King George?"

"You know I'm not allowed to do that." She placed Teddy Hawkins on the bed. "I did bring this, though."

"Rose, my friends can't see Teddy Hawkins. They'll think I'm a baby." Then Timmy saw Kade and gave him a wide smile. "Hey, Mr. Dolan."

Kade rubbed Timmy's head, happy to see the kid was no longer attached to machines. He'd even put on a few pounds and added color to his cheeks.

Rose handed Timmy a brown bag. "I brought you new drawing pencils and some M&M's. But don't tell the nurses about the chocolate."

"I won't!" Timmy smiled, opened the bag, and said, "Wow! Thank you!"

Kade noticed the Attacktix figures lining the window sill, and then he nodded to the notebook with elaborate sketches lying on the beanbag chair. "What are you working on?"

"I'm making my own comic book. It's about a rogue space alien who comes to Earth for a new heart but finds a family instead."

Kade laughed. "I can't wait to read it."

Timmy tilted his head and studied both Kade and Rose. "What are you doing here, Mr. Dolan? Rose said you had to leave town."

"I did." Kade picked up Teddy Hawkins from the bed. "But I'm back. And I have two things to ask you."

"Shoot." Timmy hopped onto the bed and started eating his M&M's. Today he was wearing blue plaid PJs, and his hair was longer.

He seemed so much older than the last time they'd talked.

"Well, the first thing is I'd like your permission to marry your sister."

Timmy's mouth, filled with candy, opened and closed a few times. Then he wiped his mouth with his arm, leaving a sticky residue on the cotton. "Really?"

Kade took Rose's hand and squeezed. "Really."

Timmy jumped off the bed and hugged both of them. "Yes! That is totally awesome!"

Rose knelt to meet her brother's gaze. "You sure you're okay—"

"We're going to be a family, Rose!" Timmy kissed her on the cheek. "Will Mr. Dolan live with us in Virginia?"

Rose looked up at Kade with tears in her green eyes. "Yes. We may even start his horse farm here. His dreams are now ours."

Timmy held out his hand, and Kade tried not to laugh as they shook.

"You had a second question?" Timmy asked in a way-too-old voice.

Rose cleared her throat and blushed.

Kade held up Teddy Hawkins. "Would you mind if we gave Teddy Hawkins to another child? A baby?"

Timmy wrinkled his nose, so similar to Rose's. "What baby?"

The question carried enough of a threat to tell Kade that while Timmy wasn't a little kid anymore, only a special child would be given permission to care for Teddy Hawkins.

Kade knelt. "By next spring, your sister and I are having a baby. And you're going to be an uncle."

Timmy's eyes widened until, suddenly, he turned away to wipe a tear from his cheek.

"Timmy?" Rose touched his shoulder. "Are you upset?"

"No." Timmy sniffled and looked at them again. This time, his tears were framed by a wide smile with two missing teeth. "But you did it, Rose. You made your promise come true."

"What promise?" Kade asked.

Timmy reached up to wipe away a tear on Rose's cheek. "Rose once promised me that we'd be safe. That I'd get better. That one day, no matter what, we'd have a family of our own."

Kade took Rose and Timmy into his arms and made his own promise. "We're a family of three, soon to be a family of four. And I solemnly swear to protect our family, no matter how large it grows, forever and ever and ever."

"Or until the youngest turns twelve," Rose said in a muffled voice.

Kade laughed until Timmy pulled his shirt. "What does that mean?"

"It means, Timmy, that you're going to have your hands

full with lots of nieces and nephews. Some of whom may want to go to Iria."

"I like that idea." Timmy snuggled into their hug, not quite as big and independent as he pretended to be.

Rose kissed Kade's cheek and rubbed Timmy's head. "As long as we're together, we're all going to believe in loopholes and rogue space aliens and fairy tales."

"So true, my love." Kade gave her the first of a million kisses, the kind that would last and last and last. "For the rest of our lives, we'll believe that happy endings are possible."

ACKNOWLEDGMENTS

While a book may be scratched out in the dark by a terrified author, the truth is no book is published without help.

Love's Last Kiss began as a short story, that morphed into a novella, and then became a full-length novel. This book took me years to finish, and I have so many people to thank.

I'd like to thank my agents Deidre Knight and Kristy Hunter for encouraging me to go on this journey into the world of indie publishing.

I want to give a huge thanks to Joyce Lamb for editing this book and helping me turn it into a novel I love more than I thought I would.

Another huge shoutout to Eileen Carey, the brilliant and creative cover designer who has done all of my Deadly Force books. I love all of my covers, but this one is my favorite so far!

A ton of research went into this story, and I want to thank Jean Anspaugh, both a friend and an expert in transplant patient coordination at Inova Fairfax Hospital, for explaining the procedures, legalities, and patient requirements regarding pediatric heart transplants. I am so grateful!

I also want to thank the Charleston Library Society, Historic Charleston Foundation, and Historic Savannah Foundation for opening up their extensive research collections.

I can't stress how much I rely on my critique parters/betareaders/proofreaders. I am sending hugs to Mary Lenaburg, Kieran Kramer, Nadine Monaco, and Christine

Glover. Thank you for your love and expertise. If not for your support, I would've deleted this manuscript a year ago.

Sending love to Abbie, Diana, and Jennie. We are, truly, all in this together!

I couldn't write all of these words without my WRW, Angela James, and Paris Writing Salon sprint groups. Thank you Keely, Angela, and Gabby for inviting me into your worlds.

To my twins and my husband... these books wouldn't exist without your love and encouragement. Thank you for never giving me grief about burnt dinners and piles of dirty laundry while I'm on deadline.

To my readers. Thank you for loving this world of Kells Torridan and his men, and for making these books such a success. I hope I will never let you, or my characters, down.

To learn more about my upcoming releases, including the next book in the Deadly Force series, sign up for my newsletter at www.sharonwray.com.

ABOUT THE AUTHOR

Sharon, a Jersey girl living in Virginia, is a chemical & patent librarian who once studied dress design in the couture houses of Paris. Although it took forever to decide what she wanted to do when she grew up, she now writes romance and women's fiction novels filled with suspense, adventure, and love.

Her Deadly Force romantic suspense series is set in a world with assassins who bow before killing, sexy Green Berets seeking redemption, and smart, sassy heroines who save them all. It's also a world where, since Sharon is slow and clumsy, her chances of making it out alive would be slim.

She also writes contemporary romances (both sweet and steamy) and southern gothic romantic mysteries.

She's repped by Deidre Knight and Kristy Hunter of The Knight Agency and blogs regularly at www.sharonwray.com.